SCARBOY

SCARBOY

RIP PAULEY

LIBERTY HILL PUBLISHING

Liberty Hill Publishing
2301 Lucien Way #415
Maitland, FL 32751
407.339.4217
www.libertyhillpublishing.com

Cover art by Tara Lehning

Paperback ISBN-13: 9781662870354
Ebook ISBN-13: 9781662870361

To our dogs and the fables that live in them.

1967

THE LATE SUMMER breeze swept across the Virginia field with a faint flutelike sound, brushing the tips of the timothy grass. It passed through a line of pines on the hillside up into the flat rectangle of the small farm bordered by ash trees and pines.

There, against the fence of his small enclosure, the young dog lifted his head and took in the scents. Their density worked at and wrinkled his nose as he sorted those familiar from those new, his young instincts seeking to identify and categorize each in its place, building his memory bank. A lighthearted human observing all this might have smiled at the puppy's furrowed brow, which, along with his silent, sphinx-like pose, offered comic contrast to the welter of farm animals around him.

In a nearby enclosure, a dozen Barred Rock chickens strutted about in martial stutter-steps outside their hen-house, foraging for any trace of pellets from a recent feeding as they nervously scoped their perimeter for signs of threat; a pair of white Chinese geese with their knurled crowns murmured nasally to each other by the driveway which divided the livestock area from the small, gray farmhouse; several pigs grunted and shifted their bulks in the pen some ten yards from the puppy; and directly behind him, a half-dozen Toggenburg goats skirmished among some tree stumps and plank ramps.

The puppy was the last remaining unsold of a litter of six. His mother, Laila, a seven-year-old German shepherd and the great favorite of her owner, Opal, the widowed lady of the farm, had died from a sepsis infection before the pups had opened their eyes. Opal, who'd midwifed many litters and witnessed more than her share of animal death, had been shattered by the loss and blamed herself; she'd been reluctant to breed Laila at her advanced age. Still, she could not resist a pairing with the extraordinary sable male from the Strongheart Kennel, which she'd met while visiting her cousin in North Carolina. The male was lean and athletic—none of the lunky, big-boned look too typical lately among shepherds, in her opinion—and displayed a focus and drive along with an appropriately aloof nature that matched the original breed standard for working dogs.

But with her days of competition training behind her, Opal realized she might have been seduced by nostalgic illusion. She'd lost Laila and was stricken with guilt, even if Doc Cash couldn't pin the infection on the pregnancy or the birthing. Opal applied herself to the whelping with a self-thrashing determination to produce the most well-adjusted pups possible and never to breed again.

The puppies were a tribute to her efforts. One by one, the healthy and happy scamps had gone to new homes—with the exception of this singular male. Unusually reserved, he hung back from the prospective buyers (more imperiously than skittishly) as they fussed over the other clamoring pups. So they'd passed him over. Opal knew most people didn't understand the complexity of the canine temperament and would naturally gravitate to the most outgoing pups. She appreciated his reserve and made no effort to explain it or to draw out the puppy for them. She hadn't yet decided whether or not she would keep the dog for herself; at one point, she'd even removed the pup from the litter.

She was emotionally inclined to hold on to it, to preserve the legacy of Laila, as the pup had inherited her coloring and markings, if not, seemingly, her sweet and outgoing personality. But, practically thinking as an aging widow and overworked farm owner enduring an economic downturn, she hesitated. To hold on to such a dog and not train it would be heresy.

So she had let the buying and selling process play out to see what fate would decree. Now the pup, nearly four months old, was still with her. And the sign down on the highway remained.

◆◆◆◆◆◆◆

The Volkswagen van veered sharply into the dirt lane, sending the loose painting gear in the back rolling and clanging against one side. Jeremy, driving, had responded instantly to Tory's excited cry and arm gesture toward the hand-painted sign—'*Pups For Sale.*' She'd even struck his hand on the steering wheel with her palm, her seashell bracelet jangling against her tanned wrists. In the back, Dev, Jeremy's best friend, perched between the seats and focused on rolling a marijuana joint, was tossed sideways.

"Hey," he said, but only distractedly, righting himself with one arm and repositioning himself between them as he saved the joint and licked it to a finish.

"Sorry." Jeremy ground down to second gear and the van lumbered with a whining strain up the red clay and gravel incline.

He glanced at Tory and took in her animated expression. There'd been nothing like it since they left Ft. Lauderdale. He smiled at her with a forced manly reassurance. His eyes scanned the light blond fuzz on her tanned arms up to her freckled profile, her perfect nose, blue eyes, and sandy-gold hair pulled back in a thick, wanton ponytail.

She was more beautiful each moment. But the realization came alongside the sinking suspicion the enchantment felt in Florida was only in his imagination. It didn't matter: this sudden burst of excitement, the quick, high leap in her voice, almost as he wished to hear it as a vocalized pant of sexual thrill, was impossible to resist.

Had Florida been a dream? It felt like it now, distant and unreal, yet hovering over him darkly like some personal storm system. He was a knot of nerves, his appetite lost, his lower intestines churning, and his heart occasionally palpitating. How did he come to this point with this girl?

◇◇◇◇◇◇◇◇

They'd met less than a week before. He was on the beach at sunset with Dev, toweling himself. He had spotted the lively clutch of friends thirty yards away, five girls and three boys. As Dev collapsed on the sand, Jeremy's eyes had quickly settled on Tory, in a bikini under a sheer, serape-style skirt and a wrinkled-silk top. Even from his distance, he was instantly fixed on her and could see how the others orbited her. He understood. Her confident expression, the easy smile, the slight upturn of her chin—she was a girl apart, an arresting mix of unattainable hauteur and girl-next-door cuteness. She was the girl you imagine meeting but never really do. As they moved past, he forced himself to turn away to dry his hair. When he turned back, she was looking at him. The others were not paying attention, but she held his eyes and smiled.

His heart skipped. He nodded coolly, but saw she was distracted by the group and had moved on.

Dev was sorting through his backpack.

"I've got wicked munchies."

Jeremy tapped his shoulder. "Did you see her?"

"Who?" Dev looked around dartingly. He now spotted the group receding down the beach. "Babes? You know, man, it's Floor-eee-daa. It's all beaches and babes."

"Never mind," Jeremy shrugged, moving off. "Let's eat."

They'd counted their money back at the motel and figured they could afford three more days before heading back to Boston. They had a contract to start a painting project in Melrose, the house of Dev's sister's boss, a dentist. Fine, Jeremy thought, his mind lingering on the girl but almost relieved to allow the moment to pass into luminous memory unmarred by reality. He wasn't a lady's man and knew it, even now at twenty. He realized he was good-looking, and a fair number of women were drawn to him. He'd heard more than once that he resembled some actor with three names. Who was it? He could never remember. But he wasn't able to be casual about relationships or sex, so he kept girls at a certain comfortable distance as if waiting for signals of seriousness and trust, which would enable him to loosen his reserve and make sense of a plunge as if it were all-or-nothing. He considered this related to his parents' divorce and his father's subsequent broken life. That's what the counselor had implied. Jeremy had only nodded in quiet assent. Why not? It made sense. And it was convenient to have an excuse for wishing to remain unattached as he tried to sort out his ambitions as a writer. It was natural, his counselor had asserted with pronounced sympathy.

But Jeremy admitted to himself that he'd always felt this way—guarded as if love was a frontier full of risks for which he wasn't yet ready. As it was, he was barely not a virgin—a fact that would have surprised anyone who saw him, with his lanky frame and dirty-blonde mop of surfer's hair. Not even Dev knew of his inexperience (though he wouldn't have cared, Jeremy thought; Dev was the most non-judgmental person he knew). Dev was friendly to all girls and was carnally rewarded enough for his guileless affability.

But Jeremy had always felt a sense of duty, even probity, around women, and this packed unavoidable stress into his notions of intimacy. He'd had one fling with the sister of his mother's co-worker. She was thirty-five, sixteen years older. Her age and experience had somehow relieved him of his inhibitions; he'd allowed her to approach him and steer the course of their brief, discreet dalliance. She was attractive, funny, and somewhat sardonic, and he was pleased to learn that he could satisfy her according to her more seasoned criteria by saying very little and simply following her lead. It had all felt honest—she knew what she was doing, and he was happy to learn. He hadn't objected at all when she ended it. She thanked him, and he felt she meant it. But that was almost two years ago, in the summer after high school.

But this girl had stirred something in him he didn't know existed. It was too immediate and weirdly overwhelming to understand. Watching her in those thirty seconds, he felt he could have picked up a sword and slain a dragon for her. His vision of her seemed to open a lighted passage toward a dreamlike horizon. In his mind, he was already writing a poem of what the mere sight of her had stirred—just the way she carried herself, her self-possessed stride, her eyes, inviting yet challenging as if she saw something worthy in him as well. He felt a shared magnetism; that moment on the beach was a moment for which all previous moments had been necessary to reach and feel.

Was it to end like that? Maybe a poem was what it was all about: one fleeting unforgettable moment, enough to know the feeling and memorialize it. He told himself it might have to be enough.

Dev had gone for food and, when he returned, was smiling with a coy but combustible eagerness.

"What is it?" Jeremy asked, waiting.

Dev nodded and put the food down.

"So this chick comes up to me at the food van. Out of nowhere." He stared at Jeremy. Jeremy waited, knowing he couldn't push Dev. But still, he was impatient.

"Okay."

"Yeah, well. She says her friend saw you on the beach. This chick saw me too. But her friend saw you and wants to know if you'll be at the boardwalk tonight to hear some folk music concert deal. She wants to meet you."

"This girl was... what did she look like?"

"The girl who came up to me? Dark-haired, cute. No, I didn't see anybody else."

Jeremy's mind and heart raced. Was it a friend of THE girl? Had he seen any other girls today? Probably. Yes. But he knew it was the girl. That was why it had felt poetic.

"Yeah," Dev said, musing. "Kind of cool. Let's do it."

"Okay." Jeremy nodded, trying to remain calm.

"Her friend said that you reminded her, you reminded her friend, of some actor. I can't remember. John something-something."

"John Phillip Law."

"Right," Dev said, jabbing his finger at Jeremy.

"I didn't remember until just now. Someone else said it once. He was in a movie I saw, '*The Russians Are Coming*,' I think."

"Cool. Okay."

They cleaned up and headed down the sandy trail to the beach and boardwalk. The flaming-peach sun was burning out into the flat sea. The smell of fried foods was in the air, and they heard the first sounds of the band testing its instruments: some microphone taps and feedback squeals.

His mind was trying to see ahead, to imagine different versions of encounters and conversations, anxiously trying to rehearse. He took deep breaths. He was thinking too hard.

Suddenly they were at the edge of the boardwalk and among the crowd. They could see twenty yards past the wall of young people (the long-haired boys in surfer shorts or jeans and tee shirts, barefooted or wearing sandals, and the girls in shorts or mini-skirts) to a raised stage with brocades of colored lights along the scalloped fringes of a striped tent. To the side were a tropical bar and a food shack. Jeremy, dressed in tie-dyed green shorts and a clean unpressed cotton dress shirt rolled up to the elbows, shimmied through the crowd away from the bar toward the boardwalk's railing overlooking the bay. He wanted to be apart from the crowd, to scan back at it. He glanced behind him; he'd lost Dev. That was all right, Jeremy told himself, though feeling a quick jab of insecurity.

He reached the railing and spread his palms out on the piping, hoping to efface his nerves. He inhaled the sea-briny air as he stared out at the tide. He felt a sudden urge to escape, to walk the beach in the spirit of a lonely and brooding poet. But yet, his hand held firm to the railing, waiting for a sign.

"Hello."

He turned quickly. There she was. Her face was slightly upturned, her expression open and inquisitive. Though not smiling, there was the hint of a conspiratorial smirk. She held two tall frosted glasses filled to the brim with a pinkish drink and offered one.

"It's a Singapore Sling. They're impossible not to love."

He took it.

"I'm Tory," she said.

"Jeremy." He sipped the frothy drink cautiously. It was both tangy and syrupy. He drank only beer, as a rule; hard liquor usually made him sick. But he felt that in this case, it would not, could not.

She wore a short, loose sundress and sandals with straps that wrapped above her ankle. Her sun-streaked hair was chatoyant against the tent lights. After all of Jeremy's imagining, her physical presence suddenly overloaded his circuitry; his mind felt vacated, which was both a relief and a little unnerving. He took a sip against the pressure to speak.

"Thanks."

She shrugged and moved up to the railing next to him.

"It's kind of unusual for me to ask about a boy. Something about you on the beach, something was different. I got the feeling of a wanderer, a free spirit, not part of all the—" she waved around at the crowd—"the whole manufactured spectacle of college kids pretending to be rebels. I wanted to meet you. I have good instincts."

He took another sip, his fourth. He had already downed a third of the concoction. What was there to say?

"No. I'm not in college. Are you?"

His response felt flat, not fulfilling any expectation of an authentic '*rebel*'.

She nodded. "I'm in my second year at Radcliffe." She shivered as she shook her head, a spasm of disgust rippling across her face. "I don't want to be there anymore. Or even here, really." She gazed out at sea. "My father..." she left it hanging. Her eyes turned inward. "I'd love to travel right now. Take a year off. Hit the road. So much is happening out there..." her arm reached out toward the distance with a pining look. "So much is changing. It feels so, I mean, I feel so stuck in Boston." Her hand touched his arm briefly. "Is that what you're doing?" Her eyes, on him, seemed to shimmer with hope.

The band was playing a catchy yet wistful *Peter, Paul and Mary* tune, at odds with what had earlier seemed *the Beach Boys* mood of the crowd and event. But he was suddenly grateful. He felt this music more suitable to the lyrical potential of the moment, and in turn, to the chords of his imagination which the girl's appearance had first struck. At the same time, this seeming perfection of conditions, the physical and emotional melding, added to the growing pressure he felt to meet and sustain it. He stared over her head as if contemplating her question, not wishing to fall short in his answer until he finally realized it wasn't a cerebral question. He shook his head.

"We came down from Boston too. We're not sure what's next, exactly. Maybe hit the road—"

She interrupted excitedly. "Are you thinking of heading out west? It's what I thought when I first saw you, the impression I had. San Francisco?"

Again, the question was a weight. He could see the expectation in her eyes, excited flickers of foreknowledge of what it must be to fulfill kismet, of what she—and maybe both of them—willed to be. Was it a vision of this one moment, one night, or was it more, and more than hers alone, something cleaved to him in some mysterious way and destined for them to share? His feeling of piercing longing when he saw her, unlike anything he'd ever felt—was that the first tease of fate? Was it now up to him?

He turned and looked up and away, beyond her, toward the west, squinting; with a deliberate but as subtle an affectation as he could summon, he released his face and concern to the worldly elements as if folding up the two of them and delivering them to a storm-tossed Cornish coast. He hoped the effort had at least masked his nerves. He took a slow breath.

"Want to walk on the beach, get away from this?"

'*This*' being the trappings of the world she wished to escape, and he the agent of their joint escape. But he had hoped for a commanding tone and lost momentum at the last second. So it emerged thin and needy. She nodded. He couldn't read the nod but was heartened by its readiness. She took the lead by walking to his left and down the weathered, gray-timbered steps to the sand.

They fell into a stride. After his weak show of initiative, he fell in a little behind her as if this was her adventure. He would play the reticent mystery man who'd made the moment possible but otherwise withheld himself and his 'secret.' A secret which, once discovered (only by her, only on this walk and on this charmed night on this dark shore), would redeem all the romantic missteps of her past and make clear her future path.

'*Secret*'? Well, it was one, in a way. Dev was the only one who knew that he kept a journal and had scratched out some as-yet-unpublished short stories and poems. But how was it to say you wished to be a '*poet*'? It was not something he'd ever admitted. Was poetry the end, poetry itself, or the means to another end—of what, he wasn't sure? He only knew his mind was constantly foraging for words and images to transcribe feelings and moments. This effort seemed more important to him than anything else he could do. He wasn't sure if or how it would come to anything, what it might mean as a livelihood beyond self-centered flailing.

Painting houses seemed a fine and healthy form of work to support him; it freed his mind to drift while grounding him in commercial reality. He was also good at it and enjoyed it, practically and aesthetically. The work was simple yet exacting and rewarding to the senses. The owners always appreciated the finished product. He didn't mind the thought of painting as one kind of career.

But he also suddenly knew that he was not interested in '*hitting the road*' as in '*going out West*' or fulfilling whatever might be Tory's longings in that respect. For him, traveling—at least as some open-ended prospect—was a little disorienting. He needed the predictable routine, the everyday work. But he wouldn't worry about that now.

Still, he wanted to understand her wanderlust, her champing at whatever bit life or family pressures had forced on her. He'd read the Beat poets, appreciated their romance of the road, and was no less aware of, if not captivated by, the hippie zeitgeist. He sensed she might be projecting her expectations onto him. It was all right; he would wait for some miraculous insight, an inevitable and immaculate offspring of the rapture of this night, to resolve the issue. He only knew his attraction to her was unlike anything he'd ever felt.

As he caught her scent with the breeze—a blend of lilac, anise, and suntan lotion searing into his memory—he sensed that his secret would become absorbed into her.

She stopped and turned, almost as if he was willing it—no, not by his will at all, something outside and beyond it and him, numinous and knowing. The light of the pier behind them seemed to cast an aura around her face; her hair was a bronze sheen with golden, breeze-blown strands, her cheeks smooth and satin-downy on each side of perfect, slightly parted lips in persimmon. The totality of her girlness before him was overwhelming.

"You're an artist, aren't you?" she asked with expectant suspense.

"I'm a writer. A poet. That's what I want to be, all I want to be." The ease of the declaration surprised him. It was exhilarating.

"I knew it. I knew it was something like that. That's amazing."

Was it? Yes, it must be. She had asked this question, and he had answered it with a sureness that a hundred hours of rehearsing couldn't have matched. They stared at each other, for how long he didn't know and didn't care. He could have stared, he thought in a flash, for as long as the stars burned.

"Write me a poem."

He was startled. The demand struck him as both perfect and off-putting. It was a challenge he should have been expecting. In some part of him, he'd been composing poetry about her since he'd first seen her. While this was true, he'd thought he would surprise her, not that she would ask for it. His mind was a silent riot, a scramble for words and images, his own and of other poets. Her demand, if that's what it was, forced him to abandon his natural and impossible romantic standard. Time was up. Nothing mattered more than proving it to her. He looked into her eyes and saw something different, a narrowing glimmer. Was it the melting surrender to the moment he was feeling within himself? It had to be.

"Yes," he said.

He didn't wait; he just relaxed and let the words come.

"All nights are now you, before me: sight, smell, and feel. To behold, but then to hold? Or is it just my dream, nothing real?"

His eyes turned upward as he spoke, his vision blurring as if under the sensory spell of his own words. They returned down as he finished. Her face was now closer, her eyes unreadable. He realized she was moving toward him. He could feel her breath on his face. Now he felt her hand on his arm. Her breasts under the tunic met his chest, pressing and becoming one with him. Her mouth went to the side, pressing into his cheek. Was this happening?

She whispered into his ear. *"All across the nation, such a strange vibration... people in motion."*

What was that, a poem? No, it was too familiar. Was it a television or radio commercial? His mind sorted through jingles and taglines, but nothing matched. But now it came to him—it was a song, a line from a song.

Something about '... *San Francisco*'—yes, she'd already mentioned that and asked if he'd come from there, the place she perhaps idealized and wanted to visit. He felt a little deflated as he repeated the words in his head. Her whisper, with its breathy intonations of importance, suddenly felt silly to him. He felt a stab of sympathy for her.

He nodded but pushed out any judgment, wanting to reassure her poetic instincts. Her hair now brushed his mouth as her mouth bent into his neck, lightly biting it. Her hand was moving down to his midriff, fingering under his shirt to his waistband.

He felt himself weakening. He wanted to gain control but couldn't resist the confident, fluid certainty of her motions or the silent ineluctable momentum of his consent. He dropped to his knees. The sand felt like powdered velvet, a soft bed. He was inhaling her hair and the dense scents of her body as only intimacy allowed it. One foot away and staring and exchanging poems is a world apart from the touch of skin and the willing, whispered contact, the point at which the need and end are revealed and bound together. Oh, it was true; there was no going back and nothing more to say. It was just happening; she was making it happen. He couldn't believe there was nothing more to do but hold himself together and be ready. But he could feel such resolve slipping from him. It gave way to the holy tingle and rising rush in his center, where her hand was sliding.

His loss of control was both exciting and perilous. There was a feeling of thrilling abandon to her, to their moment as she was confirming it. To fight off the sense of weakness and unworthy, paralyzing expectation, he pushed his mouth into her neck. But he took in only a mouthful of hair. It was no good. Her hand circled gently but determinedly around his midsection, now moved under his waistband, down, sliding across his pelvis.

He was swelling into her unstoppably, his head now arcing over her shoulder, his eyes closing, readying, unable to stop the secret, rising, gloriously venous rush, the compacted, perfected totality of his desire and being, seizing, possessing, and evacuating at once in shuddering convulsions in which the opening to a radiant infinity revealed itself in a scintilla, before closing on him, leaving him a tossed, spent and destitute soul, tears in his eyes, tears of abandonment and insolvent gratitude.

He groaned and fell to the side. She slid to the sand beside him, holding him lightly. She made a sound between a sigh and a chuckle—a mere sound but somehow loaded, more than it was. It was the last sound he would have or could have made, and in his spent state, he could feel the judgment in it. Was it a sneer, even? Or was he imagining?

The feeling of judgment began to sharpen as his body shifted into the sticky wetness at his center. Her hand was no longer in his pants. When had it come out? He didn't remember. His eyes were still closed as he rolled on his back. He opened them, staring up at the sky. He saw the stars as plain bright dots, heard the quiet sibilance of the waves as only grating, and felt the sand now lumpy and unyielding beneath him—his sensations of the world around him no longer poetically redolent and vast but hard and crowding.

His peripheral vision took her in; he could see she was also staring up. There was a long silence as they lay side by side, motionless and inches apart but without any of the electric sense of nearness he'd been feeling. He held tightly to the silence as if it was something he could will into solace or something tangible he could peel apart and spread around him like a blanket.

After how long, he wasn't sure, her voice broke through.

"I should get back. My friends must be wondering where I went."

"Yes," he may have said. But he wasn't sure, as his wish for silence was overwhelming. He watched her raise herself and brush the sand from her legs. Now he spoke, his voice too high and eager.

"Yes, that's a good idea." He stood, copied the brushing motions, and when he looked up, she was already walking away toward the distant strip of lights of the boardwalk.

◇◇◇◇◇◇◇

He returned to the motel room. It was empty. Dev was still out, no doubt winning over every girl he met. And also, no doubt, there would be at least one who would want to take him home with her, as if he were some cross between an affectionate stray dog, a long-lost brother, and a stoned knight who'd wandered off from the crusade. They would not be wrong.

Jeremy felt the stuffiness, but instead of sliding open the heavy window, he cranked the dented, paint-chipped air conditioning console to a rattling '*High.*' He wanted no more of quiet nature. He went in for a rough landing on the bed and curled up on his side. He could begin to feel the waves of cool, canned air, smelling vaguely metallic and moldy, chill his skin. He was hoping the sound of the machine would blank out his mind.

But within seconds, the memory of his failure on the beach flooded over him. What had gone wrong? Perfection had turned on itself with perverse swiftness.

He should have known. The turnabout was also poetic—a cruelly ironic cuff to his passionate illusions. He clutched at this thought for a moment, thinking he could be absolved by retroactive cynicism, that is, the conceit that he had knowingly invited the humiliation as a poetically exploitable Byronic disgrace.

What did she think of him? He'd imagined the worst the whole way home. He was a joke, a callow fool, a pretender—someone to be briefly pitied and forgotten. She'd tossed him a polite, half-wave as she rejoined her friends, and he had peeled away, affecting indifference (which now seemed even sadder when he thought about it). How could he even pretend to be indifferent after his premature... he could not say it. His face flushed all over again. How could he make it right? Should he try?

Maybe he should talk to Dev about heading out for Boston tomorrow; leave and forget all about it.

But he knew he couldn't forget about it. The girl was shot through his system, and he couldn't end it like this. It wasn't finished; it couldn't be. The feelings he'd had were too extraordinary and no less so now, only more agitated and desperate. What could he do? How could he recover whatever he thought they had without seeming desperate?

He mauled the possibilities for an hour, not realizing he was too close to his embarrassment to think clearly. After an hour, exhausted, he gave up and closed his eyes.

He snapped awake from a nightmare where he was naked on the beach, struggling to run, but his legs only sinking into the sand. Around him, he could see faces, the crowd from the boardwalk, now encircling him, watching, pointing, laughing, jeering.

The light was on. The A/C was still rattling on high. He turned around to see Dev propped up against the headboard, reading a comic book. Dev turned to him.

"Man, it's cold."

Jeremy stared at him for a moment before sitting up.

"Sorry. My fault. Turn it down if you want."

Dev shrugged. He put down the book. "I saw you wander off with that chick. What happened? Anything good?"

"Nothing. I don't know. No, nothing."

Jeremy couldn't keep the edge off his voice; he knew Dev would pick up on it. Jeremy was torn between an urge to talk and a complete loss of words.

Dev nodded, almost as if reading through Jeremy's averted glance.

"Yeah. I hung out with her friends. Silver spoon kids from Boston. She's pretty rich, I got that. She has some super-daddy. You probably know all that."

"I don't know much. I just got her name. We talked, but it was kind of... weird, unreal, about nothing really. Just sort of in code of some kind. As if we had some connection and didn't want to be obvious about it. Or I'm just imagining."

"Cool."

"What else did they say about her?"

Dev kept his eyes on the comic book, reached for the beer bottle on the night table between the beds, and took a slug, propping it between his legs.

"She has some richy name, one of those Beacon Hill names. Winthrop, I think. They said she'd split the family scene, and her old man was not happy about it. They all acted like they'd split too, to keep up with her. I got the feeling she was like their rich-kid clique leader or maybe—" He stopped short. He took a sip of the beer.

"Maybe what?" Jeremy asked, more attentive.

Dev shrugged. "I don't know."

"Come on, Dev."

"Maybe a little..." He put the beer back. "A little schizoid. Like they had to watch her to see she didn't go off the deep end but were also in awe of her and didn't want to admit that." He turned on his side toward Jeremy.

"Man, there was like... I felt no real connection with them. They knew I wasn't one of them. But I could see one of the chicks dug me. I didn't give a shit about their money and kept joking about Boston types, and she was grooving on the crap I was giving her friends. But that was it. I blew them off after a while. Then I met some townie chick, but she was stuck on her biker boyfriend laid up from an accident. She was a Dead-head. That was cool. We shared a joint and talked Jerry Garcia. She left with her friends. The music wasn't going anywhere and I looked for you but figured you were grooving on the Winthrop chick. I wandered down the boardwalk, hit another spot, and came back. Coming in here felt good. A/C, man, nothing beats it."

Jeremy didn't want to pump him for anything more. And he knew Dev wasn't going to press him more about his night; he could tell. He shifted on his back and took a deep breath.

"It was a weird night, Dev. But I'm thinking the awfulness was good in some way."

Dev nodded mellowly, accepting the riddle.

Jeremy turned sideways. "What would you think about heading out early, maybe tomorrow?"

"If you want," Dev said.

"Yeah, maybe. Let's talk about it in the morning."

Dev was now delicately picking out a marijuana roach from the bedside ashtray as if extracting a fragile insect carapace for scientific examination. He studied it, precisely placed it between narrowed lips, squinted as he struck a match, and pulled at it.

Jeremy smiled and turned over.

He'd decided what to do about the girl. It had struck him with starburst suddenness and a rush of wild satisfaction as he'd been talking with Dev. Talking with Dev always seemed to clear his head. Yes, that was it: <u>he would write her a poem</u>! It would be the ultimate poem, words powered by compressed emotion, frustration, and shame, words that would both explain away and even exalt his awkwardness, his failure. The failure, memorialized in a poem, would serve as proof of his deeper feeling and lyrically redeem his ineptitude on the beach, symbolically exalting the moment and what it meant, greater than he'd been able to express. Who else but a man worth knowing, a man of special sincerity, could or would write such a poem?

He was honest enough to consider the needs of his ego and pride to salvage his self-respect. But he had to believe that the sense of wordless attraction between them at first sighting was real and worth this effort. After all, this was who he was, wasn't it—a poet? Also, it was what she wanted to see in him, what would make sense of their instantaneous attraction. He would write the poem tonight.

He got up and scrambled through his pack for his schoolboy composition notebook with the black-and-white paint-splattered cover and his Bic pen. He clambered with them back into bed.

Dev, holding in his last drag, slowly exhaled smoke. He cast a sidelong glance at Jeremy, already bent to his open notebook, smiled, turned on his side, and fell asleep.

◊◊◊◊◊◊◊◊

The poem came together with more lines and images than he could ever use, a good sign. He sorted among the fragments for the best before assembling the connective tissue. It was how he always wrote. The poem's essence formed in a series of word-bursts before he pared it down and pieced it together. In this case, it naturally fell into a sonnet form, and he liked that. The words would be a little wild but contained within the structure, seeking to break free of it. By morning, having read it repeatedly, he was exhausted and exhilarated. He felt as if he no longer needed sleep again, but when it came, it would be as sweet as any he'd known.

But how would he deliver the poem? He knew this mattered: it was, in a sense, as important as the poem itself. He thought of slipping it under her motel room door and immediately leaving with Dev. His departure would serve as the perfect poetic coda. What it meant, the idea of him writing it would provoke and linger in her imagination; it would put fate to the test of whether they met again in Boston (even though he would make sure somehow that they did).

As he finished the handwritten work with the fountain pen and onion paper he carried with him and carefully folded it inside the plain white envelope, he noticed Dev watching him from the bed, his arm under his head. Dev arched his eyebrows lazily, then burped.

"What have you got there, Longfellow?"

"Just something. Nothing..." He turned around and looked squarely at Dev. "It's for that girl, Tory Winthrop. Because I'm a fool, and I can't stop myself. Then we can go, today, after breakfast if you want."

Dev nodded. "Groovy. You know she's staying at the Sheraton on the beach, the richy hotel?"

"I guessed that."

Jeremy smiled: Dev heard and saw—or listened to and observed—more than he seemed to.

◆◆◆◆◆◆◆

Jeremy set out down his motel walkway, across the tarmac parking lot to a sandy median with a low split rail fence over clusters of shiny, prickly scrub. He was now in a straight line toward the beach and the blue horizon of the sea shimmering under the rising run. The breeze was balmy and salty. Jeremy caught a whiff of bacon and coffee from a canteen wagon to his right, where a crew of workers was lining up. He suddenly felt energized with confidence and purpose. What could go wrong on a morning like this?

As if in reproof to his sudden brio, a cloud covered the sun, the sea suddenly looked gray and cold, and the buildings before him no longer sun-splashed and charmed with a tropical aura. As he veered to his right parallel to the beach and made his way along the access road lined with the beachfront hotels and apartments, he saw the Sheraton's large, mauve neon sign. His stomach fluttered and his heart double-pumped. Was he crazy? He pulled out the envelope and held it along his pant leg, slapping himself like a jockey with a whip, and picked up his pace. He refused to lose his nerve now.

He moved boldly through the hotel lobby to the desk. He arrived just as the short, cute receptionist turned toward him and smiled professionally.

"Can I help you?"

He held out the envelope.

"I would like you to leave this for a guest. Tory Winthrop."

She nodded without looking at him, took the envelope, and scanned the registry, swiftly and efficiently.

"Room 234." She pivoted and slipped the envelope into a slot. She turned back to her work.

So that was it. What was he expecting?

It suddenly occurred to him that he'd been imagining a brief but charged exchange with the receptionist; she would read his mind and his mission and his anxiety, sense the *billet-doux* within the envelope, and transmit back a look of female simpatico in support of his poetic valor.

He turned and stared at the floor of shiny agate tiles. He was absurd, or worse, indeed foolish. Who else writes poems and delivers them to hotel lobbies for girls he barely knows? Forget it, he thought to himself. '*You stayed up all night to write it, so now you delivered it. It's over!*'

He felt a new urge to hit the road.

As he looked up, he saw her, through the light lobby traffic thirty feet ahead on his oblique left, in an open lounge area next to the elevators and cordoned off by thick plants. She didn't seem to be alone. She was wearing jeans and a loose cotton poncho. She was reading a piece of paper, a note of some kind, with a clear concentration.

Jeremy was at once spellbound and charged with an urge to escape. He didn't want to see her again before she'd read the poem. But he couldn't break his stare.

He suddenly snapped free from his thrall and veered to the right and the doors to the rear parking area. He counted the steps. But with each step, he felt suspense build in his imagination, as if he wouldn't make it, that it was impossible given that she was there just when he was. A magnetic force seemed to close in behind him, shutting out the sounds around him. He was only a few feet from the door. Now his hand reached out to it and pushed.

Then he was out in the air, with the sounds of cars and the breeze on his face.

"Jeremy!"

He started and turned. She was moving swiftly and straight to him. Her eyes were bright pools of excitement.

"I can't believe it! I was thinking about you and our talk last night. It was so neat! What are you doing here? Is this your hotel too?"

He opened his mouth, unsure what words would come out.

"No, I was just... leaving something for a friend."

"How cool. I mean that I saw you." Her eyes seemed to lose their excited directness, looked down, then back up with uncertain entreaty. Coy entreaty?

"You know, my friend heard your friend say you might head back to Boston soon. It turns out I, uh..." she looked down again, and Jeremy could see the crumpled note in her hand. "I." she shook briefly, a dry shiver, her face turning down and her mouth curling. But she recovered quickly into a smile again.

"I need to get back there myself. I was wondering if I could bum a ride. I need a couple of days to get my head together over some stuff. I'd be cool, tag along, and pay my way. Not be a pain."

She looked up, her eyes now disarmingly direct. "It was so serendipitous to see you here! I don't want to fly, and my friends—" she made a vaguely dismissive gesture behind her. "They've got plans."

He stared at her, wondering how to agree without too much eagerness. This was so sudden a turn of events. What about Dev? Dev wouldn't care.

She seemed to interpret his silence as hesitation that needed more persuasion.

"It would be perfect. Like a way to see how we travel together. You know, when heading out West like we talked about…"

He could not have seen this coming. She seemed a different person.

If he were a true poet, he would be open to life rewriting the script. Here in front of him was unexpected beauty: one seeker and one sought (though which was which he wasn't sure), staring at each other in their respective, unexpected coordinates—awkward, suspenseful, and awaiting an answer which was his alone to give. Last night he had control of nothing; at this moment, he was in control of everything, or the *'everything'* of them.

"I'll let Dev know. I'm sure it will be good."

Her eyes lit up again. She hopped in place and settled. He thought she would embrace him, but she gave a quick shake before letting out a breath.

"Cool."

"We're leaving today. Soon. I hope that's okay."

She nodded vigorously. "I'll get my things. Where should I meet you?"

He had told her where the van was parked, and she hurried off. He watched her, feeling a quick thrill at her easy, athletic stride, the perfect shape of her legs under the perfect fit of her jeans.

As he walked back to the motel, he couldn't imagine what the two or three days in the van would be like, the arrangements they'd be making. Too many images sped across his mind. A voice in his head instructed him not to expect or plan anything, just to let it play out. As he repeated this sensible advice, he was jarred with his first hint that maybe he hadn't been in control of their moment in the hotel lobby.

◇◇◇◇◇◇◇

As Jeremy expected, Dev was unfazed by the news of their traveling companion. He became absorbed with packing his grass and paraphernalia. Once done, he sat inside the open van leaning against the sliding door, with a half smile as he watched Jeremy. Jeremy caught his look, smiled back, and, realizing his balled-up tension, relaxed his shoulders.

Jeremy and Dev had mapped out the trip according to overnight stops at friends of Dev's along the way. This plan would save them motel costs. Dev seemed to have a limitless supply of friends tucked around the country. It was Savannah (the first night), then veering a little to the hills of Virginia for the second night, and finally to Cape May, New Jersey. It would break up the trip nicely: three nights, easy driving, and back in Boston in a few days.

Dev arched his eyebrows under the tourista straw hat he was wearing with casual irony, and Jeremy turned.

There was Tory.

Dressed in the same jeans and now wearing a white vinyl fringed jacket, she was holding a small light blue Samsonite with both hands, a knitted satchel/purse hung over her shoulder. Her hair was pulled back and held in place by a beaded headband; she looked a cross between a hippie girl and an Indian bravette. She wore a wide-eyed, expectant smile.

Dev nodded approvingly.

"Tory, this is Dev. Dev, Tory."

"Cool," Dev said as he pivoted to the inside rear. "Hop in. You can ride shotgun."

Tory looked inquiringly at Jeremy.

"That means you can have the front seat," Jeremy said.

"Oh. Thanks."

And so they were off.

◆◆◆◆◆◆◆

The first day on the road was mostly uneventful. Tory sat one leg under her on the seat, sorting through Dev's cassettes and selecting their music. She seemed good at balancing the choices and order. There was Dev's *Grateful Dead, Creedence Clearwater, Crosby Stills Nash and Young*, and *The Doors*. She would nod to the music, her eyes half-closed, casting quick smiles at Jeremy, some warm, some shy, some sly. When he tried to read them for meaning and smiled back, she would bob her head and turn away. Dev was stretched out in the back reading comic books, sleeping, and now and then working on a joint to pass around.

As they passed into Georgia, she grew quieter, even withdrawn, and the music lapsed. After a long silence, he asked her about her family.

"You've never said anything about them."

She stared at him briefly and intensely, shrugged, and looked away. She suddenly laughed, but bit it off.

"My family. I could write a book." She turned back to him. "Or maybe a poem. Not a sonnet but a long, dark poem. Are you up for it?"

Her look was that same weird mix of intensity and detachment as if shifting abruptly between him and some inner scene of conflict.

'*Not a sonnet*'? Was that an allusion to his poem? If so, it was the first acknowledgment of it. But maybe not.

Now her look settled on him.

"You can tell me," he said. "I'd like to know."

"Would you? I'm not sure." Her new, challenging tone seemed to compress the air in the van. She arched her eyebrows as if expecting some equally charged ping-back.

She let out a long breath and leaned into him, shutting her eyes, her voice lowering.

"Okay. I will. Later. I want to know what you think. You're so sensitive." Another change of tone, to almost a purr, as her eyes moistly blinked. Jeremy leaned a little into her, registering her gesture. She sat back upright.

Suddenly Dev was reading the map and his scrawled directions in Jeremy's ear, guiding him to his friend Piper's house.

They found it on a sleepy street off one of Savannah's main drags. It was a shambolic three-story Victorian structure; it looked to Jeremy like a former fraternity house. Thick trees, draped with moss, bordered it.

They were met and ushered inside by a gaggle of merry hippies: the thin, tall Piper who joyfully embraced Dev; her darker and subdued husband, Drake; friends Mollie, Ben, and Sol; and a huge, excited shaggy dog with cocoa and black patches around his eyes. Jeremy guessed it to be a Saint Bernard.

"Bernese Mountain. His name's Bombadil," Piper said cheerily.

Drake nodded, roughing up the dog's flanks.

Jeremy noticed how Drake carefully watched each of them as they interacted. He looked about thirty, tall, solidly framed, and, as Jeremy saw it, with a covertly conceited manner. He seemed to slump as if to detract from the latter feature, as if aware it was more observable than he liked.

They moved inside. The house was an old Gothic Revival-style manse, vaulted and creaking and paneled everywhere, floor to ceiling, with dark wood. A wide center staircase led to a large landing, which cornered upward to stories above. He could feel the hippie clutter and lived-in disarray, the absence of a calculated layout of furniture and décor—but the house did not appear disorderly or dirty. The air held a faint scent of strawberry incense. Dev was being flocked by the group and Piper. Jeremy and Tory stood back a bit, and Jeremy returned to observing Drake, who he noticed was stealing frequent glances at Tory.

Jeremy knew that Dev's friendship was mainly with Piper—the two had been adolescent boon companions on Cape Cod, though from opposite sides of the tracks. Piper was the rich kid, and Dev was from the working class that serviced those rich kids' summer homes, families, and activities. Dev had given Piper sailing lessons, and they'd hung out at the townie snack bar, which the slumming Piper preferred to her family's upscale country club. It all made sense to Jeremy—that is, Dev making lifelong friends with girls without any sexual pressure. He had more female friends than anyone Jeremy knew. Dev knew Sol, Ben, and Mollie—all quintessential hippies—and they too hovered around him as long-lost friends reunited.

That Drake was the group's leader was quickly confirmed by the subtle but unmistakable deference of the others. Jeremy thought the blonde Piper, model-thin with a look of well-kept, graceful privilege (even while dressed down in jeans and knee-length macramé sweater jacket), was a good match.

Tory had said nothing during the disembarkation and as they moved into the house. She stuck quietly close to him, her arm looped through his almost clingingly. It didn't displease Jeremy so much as puzzle him a little. He saw that Drake spied his smiling unease.

Drake, Piper soon explained, was a musician and local performer who led a small folk band for which she was the vocalist. She proudly added that he was also a playwright who ran a local children's theater; one of his plays was recently '*under option to PBS*.' But Drake had higher '*creative*' ambitions, in which the others, it appeared, were emotionally invested.

She cast an adoring smile at Drake.

"He's a poet by nature; he's guided by a poet's vision. The artistic possibilities for him are limitless. There are so few real poets anymore, you know."

Drake shrugged.

But Jeremy could see him drinking up Piper's words. Yes, he saw himself as a genius. He also projected (intentionally, Jeremy thought) a Jim Morrison vibe. His tight, low-slung black pants looked velvety or velour, not leather, but were worn hip-huggingly and with a wide clamshell belt that seemed a conscious replication. Jeremy found it all irritating.

After a very filling stew-pot dinner, made from scratch by Mollie, they were told, they moved to the large den, a warmly-lighted room of packed bookshelves, old, comfortable easy chairs, a few large bean bags, and a long red-corduroy couch worn smooth in patches.

Through a wide opening framed by two ficuses was a large airy music studio, obviously just remodeled; the newly painted white walls were startling next to all the darker woody rooms, and the floor was a refinished honey-pine. Drake ambled across to the far end, and Piper motioned Jeremy and Tory to follow. Inside, there was a flashy and articulated array of brass and chrome instruments, an electric piano, a full drum set, and bulky sound equipment connected to black cables.

Drake casually picked up an acoustic guitar and sat on a stool in front of a musical easel. The others gathered around him. Jeremy and Tory stood behind the rest, but Piper gestured to them to come forward.

Drake picked at the strings; his face bent intensely over them. He suddenly broke in with the Beatles' *Yesterday*. He had a decent voice, Jeremy thought, but his closed eyes and look of plaintive rapture were overdone.

As it ended, there was a worshipful silence as everyone nodded. As if reading his mind, Tory spoke up with a sharp tone of challenge that Jeremy found bracing.

"Play us something of yours."

Drake didn't look up at first; he just picked at the guitar. A silence fell, though the others were nodding in expectation. The pause seemed contrived to Jeremy; he sensed that Drake planned to play something of his own and was waiting to be asked. But his response surprised Jeremy.

Still staring at his strings, Drake nodded and spoke quietly.

"How about I just make one up right now." He looked up directly at Tory. "For you." He held her gaze, then shifted to Jeremy and winked.

"Let's call it '*Wayward Girl.*'"

Tory showed no reaction. Jeremy looked at Piper; her half-smile was unchanged from earlier, and her expression unreadable. Now Drake started swaying his head a little, closing his eyes. He started picking at the strings, forming a tune. He lifted his chin as he sang-spoke in a borderline falsetto, his eyes closed.

"*Here to there, not yet everywhere, looking for a new way, away; her own way—the dream of the girl, the Wayward Girl. A little lost, this sweet young find, hoping to find, hoping to find, the one who can find her the way, the way back for the wayward girl.*"

He finished with a flourish of finger movements, opening his eyes.

It was a convincing emotional performance. Jeremy turned to Tory, and she was staring back at Drake, her head swaying slightly still to the tune, now slowing.

Jeremy realized with detached clarity that Drake was sexually interested in her and that the song was a veiled seduction in front of everybody. He was not surprised. That Tory could find Drake's impromptu doggerel (if Drake hadn't previously written it for some other '*wayward girl*') more impressive or meaningful than what he had written did not seem possible. For an instant, he felt a rush of hatred for Drake and his act, his props, and his little captive audience of acolytes.

Jeremy tensely smiled as the others clapped and looked at Tory. She gave nothing away, just smiled lightly. Good, Jeremy thought. She's being nice, that's all. Jeremy checked on Piper. She appeared unaware of any suggestiveness to the song and put Drake's guitar away as the others orbited around him. Drake put his arm around Piper and kissed her.

They drifted back to the den. Dev and Sol prepared a tall, ornate-looking bong resembling a cheap movie prop from a sultan's lair, which was soon burblingly shared by all before being set on the low, ivory-inlaid table at their center. A stoned quiet settled. The large dog was stretched beneath Jeremy. The dog had gravitated to him all evening (bafflingly to Jeremy, who'd never had a dog or felt much affinity for them).

"He likes you," Piper had said approvingly. "Bombadil has a keen sense of people."

Drake was leaning back in the largest easy chair, one leg over its curved arm, with Piper on the floor propped against its front, her back between his legs. A stereo with a turntable and tape deck on the wall behind him played soft Indian flute music. Jeremy could see Drake's lidded, cozening eyes scanning them all, finally resting on Tory, who was squeezed next to him in the bean bag.

Jeremy remained vexed at Tory's quiet, pressing physical closeness and what it meant. He'd not been able to read her reaction to the song or much else the entire evening—the mix of impassivity on the one hand and needy touch on the other, the sharp interjections and the dazed stares. When he would look at her, she'd avert her eyes. She clung to him now, maybe, he thought, as reassurance to him after Drake's indirect flirtation or just as a way to avoid conversation.

Jeremy stared back at Drake, sensing his curiosity.

"So..." Dev suddenly said from the far corner, as a kind of light rebuke to the silence. He threw a Huck-and-Tom smile of camaraderie toward Jeremy.

"So," Drake said, echoing Dev. "We're all here on this night, probably never to be here in this same spot or together like this again, as much as we might like to think otherwise. Who knows? Do you wonder why or what brought us here?"

He looked around at each one of the group. Ben, Sol, and Mollie looked limp and lost, heads nodding to some silent hypnotic rhythm, eyes drifting in and out. Jeremy knew Drake would fix on him and Tory, and he did. It seemed they were the only ones whose relationship or emotional quotient he couldn't figure out. His curiosity was offset by a faint, knowing smile and the hint of a subversive urge.

"Jeremy, you're a writer."

"I write. I guess others can say if I'm a writer."

"Oh, don't. We artists can't be so self-effacing. If _we_ don't believe it...."

His fingers were tapping out some tune on the top of Piper's head. Piper's hand reached up and stroked his hand.

"How did you two meet up," Drake said, not looking up.

Tory's voice was sharp and startled the rest.

"We met in a previous incarnation. We're soul mates." They all turned to her. She stared back levelly at Drake with no hint of irony. "And after some issues get worked out, we're going to hit the road west," she added.

Drake nodded, smiling as if it was the opening for which he'd hoped.

"Out west? I like it. Been out there before?"

She ignored him and turned to Jeremy. "And don't talk yourself down. You sound like my father. You're a poet. Whatever he says or what anybody else says."

Drake arched his eyebrows.

"Her father says you're not a poet?"

Jeremy was stumped. "No. We've never—"

"I know that it's what he would say," Tory broke in. Her eyes went flat and cold. "It's what he would say. If it's not on your resume and backed up by an Ivy League degree, or a resolution of his Board of Directors, or passed down through the ages like some decrepit Bostonian legacy, it's not equal to the code, not worth anything, and he doesn't take it seriously. None of the rest of us is supposed to either."

Jeremy looked at her, stunned at her sudden vehemence but trying to take it in stride.

"Your father," Drake said, staring at her, no longer strumming.

She nodded, not at Drake but over him, at the wall, and at the world.

"He doesn't think about art, not really. Not as something created, that artists create, live to create. Just as something to invest in or look at in a museum. Not as the stuff of lives, dreams, passions, beauty."

Jeremy could see all eyes on Tory. Dev was squinting at him over a joint, wonderingly.

Drake looked at Piper, and they exchanged a confidential smile.

"It all sounds a little familiar, doesn't it, babe?" Drake said. Piper nodded.

Tory suddenly dipped her head and eyed him like an archer.

"Why?"

Drake paused, taking the measure of her new tone—just as the others had. But as he opened his mouth, she was ready.

She delivered her words with dead calm. "There's nothing familiar about him. You don't know him."

Now she took in the others, one by one.

"He's not some cardboard capitalist from a hippie morality tale."

A new quiet settled. No one seemed to know what to say. As Jeremy stared at her, he could see a slight trembling of her chin.

Drake smiled lightly and offered a placating nod.

"I can dig it. I was going to say, you know, Piper and I come from old money too."

Piper spread her arms out to embrace the house. "We don't hate our folks. It's all complicated. But it's cool. If you want to rap about it, just let us know."

The soft words, Jeremy thought, might loosen Tory and bring her upper body back to rest. But she held her stiff, forward posture, her intense blank stare. She wasn't finished.

"I don't hate him. I love him. It's why I have to go home."

Drake nodded with a slight smirk. "It's why you have to go west?"

She looked at him, then back to Jeremy. She shook her head, closing her eyes.

"It's my problem."

Drake played a final keyboard riff on Piper's head as his hands fluttered off to the sides and rested on the arms of the chair. He looked down and smiled intimately at Piper before looking up.

"You intrigue me, Tory."

The dog stretched and slid his thickness sideways into Jeremy's legs, covering his feet. The dog was heavy. Jeremy, with Tory's arm locked around his, suddenly felt pinned. He pushed back at the dog roughly, stirring it awake. It looked at him, stood, shook and sidled sleepily to Piper, collapsing between her legs. She started stroking it.

Jeremy felt bidden to say something supportive, as the boyfriend. At the same time, a curious defiance rose within him to say nothing, an unwillingness to force what he didn't feel. The schizoid riddle of her was complicating his physical attraction; he had no answer and felt exasperated. He sensed that he wouldn't find a solution with poetry, but had no other capability or offered no further mystery or promise to her. His poem, he thought, must have been seen by her with an appreciative but condescending indulgence. A wave of defeat swept over him.

She stood, lifting him along with her, arms locked.

"Goodnight," she said to the room.

She led him firmly down the hall, up the stairs, down the long hallway, through a set of louvered doors, to the side screened-in porch. They stood before a large hammock covered in a quilt, assigned as their sleeping space. She climbed on and pulled him in, with clear purpose, nearly knocking him over as they awkwardly squeezed into the swaying hammock.

The angle and weight of their bodies pushed them in closer as they shifted; Jeremy worked to peel apart their tumbled twining into some passable position for rest. Finally, their bodies found the spaces to fit and fill, even though their thighs and legs were smeared along each other, and her head and hair against his cheek and ear. There was a spell of hard breathing, which finally eased. It might have gone on for just a few minutes or an hour. He didn't know. He had no idea what to say. Something was going to be said, though; that's what this night was about, he knew. He felt no physical urges, just suspense.

And then she began. It was a thready whisper at first, alternating between high and hoarse. The words were not always clear. He said nothing for fear of interrupting and strained to listen. Her breath was warm, and sometimes when her voice picked up pace, the quick, moist puffs of stressed words tickled his ear. But he didn't move, didn't brush at it. At first, he thought she might suddenly shout and shatter his eardrum, as the words seemed driven by deep, inner force; but that concern dissolved away under the steady, discursive whispering punctuated by low sobs and tense silences to catch her breath.

"I was trying to be good... I couldn't help myself. I couldn't control... I was tiny, a tiny girl in a huge bed... tiny and terrified of the wet, knowing I would make it wet, not knowing what to do, knowing he would know before I even knew... How did he know?"

Was it a strangled confession of bed-wetting? In his mind, Jeremy saw an image of a tiny twig of a girl in a nightdress huddled at one end of a bed, shivering, waiting with trembling expectation, looking into the darkness for something.

"I didn't ask to go. The tall ceilings, dark overhead, I can't see the top, just dark and echoing, the long stairs... why didn't you smile? 'Smile,' he said, 'you have a name, don't be a baby, they're judging you, are you strong, a strong character? That's what they'll be looking at. Are you just weak like so many others?'"

Who was she talking to, who was talking to her?

"I hated it. No one listened. No one. I was the only one. I couldn't... couldn't..."

Her voice grew low, with a new timbre, fierce—someone else's voice.

"'Yes, you can. Quitter. You won't quit.'"

Back to her voice, *"I can't."*

She was hiccupping sobs now, like a child caught in a panicking, despairing cycle of sobs.

"I don't know... I don't know... I can't... I can't."

There was a pause, her breathing slowed, and she pulled him in tighter as if now speaking to him. But her voice was remote.

"I like him. But I shouldn't. What is he? I don't know what he is... does it matter? Don't look at me that way. Why couldn't I say it – I wanted to say

'*don't look at me like that. He's just a boy who likes me. Why is that something I should be ashamed of?*'"

She released him a little. Another tense pause. Suddenly her fingers gripped him, clawed into his upper arms.

"*I was stuck, trapped. He looked down at me, rising over me. I couldn't stand up. I was down, stuck, stuck, stuck. Daddy, I want to call him Daddy, other people call their daddies ... but just Father. Father.*"

She pulled away and turned on her back. She was whispering more faintly now; he couldn't hear. He shifted closer to her; the hammock swung and creaked.

"*I am something. But I don't know what. What am I? Do I have to be something? If I'm not his daughter, who am I? I can't go and find out. He said that. That's what the stupid masses are doing. That's what he said. I'm smarter. I'm like him. Better, smarter. The rest is a sham, 'find yourself,' an idiotic sham, foolishness, throwing it away. What am I throwing?*"

Her hand reached to her left and rested on his thigh, and she turned back into him.

"*I want to throw it so badly. How do I throw it? You'll show me, won't you? Throw, throw, throw, far as you can, it has to be far, past anything he knows, far out, far out, far out.*"

Jeremy didn't know if she was asking him—it all seemed part of her delirious dithyramb.

"*Out west.*"

Now she burrowed her mouth into his neck, and he could feel her tears on his cheek, her hot breathing in his ear, now her lips dropping and parted, stroking his neck.

"*Beautiful poem. You see me as something beautiful. Will you break me? Break me open, break me into pieces. Will you take me away in broken pieces, will you take me away? Far away. Far out.*"

Now she giggled, a broken, muffled sound, but then a crackling squeak that stopped as abruptly as it began. She was utterly still.

He dared to take a deep breath, but she didn't stir. What was it all about? What did she want, or need, from him? He wracked his mind for every clue drawn from every moment since they'd met, but images ran together into this moment, this hushed, static, indecipherable intimacy, the mere bodily comfort, its innocent warmth. Was that what she wanted? Or what did she *need*?

What did he want? He had craved her physically. But he knew, as the poet, that now was the wrong time, the wrong moment in the verse.

He wanted to rouse her, take her outside and talk to her. He would tell her, yes; they would head out west. Whatever it was that held her back, was haunting her, he would help her, lead her away, out west if necessary, far out, as far as they could go. He would be the man for her; he would become the poem himself in a way she could see, in the way he'd envisioned and written for both of them. They would become the poem together.

But he felt as if she were too fragile and would break if he shook her awake; he also felt, simultaneously, that she would forget everything she said and wonder why he woke her. His romantic midnight courage would crumble in the reality of the simple question.

◆◆◆◆◆◆◆

Jeremy woke with a start. The sudden and disorienting sway of the hammock, the gray darkness all around him but for the outline of the darker head of the dog inches from his face, made him jerk backward, rocking the hammock further. It took him seconds to remember where he was. Tory was gone. He slid upwards and looked at his watch. Two-thirty. The dog had his head flat on the hammock, and Jeremy could feel it looking up at him. What was it with this dog?

Jeremy shifted his legs over the side of the hammock. He cleared his eyes and could see the faint light through the louvered porch doors. He stood, getting his balance.

He moved to the doors and peered through the louvers. The long hallway was empty, its dark wood barely reflecting light from the stairwell at the far end. It felt like a movie set of a haunted house. He cracked the doors and stepped through, closing them behind him. He didn't want the dog to follow.

He stepped lightly down the hallway. The heavy doors with their bulbous antique black knobs were closed. He saw a strip of light under one door and heard quiet sitar music playing behind it. He smelled the rich leafy odor of marijuana.

He reached the stairs and saw another low light coming from the den. He imagined Tory alone, staring at nothing, wondering about him. He moved down the stairs quietly.

At the bottom, he looked left—only shadows of alcoves toward the pantry and kitchen. To his right, the den and flickering reflections of candlelight against the hallway wall. There was a palpable feeling of human presence. He stepped closer, and his narrow view widened. He stopped. Now he could see the sliver of a human form, the naked back of someone sitting on the floor in a straight-backed meditation posture. Not on the floor directly but atop some makeshift flannel bedding.

He moved a little closer. Now he saw the hair, golden-brown, released from its ponytail and spread over the shoulders. Tory was nude from the waist up. He stepped off to the side against the hallway panel.

Was she meditating? Alone? Was this some aftermath of her stream-of-consciousness confessional (if that's what it had been) in the hammock? There was a thick silence; he felt as if his quiet breathing was loud enough to be heard and that it mattered not to be heard, that he was somehow in a strange contest of silence. He didn't move, distrusting the old wood flooring. But after a minute, his upper body leaned forward. With aching slowness, he inched out for a broader view.

The two figures, Tory and Drake, sat facing each other about two feet apart. Semi-circles of squat candles bracketed them, flickering and framing them against the sphere of shadows around them. Drake was also shirtless. His torso was thicker and more muscular than Jeremy would have guessed, and his chest was heavily matted with black hair. He was in a formal Lotus position, and looked comfortable and practiced in it. His hands were up, palms facing her, rotating as if massaging her aura. He was staring intensely into her eyes. Tory was in a more diffident kneel, her hands on her thighs.

She stared back and now swayed slightly, her head nodding in a slow pendulum, uncertain but enthralled.

Jeremy watched, also enthralled. The scene did not seem an unnatural end to the evening if this was the end. He had sensed Drake's motives. Jeremy had imagined Tory's fevered outpourings in the hammock were confidences exclusively for him and cathartic for her. But he'd said or done nothing to comfort her. Or was it instead nothing to satisfy her? She needed something... something else. That must be why she was here. He pulled back.

What was it for him to do? A fit of jealous rage? How would it look and feel?

He peered around the corner again. Now he could see the pale, bell curve of her breast, impossibly perfect in profile with its smooth dipping undulation. The way she jutted her chest forward but held her back straight and her head tilted and slightly arched over Drake was naturally bold and yet betrayed a sense of remove. She was a little unsure, it seemed, waiting. Drake's hands moved toward them, within inches, and then touched before wrapping around them and pushing in suddenly and manhandlingly.

Without knowing what he was doing, Jeremy walked into the room. His body was moving past his mind, something foreign to him. It was strange, as his mind was sharpened to a purpose yet empty of any idea, plan, or words.

The sound of his entry sent Drake falling backward. His elbow caught him, so he was on his side but cantilevered up in a position that forced on him the appearance of lounging. He took advantage; instead of trying to sit up, he leaned back a little as if he'd been expecting the interruption and was now slyly assessing Jeremy and his own options. Jeremy didn't care. He looked down at Tory.

She'd picked up her shirt to cover her front. Her expression was blank, and she stared straight ahead at nothing.

"Let's go," Jeremy said.

"Where?" she said quietly.

His mind came back suddenly, and he thought how absurd *'to our hammock'* might sound.

"Anywhere not here."

"Stay cool, man." Drake's voice, just the sound of it, jabbed at Jeremy like a needle. He didn't want to speak to Drake, and the voice only fortified his determination to ignore him.

"Let's go," he repeated to Tory.

She stood, gathering her sandals and clutching the blouse to her chest. Without looking back, with his hand under her elbow, he led her out.

◆◆◆◆◆◆◆

He woke not in the hammock but in the back of the van.

He'd returned to the porch with Tory and watched her climb into the hammock. But he was unable to climb in beside her. Something told him to leave her alone just now; the forced intimacy of the hammock wasn't going to work. She didn't say a word or urge him in next to her, just lay quietly as the hammock rocked gently.

He'd moved around the corner, found an old white wicker couch, and lay on its soiled terrycloth cushions. He'd hoped the sounds of insects from the thick darkness beyond the screens would be sedating, but the crunching of the wicker under him was too much.

He'd gone back down the stairs, ignored the flickering light in the den to his right, turned left and through the kitchen and out of the house.

He was instantly calmer in the van; the scent of Dev's pot and the feel of the sleeping bag were comforting. He locked on the image of the drive, away from here, with Tory to himself again.

When he stepped stiffly out of the van in the morning and looked up at the large house, which seemed less gothically impressive and even shabby in the morning light, he suddenly worried if it would be that easy to get away. They were Dev's friends. He stared at the house for a few minutes in a trance. He wondered where Dev had slept and wished he would now join him. He felt something brush his leg. The dog was looking up at him, tongue out.

He struck out on a walk around the neighborhood, the dog keeping pace. The crisp air felt good, and he was encouraged in his conscious effort not to think about the night before—at least not now. In time, it might become clearer. Yet beneath his temporizing, in the hold of his gut, he felt the same tightening knot over her. What was it she wanted from him? Anything? Was he wrong or vain in assuming she did? He had no idea.

He started running as fast as he could, madly pumping. *Stop thinking! Stop it, stop it*! He realized the dog was running with him, a heavy loping. The contrast between his teeming, tortured thoughts and the easy lope of the dog, its open, flapping mouth, which seemed to be smiling, brought Jeremy back, and he slowed. He stopped, leaning over to gasp for air, putting a hand on the broad back of the dog, which panted and stared back at him with untroubled brown eyes.

When he returned, Dev was sitting in the back of the van against the open door, smoking a joint. Dev cocked his head, one eye open and one closed against the smoke.

"You crashed out here? Man, what went wrong?"

Relieved to hear Dev's voice, Jeremy shook his head.

"I don't know, Dev. I don't. I want to get on the road and back to work."

Dev nodded. "Me too." He gestured toward the house as he took another long drag, his chin tucked in and his chest expanding. He exhaled, speaking through the smoke.

"Those guys are under some kind of weird spell with that guy Drake."

"You saw it too."

"Not our problem, man," Dev added. He stood, packing the tiny roach away inside a breath-mint tin. Jeremy felt a charge of affection for his friend.

"Right," Jeremy said and patted his shoulder as they moved to the house.

Mollie was up and helped them with a small breakfast of granola, orange juice, and coffee. There was not a sound otherwise. Jeremy decided to wake Tory. They had a schedule to keep and couldn't tarry, he thought. But it was Sunday; they had plenty of time to be back in Boston on Wednesday, even with the stopover in Virginia that night.

He went up to the porch. Tory was in the hammock, on her side facing away, appearing asleep. But as he moved to touch her, she turned and stared up at him. Her eyes were flat.

"We need to get going," he said. He waited for an acknowledgment.

She nodded and turned back on her side.

To his surprise, they were on the road in forty-five minutes. No one else had appeared. Tory had silently declined breakfast but carried a mug of tea Mollie had given her, along with her knitted bag, to the van. She sat huddled in the front seat, saying nothing. Jeremy couldn't tell if she was sullen over him, sad generally, or whatever else. He could not honestly plead surprise. In a way, the figure next to him was not different from the maundering and riddling girl in the hammock or the spellbound partner of the wanna-be Jim Morrison. It was all of a puzzling piece somehow—as was the girl on the beach in the glow of the setting sun who'd inspired a poem (who had perhaps appeared as a transfigured poem herself).

As Jeremy drove off, with Dev in the back propped up against the side, he looked in the rearview mirror. Mollie had retreated to the house, but the dog stood still, watching even as they turned a corner. He felt a sudden, strange pang of sorrow.

The first few hours of the drive north passed without event and with few words. Tory's motionless silence seemed to set the mood. Dev said little, shifting now and then in the back, resting, reading. Jeremy made a few lighthearted attempts at conversation. He asked her if she was happy to be going home.

She said nothing for a minute and then shook her head dully. A minute later, abruptly, even brightly, she said, "Yes. Yes. It's right. It will be good."

For the next few hours, it was a kind of bipolarama. Tory apologized for her confessional effusions in the hammock (which he assured her were no problem for him) but said nothing about the scene with Drake. Nor did he. She withdrew again. A few moments later, staring straight ahead, she lapsed into quiet, murmuring declamation of her father, almost to herself. Her father was obsessed, she said, with his patrician code and blind to the wild and exciting changes around him in the culture, no matter how patiently she tried to acquaint him with them.

But then she would backtrack, explain away his coldness as a kind of generational stalwartness, not his fault. She would even throw in boasts about his accomplishments, his brilliance among his peers, and how this incited resentment and cost him, though he didn't flinch or compromise.

She would talk lightly about a deceased mother she hadn't respected and friends who didn't understand her dream to break free. Then she would loop her arm around his, leaning against his shoulder, and sing along to the music. She would, with almost cloying, sugary insistence, ply him to tell her what it was to write a poem. He didn't know how to answer. But she would spin off to another subject before lapsing into more moody silence.

They'd crossed into Virginia by noon and were closing in on the Staunton area—where Dev's friend Harper lived. At Jeremy's prompting, Dev started to tell some old stories of his friend Harper and his adventures as an Army Ranger and his mushroom trips in Cambodia before being cashiered and making friends with Ken Kesey. But she only leaned her head low against the windowpane.

◇◇◇◇◇◇◇◇

Not long after, she looked up, saw the hand-painted sign, and clutched his arm.

"A puppy!" She silently mouthed '*a puppy*,' staring at him as if they were suddenly trusted lovers exchanging a soundless code of connection.

"It's perfect! A perfect sign! When I was thinking about what we could have to symbolize..." Her arms reached out. "This, our trip, and the trip out west. The future."

The animation and conviction on her face were too much for Jeremy. He couldn't stop to question any of it or its meaning. He yanked the wheel up the dirt road.

As they turned the final bend of the crushed gravel and dirt lane, an old, graying split rail fence appeared on both sides. Suddenly there were two large oak trees before them, grand leafy portals to what looked like a miniature fairy-tale farm.

"Oh my," she said.

A handful of small, red clapboard sheds and outbuildings bordered the left side of the clearing on the pan of hilltop acreage. Straight ahead was an opening to a field beyond framed by large ivy-covered stone plinths. On the right was a small wooden farmhouse with a porch.

Jeremy slowed to a stop and shut off the engine. A cool breeze blew through the open windows. They were all still, the road sound in their ears. Suddenly the honking of geese and trebled bleating of goats broke the quiet.

Tory was first out, almost leaping. She stood, opening her chest with a marveling deep breath as she looked up. Jeremy walked around the front, sizing up the small, neat spread and Tory's wild smile.

She turned to him, incandescent. "Look at it. It's perfect!"

'Perfect' for what? He wasn't sure. But it did look like a scene out of a storybook.

Having tucked away his roach, Dev opened the back, stepping out as a large goose swaggered toward him and made a quick nip at his pants.

"Dude," he said, moving behind Jeremy.

As the screen door slapped, they looked up to see the stocky, bow-legged woman, out from the shadowing overhang of the porch, in ample jeans and a man's work shirt. She peered at them under a sun-visored hand.

"Welcome there, young folks," Opal said. "What's your interest?"

A few minutes later, the group stood at the split-rail and chicken-wired enclosure and looked at the pup at the far side. The pup, lying down with paws extended in front, in an alert, if relaxed pose, stared back.

At sixteen weeks, its ears were erect, and its stare was attentive but neutral. *It did not glean anything of particular urgency or interest from the group to necessitate an approach; it trusted the farm lady, and that was enough.*

Tory fixated on the dog with a wondrous stare.

Jeremy stood slightly behind her, just waiting it all out.

Opal, a few feet away, grinned at the dog's detachment. It was what she expected. She glanced among the three and the dog with her shrewd hillbilly eyes. She was conflicted about selling the dog and didn't usually feel that way about anything. She knew it was an exceptional dog, but she also understood that she could not realistically fulfill its future as she felt obliged.

But still, she was partly hoping the dog's aloofness would discourage these kids, just to put off her decision. But the girl did not seem discouraged. Opal watched as Tory stepped closer, leaned over the fence, and slapped her hands against the front of her thighs.

"Look at it. It's so regal." She turned to Jeremy. "Don't you think?"

Opal made a clucking sound and tapped her thigh. The dog looked at her, stood, and trotted to the fence. As it approached, the girl's hand reached toward it. The dog slowed, turned its head to the lady, and paused so that Tory's outstretched fingers could just brush its sable and tan coat. As Opal signaled with her head, the dog stepped into the girl's strokes.

The dog was not deeply, organically 'aloof' (and Opal understood this). It was naturally confident and not uncomfortable with solitariness. It was a confidence embedded through its bloodlines. It did not seek affection as a thing unto itself or a matter of needy impulsion. It was a purpose-driven animal and related to the world through work. Part of this instinct was a sense that humans—or one human above all others—must be and would be involved in defining his purpose.

Opal felt the dog was exceptional because it understood—or would come to understand—where humans fit in its scheme of life and to co-exist without recourse to undue solicitation or undue worry. It was a dog who would take much of life and the people around it in stride. It was not something one could teach. The other puppies had it, though not to this one's extreme. They would be socially adaptable and equipped for happy lives, given care from decent and fair owners. This dog would be different; its judgment, its natural sense of discrimination, would be keener and play a more significant role in its life. Judgment in a dog—it was a rare thing. This dog would be a detached and resilient dog around human challenges, but once he found the individual who could reach down into its core and inspire him with trust and leadership, the dog would give more than could be measured.

Opal cut short her reverie. If she thought so highly of the dog, how could she—at the very least—ensure these kids understood their responsibility?

Dev's voice cut the silence. "That's a police dog, man."

Tory now leaned in and picked up the pup with some effort. The dog relaxed into the hold and sniffed her chin. She squeezed him slightly, and he grunted.

"He's a free spirit," she said. "He can be whatever he wants."

"Yeah, like a police dog," Dev repeated.

Jeremy looked at Opal as if for help. But Opal was rock-faced, waiting.

"Tory," he said carefully. "Is this going to be your dog? I mean, is this what you want?"

She turned to him with a giddily chastising expression.

"It's going to be our dog. Our mascot, a way of symbolizing our time together, whatever we do together."

She seemed possessed, Jeremy thought. He wondered if the others saw it. Opal, with her crows-feet squint, was inscrutable. Dev was looking off again.

Tory now turned into Jeremy, holding the puppy.

"Look at him. You can't tell me you can look at that and not see poetry. I'll bet you'll write one for him tonight."

Jeremy stared at the dog and smiled wanly. "It's a big commitment. Who's going to—?"

"Don't be so bourgeois." She softened and bore in on Jeremy like a snuggling lover. "We'll share him. I've already got a name. You'll love it."

She seemed to be taunting him, swaying slightly with a sly smile, before leaning in to whisper in his ear. Jeremy listened and nodded blankly. He stared at her as she pulled back, searching for some sign of self-mockery or sarcasm. But he saw nothing like that, only pure, ingenuous sincerity.

These intimate exchanges and looks were beyond Opal's reckoning. But, she admitted, the girl was at least enthusiastic. Opal needed to know more. She picked up one of the sassy geese pecking at Dev's ankles.

"Why don't y'all come in for some iced tea while you're fixin' to decide."

The farmhouse inside was what Jeremy expected—close and rustically homey with exposed ceiling beams, knotted wood walls, and oak floors. It was impeccably tidy. The fine-looking, handmade wood furniture was in perfect scale to the size of the main living area, which opened up a few steps down from the entryway. To the immediate side was a small kitchen with a single white porcelain sink and old chrome fixtures. Copper-bottomed pots and pans hung from a center rack. A collection of old chinaware filled the recessed shelves, along with dozens of porcelain and clay figurines of animals.

Jeremy sat at an old gingham-covered table next to the kitchen, where Opal prepared the iced tea. Down the steps, in the living room, Tory and Dev stared at the near wall lined with photos of dogs, some faded and old, some newer, and a plethora of faded ribbons and awards.

Opal poured tea from a frosted pitcher and handed it to Jeremy. She put it down and moved to the others. She pointed to a nearby picture of a German shepherd, posing in classic stretched profile alongside a younger Opal.

"That's the boy's granddaddy, Tobias. '*Toby the terror.*' He done herded ten horses from a burning barn. Burned badly in the bargain. He weren't nothing like a terror to us, so that's the joke."

She pointed to another, a black dog looking straight on at the camera, a blue ribbon around her neck.

"And there's his daughter, Helen of Troy. Real fine bitch. I sold her to a fellow down in Raleigh. A year later, he drove up to tell me she hauled his drownin' little girl from a swimmin' pool. That line, it's some line."

Tory turned to Opal.

"It's always bloodlines and breeding, isn't it?"

Jeremy detected an ironic edge to the comment. But Opal looked at her thoughtfully.

"Yes indeed, mostly it is. That's the science of it. But one can never be sure either way. You just do your best to honor the breed, the model old Max set for us back in Germany."

"Hmm," Tory said.

They moved back to the table and sat. There was a silence as Opal glanced at each in turn. She removed a worn manila folder inside a thick album beside her, opened it, and sorted through some papers. Jeremy had intended to remain silent; he imagined that the reality of an actual purchase of the dog would hit Tory, and they'd soon be on their way.

Opal put her palm on the papers, nodding with a new gravity.

"I'll confess to you folks, I haven't been sure about selling this pup. He's not like the others. I'd like you to understand how he's different."

"I can see he's different," Tory said, with new calm and directness that surprised Jeremy.

Tory had her hands in her lap and her legs crossed like a self-contained diplomat at a tricky juncture in a peace deal.

"That's why I was drawn to him. I was drawn to him before I even saw him. Your sign told me something. You know what I mean?"

Opal stared at her with a slight frown. Being of a mystical bent, she understood or wished to; simultaneously, she felt uncertain. People will say what they want you to hear when they want something. She'd sat at the table with many an unworthy prospect, and her dogs deserved the best.

"This is a strong dog, and he'll be stronger in the mind and body. And soul, I'll add. He'll need work and training from those who can respect him, and he can respect. He's not an ordinary pet."

"You've sold the others, right?"

Opal nodded.

"You held onto him because no one wanted him or because you want him?"

"A little of both."

"You have to decide if you want to sell him. I'm prepared to pay you whatever you want. He's the dog for me. I mean, for us..." she turned and clasped Jeremy's arm and smiled, her eyes glimmering. "We're going to love him and show him the wider world. Isn't that enough?"

To Jeremy, her look, her touch, and the earnestness of her words were a revelation. From where was it all coming? He wanted to believe it, but at the same time, couldn't shake the sense that this was a kind of battle of wills to Tory. As if she wouldn't be denied. Looking at her, he felt everything he'd thought he'd known wiped away. It didn't seem possible that she didn't know what she wanted and couldn't have it; *'going west'* never seemed more thrillingly possible. He tried to think of what a dog would mean—the details of its care. She was implying she would handle all this, wasn't she? Her intention and will at the moment seemed a force to obliterate all doubt.

"You mentioned $200, I believe," Tory said. "I'll give you $500."

At one time, this would have been the worst thing anyone could say to Opal. To her, it wasn't ever about money. But she held back her first bristling instinct and thought: why was this so difficult? It was this particular dog. Wasn't there a reason it was still with her? So that was it—she was going to keep it? But was that fair? She was older now. That was just the truth. She was holding on to an image and a past and its possibilities which were no more.

Tory asked calmly, "What is your hesitation? Why do you think we won't be good owners of your dog?"

Opal was startled out of her thoughts. A breeze fluttered the kitchen curtain, and she felt its cooling touch. The papers stirred as if to scatter. She put her hand on them. Suddenly, she felt a sense of great relief, an unburdening. She would let the dog go. The dog would have its own life, adventures, and fate—apart from her. Who knew where it would lead? But with a calming resolve, she knew this dog needed the world, and perhaps some part of the world needed it. That was what she'd felt from the beginning, she realized in a flash—this dog's destiny was beyond her. She just had to set it in motion. The presentiment of the truth had shaken her, and she'd been holding on to hoard the dog's specialness. It was of strong stock, the strongest, and it would be fine, as God would have it.

"It's not the money," she said, finally. "The price is $200."

SOMERVILLE, MA

THE DOG SAT *in the small apartment, watching the man watching TV.*
The dog was waiting without knowing it exactly; a vast, if conditional, patience
was part of who he was. Nothing was being asked of him, and so he waited. The
patience was in inverse proportion to what he had to give, the intensity of his
drive and loyalty, but the giving required the human to draw it out. The dog
instinctively understood this man was not the one to do so.

The dog had been lifted into the van and left the farm without objection. He
thought of the lady for a while and felt some expectation of returning. But after
a few days, he accepted where he was. Once in Somerville, in the apartment, he
quickly adapted as well. The two men fed and walked him. He'd already come
to understand their body language, the intentions and emotions behind it, and
the inflections within their voices. Reading people was natural for him; his
self-confidence allowed him the tolerance and mental space. It would be diffi-
cult to rattle him, though as a very young dog, he was always ready for physical
challenge or action or play, at the right moment.

He could feel the tension of the taller man. It radiated from him—the tight-
ness in his body when he gathered him for a walk, the identical path they took,
and the quick, impatient jerks on the leash. He seemed uncertain and conflicted;
the dog read the switches between the man's frustrated jerks and stroking apol-
ogies as marks of unseriousness. In this case, it wasn't a judgment, as we might
call it, just a way of adapting and understanding. The other man was looser in
his body, but his walks were scattered and inattentive. The dog was inclined
to dismiss this man as well. But they fed him, and this mattered. He waited.

Jeremy was at wit's end. The last day and a half of the drive had been
weirdly flat. Tory had paid little attention to the dog sitting with Dev in the
back. She mostly read from a French book. She would occasionally glance

46

back at the dog with a vaguely beatific smile, then at Jeremy, and place a soft, saintly hand on his arm. He took this to mean an assurance all would be well. His urge to trust her was nearly as overwhelming as his physical lust for her. Trust was the only path to satisfaction or a clearer understanding of a future. It was in her hands. Had it ever not been? He felt now he was playing a part and was lost in it. His intervention that night at Drake's seemed to have not mattered. He was again the slightly bewildered poet, waiting on her. The thought frustrated him, but the frustration mingled with fatalism. He knew no other way. He didn't understand yet that fatalism was just a means of coping and was a self-deception.

When they reached the outskirts of Boston, she gave directions to the downtown. She didn't say anything about '*home*,' Jeremy just assumed. He navigated the narrow, cloistered streets of Beacon Hill. He had always disliked the area. He saw the dirty brick, tarnished brass, and chipped-black iron gates of the frontages as a kind of inverted ostentation, an effort to give meaning to anguished emptiness. He smiled at his fraught phrasing—but he didn't care for the dowdy, understated wealth of old Boston and found relief in the brash *nouveau riche* money of the suburbs with the red Corvettes in the driveways of the houses they painted. He'd understood Tory was a '*rich kid*' but had not associated her with this, perhaps as avoidance.

When they reached a non-descript three-story brick townhouse, she put up her hand, grabbed her bag, kissed him on the cheek, reached over and awkwardly hugged the dog, and slid out the door. She looked back at him.

"Let me sort things out with my father. I'll give you a call. Thank you so much for everything. The poem is a keepsake, a treasure. I'll call..."

He was speechless.

"You guys have a place to keep him for a while, don't you?" she said. "You're in Somerville, right?"

"They don't allow dogs." It was all Jeremy could think to say. Words were rushing and crowding the gates of his mouth like rioting prisoners, but none could escape.

"Oh, you're clever. Both of you. You'll work it out."

She blew them both a kiss, shut the door, and ran toward a side door through the open garage where an old Volvo and equally old Mercedes convertible were parked.

Jeremy looked at Dev, who just shrugged, squinted against his joint smoke, and smiled with the *sans souci* of a Foreign Legion soldier. Jeremy laughed but grimly, out of solidarity. Dev ruffled the dog's coat.

◆◆◆◆◆◆◆

Tory had wanted to name the dog *'Frisco,'* as she'd seductively whispered to him that day at the farm. Jeremy and Dev rejected that, but they only called him *'dog.'* (Somehow, *'pup'* did not seem apt for this dog.) They'd been able to sneak him in and out of the apartment, but the effort to avoid the manager and other tenants was becoming exhausting. They'd taken the dog with them on their painting job in Melrose, but the job had been scuttled; Dev's brother-in-law had sudden money concerns.

The entire scene of the two of them and the dog in the apartment had become, to Jeremy, a constant reminder of Tory, whose silence and non-responsiveness to his calls were stacking up as a kindling pile of frustration. Dev had tried gently to tell him that Tory was gone. It had been just a *'summer thing.'* It wasn't worth the stewing.

Jeremy sensed Dev was right, but still, he couldn't absorb it.

Jeremy hadn't felt her shimmering image without a deeper reason, hadn't written that poem for something so fleeting and unreal.

The dog was proof of it, of the meaning of it all, proof that he and Tory would find a way or she'd call him and set their newly defined relationship in motion. She seemingly had profound issues with her father and needed the time, that's all.

But with each day, he dog became more of a reminder of failure and crashed illusions; at the same time, he was a symbol of her capriciousness and manipulation. Jeremy's longing for her and the relationship reconstructed was collapsing. Increasingly, he craved a reckoning.

For days leading to Thanksgiving, he'd been working out the confrontation in his head, tormenting himself to take action. He kept balking. He wanted nothing more than to see her, but still knew how it would end; he feared the words out of her mouth, or worse, those written on her face; he feared what he might say in response (even that words would fail him, and his frustration would find no relief). But there was the dog; the issue had to be settled.

On the Tuesday before Thanksgiving, while walking the dog, he ran into the building manager. She was a morbidly cheerless woman in her fifties with a face and expression that seemed only to take on life—like a miser when counting his secreted gold—when the opportunity for gossip or the exercise of petty authority offered itself. He had told her the dog was a friend's dog and only there for the day while the friend was at a hospital for medical tests. She didn't want to accept the story but, as Jeremy knew, had no choice—this time. So that was it. He was committed.

He drove into Boston in the cold rain. The dog sat quietly in the back. He glanced at it—calm in the face of what was likely another disruption in its life. He felt admiration for its... what? Grace under pressure? Something. The dog had never caused them a single problem. That seemed unusual for a young dog. It had yet to bark, whine, act up, or make a mistake in the house. And it was, he admitted, stunning in its appearance. It had taken on an even more imposing adult demeanor at seven months. Was it possible that he and Dev could keep it after all? But he checked himself. That wasn't the point. It was her dog, she wanted it, and she bought it. It was her responsibility. Yes, this was about responsibility.

More nervous as he neared Beacon Hill, he tried distracting himself with a recitation of his disgust with Boston. All about him, the city looked rusty, crusty, and oppressive, a joyless place and people trudging through the motions of an endless endurance test. It was a dismal city, with its ancient and supercilious aristocracy in its lofty precincts and its mean and brawling natives in the lower ones. Its 'Southie,' whose stretched vowels made Brooklyn's accent sound melodious, and the equally clannish and congested North End. And it was a physically drab city, really—its so-called historic charm a big lie. The city had been built by piling dirt from donkey carts over a great swamp. Historic landmarks were dotted here and there but were surrounded by a trashy low-rise sprawl of sex parlors and sailor haunts. As he neared Park Square and the fringes of the 'Red Light District,' the sense of it was thick. He looked at the commuters emerging from the subway, huddled against the buckshot rain and wind. He thought back to Florida. The world was a wider place; he suddenly wanted out, and a resolve fortified him for a moment: '*Go west, young man!*'

He was on her street. He parked, cramming the van between a Fiat and a Jaguar, got out, and cranked open the rear van door. The dog sprang out, and Jeremy took the leash.

The gate to the house and its short driveway was open, and he walked up the apron of smooth embedded stones under the multiple oblong eyes of large uncurtained windows. He reached the concrete stoop with the curled wrought-iron handrails and stepped up to the lacquered black door. He was all momentum now. He lifted the horseshow-shaped knocker, and it came down as loud as a shot.

There was no sound from within before the door opened suddenly, but only partially. A black woman in a white smock and holding a rag stared at him sideways. Her voice was low and reluctant.

"Can I help you?"

Another voice, deep and resonant, sounded to the side. "What is it, Sally?"

A hand jerked open the door, and a tall man in gun-metal gabardines and a blue, double-breasted blazer with a crest stepped in front of the woman, entirely blocking her. He had a mountainous head, and oversized features—nose, lips, and precipitous cheekbones—with steel-gray hair piled on top but trimmed to a buzz at the sides, exaggerating his height. Jeremy had an image of Herman Munster without the jolliness. He looked to be a hale fifty-five. He scanned Jeremy and the dog sharply, his voice peremptory.

"Yes?"

"I'm looking for Tory. Tory Winthrop."

"And?"

Jeremy could detect a moving shape behind the man, in the shadows, coming down a large staircase.

"I've got it."

She was suddenly at her father's side. The man looked at her, back to Jeremy, but didn't budge.

"It's all right, father," she said. "I know him. I can take care of it."

'*It.*' Jeremy registered what it augured.

The man held hard eyes on Jeremy. After several seconds, he stepped off to the side. From down a hallway, Jeremy heard: "I'll be in the study."

Tory nodded and turned back to Jeremy.

She wore flannel pajama bottoms, slippers, and a too-large, shaggy sweater whose sleeves hung below her hands. Her face was a shock to Jeremy. Recalling and expecting his Ft. Lauderdale vision, he saw another person's face. The bronzed, radiant sun goddess was gone. Her hair was pulled back tighter, with no more shimmering, wayward strands of gold thread; it looked flat as straw. He had the impression of greeting a prisoner brought out from a cell to see him.

She plastered on a thin smile. She still had not acknowledged the dog, sitting quietly by his side.

"How are you?" he said, unable to think of anything else.

"Fine. It's nice to see you. What's up?"

'*What's up*'? The words loosened him a little.

"You're back at college?"

"Uh-huh. Radcliffe."

"I remember." He heard the words come out of his mouth before he could stop them: "How bourgeois." Frustration and anger, he knew, often first appear as sarcasm.

Her eyes glazed over. For a moment, Jeremy saw before him the corpse of their relationship. But she ignored the words.

"What about you? Any plans?"

"Dev and I may go out west," he spoke the lie without thinking. "You know, like we talked about doing." There it was again, the sarcasm. He didn't want to sound like that.

Her eyes dulled but stayed on him.

"Good for you."

Jeremy looked down at the dog and held out the leash.

"I came by to give you your dog."

She gave a quick laugh. "I can't take him. His home is with you now."

Jeremy felt the words rising and rushing.

"He's your dog. I can't keep him. That's why I'm here. I'm not here for anything else." He stabbed the leash at her.

"Jeremy, please. I'm at college. My father's got three Jack Russells." She shrugged her shoulders with a half smile and with confident finality.

"Let's get your father then. He's your dog. You bought him. I didn't want you to—"

"Why didn't you try to stop me?"

"What? *Stopped* you? How could I, I couldn't—"

"Why couldn't you? You sat there and said nothing. You know you might have, I wanted you—"

"What are you talking about? You were crazy for the dog. What did you expect me to do, just say '*no*'?"

"You never said anything. I thought you'd speak up, you know, or..." She glanced briefly, anxiously down the hall.

"You thought, I... I..." He couldn't speak. He was throttled with confusion, feeding the anger. But he knew the anger could only choke him like this if there were some truth in what she said. Yes, he had desperately wanted to tell her '*No*.' He hadn't. The searing realization seemed to open the gates for a dozen other moments, memories of tense silences when he'd possibly failed some test of worthiness.

"So that's what the father issues are all about? He tells you what to do and not to do? Because he's '*stronger*'?"

His words surprised him, and it thrilled him to utter them. But if this was 'strength,' it was a bitter and belated kind, he knew. He could see that the words had stung. Her face shrank into itself, and her eyes deadened. She shook her head.

God, this wasn't going in any way he'd hoped but in every way he'd feared.

"Forget it. It doesn't matter. Jeremy, I'm sorry. I can't take the dog. He's your dog now." She smiled thinly, and her eyes frosted over with finality. "You'll do fine with him."

She leaned over, gave the dog a quick indifferent rub, and took a step back behind the threshold.

"Take care, Jeremy. Keep writing. You know what I mean, your poems."

"No," he said, and she paused.

"This isn't what... I wanted to say. The dog, it's all right, it doesn't matter. It will be fine. You were so happy that day. I wanted you to be happy, that's all. I wanted you... I wanted you."

He stood, staring at her, trying to see in her the girl he saw on the beach, knowing at the same time it was impossible and the knowledge hollowing out his insides. He could suddenly feel the weather now as a hostile element, as an ally in his humiliation.

"I'm sorry I didn't do better... I want..."

Her eyes seemed to take on a shallow luster as she listened. Was it his imagination? Was she listening at all? Or just waiting him out, out of old Bostonian cordiality?

She glanced down the hall, then back at him.

"I'm sorry, Jeremy."

The door shut with a solid, weather-stripped smack. He stared at its black massiveness. There was nothing else to do.

He felt something he'd never felt in his life: from the deep, a rising rage. He could feel it as an actual heat spreading in his body. He'd forgotten the dog. It was sitting, just watching him. Suddenly, the dog became the physical totem of the relationship's disintegration, from a shining dream on a beach to a shivering, sopping failure on a doorstep in the rain.

Jeremy dropped the leash and pivoted down the steps. He walked halfway across the apron before stopping. He turned. The dog hadn't moved. The fact only enraged him more. Now he saw the maid peering at him through the narrow strip of leaded glass to the side of the door. He pointed to the dog, then at the house.

"Take it! It's not mine. It's hers!"

He walked to the end of the driveway. There was no sign of response from the house. The dog still didn't move. Jeremy said to himself, *'just go, leave it there.'* But he couldn't do it.

"Goddammit," he said. He spun and walked rapidly back to the dog, picking up the leash.

It had all been an illusion, his infatuation. But there was nothing illusory about this moment. The rain had picked up and was lashing the side of his face. He could feel the cold wetness against his legs. He was close to soaking through.

He'd failed to read through the illusion and to flex the will to win the actual girl, to extract her from the illusion. He was a double loser. For a moment, he was caught cowering between the terrible twin revelations, made clear and harrowing in an instant by her presence and words: that he could have had her but never could have had her and that everything he did was of one willful folly he could have stopped at any time but also never could have stopped.

His prideful poetic conceit had willed her to be something she wasn't. He couldn't blame her for not being or becoming the girl from the poem. He also wanted her body? Right? God, yes! Say it! Admit it! He failed at that, too. It was probably there for him at any turn, but he was too noble to lower himself! But it wasn't nobility at all, just cowardice. He lied to himself to exalt his artistic ego. A pitiful self-deceit—he wanted to grub around her and have her as much as Drake did. She had contempt for him as a result. Yes, he saw the contempt in her eyes, face, and voice. He was a fraud, a pretentious play-artist.

She'd even given him a final test, and he'd been too stupid to recognize it and scared to face it. He couldn't even thwart a crazy whim. She'd wanted him to stop her. Really? This burned the most. She despised him for not standing up to her when he could have, so easily.

The compressive force of his self-loathing and his hatred of her was squeezing him like a tin can tumbling into the ocean depths.

He looked at the dog. He was stuck with this, the living reminder of his weakness and failure.

He still held the leash—the mental image of handing it to her in decisive comeuppance now mocking him.

As he stepped down, he slipped into the dog and fell, one knee cracking into the pebbled concrete. The stumble released his rage. He stood and kicked the dog on the flank, in the soft cleft between the rib cage and the hindquarters. It was a violent kick, and the dog let out a deep grunt and short yelp as it spun and fell backward down the stoop, its front paws spreading out and its rear end collapsing.

It lay there panting, momentarily bewildered, watching him.

Jeremy, struck by what he'd done but caught in the awful momentum of his rage, unmoored from himself, seeking repudiation from the universe through the dog but seeing nothing from it at all, just innocent puzzlement, grabbed the leash and jerked the dog forward.

He zigzagged like a drunk down the driveway, nearly tripping again as he snapped the dog this way and that, hoping for it to cry or growl or bite. But the dog only followed quietly and obediently. The dog was large enough that now, aware of Jeremy's state and no longer caught off balance, the yanking didn't have much effect.

When he reached the van, the dog sprang inside before he could yank it.

He slammed the door and caught the dog's tail. He heard another yelp, more like a short, upper-register cough, but this time capped by a growl, then silence. Jeremy opened the door a crack, re-slammed it, and crashed his fist against the side of the van.

◆◆◆◆◆◆◆

He drove toward Cambridge, trying to empty his mind. He just wanted to get drunk with Dev. He neared a favorite tavern of theirs, *Rory's,* on the Cambridge/Somerville line but couldn't find a place to park. It was still raining, the frayed wipers leaving streaks as he strained to locate a spot. He finally came upon one and shoehorned in the van. Opening the window vent for the dog, and pulling his jacket over his head, he ran into the bar.

55

Dev didn't answer Jeremy's call from the bar's payphone. After walking back to his table, Jeremy thought it was for the better. He deserved to drink alone.

He nursed beer after beer at a corner table as he cracked peanut shells from the wooden bowl, brushing the remnants off to add to the bar's most well-known feature, its carpet of shells.

Two hours later, he'd had enough. He no longer cared about the day or had convinced himself he didn't. He walked outside. The sky was clear; the temperature had dropped sharply. He inhaled. All right, it was over. He didn't have to think about her anymore. He felt a rush of drunken exhilaration, eager to plan what was next. He was serious about leaving, striking out west—with Dev. The universe was telling him it was time; it was a perfect time. Nothing was holding them. They just needed to get the money. And they would, by the spring, after another house or two. He teased himself for a moment, thinking of sending Tory a gloating postcard from California. He shook his head and brushed the notion away. No, he was done with it all. The world was new and open. He started walking home.

◇◇◇◇◇◇◇◇

The hours in the van had passed uneventfully for the dog. The sounds of the cars on the wet street were repetitive, and he soon ignored them. It was true that the man's actions had been shocking in that they were new to him: his first experience with violent human behavior. But the sensation of shock was brief and had little emotional reverberation. He added it to his growing awareness of the world. The dog had sensed the man's tension; a keenness to somatic signals was in the dog's genes. And he was predisposed by breeding to accept and cope with surprises.

Most importantly, the man was not his handler—not the individual committed to his training, not the leader with whom he was destined to develop a bond. He'd known this from the beginning. So his actions meant less personally to the dog. The dog had never felt in danger, and it was not in him to overreact when the circumstances did not exceed his temperamental thresholds.

The dog was thirsty. He stood as he now heard sounds against the van's sides and back, some thumping and scraping, and men's voices quite close. The voices were rough and clipped. He heard new sounds of chains and, shortly, the grinding of a winch. With a sudden jerk, the front of the van lifted. A few moments later, it bucked and lurched forward. Some paint cans rolled to the back, and the dog braced his legs for balance. The sensation of movement without a driver was new, and the dog filed it away as another experience.

◇◇◇◇◇◇◇◇

Vic Tolivaro of Vic's Towing stood behind his warped and grease-stained plywood counter and looked over at the dog sitting on the shipping blanket. He couldn't get over its magnificence and shook his head again with disgust at the negligence and even abuse to leave such an animal in a beat-up hippie van. He silently repeated the refrain his conscience was practicing: '*what good fortune I was able to save it!*'

He went over the events of a month and a half ago when the van was hauled into the yard, one of two official police impound lots in the Cambridge-Arlington district. It was an ordinary tow job for unpaid parking tickets. Vic hadn't intended to look more closely when he came to work the following day. But as he approached it through the vehicle-packed yard, he noticed a slight movement and moving closer saw a quick fogging on the window. Vic peered in carefully and jumped back at the sight of the black snout of the sniffing dog.

He jimmied open the back door and saw the German shepherd staring at him, panting. There was a smell of urine. The dog made no motion to leap out past him. He found a piece of rope to loop around his head, led him out, then inside his office, and he offered him water. The dog drank thirstily; once satisfied, he sat down. The dog was a stunning specimen. Large but not heavy and leaner in the frame, more like a wolf. Its eyes were the sort he always associated with dogs that perform jobs—distinguished by seriousness and intelligence. Who could have given up such an animal?

Vic concocted a cover story about where and how he'd found the dog (well away from there, in Wakefield square, while visiting his mother). He would say he'd posted notices on telephone poles and around town to no avail.

He would keep the dog for the yard. But for the next few weeks, at least until the van owner appeared to reclaim the vehicle, he'd kennel the dog at home.

And so it worked out for him. The van's owners, two kids, about twenty or so, did appear the next day to bail out their vehicle and had indeed asked about the dog. One seemed quite upset. The truck drivers were summoned but, of course, knew nothing. Vic took offense that anyone in the yard had tampered with the van. Someone must have broken into it on the street, he said. Vic made a sympathetic noise to the kids while at the same time suggesting in a streetwise manner, '*that's what you get for neglecting your dog.*' The hippies looked broken.

A few weeks passed, and the dog was now moving about the shop. It didn't seem to warm to any of Vic's workers or customers; it cut a stand-offish and imposing figure. That was fine with Vic. He took it out for short walks, fed it, and left it in the shop at night. '*Striker,*' as he'd named it, would become a guard dog for the business.

But Vic wasn't prepared for Sgt. Brian Doyle. If he'd known about the beat sergeant's application for transfer to the Cambridge Police K9 unit, or just a bit more about Doyle's real nature, he might have kept the dog out of sight. Doyle issued a lot of the towing calls to the yard. He stopped by occasionally to swap local gossip and seemed to strut about as if Vic and the yard owed him (which they did, Vic admitted). And Vic would slip him skim money now and then—nothing regular, just depending on how busy they'd been. Unlike the other locals that Vic knew well, Doyle was socially awkward. His stories of the street were often more cruel than funny, and his racial slurs were over-eager.

Doyle was tall and broad, with what once might have been described as rough-hewn Irish handsomeness. But now, at thirty-six, he looked past his prime (a fact no doubt accelerated by drinking). His face was a florid slab, his cheeks flushed by burst capillaries, and he carried a decided paunch.

Doyle eyed the dog almost immediately after he came in. The way he moved toward him made Vic's heart sink.

"That's a hell of a dog," Doyle said lowly. "Where'd he come from?"

"Found him on the street a month or so ago, up in Wakefield," Vic replied casually. "No collar, no tags. Put on a local search, but nothing. He's working out nicely here."

Doyle nodded, drawing closer.

The dog had accepted Vic as his caretaker, seeing him as another figure capable of serving his needs. The dog did not measure time or frustration as people did but merely understood his station in life to be what it was until it wasn't. The yearning to meet the right individual still held. He examined every person he saw and met, innately measuring their character and potentialities of leadership, elements he could sense. The process was unnoticeable to people. The dog had eyed Doyle and, still young and inexperienced, saw something different and worth noting in his features and body language. His approach was confident, which impressed the dog. At the same time, he put the dog slightly on edge, and the contrast confused him. It was new and unsettling. He quickly sat up and stared stiffly at the large man in the uniform.

Vic noticed the sharpened intensity. Doyle paused, nodding, and turned to Vic.

"Yeah," Doyle said quietly. "That's some dog."

He pulled out a small notepad.

"Would it surprise you that a dog like this was reported missing a few weeks ago?"

Vic shrugged. "Dogs go missing all the time."

Doyle nodded. "Righto. But the description is an exact match. What do you say to that?"

Vic had nothing to say. Doyle's stare said it all—he was taking the dog. Vic accepted the fact and quickly realized it was probably for the better. His business mattered more to him than any dog. He'd stolen it, and the thought of that, the trace of guilt over it, would never completely disappear. Doyle had probably detected it. He was a cop, after all.

Vic, sorting through his mail, said out of the side of his mouth, "Do what you gotta do. I found him, that's all."

Doyle glanced at Vic's back and turned to the dog.

"Righto."

CAMBRIDGE, MA
1968

IT WAS A hazy, rather cool August day on the Harvard soccer field. The new Cambridge Police K9 unit was mustering, with four German shepherds in heel positions next to their handlers, the officers in gray sweatpants with blue jerseys. They waited as they watched their commander.

Lieutenant Darius Lockwood observed them all in turn. The pilot program was Lockwood's idea. Still a young man and already a ten-year police veteran, his abiding passion had always been dogs and training; since he was a boy, he'd wanted to train police dogs. It had taken two years of patient lobbying of the police and other civic hierarchy, all the way up to the chief and mayor. In addition, he'd helped raise the funds. The months of training with these officers and their dogs were now bearing fruit.

While K9 teams and dogs had been deployed in other parts of the country, Lockwood's training model, based on his ideas, research, and testing, was a radical departure. Most training was based on compulsion and drills to enforce strict behavioral requirements for police work. It looked martial and borrowed much from military dog training. Lockwood's methods, which he called '*Play to work*,' developed a dog's natural love for play, layering higher expectations and obligations into the play. But the essential feature, the driving force of the training process, was the dog's core enthusiasm for play tempered into a reliable discipline by his handler and through their bond.

He'd sealed the deal by demonstrating with his dogs. And his dogs outperformed anything the observers and 'experts' had seen—they hit harder, gripped tighter, held on longer, let go faster, and moved with alertness, speed, and intense enthusiasm. Lockwood anticipated the skepticism and professional resentment, which were revealed in questions about how they'd perform under '*real pressure*.' Lockwood knew he'd trained his dogs in the most exacting simulations of reality possible but responded simply by asking for any volunteer to come at one of his dogs or serve as a mock criminal in any simulation of their own. No one had volunteered. Lockwood had taken a risk. He knew he could not re-create all the possible circumstances and hazards of the street and that dogs would always interpret actual conditions differently from staged ones (he never underestimated their instincts for the organic moment). But he knew his dogs were giving him the best they had.

Of course, this meant finding suitable top-tier dogs, and the handlers to develop bonds with those dogs. It hadn't been easy. As he looked over the three dogs and cops in the line, he was mostly satisfied.

Zeus, the two-year-old gray shepherd, who Lockwood had trained from a pup, met all the criteria. He was on the heavy side (ninety pounds—Lockwood preferred leaner and more athletic representatives of the breed), but that shouldn't be a problem, he thought. Funnily, Zeus's handler, Sgt. Arvin was short and thin. But he was dedicated and had sailed through training. They were bonded; it was a good team.

Comet, the sixty-five-pound all-black female, was a pure athlete with all the heart he could hope for. He'd found Comet in a litter of dogs on a trip to Canada, saw the signs of a fun-loving and unstoppably-driven prodigy, and grabbed her. Sgt. Reilly, her handler, was a slow but steady learner, less quick a study than Arvin but just as dedicated. They both loved their dogs, and their dogs loved them.

The third man was the odd one out. Sgt. Doyle had approached him about a year before Lockwood had started the program. Doyle had heard about Lockwood's history and the rumors of his plan. This fact was in his favor. Doyle had no experience with working dogs, and Lockwood wondered if he was more interested in the status and trappings of patrolling with a dog than the responsibility it entailed.

His interview with Doyle was interesting and inconclusive—at times, Doyle seemed to confirm Lockwood's doubts, but at others, betrayed a humble sincerity. Was it an act? He couldn't pin him down. His work history was spotty, including a lot of sick time and two disciplinary hearings for excessive force involving young black males. The department had taken no official actions. That was in Doyle's thirteen years on the force; the most recent incident was three years ago. Lockwood was willing to overlook it. However, Doyle had come into the interview reeking of mint mouthwash, and Lockwood wondered about alcohol. He had the appearance of a drinker.

But it was Doyle's dog that sold it for him. Lockwood met him on the field soon after and instantly could see the dog was exceptional. It wasn't any particular physical feature, though the dog was an exemplar of the breed: solid but trim at around eighty pounds, with the faintest, intermittently visible outline of his ribcage, a straight rather than sloped back, a large head, eyes simultaneous direct yet dispassionate, with a steady, curious but somehow knowing stare—all this within his striking tricolor coat. He moved with an authority, economy and purpose Lockwood had never seen.

The dog was probably around fifteen months old, but he looked experienced and dog-wise beyond its age.

Lockwood needed to test the dog for the presence and quality of his 'drives.' He quickly realized the dog's inexperience, and Doyle looked flattened when the early work with the tugs and rags did not stir 'Chaser' as wildly as the other dogs.

But Lockwood knew better. The dog had it in him but wasn't one to trifle or to respond to cheap excitements; he demanded a serious partner. Lockwood adjusted his style, slowing his pace and adding drama and frustration to his approach.

The dog responded. Once he'd drawn Chaser out, Lockwood built the challenges. He discovered in the dog—just as the dog discovered in himself—the joy and meaning of the bite. Chaser's grip was deep and committed, with no double bites, munching, or hectic shaking. He bit for all it was worth and, unlike many dogs, pushed in as if there was nothing Lockwood could do, no distraction he could throw at him, to stop him. At the same time, Lockwood could see in his eyes that there was no crazed emotion, no loss of control, just flat-out commitment to the exercise. And the dog learned the *out* command faster than any dog he'd trained. No hesitation, no reflexive snap-backs or 'dirty' bites. He just understood that Lockwood made the rules. While Lockwood appreciated this responsiveness, he also knew the value of precisely the opposite—total abandonment once in the struggle, the battle. Yet he didn't doubt it was in Chaser, just that he was smart enough—had the inherent judgment—to know its time and place.

Lockwood admitted that he was jealous of Doyle and had to be careful about how he trained both around the others to refrain from favoritism. But Doyle was slower to learn handler skills, and it frustrated Lockwood to see Chaser poorly served; the dog had such enormous potential. He saw Chaser making adjustments to Doyle as if the dog understood and compensated. It was difficult to get a good read on their relationship. Doyle made very few gestures of affection to the dog. At times Lockwood felt as if Chaser's lack of expressive displays, the dog's essential stoicism, frustrated Doyle, as if the sergeant wanted more of the flashier, thrashing behavior of the other dogs. He recalled his initial doubts about Doyle's real motives for K9 work.

One afternoon at the field, Lockwood was working on 'civil' bite training. The dogs had advanced beyond bite work on the full-body suit, and now the decoy officer who worked with Lockwood was in regular clothing; the dogs were equipped with full-face vinyl muzzles. The exercise was to show the dog's willingness and commitment to bite on command without the help or targeted stimulus of any padding (which obviously no criminal would be wearing).

Zeus and Comet performed heartily, punching in with a racket of snarls, growls, and frantic whines as their bites were stymied by the muzzle. They outed reluctantly but returned to heel position, ready for the next chance.

Lockwood nodded in approval but reminded them—'*Aggression is easy. Control is what makes them police officers. They need to turn off as fast as they turn on. We'll keep working on that.*'

Now Lockwood instructed Doyle to approach and lead the decoy officer off the field and, when the decoy made his break to run, to issue the command to Chaser.

His head sealed in the muzzle uncomplainingly, Chaser stared at the decoy and then up at Doyle, waiting. Lockwood nodded. "*Foos,*" Doyle shouted, the 'heel' command, and started walking, Chaser moving alongside crisply in sync. They reached the decoy. Doyle ordered his mock prisoner to move and led him toward the parking lot, Chaser keeping his perfect pace. Suddenly the decoy, on Lockwood's signal, bolted. Doyle yelled, "*Blitzen, blitzen!*" Chaser leaped after the decoy, now thirty feet away.

But instead of slamming into him like the other dogs, Chaser pulled up short, braking almost like a cartoon character. He stopped and circled the decoy like a herding dog. Lockwood watched, amused despite himself, but he directed the decoy to lunge toward Chaser with violent gestures. Chaser just kept a tight and more active circle on him, barking evenly in time to each of the decoy's shouts and gestures.

Doyle, his face reddening, gritted his teeth and cursed. He shouted at Chaser again. "Blitzen, goddammit!"

Lockwood signaled to Doyle with his hand.

"All right, it's all right." He pointed to Doyle, and Chaser quickly trotted back to his side.

Lockwood knew that the dog's self-restraint, its apparent reading of the moment as a simulation, and his decision to adapt to it were unusual, yet not unreasonable. He was quietly pleased with the dog's discernment and control.

But he could see from Doyle's clenched jaw line and his tight hold on Chaser as they moved off the field that the sergeant felt differently.

As Lockwood was packing his equipment in the back of his old Willies, he saw Doyle approach after loading Chaser into his patrol car. Doyle neared Lockwood and stopped. Lockwood kept loading, waiting.

"Sorry about the dog today, Lieutenant."

Lockwood turned and studied him.

"Your dog's got what we call '*intelligent disobedience*,' Doyle. Judgment. You can't teach that."

He watched Doyle for a sign of comprehension, even interest. Like dogs, it would be in the eyes. But Lockwood only saw concern.

"But how will this figure in our scores?" Doyle asked.

Lockwood gave no indication either way in response.

"Sergeant, think about this. We can't take all deviations from our training norm as a problem. We have performance standards for good reason. But we're dealing with animals and ones working under enormous pressure. Dogs at this level deserve our respect and the benefit of the doubt. You've got an extraordinary partner and dog. That he would throw off the pressure he saw as unnecessary in the circumstance is worth our understanding."

He saw Doyle stare back, but his eyes were hard to read. Lockwood propped his arm against the open hatch of the Willies.

"I was told something by a trainer when I was a boy with my first dog. He said, '*the dog is always true.*' I didn't understand it. So I just filed it away at the time as a riddle. How could that be right? Dogs make mistakes; they need training. But he didn't say they always knew what was right. He was talking about moments like we saw today, those you can't immediately explain when the dog seems to defy us, and we're tempted to force ourselves on the dog because that's what 'training' tells us to do. We should step back and consider what the dog is saying to us. Consider the idea of '*intelligent disobedience.*' Does that make sense?"

Doyle didn't move or make a sign. Lockwood shut the door.

"It's all right. Just think about it. Good night, Sergeant."

◆◆◆◆◆◆◆◆

It was the Monday after Thanksgiving, and students were returning to the college. Doyle enjoyed the Thanksgiving break: the streets around Harvard Square were quieter. Now the grubby hippie students were back in numbers. He stood at the corner of Mt. Auburn and Holyoke Streets in his civvies, his heavy vinyl cop jacket with the protruding padding of fake fur around the neck, and holding a grocery bag from Purity Supreme. His eyes took in the scrums of overgrown children posing as '*students*'; the boys with their mops of hair or ponytailed like girls, in their frayed and patchwork denim; the girls in their tight, tattered bell bottoms or slatternly miniskirts, most of them in oversized Army jackets with its implied mockery of the military and authority.

Worse, he thought, were the blacks in their Afros, strutting about as if they owned the college. This was Harvard, a place he'd been conditioned by his father to respect. It was all a filthy insult now. His city was overrun by spoiled and ungrateful punks who'd never struggled and couldn't appreciate where they were or what they had.

He suddenly noticed a black student staring at him and turning to a white girl—his girlfriend?—as he pointed to Doyle's shoes and snickered. Doyle looked down at his white socks, exposed under his short, cuffed pant legs. Doyle returned his stare, holding the black man's eyes until the other moved off. '*That's right*,' he said to himself, '*you better be afraid*.'

Doyle's house was an old three-bedroom in a working-class neighborhood of North Cambridge. It was the house he'd grown up in, and which had been left to him and his mother four years ago when his father passed from lung cancer.

Doyle didn't date anymore—his work was his life, as he told himself, and marriages for police rarely worked anyway (in his case, he'd long foreclosed on any possibility of that). Hence, the living arrangement was fine with him. At times Corrine could annoy and frustrate him, but she was proud of him and his work, and while he wouldn't admit it to himself, this pleased him.

The walls were painted a light tea brown, and the carpet was a darker brown with orange flecks. From the heavy sofa cushions to the sepia-tinged photos and realist landscape wall paintings, to the porcelain Hummel figurines and an array of other kitsch, along with Corrine's endless string of Pall-Malls and the cooking smells, it was a stuffy, widow's dwelling. To Doyle, the space seemed dimmer than ever, especially since he'd installed, on her insistence, new, heavy curtains on the windows.

But it was a tolerable existence for him. He had his room when he wished to be alone, and as much as he would privately gripe about Corrine, he looked forward to having her there when he returned from a long shift.

And she had not minded the dog at all. This reaction was odd, he thought, as he'd never been allowed dogs as a child. But she instantly accepted Chaser. It may have been Chaser's perfect house manners or the security of having a '*police dog*' in the apartment. Chaser, for his part, seemed to listen to her better than he listened to Doyle. It was an observation that Doyle didn't like making.

"Head of his class," she said as she shuffled in from the kitchen, holding a ladle with some stew meat. "That calls for a treat."

Doyle was nursing his third beer as he watched her lower the meat to Chaser.

"No," he said.

She looked up, surprised. The same surprised look she'd given him for the last hundred times he'd told her not to feed him.

"And why not?"

"Just no. I don't want him spoiled."

She sniffed in protest but read his dark expression and stood up.

"Honestly," she said and shuffled back to the kitchen.

Doyle watched Chaser, whose ears had pricked as Corrine approached and who now glanced at Doyle.

"I don't like him staring at me," Doyle said, as if to himself but wishing to be heard.

Corrine shook her head.

"I don't know what's wrong, Brian. Why can't you be happier?"

She set the small card table in front of the black and white console TV. Doyle stared at Chaser, then up at his mother.

"They think he's too good for me. I can see it in their faces."

The dog understood his arrangement with the large man. While he accepted the commands and efforts at training, his consent was conditional, a matter of necessity. The man demonstrated sporadic leadership characteristics, enough to interest the dog. But it wasn't long before the dog realized something off-kilter in the man. The dog's drive to bond and his unease with the man abraded against each other. He came upon a truce in his canine mind, a guarded consent to go along. Without knowing it, he was learning to live in a world of men with the least trouble.

He felt more comfortable and motivated around Lockwood. For this, the training became a rewarding experience. He could sense that this somehow disturbed Doyle and assimilated this realization into his living 'arrangement' as best he could. Though he did not identify Lockwood as that singular leader for life he sought, there could be no disguising his preference.

Late one night, as almost every night, they sat in the living room in front of the large TV. Doyle was in his father's heavy, old Naugahyde recliner, a beer at his side, his eyes drooping as if asleep but narrow and focused on the television. Chaser was between him and Corrine, who sat in a padded chair at the tidied card table, working out a jigsaw puzzle of Boston.

Images flashed on the screen of student protests, hand-painted anti-war messages on bed sheets, and banners hanging out of windows with the angry faces and flailing arms of mixed-color students. Bottles flew through the air at a line of police cars, the police before them in riot gear. It was a news special: *'Campus unrest sweeps the nation.'*

Corrine looked up, shaking her head.

"So much violence. I don't understand." She sighed, returning to her puzzle. "I'm glad your father didn't live to see this. I don't think any war is ever good, but if your country needs you, you answer the call."

She glanced self-consciously at Doyle and smiled gently.

"We know you couldn't, Brian. He understood."

Under heavy, hateful lids, Doyle's eyes were fixed on the TV.

After his mother had gone to bed, Doyle walked Chaser and returned to the quiet house. He turned off the lights; the light from streetlights seeped through the curtains, and a kitchen nightlight palely illuminated the living room. Doyle quietly commanded Chaser to *'platz'*—his down command— and stood over him. He tore off a piece of corned beef from the hunk in his hand and dropped it next to the dog's nose.

Chaser sniffed and shifted slightly closer.

Doyle's hand gripped the rolled newspaper, rolled tight as a baton, and held it over the dog. Chaser hesitated. He suddenly stood to a sit position, took a step forward, and dropped down over the beef now under his chest. Doyle stared at him, a harsh smile stretching his mouth. He walked into the dog, pushing him back, and then whacked him across the jaws with the newspaper. Chaser growled reflexively but cut the growl short just as the second swipe of the hard roll struck him on the snout.

"I said '*Platz*'!"

Chaser slowly lowered himself.

The blows didn't hurt the dog; he could absorb far more pain. He wasn't surprised; he knew violence was in the man; he'd felt the intimations for a while. It was a confirmation of instinct and another lesson about men. He tucked it away. This was his life for now, and he would abide it.

Doyle couldn't sleep. At three a.m., he got up, went to the window, and stared at the cold street. He took a deep breath, let out a throat-scraping cough that made him wince, and decided. He turned to the dog.

"Let's go."

A few minutes later, in civilian pants and his plain, stained parka, and with Chaser fitted in an unmarked leather harness with a fifteen-foot line, Doyle climbed into his Plymouth Duster. He began to cruise the streets around the college. Chaser sat in the back, his nose at the slightly cracked window.

Turning down a side street, Doyle spotted a trio of students moving across a grassy section of the campus. A few trees dotted the area, trisected by asphalt walkways. He slowed and turned off his headlights. He rested his hand on the side-mounted swivel beam he'd installed, watching. He could see the figures well enough from the illumination of a single streetlamp at the far edge of the yard. They didn't seem to have noticed him and were moving with what he saw as a furtive purpose, removing leaflets or small posters from a backpack the woman was toting and tacking them to the trees. They paused, about thirty yards away, at the pathway bordering the yard on the left from a line of academic buildings and the street beyond on the right.

It looked like a young white man, a white girl in the middle, facing him, and a black man. The woman had dropped her sack, and the white man was lighting a cigarette or joint. He took a long pull and passed it to the girl. The black student—they were all students, Doyle assumed—was staring in the opposite direction.

Doyle played with the switch on his beam. He decided and flipped it. The strobe exposed the three with an unsparing blast of white light. The girl stumbled back and fell over her pack. The white student instantly ran back in the direction they'd come. The black student turned directly into the light. The girl now stood, glancing between the light and the student who ran away and shouted something Doyle couldn't hear. Now she ran after the white man. The black student, staring at the light, suddenly turned and trotted toward the closer line of darkened buildings and the street on the right.

Doyle smiled grimly, quickly stepped out, leaving the door open, and grabbed Chaser's line, leading him through the open door and after the black man.

Doyle made sharp vocal sounds to motivate Chaser. The dog broke into a run; Doyle felt the line sliding through his hands. They passed the spot where the trio split, and he caught a quick image of the white couple under the distant streetlight peering into the darkness at them. The girl, seeing the black student running and the dark torpedo of the dog in pursuit, screamed.

Doyle had given Chaser the command to take down the subject, and the distance now closed to thirty feet. Doyle held his flashlight, and the thin beam bounced as he ran, catching glimpses of the student looking back wildly, seeing the dog closing, unsure of the distance, and throwing up one arm against an attack. Doyle could hear his panicked bursts of breath.

Doyle's heart was racing partly from the strain of the run and partly from adrenalized anticipation. A visceral grin creased his face as the dog closed in.

The black student fell and turned on his back, both hands now up around his face. Doyle's flashlight illuminated his face, his lips pulling back from his teeth in fear. Doyle had ten feet of taut line on Chaser, who stood three feet away from the student, rigidly aimed at him and silent.

The black man, now up on his haunches, scuttled further back. His shock was giving way to anger.

"What the fuck, man?! What are you, man, a cop?"

Doyle said nothing, just held his stance, his light directly on the student's face, blinding him. He spoke sharply to Chaser, but his voice lacked force.

"Blitzen!"

Chaser knew the command, and it excited him. He felt the urge to bite, reinforced by the chase and the taut line. But he was conflicted—he also felt the unnaturalness of the scene, at odds with his instincts. The sense of purpose of the chase and the frenzy around the prospect of the bite drained away as he came upon the student. And it mattered that his handler's command was tinged with uncertainty. To the dog, the moment seemed simply 'wrong.' He barked once, however—to release his tension; it was a deep and convincing bark to someone inexperienced in the character of barks. But Doyle recognized it for what it was—empty noise.

The student scrambled backward. "Fuck you, man," he said, pivoted, and ran.

❖❖❖❖❖❖❖

Doyle woke late, feeling awful. He had returned home at four-thirty a.m., downed several shots of cherry brandy, collapsed in his large recliner, and finally fallen asleep. He'd wanted to drag Chaser around after the excitement to remind him of what a command meant, but some inner voice of guilt stopped him. The truth was he was glad Chaser hadn't bitten the student. But he'd scared him, and Doyle grinned at the memory of the student's terrified face. There was no way he could have seen Doyle clearly. Doyle had retreated without saying a word, and as he walked back to the car did not see the other students. No one else seemed to be around.

With the aftertaste of the brandy in his burps, Doyle showered, washed down two aspirin with a cup of instant coffee, and made his way into the precinct station at noon, when his shift was scheduled to start. He placed Chaser in the holding kennel. At the desk, he was told Captain Bixby wanted to see him.

The Captain? What the hell? But Doyle's spike of fear faded as he made his way through the crowded central hallway. The caffeine high was kicking in. And what chance was there that his little game last night on a nearly deserted patch of the college had been reported?

Bixby's door was ajar, and Doyle knocked as he peered in.

Bixby was a no-nonsense type with a drill-instructor bearing—slender and taut under an ever-neat, crisply pressed uniform and with eyes that swept and saw everything around him and stored it away. Doyle had only crossed paths with him a few times and practiced avoidance. The less Doyle was seen, the better Doyle felt. Bixby looked up from his desk and gestured for him to come in and sit.

"Close the door behind you," Bixby said.

Doyle did and sat. He waited with a blandly innocent look on his face.

Bixby picked up a sheet. Doyle knew the form of the sheet—a citizen complaint.

"We have a report of a disturbance on campus early this morning, Sergeant. Allegedly a plainclothes cop with a dog was harassing some colored student. Harvard police called me this morning about it."

He put the paper down and leaned back.

"Know anything about that?"

"That's not my shift, sir."

"It's not what I asked."

"No, sir. I don't know anything about it. How do they know it was a K9 officer, not just someone with a dog?"

The captain swiveled his chair a quarter turn and looked out the window. The silence worried Doyle, but he kept the worry out of his voice.

"Have you talked to the other officers? Sir."

Bixby flicked the report with his fingers.

"It was a statement taken from some kids at 4:30 in the morning. They may have been stoned. That's it."

"Kids? Not just one kid?"

Bixby studied Doyle for a moment and swiveled his chair to the front again.

"Officer Doyle. I've been told that a K9 unit is being requested in the Mattapan area by the Boston PD. That's where you're being reassigned for now. You'll still operate under Lt. Lockwood but in conjunction with Boston PD. You can go over the details with Lockwood."

Doyle recoiled.

"Mattapan?"

Bixby just stared at him. He noticed the reaction and the sudden washed-out look on Doyle's face.

"That's right. Mattapan. Is there a problem?"

Doyle struggled for words; he knew he had to control himself.

"I, uh, it's just I've been here, I've always been here. I've always had the college beat."

"Change is good. You're still part of this team. And it's temporary, I'm sure. Boston has had some issues with K9s. They know we have a good team, so this is a chance to show our work. Lt. Lockwood has impressed a lot of people."

Doyle felt himself sinking further into his seat, wanting to anchor himself for the time to talk himself out of this. But Bixby's face and voice were unyielding. Doyle knew it.

"A problem, Sergeant?"

"Problem?"

"Do you have a problem with black people?"

Doyle shook his head and put on a look of concerned surprise.

"No, sir, no problem. It's just that I like it here, I don't want—"

The captain closed the file. That was it. Bixby watched Doyle's large bulk move out the door, leaving it open. A few moments later, Lockwood came in. Bixby shook his head and put up a hand.

"Don't bust my balls. There's nothing I can do. He's a fifteen-year veteran, and that's what they asked for. They only look at numbers, you know that. Now, do I need to worry about this guy?"

Lockwood wasn't sure but didn't want to sound unsure. He only had his instincts. He wanted the dog Chaser around him as much as possible, but couldn't tell the captain that.

Lockwood said, "No. And like you said, he'll still be reporting to me."

Bixby grunted.

"Fucking Boston. They need to find their own fucking K9s." He turned back to his paperwork, then quickly up at Lockwood.

"Is Doyle some crazy racist? Did he roust that black kid? The report said it was a big guy with a German shepherd."

Yes, Lockwood thought: Doyle had done it. But he couldn't prove it or say it. He arched his eyebrows and shrugged.

"I don't know," he said. "I haven't known him long enough to say. He probably drinks. That doesn't make him different than a lot of cops."

"Not very reassuring."

Lockwood smiled resignedly. "Dogs, I know. People, not so much. Maybe at some point, I can work only with the dogs."

◆◆◆◆◆◆◆◆

Doyle deliberately avoided Lockwood the rest of the day. He wondered how long before he'd get the briefing and what the logistics would be for his relocation. Maybe the whole matter would be forgotten or scrapped. It was possible. This was police management, after all—a running joke of bureaucratic screw-ups, delays, and policy reversals. But Bixby didn't seem like one who would be caught short or recant an order. Likewise, Lockwood.

Doyle was convinced, more and more as he reflected on the captain's manner and his question about '*black people*,' that both Bixby and Lockwood suspected him, and this was the real reason for being exiled to Mattapan. They thought throwing him among a heavier black population would send him over the edge, and he'd quit the K9 team. Lockwood always talked down to him like a child, trying to explain dog behavior to him as if dogs were humans requiring some sensitive, psychological insight to handle. Lockwood didn't think Doyle was good enough for Chaser. But Chaser was only there because of Doyle. Lockwood wanted to take credit. Doyle saw through the big-brother condescension, the pretense of mentorship. Lockwood coveted Chaser and was trying to demoralize Doyle. Well, he'd never get him. Doyle would kill the dog before he gave Lockwood, or anybody else, that satisfaction.

Doyle had looked into Lockwood's background. Not a lot of street experience, but he'd been to college, Boston University. Lockwood was another fair-haired, ass-kissing college kid; this was how he'd risen to lieutenant so fast.

Putting aside Lockwood, as there was little Doyle could do about him at the moment, he finessed a copy of the citizen complaint.

The black student's name was Ahmed Carson, 24, from Yonkers, NY, and a student at Harvard. Doyle made inquiries at Harvard and learned Carson was a junior studying political science. He lived off campus in Inman Square. Using his police authority, Doyle asked for and received the address. This wasn't over.

Doyle learned that the Mattapan transfer wouldn't be happening right away—good old police inefficiency!—and he was now excited at the prospect of tailing Carson. His instinct told him he could find something on him. He channeled his rage at the untouchable Lockwood and Bixby into his focus on Carson.

Doyle waited within sight of the residential house Carson seemed to share with other black students. Doyle was patient; this was fun. And his mother seemed pleased over his new mood. He hadn't told her about the transfer (as he was hopeful it would fall through). He'd eaten a TV dinner earlier and told her he had some overtime work. She was proud of her son's *'work ethic'*—he was just like his father, she said.

Doyle saw Carson emerge with a handful of other blacks and climb into a large Pontiac. It was easy to spot him—he'd trained his mind to the photo in the Harvard records. This came naturally to him; he was a good cop, he said to himself. The Pontiac swung onto Mass Avenue, and Doyle followed.

The car led Doyle a few miles deeper into a more blighted area of the city. It finally pulled up at what appeared to be an abandoned brick building in the foreground of a tenement project. The students got out, moved to a chained door, dropped the chain, and slipped inside.

Doyle watched, wondering what the hell was all this. The building looked like an old lodge or meeting hall. A familiar-looking symbol, partly eroded, was etched into a grayish concrete triangle over the entrance—a large 'G' within a compass atop it and a V-shaped set of rulers beneath it. The streets were relatively empty, and the streetlights almost completely yellowed out. After a few minutes, another car stopped, and two more black men got out and moved inside.

This was enough for Doyle. Something was going on here. Doyle glanced around, got out, put Chaser on a leash, and made for the building's entrance.

Doyle gripped the door and pushed, stepping over the chain. He walked inside. It was dark and silent. He adjusted his eyes, and after a moment, the weak light through the wide windows was enough to see the long hallway between cracked-plaster walls. He moved forward as Chaser stepped gingerly over various bits of debris. Chaser's ears pricked up at noises at the rear, and Doyle moved toward them. They reached a door and could see dull light at the threshold gap. He heard muffled music. He reached for the handle to feel if it was locked. It wasn't. He looked at Chaser, who seemed calm but alert, as his hand inched open the door, cracking it open enough to peer inside.

He saw two long tables with rows of pamphlets and posters in stacks. On each table was a kerosene lantern, which broke the room into geometric slices of alternately uneven yellowish light and murkiness. One of the tables held an assortment of drug paraphernalia and bags of white powder. Carson was studying the posters. To the back of the room, the rest of the group sat in old, shredded armchairs, nodding to music from a transistor radio (Reggae, Doyle guessed) as they smoked joints, inhaling with long, luxurious chest swellings and equally long exhalations. Doyle quietly closed the door. His heart raced. This was a drug bust and more. But how could he perform a raid with no warrant and without revealing his earlier misconduct? Goddamned radical blacks plotting violence! Maybe he couldn't do anything officially, but he could scare the life out of them. He knew Carson wouldn't, couldn't say a word about it.

He thought for a moment. He pulled his police revolver, his eyes wide and frightened, and looked at Chaser.

The dog saw Doyle's eyes and read his body language. He knew something was imminent and that it wasn't training. He'd picked up the mishmash of odors—the marijuana, the vermin in the building, dried urine, the kerosene, and even the student from earlier. He didn't know what to expect. He didn't trust the man, and this added to his unrest. He understood what training might compel him to do and was prepared, but sensed that he might be on his own.

Doyle opened the door with the hand holding the leash. The other hand held his revolver. As he stood staring at the scene, one of the students looked up, saw him, and stared open-mouthed, momentarily stunned at the sight of the large white man in the parka with the German shepherd. It wasn't until a second student looked up that a scream went out. The effect of the sudden sound in the quiet, cavernous room with the lilting music was dramatic.

The blacks in the chairs, images of lost stupor, erupted and bolted to a back door partially obscured by boxes, which Doyle hadn't seen at first. The door burst open with a metallic crash. Carson looked up at the others, turned, saw Doyle, and backed into a table, knocking over a kerosene lamp. The lamp fell on a pile of papers. The entire floor was covered in old newspapers and rolls of old carpet. Doyle could see the fluid spill and ignite. Another black started shoving the bags of white powder into a backpack, but when he saw the slick of fluid and track of speeding flames ran for the exit. Carson stumbled to the side, saw the flames hungrily spreading, and turned and slammed into another table, spilling a second lamp. The flames raced along the new rivulets of fuel; the fire was already making a terrifying munching sound and producing thick, choking smoke with no egress.

As Carson retreated, he pulled a gun from his waistband and fired crazily in the direction of Doyle. The shots echoed loudly. Doyle hit the ground, let go of the leash, and covered his head. Carson had also fallen and fired again and again as he crawled backward. The bullets hit the wall behind Doyle. Panicking, imagining the pain and terror of being shot, Doyle scrambled back to the door, leaped out of the room, and slammed the door behind him.

He breathed a huge breath and felt a swell of relief. It lasted only a second. The dog! He was still inside!

Doyle opened the door but met a blast of acrid, choking smoke. The swiftness of the fire's spread astonished and scared him, and he slammed the door. He could feel and hear the devouring flames through it. He couldn't get back inside; it was hopeless. He only knew he had to get out of the building. He shouldn't be here; he must get away. He ran.

Inside the room, Chaser turned in every direction. He'd never seen fire and had no chance to collect himself. Flames were now racing up the wooden table legs, and he could see the brighter, roaring balls of heat from the old chairs being consumed. His way was blocked, his paws already feeling the burn. He retreated to the door they'd entered, and scratched at it, barking. He turned and sprang through what looked like an opening between the flames toward the rear. He dodged around hot spots to the back but faced a shut door again. The smoke was filling his lungs and the fire closing in around him. He suddenly felt the floor sagging.

◊◊◊◊◊◊◊◊

From an open window of the apartment in the large tenement a block away, twelve-year-old Samuel Broussard watched the spectacular blaze of the abandoned building, the mighty, arcing geysers of pressured water from the fire trucks, and then the collapse of the roof followed by a sizzling, sparkling fountains of fiery matter. He wondered if any of it would reach them. He wasn't scared, just fascinated by the spectacle of destruction and the efforts of the firemen and police.

"Samuel!"

The boy scampered back to his bed.

The door opened; his mother looked in and then stepped in.

Rosalyn Broussard was thirty-one, a severely handsome black woman as thin and straight as a ramrod. She wore a one-piece house dress, one of four, two of which were always cleaned and pressed for her next day of work on Beacon Hill as a maid.

"What did I say, Samuel?"

"Stay away from the window."

"That's right."

She walked up to it and peered out, staring at the conflagration. She wondered if the fire was an arson case.

"I went down and talked to the firemen. There's no danger of it spreading. You don't need to concern yourself."

"I wasn't worried."

She nodded to herself. No, he wasn't. It made her heart glad. She'd mostly stopped fearing that any genetic traces of her no-count Cajun husband or her no-count father had made it into the boy. She knew Samuel was not the same and blessed the Lord for that. It didn't mean she would stop pushing him.

"Did you say your prayers?"

She gave him a sideways stare, and he nodded back solemnly. She fought back a smile, lowered the window, and leaned in to kiss him goodnight again. But she sniffed and stepped back.

"I don't smell toothpaste. You didn't brush your teeth."

Samuel sighed and pushed the sheets back.

"You want to be like Uncle Jimmy?"

Sam looked up and tucked his lips over his teeth to mimic the gummy motions of a toothless mouth. She smiled and pushed him off to the bathroom.

She turned again to the window and the scene of the fire. Another blow to the neighborhood. Oh, but maybe not. Fire can be cleansing. The building had attracted addicts and bums and caused some of her anxiety around Sam's walk to school.

Sam moved back toward the bed, but she waved him to the window and put out her knee for him to rest on.

"We're safe here. You understand that?"

He nodded. His mother's words were the sum of all strength and truth. She'd never told him a lie and never let him down. They'd left Virginia as she'd promised and found a life in Boston, as she'd promised. And the fact was he didn't feel unsafe at all. He saw the neighborhood as a place of adventure. He just wished he had a dog with which to share it.

"Now to bed." She patted his rump as he scooted back to it. She stood now and moved to click off the light.

"We'd be safer with a dog," he said, knowing but hoping against her usual response.

"We weren't going to talk about that again, Samuel. You know we can't have a dog here. It's not..." She thought better of it and clicked off the light. "Good night."

◆◆◆◆◆◆◆◆

Doyle sat in his Duster, staring at the fire-razed building as more of it appeared to him in the chill light of dawn. He'd sat there for hours, unmoving; forcing his mind into a numb emptiness; knowing the enormity of what had happened and what it meant and unable to consider it. From a shadowy distance in the Duster, he watched the inferno, the fire trucks and police do what they do as they put up cordon tape, and finally as the vehicles pulled out.

His dog was dead. But what could he have done? He was only trying to do his job. It was a tragic and freakish sequence of actions and reactions— beyond his control. They were criminals, radicals, maybe drug dealers, or worse. He been bravely acting on his own, doing the right thing, taking on a band of radical activists, and in the chaos, his dog was killed, and he was nearly burned alive. He should get an award. He tried to go back for the dog. But the fire... he never saw one spread faster or more wildly. Fire terrified him. Why not? We're all afraid of something. He'd seen burn victims. He couldn't go through anything like that. He'd rather be shot, and he almost was. He could deal with being shot. But not burned.

He would be out of the K9 team. What was he going to say? That Chaser ran away? No, that would humiliate him. Chase was stolen? Yes, that was it. It was also somewhat humiliating, but not as bad. He'd left him in the car, his personal car, and the window had been broken. It all happened in a few minutes. Of course, he'd have to break his car's window and pretend to search for the dog, and maybe other cops would look out for the dog for a while. He'd say it was a dog-stealing ring, something he'd heard about, and that Chaser was probably in another state by now. That had to be it.

Some of those black kids had seen him, but they couldn't identify him in the poor light and the chaos. And why would they try?—they were caught in the act. In his fever of plotting, he thought about quitting the force. The loss of his dog was too much for him; he'd let them think that. It might evoke pity for him. But he was still short of the years for his pension. He didn't think Lockwood would give him another dog, so his dream of working a K9 unit was over. There would never be another dog like Chaser. Even in his ramblings, Doyle acknowledged how much the dog had compensated for his shortcomings.

He suddenly realized his exhaustion, from his scalp to his feet. He was also freezing. He'd call in sick—he was too traumatized even to bring up the subject of Chaser's theft. A great meliorating wave of self-pity rose from his depths and soaked him in its soothing warmth. He felt momentarily lifted and started the car.

◆◆◆◆◆◆◆◆

Samuel, dressed in his St. Aloysius elementary school uniform of a white shirt with blue tie and black trousers over saddle shoes, slurped down his Wheatena at the folding kitchen table in the small, neat-as-a-pin apartment. In her maid's uniform—an olive green dress and white rubber-soled shoes and her hair in a hair-net—Rosalyn tidied her small desk to the side of the kitchenette with brisk efficiency. She rose to the counter, finished packing Samuel's bag lunch, a cheese sandwich, apple and cupcake, and counted out her bus and subway fare.

She scanned the table and the surround.

"Homework?"

After finishing the Wheatena in one last slurp, Sam dropped the spoon in the bowl and slid out of the chair to retrieve it from his room.

After she'd cleaned up the dishes, he returned. She helped him with his second-hand loden coat, and out the door they went. It was a practiced routine.

Rosalyn tried taking his hand as they moved down the hallway, but he shook it off. She did it to be able to give him a scolding tug if he looked anywhere but straight ahead. Rosalyn was fiercely strict about good behavior inside and around their apartment building. Samuel knew it well. He was able to steal some glimpses through open doors at what looked like interior messes. He thought his mother would be appalled. On one occasion, he'd seen a dog and used it as leverage in one of his pleadings. She'd batted it away with some simple Biblical injunctions and made a point later of impressing on him the importance of upholding personal standards no matter—and even because of—the degradation around him. She told him to look up the word '*degradation*' and tell her in his own words what it meant and why it was such a sin, not just against the people around him but against himself and God's love for him. Samuel had turned the word into a little jingle to himself, '*Deg-ray-day-shin, shin-shin-shin-shin.*'

They passed next to a ladder. Sam looked up and saw Mr. Sturdevant, the fifty-ish, white-haired superintendent, replacing light bulbs. The man coldly returned the look. Sam had never seen Mr. Sturdevant smile. His mother was unfailingly polite to Mr. Sturdevant and made sure to personally deliver their rent check or order Samuel to do it and return with a receipt. Mr. Sturdevant always sighed when asked for the receipt.

They opened the outer door and stepped on the landing. The wind bit into them. Rosalyn tightened the collar around her JC Penney polo-style overcoat. She looked at her tiny Timex wristwatch.

"You have the number at the Fitches. I want you home right after school."

Samuel nodded; he heard this every day. She scowled.

"Yes, ma'am," he said.

"And don't forget to bring your lunch bag home. And you're not to go near that burned-down building. You understand?"

He nodded. "Yes, ma'am."

She planted a firm send-off kiss on his forehead.

Samuel turned up the street toward St. Aloysius, five blocks away going east. He walked toward the grayish light of the overcast sun and into the wind. He reached the intersection directly parallel to the burned building and peered down the street. It was odd to see the empty space where the building had been now marked off with yellow tape. A few angled beams stuck up like charred spears. The urge was irresistible, and he turned and made toward the building.

Halfway down the alley, a figure stepped out in front of him, blocking him. Samuel jumped back. It was Cuz, a street wino. Samuel knew him only by sight and reputation; he'd noticed him before on his walks, as he would eye Sam from a building stoop while huddled under a blanket or leaning against the side of the alley near a dumpster. Sam didn't like the hooded glare and kept his distance. Sam had seen Cuz gabbing away with other men or accosting passersby for handouts; he didn't look as menacing to Sam then.

"What's in the bag, boy?"

Sam didn't want to say.

"Nothing."

"Don't look like a bagga nothin."

Sam felt a sudden rush of boldness. Why should he not say what was in the bag?

"My lunch."

Cuz leaned slightly to the side, nodding.

"Well, lunch ain't nothing. Don't they give you lunch at school? They give lunch in prison. You too good for their lunch? You think you deserve two lunches?"

As quick as a lizard's tongue flicking to an insect, Cuz's hand grabbed for the bag. But Sam was ready, and when he yanked his hand back, the bag tore open and the food spilled out.

Sam knelt to pick it up, but Cuz's boot pushed him off. Sam pushed back at the boot with his hand. He looked up, the sandwich wrapped in wax paper in his hands. The wino's face, his eyes yellow and his teeth either missing or rotted, the strands of greasy hair leaking out from his filthy Red Sox watch cap, suddenly struck Sam as sickening and pitiful.

Sam handed up half of the sandwich. Cuz took it. But now he lunged downward to grab the rest, the cupcake and the apple. Sam pulled against the grip, and Cuz now seized Sam's hand, holding on with a bony strength. Sam reflexively twisted and pivoted and through the angled motion, caught

Cuz full on the nose with his elbow. Cuz cried out, dropped the food, and clutched his nose, cursing. Sam ran, with Cuz cursing and chasing.

◇◇◇◇◇◇◇◇

After her twenty-five-minute ride on the Red Line, Rosalyn walked up from Park Square and reached Beacon Hill. She moved purposefully, her eyes straight ahead and hands joined at the waist, holding her duty bag and purse. She walked down the line of brick townhouses of Louisburg Square with their cobbled frontages, short driveways and tidy, modest shrubs and gardens. The shows of wealth and power were inverted, seemingly in a competition of austerity. This was old Boston money, but the newly wealthy were taking up residence, seeking to ease themselves into the precincts of influence.

The Fitches were a mix of old and new, as Rosalyn understood. The husband, whom she rarely saw at home, was some marvelous real-estate investor with family money and his own company, as he'd been written up in *The Globe* and local magazines. She'd seen the picture—a well-padded man in a pinstriped suit astride a polished wood desk, his eyes deep-set under thick brows and an unruly mane of salt-and-pepper hair. The stories referred to his *'plans to change the face and image of Boston.'* Rosalyn could see the resemblance to him in one of the two sons.

But Rosalyn dealt only with his wife, and Abigail Fitch seemed the opposite: a soft-spoken, diffident, honey-blonde woman. As far as Rosalyn could tell, her activities involved serving on various charity boards and playing tennis. She had a mild Southern accent, and Rosalyn had guessed she was a Virginian. The similarity of their accents had endeared her to Abigail from her first interview. Rosalyn was pleased and grateful to be hired but had been slightly unsettled by Abigail's instantaneous fondness for her. After a few weeks, however, Rosalyn saw it to be the nature of a rather sweet, timid, and insecure woman who perhaps needed affirmation of her goodness from a black housemaid. It wasn't in Rosalyn's own nature to make friends with her boss or a wealthy white woman. Rosalyn didn't fully understand that

Abigail was, in some way, in awe of Rosalyn as a single mother who worked so hard. It was more than that—it was Rosalyn's simple bearing, suggesting reserves of character, which sometimes even intimidated Abigail.

It was a good arrangement for Rosalyn, and she knew it. The only part of the job that presented a challenge was the two stepsons, thirteen and fifteen, and Rosalyn's unspoken disgust for Abigail's failure to manage them.

Rosalyn had her key and knocked twice, then entered. She hung her coat on the brass hooks to the side of the door. She looked up the stairwell with its Oriental runner and fox-hunting prints lining the wall and down the short hallway to the den and living room behind the closed doors. It was quiet. Now she heard some sounds from the kitchen to her left. She placed her bag on the foyer table and moved toward it. Suddenly the door to the den opened, and the two boys, in private school blazers and flannel trousers, burst out. They saw Rosalyn and quickly stiffened, putting their hands to their mouths. One grinned, chuckled, coughing and choking as wisps of smoke seeped from behind his covering hands. The other did the same, with the same result. They shuffled past her and rushed up the stairs, laughing.

Rosalyn moved through the dining room and pushed open the swinging kitchen door with its small porthole window. Abigail Fitch turned with a look of exhausted relief.

"Rosalyn. Thank God you're here."

She was in her short tennis dress, in sneakers and socklets with tiny pompoms. She wore a bulky cable-knit sweater, sleeves pulled up to her elbows, and a small, expensive-looking gold watch.

"Ma'am," Rosalyn replied, waiting.

Abigail had insisted that Rosalyn call her '*Abby*.' Rosalyn had simply smiled and maintained the '*ma'am*.' Soon enough, Abigail gave up.

"Oh, dear. Rosalyn, would you mind taking care of Digger today? The boys forgot." She shook her head. "But you know, they have midterms now..." She smiled with a look of wincing apology. "He's in the rec room."

Rosalyn smiled back, betraying none of what she felt.

Digger was the Fitch's Great Dane puppy. It had been a gift, she'd been told, from Mr. Fitch to the boys—an effort to help them learn some responsibility. But Rosalyn understood it to be Abigail Fitch's idea, that Banistre Fitch wasn't one for imposing discipline. So far, Rosalyn had had no run-ins with the dog, which was kept in the large rumpus room at the back of the townhouse. The room led to the garage and an exterior brick enclosure with a small garden. She'd occasionally heard the dog but never seen it.

Rosalyn detested dogs; she hadn't told Samuel and didn't believe she would ever need to. Dogs were too close to the bone of her wretched youth in Virginia. Her father, a man whose failed pursuits of varied vocations were only matched by his attraction to drink and women, had decided that training hunting dogs for the wealthy white landowners in the area was a profitable idea. But the burdens, as usual, soon fell to her. In addition to managing the house and her sick mother, she now had half-dozen brainless, frenetic hounds in a chicken-wire kennel to feed and clean up after. Dogs—any dog—reminded her of the stink, squalor, and hopelessness of those days in the tin-topped shanty and the sweltering, sleepless nights of crazed barking at the slightest sound and of nearly drowning in the despair.

Behind it all, was the drunken, volatile figure of her father, with his fits of rage at her for not '*backing up the breadwinner*,' when it was only her swing-shift job at Jeeter's Grocery Store which saved them from indigence. Limousine driver, sharecropper, Fuller-Brush man, bartender, blues band roadie—she'd lost count of his ill-fated fancies. Rosalyn wondered at times if she should feel pity for the fact he tried as hard as he did, until she remembered the slaps and insults. How many years out of that pit would it take not to feel the cold breath of poverty at her neck? She'd married to escape it but only ran into more turmoil and trouble. She was out now and would never slip back.

She shook off the memories. It wouldn't happen. Her will was stronger than whatever would challenge her. She grabbed the bucket and cleaning equipment, walked down the hallway and the small down-steps, and opened the door to the rumpus room.

It was an unholy mess. Bunting from shredded cushions and splintered shards of wood chewed off the legs of an old billiard table littered the tiled floor. The curtains bracketing the French doors leading to the garden were torn down and shredded, and scattered puddles of urine and piles and skid-smears of soft, chunky feces were all over. The stench stirred her worst memories. She gritted her teeth and forced herself to focus.

The dog, a huge, harmless, and stalky-limbed beast, stared at her from the dismembered couch. Its look of furrowed concentration was stupid, she thought, but also defiant.

There wouldn't be any defiance. She put down her equipment and stared at the dog. It cocked its head, and turned away. '*That's right*,' she said to herself, '*wise move.*' She walked calmly to it, reached for its collar, and pulled it off the couch. It yielded easily. She led it straight to the French doors, opened them, and pushed it out with only a light motion of her wrist. It took a few steps, turned, and sat. She slammed the door.

In forty-five minutes, the room was immaculate. After a thorough spraying of disinfectant, she was finished. There was no stench, and she took a deep breath as she leaned against a line of storage cubby holes. A good cleaning always felt satisfying; she never tired of the feeling. Outside the doors, the large dog sat on its haunches, watching her, as it had the entire time. She felt a sudden pity for it. But just a little. She smiled to herself. Hard work usually opened the door to feelings of charity.

Abigail was gone when Rosalyn finished her chores, and her payment was in its usual place, wedged under a fruit bowl in the kitchen. She took it and, bundled in her coat, stepped out the front door.

She stared out into the slanting sun of the clear, cold afternoon. The way it caught the bricks, slightly bronzing them, looked like a painting. Something caught her eye to the lower right, and she glanced down. The two boys, dressed only in their school garb and blazers, were under the iron-grated stoop and passing around a joint as they stamped their feet to stay warm.

Rosalyn turned her collar up and walked straight-backed down the steps and to the street, eyes on the horizon.

◆◆◆◆◆◆◆◆

After leaving school, or escaping the nuns as he liked to call it, Sam reached the perimeter of the burned building. Remembering his morning skirmish with Cuz, he was even more determined to visit the site. He stared at the skeletal remains of the structure and the ground of ashes and debris. He walked around the edge, occasionally stepping over the exposed foundation into the carpet of ashes. He reached the other side, next to an adjoining building, its bricks blackened by the fire. The ruin was more open here, and he walked into it, his shoes sinking a little. Sam thought that walking on the moon would be like this. He leaned down to feel if it was still hot. It was warm, and he was disappointed.

He stood and turned around, straight into a snarl of rotten teeth. It was Cuz. Suddenly both of Sam's arms were gripped. Sam struggled, but the fingers were iron pincers. Sam kicked hard, his saddle shoe striking Cuz on the shins. The man cursed, the spittle spattering on Sam's face. Sam wrenched himself free and ran.

He sped straight and ducked into the first perpendicular alley he came to, took another hard right, looking back. He saw nothing and continued fifty yards until he came to a heavy chain-link fence at the rear of the adjoining building. The fence was lopsided, and the gate bent, leaving a thin aperture. He pushed to widen it and squeeze through, but while it heaved back and forth, it was too high and heavy to widen. He jumped up to grab the top horizontal bar but couldn't reach it. He was trapped. He looked back; nothing, still no Cuz. But he might come around the corner at any moment. He caught a glimpse of a windblown wrapper skipping toward a narrow oblong opening of a crawl space under the building. A loosened panel of latticed wood half-covered the opening.

He leaned down, pulled the flimsy section of wood off, peered in, and backed himself in.

The dirt ground was hard and cold as he scrambled backward. The space was about thirty inches high, and he guessed that it covered the width of the building. He couldn't see that far. Aside from the darkness, the tangle of pipes with decayed asbestos insulation draping off them like gray moss obscured his view. Sam squeezed further back along the slimy dirt in the dark, foul space. He scooped dirt and bits of trash around him for concealment. Something was wrong, he felt. His book bag! He peered over his hedge and saw the bag next to the fence. He couldn't go back now. The thought of Cuz seeing and swiping his books—and how he would explain it to his mother—sent a tremor of fear through Sam.

He heard a shuffling. It had to be Cuz. Yes, there were his ratty sneakers and trousers. Sam pressed his head down and prayed he couldn't be seen. Cuz couldn't miss the books, could he? Would he think Sam had dropped them in climbing over the fence? There was a long silence. Sam could feel a draft on his scalp and wondered if he was exposed to view. He dared to peer up. The sneakers were still there, unmoving. Sam slid back a bit more.

His eyes adjusting, he now saw to his right a small, rusted and overturned wheelbarrow. It would be the perfect cover. He slid sideways and curled up behind it. He was well out of the light of the opening. He snuck a look around the edge of the wheelbarrow. Cuz's face appeared, staring into the dark space; it was an ugly, grimacing but blessedly brief sweep. There was nothing to see. Sam didn't think the wino would attempt to crawl inside. He was right. Cuz stood, paused for a moment, and retreated. He'd left Sam's book bag where it was. Sam suddenly realized books held no interest or value for Cuz. Sam let out a breath of relief.

He waited another few minutes without moving, thinking Cuz was crouching and eyeing the space from around the corner. Now he shifted, stretching his legs out to dig in for a purchase.

He heard and felt something behind him that chilled and stopped him. It was a growl—the last sound he would have expected in the tight, dark space. His foot had touched something—solid but not hard. His mind flashed with images of wild animals cornered in dark spaces—rabid raccoons, possums, badgers? But these were animals from his mother's stories of Virginia, not of the city, not Boston. Sam wanted to turn and look but held still. He decided to move his foot back again. He felt the resistance, and again, there was the growl. It was low, gravelly, rising from some animal depth. It was not a small animal. What could it possibly be? Sam couldn't stop himself from turning. He closed his eyes as he inched his head around as if this would help cover his movement. Once he'd turned, he cracked them open.

It took a few seconds before his eyes adjusted again. He saw the shape of the animal. His first image was of a wolf. It looked large and black; its head also large and long-snouted, like a wolf. He could now see that it was looking at him in a sidelong way and listlessly.

Its eyes looked yellow from the reflected light. Sam's neck began to ache from the twisted angle, and he carefully shifted sideways. He could now see the animal's lips curl back in response to his movement. He saw the long, whitish teeth under the upturned snarl. Sam was frightened but also fascinated. He somehow felt as long as he moved very deliberately, the animal wouldn't do anything.

Now the dog's mouth relaxed, and its jaws opened to pant. Sam stared. He saw a blackened-burnt harness around its midriff. It wasn't a wolf, but a dog. And it was hurt. Something about the way it remained so still and panted; there were fatigue and pain in the pant. Sam could see scraped skin on its legs and patches on its coat where the fur had been scorched. Burns, that was it! The animal had been caught in the fire!

Sam eased his hand forward. The panting stopped, the dog's brow furrowed, its ears pricked, and it stared back glassily. But no growl. Sam could now see its face directly and the blood-matted gash running straight down between its eyes, veering in a boomerang shape across the side of its snout. The dog's panting revealed a cracked-dry tongue.

Sam was transfixed. There was something all magnificent, menacing, and terribly wrong in the sight. This animal had crawled in here to die, and Sam could see a stolid acceptance of death on its face. Its growling wasn't from fear or ferocity but from a wish to be left alone. These impressions were all entirely new for Sam, but he felt them with flooding certainty. He suddenly realized that his fear was gone. The absence of fear thrilled him. But he was also sobered by an equally new and demanding feeling of responsibility.

Sam shifted again, this time toward the dog. He raised his extended arm and held his hand out. The dog stared at it. Sam moved still closer and was now about three feet away. He heard a low growl, but the dog's lips didn't move. He waited, and the growling stopped. Without thinking, Sam started humming. He modulated the hum up and down; it was no conscious tune, just, to his mind, a low, soothing sound. The dog resumed panting and watched him. Sam noticed the dog's breathing ease and its eyes lower slightly. Sam's hand was now six inches from the dog's shoulder. If the dog lunged at him now, he'd have no quick escape. The effort to turn and crawl out would leave him at its mercy. While Sam understood this, he couldn't imagine it.

Sam's hand closed in, and now he felt the fringes of the dog's coat. He brushed lightly. The dog didn't move. Now his hand reached through the coat to feel the firmness of its flank. The dog slightly turned its head to acknowledge, but that was all. Sam's hand stayed on its body, making a slow back-and-forth motion.

Sam maintained his contact and humming sound for ten minutes. He could have done it for an hour, but he knew he was already late. His mother would be home. He began to panic—what was he to do about the dog? He riffled through various schemes. He only knew he had to get the dog water and food. This dog could not and would not die; he would not let it happen. He'd never felt such purpose in his life. He pulled back his hand and looked the dog in the eyes.

"Wait here; I'll come back. I'll have food and water. Wait here, boy. I think you're a boy. You look like one. Wait here. Please." Sam backed out, his eyes on the dog the whole time. He emerged from the space, replaced the latticed cover, collected his books, and raced home. Woe to Cuz if he tried to stop him.

The dog had been in the crawl space since the fire. He was hungry and thirsty but without any urge to leave. He felt an overwhelming need to be still; he was in pain, and resting in the cool dirt offered some relief. He'd escaped the inferno when a beam had fallen next to him, knocking out a section of the floor. In falling through, his head had been slashed by the jagged edge of a floor joist. His paws and legs had already been singed from weaving among the pockets of flames in the large room. The blow across the face had stunned him, but he'd been able to limp around the building and find refuge in the crawl space. The darkness and coolness were what he sought. He had no thought of what to do next. Time would heal or kill him. There was no handler to think about any-more. There never really had been one. Now and then, the cool dirt would remind him of his pen at the farm, and the sight or sounds of chickens, goats or geese wouldn't have surprised him.

The smell and shape of the boy had evoked humans again and his growing distrust of them. The wounds and burns seemed to flare and hurt anew. He wished to be quiet, to melt into the dirt, but he also could not stop his growl. He couldn't sustain the uneasy feeling for long. The movements and sounds from the boy were different, and the dog hadn't any reference to them. So they gave him pause. He only knew he didn't sense a threat. And so he allowed the boy to come closer. He was a dog with a deep genetic affinity for humans; the boy fit within his tolerances. The dog also associated humans with food and water. The boy's sound and touch were a new kind of relief. When the boy backed out, he sensed he would see him again.

Sam ran up the stairs to the apartment and stopped, breathless, at the door. He listened. By some miracle, she wasn't home yet? He worked the key and entered. No overcoat on the hanger! He rushed to the kitchen cabinets, dug among the pots, and pulled out one from the back, an old tin one she wouldn't immediately miss. He also grabbed an empty milk bottle and filled it with tap water. He looked in the refrigerator, peeled off some ham slices from a slab on a plate, stuffed them into his jacket pocket, and rushed back out.

Sam ran or walked at a fast pace back to the building. He didn't even think about Cuz. He looked around the area for anybody watching before stooping to crawl into the space. He wormed his way forward.

The dog was right where he'd left him, having turned his body toward the front. He stared at Sam. Sam stopped a few feet from the dog, sliding the pot forward and carefully pouring the water a foot in front of the dog. The water splashed and gurgled. The dog watched intently but without moving. Finished, Sam pushed the pot directly under the dog.

The dog arched his head up. Sam twirled his fingers in the water. Still nothing. He cupped some water in his palm and brought it up.

The dog's tongue touched the water, and he feebly licked. Sam held his hand up until the water was gone, then lowered it to the pot. The dog's head now dropped and delicately lapped the water. Sam felt an electric charge of satisfaction. He now brought out the slice of ham, tore off a piece, and offered it. The dog pulled its head from the water at the scent but didn't move toward Sam. Sam found a section of cardboard packaging from *Hostess Twinkies* in the dirt, brushed it off, put the ham on it, and slid it to the dog. The dog stared at him. Sam noticed its eyes were different, softer, he thought. Softer? Yes, that was it. But the dog seemed to ignore the ham. Sam realized he couldn't stay any longer.

"I'll bring much more as soon as I can, boy. Tonight. Stay here for now, please. We'll find a way to take care of your burns and everything else. I promise."

The dog just stared. Sam backed out.

It was five o'clock by the time Sam reached home the second time, and dusk was giving way to darkness. He suddenly looked down at his school clothes smeared with dirt. He brushed them as hard as he could, to little effect. The black pants wouldn't show it as much, and he'd cover the shirt with his overcoat. He stopped at the door; he could hear noises in the kitchen. He braced himself and entered. His mother must have heard the door but didn't look up, so he went straight to his room and threw off his clothes.

"Samuel?" her voice carried sharply in from the kitchen.

"Yes, ma'am. We were playing football at the high school field."

He had on his regular clothes when she knocked, then leaned her head into his room.

"I'd like to hear a respectful greeting when you come home."

No word on his lateness. That was a relief.

"Yes'm. I'm sorry."

"It's all right." She paused, holding her look. "When I came home your books were here."

Sam had a jolt of panic. He forced a matter-of-fact tone.

"Yeah, I came home first, then went back out."

She nodded. "'*Yeah*'?"

"I mean, yes, ma'am."

She nodded with a faint smile and stepped out.

An interminable hour later, as they sat down to eat, Sam did everything he could to still himself. All he wanted to do was get back to the crawl space and the dog.

A candle burned on the table. The dinner setting was, like everything in Rosalyn's sphere of control, of the highest standard possible under the circumstances. She'd found the tableware china, a Lenox Wheat set, at a yard sale in Cambridge. It was mostly complete, with a few chips. Abigail Fitch had offered her a nicer set of china, but Rosalyn primly declined. She wouldn't accept charity. In retrospect, she considered that maybe it wasn't charity but a gift. No matter. The silverware was her mother's—it wasn't fancy, but it seemed real silver. She'd salvaged it after her mother died, before her father could hawk it.

Rosalyn bowed her head for prayer.

"We're grateful for all we have, Lord, and for your grace and guidance. We take all that comes to us as your blessing. Amen."

"Amen," Sam repeated.

She unfolded the napkin, and Sam did the same.

As they ate, she caught his fidgety glances at the clock.

"Don't play with your meal, Samuel. Supper is a blessed moment and deserves your attention and appreciation."

She could see her words falling away before his furrow.

"Now, what's the matter? Did something happen at school? You want help with your homework?"

"No," he said quietly. He suddenly looked up and blurted: "Other people here have dogs. I've seen them."

Rosalyn's mouth tightened, but she paused for a moment before speaking. "We're not '*other people*.'"

Sam looked up at her, his frustration rising uncontrollably.

"No one cares about the rules except you."

He both regretted the words and yet felt exhilarated to utter them. It was true, he thought. It was a truth he'd felt vaguely for some time, but the event of the dog crystallized it in his mind.

The change in Rosalyn was striking. She straightened herself into a dark angel, glaring fiercely at him. Sam knew this look, and it scared him. But he still felt he was in the right and maintained himself under her glare.

"I won't have that tone, Samuel. Do you understand?"

But he just stared back.

This little defiance was new, she thought. She paused as she stared at him. She realized she was open to an anger he hadn't seen. But she stepped back from her brink and slowed her words down as she quieted her voice.

"Yes, I care. And if I'm the only one in the building to care, that's how it is, and you'll accept it. And you will care, too. Don't ever let me hear you say you don't care."

"I didn't. I said no one else cares."

Now her voice whip-cracked.

"Don't smart-mouth me with word games. You know what I'm talking about."

She saw the tight grip of his hands on his utensils. She'd never seen him like this. She wanted to know more, the reason, but didn't know how to relent in the moment. She remained still, waiting, watching him.

Sam didn't know what to say anymore. He shortly realized that any more words were futile. He could only dig himself deeper.

"The life for people who don't care is all around you, Samuel. You'd better care, long and strong. You hear me, young man?"

She pulled his dinner plate away, pushed back from the table, and stood.

"You can go to your room. We'll see if you care enough for your breakfast tomorrow."

She turned to the sink, her lips clenched and trembling. She heard him slide off his chair and walk to his room. As the door shut, she immediately felt shame and berated herself under her breath. Her moral and parental compass was spinning at this first challenge to her authority, and she was sure she'd failed the moment.

Later, Sam lay in bed, fully awake. His mother had come in around eight-thirty and said goodnight. There was no mention of the earlier incident. He could sense that she felt bad, as he did. But he felt driven to help the dog, like nothing before in his life. He was energized by the feeling but not entirely unafraid of it. He was willing to face the fear.

He got out of bed at midnight, dressed, and tiptoed into the living room. He prepared his mercy packet, stuffing more of the ham slices into a plastic bag, and quietly slipped out, terrified at his unheard-of transgression yet also feeling intrepid.

Sam moved swiftly and carefully among the shadows of the street. The scarred neighborhood looked meaner and colder under the pale streetlight. He saw a police patrol car and ducked out of sight. He saw a few figures walking; saw a bus drop off some people. He no longer cared about Cuz. He'd inflicted pain on him twice, and he'd do it again—whatever it took.

He reached the crawl space. He bent down and clicked on his cheap toy flashlight, and peered in. He could see the dog's eyes, the reflection. Sam made his way on his belly, the dog simply staring at him as before. He poured new water, and the dog seemed to nod in acceptance. Or was he imagining it? Sam touched its flank, pressing in more firmly than before. The dog's breathing was quieter and more regular. The food and water were helping.

Sam fingered out the ham from the bag and offered a slice on a paper plate he'd brought. The dog sniffed it more readily this time and nibbled at the broken-up pieces.

Now for the tricky part. He pulled out the old Army blanket he'd brought from his closet and, with difficulty, spread it out on a section of the dirt he had cleared. Sam patted the blanket, trying to coax the dog. The dog didn't move. He gently tugged the dog by the burnt leather harness. The dog made a low, half-hearted growl. Sam let up on his hold.

"It's all right."

Sam started stroking the dog's head. The dog accepted this.

Sam lay there with the dog for an hour, his hand moving down the dog's back and over its legs. He gently brushed over the caking abrasions and could see areas of oozing. He traced, from an inch over the dog's head, the wide boomerang-shaped slash between its eyes and running down its snout and to the left. The blood and dirt were caked within it. The dog needed serious cleaning and care. Sam was conceiving his next action, and his mind started bearing down on it.

Sam was back at home at one-forty-five without incident. He was tired but knew he had to complete his homework. He looked greedily at the bed, feeling already its soft embrace, but remembered the dog and its deprivation. He had to stay focused.

He woke at six o'clock at his desk, his head flat on its side, his hands hanging down. He could hear his mother making kitchen noises. He rubbed his face, closed his school book over the homework pages, and stood up. He'd worked out the next step in his plan and was pleased. He moved out to the kitchen.

"Good morning, Samuel. It's a little early for you, isn't it?"

"I volunteered for 'early bird' clean-up crew at school," he lied.

He watched her preparing his Wheatena. He was starving. While he'd hoped the conversation the night before was forgotten, he felt impelled to say something.

"You said no breakfast."

She turned, arching her eyebrows at him. "Did you think about what we talked about?"

He nodded. She frowned.

"Yes, Ma'am."

"Sit down."

He did.

"Would you like a ham sandwich today?"

"No. No, thank you," he said quickly. "Cheese, please. A thick cheese sandwich please."

She looked at him, taking a quick appraisal with eyes that tried to see freshly. Something was different with him. If it was anything other than just a growth phase, she would find out what it was. She couldn't spend another troubled night like last night. She realized she'd been taking him for granted. That is, his steadiness, resilience, and qualities of adaptability during all the disruptions in their lives—the move, this resettlement in Boston, and a new school. It wasn't fair. He was a strong child. She was maybe expecting too much. Also, with strength came defiance. She knew this, as she remembered it in herself with her father. She'd put up with so much until one day, she hadn't.

She also realized that her natural defiance didn't necessarily make her tolerant of it in others. And that wasn't fair. But unlike with her and her father, defiance wasn't necessary or reasonable in Sam's case. But then again, wasn't it? Was that her pride and rectitude speaking, her fear of losing him to the degradation around them in this fallen world? But he was stronger than that, wasn't he? Did she need to trust him more? Could she be turning him against her and the values and discipline which had pulled them out of the sinkhole of their lives? He was only twelve. Wasn't that too young to trust? But he was no ordinary twelve-year-old.

These were the conflicts she'd been hashing through all night. She was tired.

◆◆◆◆◆◆◆

Sam, careful he wasn't watched, made his way to the building as quickly as he could. Everything looked the same. He'd smuggled an old pair of pants into his book bag and made a quick change outside the crawl space.

He was excited to see the dog on the blanket, panting easily as it stared at him. Sam poured more water into the pot. He pulled out his cheese sandwich and eyed it longingly before breaking it into pieces and laying them on the blanket before the dog. The dog ate the pieces without hesitation and then drank from the pot. Sam stroked the length of his body while the dog put his head down, his eyes drooping. Maybe he trusts me now, Sam thought. His own eyes drooped.

The sound of a jackhammer down the street jolted Sam awake. He'd fallen asleep! For how long? What time was it?

After rushing out into the light, Sam could see from the sun's position that it was mid-morning. Oh God, the nuns! He started running but realized he was still in his old pants. He frantically changed in the alley, threw the old pants inside the crawl space, and bolted off toward school.

◇◇◇◇◇◇◇

Out of breath, he collected himself at the heavy double doors and entered as quietly as possible. The wide empty hallway with its black and green tiled linoleum floor, buffed to a shine, yawned at him. He could hear the muted tapping of a typewriter from the school office to his right. He walked far enough to see the clock through the large, wire-meshed safety glass. Ten-thirty. World history class with Sister Josephine had started. He moved past the office, ducking his head under the paneled glass.

He reached the room and looked through the oblong window. There the nun was, at her desk. He angled his view and saw all the students writing.

A voice behind him startled him, and his heart skipped a beat.

"May I see your tardy excuse, Samuel?"

He turned into the towering Sister Jewell. *'Jewell the ghoul.'* Tall as a basketball player (as he saw it), rail-thin (adding to the impression of unnatural height), with a long face, high cheekbones over hollowed cheeks, Sister Jewell's most distinguishing feature were piercing eyes set contrastingly within an emotionless expression. To Sam, they were eyes that had seen it all and could wring the secrets of the ages from the stones with a mere stare.

She studied his grasping expression and opened the door to the room.

"We'll discuss this later, Samuel."

Sam fought to keep his eyes open throughout the rest of his classes. Aside from his spasm of fear over Sister Jewell, he could think only of the dog and his plan. He saw the boldly chalked notice of the *'Test Tomorrow,'* realizing he could probably get by on the studying he'd already done. His grades were good, though he was no star student and wasn't interested in being one. Sam accepted his mother's exhortations about education; they made sense, and he would do as well as he could. But this wasn't his world, not what excited him. He only knew he constantly thought of dogs and dreamed of what it would be to have one of his own, wherever that might be. It could be the city; he would make it work. It might not be as exciting as the wide open spaces, like those in his favorite comic book series, '*Terry and Scout*,' about a Ranger in the Pacific Northwest wilds and the huskie/wolf cross he'd found in an abandoned mining shack and raised and trained to be his partner. It wouldn't matter to Sam. Once he had his dog, he knew he'd contrive endless activities and adventures and learn how to talk to it, train it, and develop their partnership. He just knew it.

At lunch break in the small cafeteria, Sam watched the other kids eat, noticing the scraps and uneaten portions dumped into barrels near the kitchen. As the students dispersed, he approached the large barrels and, looking around carefully for observers and seeing none, quickly grabbed the choicest items and stuffed them into his book bag.

Finally, the bell rang, and he was free. He hadn't heard from or seen Sister Jewell the rest of the day. He made his way out with a purposeful face and stride, holding his breath past the office windows. He pushed through the doors and was outside. He couldn't believe Sister Jewell had somehow forgotten his tardiness. He willed himself to believe it. He would add her to his prayers tonight.

Back in the crawl space, Sam laid out his stolen food treasures for the dog and watched him probe it with his snout, sniff, and eat. Sam took a little back and smiled at the dog's keenly watchful expression. He refilled the pot with water. He loosely encircled the dog's neck with two hands, making a rough measurement. As he pulled his hands back, the dog nudged him gently—its first overt gesture of acknowledgment. Sam swirled his hand over the dog's head. Suddenly the dog shifted and, to Sam's pure joy, stood. The space offered just enough clearance. The dog stiffly turned, circled the blanket, and moved off a few yards to relieve himself. In a moment, it returned and lay down.

"Tomorrow, boy. We'll be out of here tomorrow."

The evening was uneventful, and Sam made sure of it. He finished his homework, set the table, and calmly sat for dinner. They could hear a dog whine and bark somewhere on the floor, then through the walls the sound of a quick exchange of angry voices before it was quiet again. Rosalyn sat, and Sam bowed his head and closed his eyes for the blessing.

"Why don't you say something tonight, Sam."

He thought for a moment, looked at her, and saw that her eyes were closed.

"We're grateful for all that you have given us, God. If you gave it to us, or if we found it, then it must be ours, and we should be grateful. We are. Amen."

Rosalyn looked at him oddly.

"I wouldn't call that a very pious appeal, Samuel, not from a Catholic School student."

Sam looked up at her.

"I'm tired."

She nodded. "What is it you've found and are grateful for finding?"

Sam turned and stared straight ahead. What could he say? He was mad at himself for saying what he said. But he'd never meant anything so much. His mouth tightened. Before he knew it, he was brushing a tear from his eye. He couldn't help himself and rubbed his eyes with a controlled fury before stopping suddenly and staring down.

Shocked, Rosalyn forced herself to remain composed. She'd never seen anything like this from him; she had no idea what it was about. But she sensed it was not the moment for questions. It was an act of will to let it pass.

"Never mind," she said. "Eat up."

In his room, after lights out, Sam carefully cut one of his belts into a makeshift dog collar, hand-pressing notch holes with an ice pick from the kitchen. The vet clinic he'd scoped out was six blocks away, but he had a plan for delivering the dog. It was a '*Free Clinic.*' He wasn't sure what that meant; despite the grimy frontage of the clinic, the '*Free*' sounded promising. He'd seen the veterinarian, or one of them, moving about through the door. He was young and black and looked friendly, or at least approachable. Sam would make it work.

Sam crept out into the living room area. He saw the light under the door of his mother's room. But it was quiet; she was reading or asleep. He tiptoed to where her worn blue vinyl purse rested on the small desk by the door: the source from which all things, such as they were possible, became possible. He glanced toward her room again. He quietly unclasped the butterfly snap on the purse, reached inside for the smaller, cracked-vinyl wallet, and carefully, silently opened it. His hand grasped some small bills but stopped. He couldn't do it.

He heard a sound from his mother's room, balled his fist around the bills, and pulled back as he closed both purses.

The nightly mission to the crawl space had become something of a thrill for Sam, and the flashlight stabbed probingly through the blackness, catching the eyes of the dog as he made his way toward him. He looked different and was panting rapidly. He ignored Sam's offered bits of salami. What was wrong? Sam brushed his hand down his legs, and the dog flinched. He shined the beam on the leg, noticing pale yellowish oozing around the blood. He stroked the dog's head.

There was nothing to do until the next day. He would need to speed up the plan, for the morning no longer the afternoon. He couldn't wait. He'd be late again for school. So be it.

In the morning, Sam made an effort at good manners as he briskly ate breakfast. He again fibbed about his early duties at school. Rosalyn nodded but observed him with no less scrutiny. She wanted to feel relieved by his attitude, but the strange shifts in behavior were unsettling.

His excitement building at the execution of his plan, Sam felt braced by the morning chill. The sun was bright as he jogged to the building; the agreeable weather felt like a co-conspirator and support. He'd seen the vet clinic's posted hours, and they'd be open early for emergencies. That's what this was. It had pained him to wait this long.

In his tunnel vision to reach the crawl space, Sam didn't notice that Cuz had seen and followed him. As Sam removed the lattice-wood section to the space, he felt the claw grip on his forearm. Cuz yanked him up, twisting him around. Cuz bore into him with fiercely squinting, bloodshot eyes.

"What you hidin' down there, boy?"

Sam stared back into the eyes unflinchingly.

"Nothing."

"Don't give me that 'nothin.' Smart ass kid with your stuck-up mama. I've seen you around. Who you runnin' for?"

"Nobody. I'm not running for anybody."

Cuz forced him back, pinning him against the wall.

"You gave me a bloody nose. You're gonna learn some respect, boy."

"Let me go or you'll be sorry."

Sam kicked out, but his feet missed their targets, as Cuz had spread his legs. Cuz cackled at his forethought, coughed, and spit, the phlegmy spittle landing on the brick wall inches from Sam's head. Sam grunted and cried out as he struggled; Cuz's smile grew wider, revealing the rotting, crenulated teeth.

"Answer me, boy. Show me respect."

As Sam struggled, kicking the wooden section, they both heard a low animal growl, startling to the ears in the urban alleyway. Cuz glanced down.

The dog's head was out of the rectangular opening, its eyes aimed at Cuz's. The rest of the dog slowly emerged, with a stalking motion, until it stood at the side of Sam, his eyes holding onto Cuz. His legs wobbled as his lips drew up in a snarl, revealing the gleaming white teeth. Burned and blood-matted, he looked like some demon dog.

Cuz stared, stunned. But Sam realized that he wasn't surprised. He pried himself away from Cuz's grip. The dog never took his eyes off Cuz, growling again, a low, chesty rumble, but quieting as Sam stepped closer to him. Sam put his hand on the dog's head.

"It's all right, boy."

He looked up at Cuz.

"This is my dog. You better not touch me again."

Cuz lowered his hands.

Ignoring Cuz, Sam unpacked his book bag, slipped his homemade collar around the dog's neck, and cut off the remnants of the damaged harness with his cheap jackknife. The harness dropped. Sam now scrambled back into the hole. The dog lay down, panting, glancing between Cuz and the space, where they could hear scraping and straining sounds from Sam. After about a minute, Sam reappeared, dragging out the rusted wheelbarrow.

Sam caught his breath as he stared at it. The warped, hard-rubber wheel assembly was fixed to a bent axle, and the metal bin was loose from corroded bolts to the wooden frame. Sam disappeared again and emerged another minute later with the blanket, which he folded and pressed down in the bin, creating a rough bed.

"Come on, boy."

Sam eased the barrow to its side and encouraged the dog to step in. But he quickly realized the physics of this wouldn't work. Instead, he removed the blanket, folded it for thickness, and laid it out to create a loose stretcher. Sam patted it roughly, encouragingly.

"Come on, boy."

This time the dog stepped onto the blanket and lay down. Sam stood, satisfied. He looked up at Cuz.

"Help me."

Cuz had watched all this, dumbly fascinated.

"Come on. We can do it." Sam's voice was now bright and commanding, leaving no room for doubt.

It took Sam eighteen minutes to reach the clinic. It felt harrowing, and Sam quietly prayed as the wheelbarrow seemed at every instant to be falling apart. Sam was grateful for each step they made; he marveled at the dog's silent acceptance of the rough bumps and shakes of the ride. Maybe the dog thought nothing mattered anymore, but Sam did not believe that was it. The dog trusted Sam; he was sure. The trust gave Sam strength. People stared at the odd sight of the black boy wheeling the large dog. A gray-haired man wearing an MTA uniform and carrying a newspaper offered to help him, and Sam thanked him but gestured ahead, saying he was nearly at his destination. A woman with her child stopped and asked if he needed money. Sam just shook his head. He felt infused with a sense of high responsibility.

When he reached the clinic, the black vet signaled for Sam through the front window to wheel around to the side. There, the vet emerged through two wide doors and, without greeting, scooped the blanket and dog up and hauled the blanketed weight into the back. Sam saw through the swing doors with rubber skirts a bright room with aluminum tables and wired kennels. As the outer door opened, he heard an eruption of barking, which rose to a clamor. Sam assumed it was from the back of the clinic. The swing doors shut.

He sat on some milk crates in the hallway. After a few minutes, a young dark-haired girl in a white smock with a clipboard asked him his name, address, phone number, and parents' names. Sam answered, letting her know he lived only with his mother. She nodded without reaction, then guided him to the lobby and asked him to wait.

It was eight-thirty. Sam stared at the chipped linoleum floor and the mismatched plastic chairs in the lobby. There was a small waist-high painted plywood booth against the back wall, and the dark-haired girl occasionally appeared from the back through swing doors to answer the phone. Sam caught brief glimpses of the lighted treatment area each time but no sight of the dog.

Sam realized the test at school had probably already started. He wasn't surprised at his lack of anxiety. In one sense, it felt incidental to him, as if it were part of another person's life, but Sam also understood there would be a reckoning. He felt his decisions and actions, which led him here, were fated and correct. The reckoning would take care of itself. Sam was only anxious now about the dog. His dog.

By ten-thirty, three other people had come in with small dogs. The girl ushered them in their turn to the back exam area, where they would emerge a little later. There didn't appear to be any other doctors or assistants.

At eleven, the swing door opened, and the young black doctor emerged. He didn't look at Sam, went straight behind the booth and collected some papers, then turned suddenly to Sam at the swing door and crooked his finger for Sam to follow.

Sam did, through a spotlessly clean treatment room with barking dogs in cages. Toward the back, they came to his dog—he was resting in a large cage. His legs were wrapped in a white bandage, and large patches of his sides were shaved and coated with a dark yellowish stain. Likewise, the wide curling wound between his eyes and across his muzzle was also coated in the stain.

The vet attached his papers to a clipboard, rested it on the cage, and looked down at Sam. He seemed to study him. Unlike the look Sam was conditioned to expect from an adult under the circumstances, the man's look was relaxed and even held some friendly curiosity. Sam had worried about the vet and whether he would try to take the dog away from him, but the worry was dissipating.

"Your dog will be all right. He was burned and dehydrated, as you probably figured out. He also has some minor infections. We've given him intravenous fluid, antibiotics, and a sedative. You know what all those things are?"

Sam nodded, though he wasn't entirely sure.

"I think he just needs rest, sustenance, and time to heal," the vet added.

Relief flooded Sam's face. The doctor could see it.

"I'm Dr. Colin Davis. My assistant is Marie. You want to tell me something about this dog?" He turned to it for a moment. "He's an unusual dog. Maybe a police dog?"

Sam looked the doctor square in the eye.

"I found him under a building. I think he crawled there to die. I'm going to keep him."

The doctor nodded appreciatively. "What's his name?"

Sam paused. He'd been thinking about this while he was waiting in the lobby. It was the first time he had. '*Boy*' was all he'd considered, but that no longer seemed adequate, not equal to the dog.

"His name is '*Scarboy*.'"

It just came to Sam, and he enjoyed declaring it. He looked around the room, then back at Scarboy.

"I can work to pay for this. Before I go to school, or after. Or both. Whatever you need me to do."

Davis nodded solemnly and looked at his clipboard.

"Let's not worry about that for now."

Marie came in and walked up to the cage, smiling.

"He didn't make a complaint when we treated him. He understood we were helping. I'll bet you'll be glad to get him home."

Sam glanced at them both. He looked at the clock with a sinking feeling. "Thank you for taking care of him. I'll be back this afternoon."

◆◆◆◆◆◆◆

The dog had been willing to listen to the boy and to follow. The boy showed leadership traits the dog recognized, which he was more open to accepting in his debilitated state. At the same time, his injuries had sensitized him to insult and heightened his wariness to an approach. At first, he'd resolved to let no human near him again. But the boy's persistence was notable, and the dog felt the intention and the strength behind it. The boy had driven through the dog's immediate need to withdraw. The boy had given him food and water and restored him. The boy's hands on him were hands that revived his 'pack drive.' Tuned into the boy, the dog identified his distress from the sounds outside the crawl space and was irresistibly drawn to it. It was not a question of whether or not to defend him or whether or not he would reach the opening. It was what he had to do.

Submitting to the wheelbarrow was also all he could do; whatever way it went, he was resigned to it, and the boy was there. The dog was spent and sensed it was this or nothing.

◆◆◆◆◆◆◆

Sam had again slipped past the school office and stood outside the classroom. The students were bent over papers, making careful, silent scrawls. Sister Josephine, a stern proctor, patrolled between the desks, glancing hawk-eyed among them. Sam almost felt relieved. He didn't wish to pretend anymore. He'd known it would be too late for him. He turned and walked toward the office.

Ten minutes later, Sam sat across the desk from Sister Jewell in the '*detention room*.' She held a blank test in her hands, staring at it before raising her eyes to meet his.

"You know the rules, Samuel. I understand your mother's work schedule, and I'll call her this afternoon. Do you have anything to say for yourself?"

"I was at the doctor's."

Sister Jewell's dead-eyed stare, typically dreadful, took on a new character to Sam at this moment. He felt no more fear of her but felt a sickening lump in his gut about the confrontation with his mother. At the same time, he realized it was no longer avoidable.

"You were sick? And your mother didn't know about it?"

"I wasn't sick. It was a friend of mine."

Jewell arched her head slightly, peering down her nose with scornful doubt. She leveled her head and shook it in sadness.

Her pose, with its presumption of guilt, angered Sam. He was telling the truth.

She put the test down.

"You will be disciplined for your tardiness according to school policy. I will yield to your mother's choice of discipline for your actions outside the school. Do you believe you have forfeited the privilege of taking this test?"

Sam wasn't sure of the question; he felt it might be a trap. She wanted a confession. They always want a confession of sin. He didn't feel as if he needed to make one. He had not sinned; he had done what he thought was right and what he had to do. But he could confess to being late and apologize. That was different.

"I'm sorry I was late. I couldn't help it. But I'm sorry."

Sister Jewell's lips pursed, and her eyes hardened.

◇◇◇◇◇◇◇◇

Rosalyn arrived at the Fitches early and found Abigail sunken in a butterfly chair in the sun pantry adjoining the kitchen. Her eyes looked moist and bleary, and she held a handkerchief. She looked defeated.

"It's the dog again, Rosalyn. I hate to ask you."

Without saying a word, Rosalyn marched to the mudroom, opened the door, and stared at the same catastrophe. It looked like the first mess had never been cleaned—the same array of shredded fabrics, dog waste, and the assaulting stench. She felt the heat at her neck rising into her cheeks, and her heart rate quickened. She took a deep breath.

She forced herself to move calmly back to the kitchen. Abigail registered the look on her face, one she'd never seen. Abigail waited for the words; upon hearing them, her face went pale, she stared back tremulously, and their roles reversed.

"You mean now?"

Rosalyn nodded.

They moved up the stairs and down the hall to the room. The door was shut, but they could hear muffled throbbing music behind it. Rosalyn knocked with authority. Abigail hung back. There was no response, and Rosalyn opened the door.

The two boys, Christian and Eric, were leaning back in their beanbag chairs. Dressed in school uniforms, with shirttails draped outside the pants, they brushed away the smoke and stared up in glazed-eyed astonishment at Rosalyn.

Rosalyn stepped aside and motioned for Abigail to move forward, and she did. Rosalyn kept her eyes on the boys.

"Eric, Christian?" Abigail said. "We'd like you to clean up Digger's mess in the mudroom."

The boys made no show of hearing. But they exchanged glances; then Eric spoke with throwaway casualness as he pointed at Rosalyn.

"That's what she does."

Christian seemed to be amused by this. He nodded, adding, "Yeah, that's what she's paid for."

Abigail seemed to waver and looked at Rosalyn. "Now boys—"

Rosalyn's voice cut her off. It was of a deeper pitch, clearer and without inflection.

"Your mother asked you to pick up after your dog."

Christian's head pulled back a bit and he looked uncertainly at Eric. Eric suddenly lifted his arm dangling to his right behind the bean bag, a cigarette in his hand. He took a puff.

"She's not our mother; she's our stepmother. And we didn't ask for the dog. It was her idea. You can go now."

Christian laughed quickly but choked it off. He nodded his head with tentative solidarity but was staring at Rosalyn, who stood in front of Abigail, and whose expression concerned him. He took another puff, blowing smoke toward them.

Rosalyn looked at Mrs. Fitch, whose pained face slid sideways, averting her stare. Rosalyn nodded, set her jaw, and moved fully into the room. She delicately picked up a towel, revealing the bong hidden underneath. Just as delicately, she walked to Eric, reached out, pincered his earlobe between two fingers, and twisted it, lifting him off the beanbag in a stooped and shocked stumble. Christian drew back, stunned.

"I'm not a '*she*,' and that," Rosalyn said, gesturing to Abigail, "is not a '*her*.' She's the head of this household, and you'll do as she says and be glad she doesn't make you sleep down in that mess with the dog."

Eric whimpered and tried weakly to push away from Rosalyn, but she only added more torque to her grip.

"Do you understand?"

Eric nodded vigorously. Christian was now standing behind the beanbag as if it might serve as a shield to this strange black Fury who'd just shattered their sanctum.

Rosalyn let go of her grip with a snap. Eric stepped back, rubbing his red, stinging ear. Rosalyn made way for the boys to exit.

"It's simple to do the right thing," she said to their backs. "It isn't easy, but if it were, it wouldn't be of much value."

Abigail stared at Rosalyn with awe as she watched the boys move down the stairs.

◊ ◊ ◊ ◊ ◊ ◊ ◊

Sam sat alone in the detention room, watching the clock. Sister Jewell had left. It had not escaped his notice that the test form was where she'd left it. There was also a pencil next to it. How long would he be here? She didn't say. He suddenly stood and picked up the test and pencil.

Forty minutes later, he'd finished the test. He thought he'd done well. He wasn't clear on some questions about the timeline of the American Revolution, but he felt good about the rest. School had never been difficult for him—he quickly captured the gist of a lesson, was efficient with his study time, and retained information well. He put the completed test back on the table. The clock said one o'clock. When would she return to let him out? If it weren't by three o'clock, he'd decided to leave or escape. An hour went by with aching slowness. The test had only briefly taken his mind off Scarboy at the clinic. The bell rang at two-thirty, and he shortly heard the clamor of liberated lungs, the clomping and shuffling of fleeing feet.

He stepped into the hallway. It was quiet, with only a few straggling students. He walked down to the office and saw Sister Jewell's door open but no one at the desk.

He returned, gathered his book bag, and slipped out a side door.

◆◆◆◆◆◆◆

With a dignified resolve, Rosalyn put on her threadbare overcoat at the Fitch's door. Abigail stood next to her, at a loss, her expression shifting between appeal and apology. She stepped between Rosalyn and the door.

"Please, Rosalyn. You don't have to quit. There's no need. No one wants you to quit." She paused. "I don't want you to quit."

Rosalyn stood still, erect, seeming to tower over Abigail. But her face was blank, inscrutable.

Abigail suddenly held Rosalyn's shoulders, her eyes wet with tears.

"Please. Don't quit." She stared straight into her eyes. "We all need you... I need you."

Abigail looked stricken by embarrassment, dropping her eyes, and shifted her body to clear the way. A few seconds later, she shook her head as if clearing out a fog.

"I don't mean to make you uncomfortable. But I have to be honest."

Rosalyn had never experienced anything like this with an employer, such a personal plea. It had not occurred to her that she was indispensable. She knew she wasn't. That is, whatever Abigail Fitch's feelings of distress at this moment, they would pass. She would find a replacement, probably one who didn't mind cleaning up dog messes and wouldn't accost her children. Rosalyn had been prepared to be fired. At the same time, she felt Abigail appreciated her act of decisive corporal punishment. Rosalyn's hope was that Abigail would learn something. The idea that Abigail would allow these two spoiled brats to cow her into submission was impossible for Rosalyn to accept. Rosalyn knew such relationships existed. Hadn't she put up with an abusive father for many years? But Abigail wasn't fifteen; she was a grown woman. How could this have happened?

But there was more to it, and Rosalyn knew it. There was the husband, of course—a piece of the puzzle she hadn't seen and couldn't understand. And step-children—another unknown piece.

She looked at Abigail, her slowly recovering pride behind the wet eyes, and wondered if it would be possible, if she stayed, to restore some respectful structure to their relationship. Rosalyn had crossed a line. While grateful in the moment, would Abigail come to resent her action; that is, come to depend on it, invite it again, and resent the dependence? Rosalyn only wanted Abigail to fulfill her role, as Rosalyn fulfilled hers. That's what we do in life, whatever role we find ourselves in—fill it fully with strength, faith, and responsibility. It wouldn't do for Abigail to need Rosalyn to do this for her. As much as Rosalyn needed the job, she couldn't keep it under compromised conditions and roles. How could she say this to the woman?

Rosalyn looked at Abigail, and the intensity and clarity of how she felt was a torch in her eyes. Abigail held the stare and smiled, suddenly composed.

"I know this is difficult. It is for me. I'm not asking you ever to do anything like this again. But I value you... I value your work and your... principles. Please think about it."

◆◆◆◆◆◆◆◆

Sam ran the entire way to the clinic. When he entered, breathless, Marie smiled broadly and arm-waved into the back. Sam went straight to the cage. Scarboy looked to be sleeping on his side but sat up as Sam slid in front of the wire kennel.

He heard the swing door flap and looked up to see the vet, carrying a leash.

"He's better. I'm very pleased. Care to walk him around the block?"

Sam stood, holding out his hand out.

Marie said they'd walked him once, and he'd *done his business.* The wound on his head was already healing but, true to the dog's name, would no doubt form a striking and lasting scar.

As Sam attached the leash to the new red nylon collar around Scarboy's neck, his head was filling with plans about working off the clinic fees after school. He had about two hours every day between the final bell from school and Rosalyn's return, and this would be his commitment. Also, he'd offer time on the weekends. He wasn't thinking about how to explain it to his mother—he'd blocked out that detail from his mind. He meant to raise his plan with Dr. Davis later that afternoon.

Scarboy stood and walked out on the leash easily with Sam. He stopped at the door, looking up at Sam. Dr. Davis smiled.

"See that look? He didn't give me that look. Just take him for a little bit, stretch his legs."

Sam was astounded at the dog's smooth gait, considering his bandaged injuries and hobbled condition that morning. He could see the dog was underweight, with the outline of his ribs showing. But it was a stunning dog—to Sam, a picture-book dog, even more impressive than Terry's dog from *Terry and Scout,* and come to life at the end of his leash. He noticed the glances of passersby and swelled with pride. He knew they were quite a sight: the large, tricolored German shepherd dog with four white bandaged legs, patches of bare, iodined skin, and being led by the black boy.

◊◊◊◊◊◊◊

As Rosalyn entered the empty apartment, the phone rang. After hearing it was Sister Rosa Jewell of St. Aloysius School, she felt a flutter of panic but kept her poise.

"Is Samuel all right?"

Sister Jewell assured her that Sam was fine and asked if she had some time to talk.

"Of course."

Rosalyn listened without interruption as Sister Jewell told her the story. Jewell prefaced it by saying that Samuel was one of the brightest and most *'intellectually agile'* students she'd ever had. In her son's capabilities and generally studious demeanor, Rosalyn should be very *'gratified'* —Sister Jewell did not employ the words *'proud'* or *'pride'* in such contexts. Sam was a credit to her care and upbringing. Rosalyn thanked her but warily, waiting for the bad news.

"Often, such talents are accompanied by a certain recusance, if you're familiar with Roman Catholic history, that is, a resistance to authority and convention," the Sister said, choosing her words carefully. "I am not unfamiliar with this tendency, and I qualify it not as wanton disobedience, but as a certain specific, willful defiance related to something of great personal importance to the child, that is, a matter of a values judgment."

Rosalyn was becoming impatient.

"What has this to do with Samuel, Sister Jewell?"

Sister Jewell understood the impatience but was not to be waylaid.

"I say all this as a means of understanding, which should pertain to proper punishment."

"What did Sam do?"

"Hear me out, please, Mrs. Broussard."

Sister Jewell explained Sam's repeated tardiness, his absence from a test, and the excuses he used. She made clear that Sam had taken the test during detention without permission, and therefore his score was not to be accepted as legitimate, and he would have to accept a failing grade. He also left detention without being excused. Sister Jewell listened for any reaction from the mother over the line but heard nothing. She'd delivered her report on Sam in a calm, non-dramatic recitation and concluded with the hopes that the cause of the tardiness could be identified and corrected to restore the exceptional student to his high standard of scholarship and behavior.

Sister Jewell felt she had achieved her goal in the conversation.

Once she was sure Sister Jewell had finished, Rosalyn waited to respond. The evenness of Jewell's tone surprised her a little. But she was impressed. Rosalyn had felt rising anger at Sam during the call; she forced herself not to interrupt. Now she felt challenged to match Jewell's manner. After a few seconds' pause, Rosalyn thanked her.

"I appreciate your attention and concern, Sister. I'm sorry for this. You can be assured I will address it."

Before signing off on the call, Rosalyn surprised herself. On an impulse, she added, "Please allow us a little time to work this out, Sister."

Rosalyn set the phone down. Free of any constraint now, her suppressed anger flared. She felt the urge to find Sam immediately and wring the truth out of him. But picturing the confrontation, Sam silent before her and watching her, her flush of anger receded. She suddenly was relieved she'd asked for a little time.

She had an image of the timorous Abigail Fitch. She recalled the scene and how she'd made a silent gesture of concession to her employer, resolving to wait at least one week before the decision to quit. What changed her mind? Of course, she needed the job. But she was steeled to quit anyway. She couldn't browbeat and manhandle her employer's sons and not have the decency to resign, nor could she remain working for a woman who wouldn't fire her for that.

But she'd never seen anything like Amanda Fitch's response; she did seem to *need* Rosalyn and as more than a maid. But Rosalyn would not fulfill such a need. She would continue her work just as she had, and if the boys gave her a problem, she would quit, and if Amanda Fitch called on her to serve as a substitute, strong-arm parent, she would quit.

But she'd felt pity in that moment. This sensation had ambushed her. And now, she thought, if she could show Amanda Fitch pity and, in turn, had been granted pardon, why couldn't she do the same with her son? Didn't Sam deserve the benefit of the doubt, if that's what it was? So Sam would get a week; she would say or do nothing concerning the Sister's call. The decision felt better with each passing minute.

◇ ◇ ◇ ◇ ◇ ◇ ◇

The dog felt comfortable with the boy. This was a new sensation after the erratic and violent Doyle. The ancient genetic compulsion to obey and perform for a leader was powerful in the young dog.

He had learned something already of human nature: its limitations, jarring inconsistencies, and cruelty. While he was trained – as all dogs in his world — to target criminal behavior only on command, and to leave judgment to the humans, he was not able to suspend his own judgment, and it generally leaned toward greater tolerance. Though strong and capable of surviving with little human encouragement or affection, he was still born to follow. He had wanted to believe in Doyle and in a reliable, predictable pattern of leadership.

He didn't realize that the fire may have saved him; if he had turned on Doyle, it would have been his own end too.

His instinctual sense of the boy had been different from the start. The boy was small, and though he did not fit the typical profile of a leader, he exhibited confidence and force of will, which relaxed the dog. The dog was content walking with him. The pain and memory of his wounds were disappearing fast. He was young and healthy, and his stride was returning.

◇ ◇ ◇ ◇ ◇ ◇ ◇

Sam made his case to Dr. Davis and Marie. Davis studied the boy. Marie looked at Davis with hopeful eyes.

"Did you discuss this with your mother?" Davis asked.

Samuel wanted to lie. It would be so much easier.

"It doesn't matter, does it? She works all day. I'll be home alone if I'm not here working for a few hours after school. I don't want to talk about it with her. She... she hates dogs. This is only a few blocks from home. I know my way around. I can take care of myself."

He looked at Dr. Davis with more fierce need than appeal for mercy.

"Okay, for now," Davis said. "We'll give it a week. We'll find some things for you to do. You and Scarboy," he added, smiling slightly.

Sam let out his breath, nodding. He didn't want to discuss where Scarboy would spend his time beyond the next week. Sam felt sure of his ability to think problems through, to form a plan. Scarboy seemed fine in the crate around Davis, Marie and the other dogs for now.

The arrangement was for Sam to arrive early before school, walk and feed him; Marie would walk him a few times during the day; and Sam would return in the afternoon for his chores, walk him some more, and feed him his dinner.

Sam was exultant.

As the week unfolded, Rosalyn closely observed Sam's manner and actions. She couldn't find the slightest hint of trouble in him or a sign of a problem. Indeed, he woke early, prepared breakfast, and left for school. Rosalyn had not thought to ask Sister Jewell about the volunteer morning work. She would. But then Sam was home when she got home, or just after— all normal. There were no further reports from the school that week. She wondered if it had all been a hiccup, a typical and temporary deviation in behavior for a twelve-year-old.

By the fourth day, Scarboy was ready and greeted Sam with a brief lick on his hand and a single whine of expectation for the walk. Sam's sense of purpose to claim and train Scarboy grew by the hour.

Davis saw this. There weren't many boys he knew with Sam's dedication; it reminded him of his own. He thought of the obstacles on his path, of making it to Ohio State, of the difficulty of securing an internship, and of gaining the support and funding to open his clinic here. And he did not remember a bond he felt for any dog as he saw Sam developing with this dog. He wondered where the dog came from; it seemed too unusual and valuable to be lost and too self-possessed to have run away. This was a dog with extraordinary powers of recovery, iron nerves, and other work-ing-line breeding markers. Davis couldn't avoid the suspicion the dog had been involved in some police activity, possibly related to the fire nearby, and was presumed lost or killed. Sam had found him. This could mean there was a police officer somewhere looking for Scarboy. But for now, Davis would keep that to himself. He only knew what he was told. He wondered when the question would come up about who would ultimately house the dog. Sam had yet to disclose any plans to bring it home. His mother's 'hatred' of dogs was part of the boy's dilemma. Davis was prepared and happy to kennel Scarboy for the time being. He would wait for Sam to broach the subject.

By the end of the week, Rosalyn had made a few discoveries that wrin-kled her perfect picture of Sam and stirred up Sister Jewell's report. One, she noticed that several dollars were missing from her purse. Rosalyn kept punctilious accounting of her cash and had no doubt. Two, she'd confirmed from Sister Jewell: there was no 'voluntary morning cleanup.' Sam was rising and leaving early for another purpose.

Her three days that week with the Fitches (she worked two other days on Beacon Hill, with houses of childless Bostonians who'd hired her through her references from the Fitches) had been uneventful, but still startling. To Rosalyn's honest surprise, Abigail Fitch seemed a changed woman, and the boys had made no trouble. The rumpus room was not immaculate, but it was maintained, and Rosalyn was not asked to do anything more in it. Still, she had tidied it up on her own. However, she wanted nothing to do with the dog, who sat in the rear garden staring at her forlornly.

On that Friday, Sam took a more wide-ranging walk. It was 3:45. His eyes fixed on Scarboy, fascinated by his straight back, limber stride (the dog seemed to be improving by the hour, Dr. Davis said), and forward alertness of his stare that took in the scene around him, Sam lost track of his turns and location. He had reached the area around his building. He turned left down an alley that emptied onto the street leading home.

Rosalyn, meanwhile, off the subway, was moving down the perpendicular street.

Sam reached the end of the alley and leaned down to Scarboy, placing his head in the thick cinnamon-colored fur around his neck. Just as Rosalyn marched by, Sam straightened, missing her.

But Rosalyn wasn't as distracted. As she passed the alley, she picked up the shape of a boy and a dog in her periphery. Something told her to stop, and she did and stepped back.

She now stared at Sam, holding a leash to a large German shepherd. Sam stared back, frozen as a bush mouse before a cobra.

After a few seconds, she motioned with her arm.

"Follow me."

She didn't need to say it; Sam knew the look. And it wasn't as if he hadn't been thinking about this moment; in that instant, he wondered if he'd been willing it to happen.

Rosalyn led them up the stairs, through the doors, and down the hallway. She kept her head up and eyes dead ahead as they passed open doorways. Sam led the obedient Scarboy as a few little dogs yelped and others joined in the clamor. A few residents stepped out to gawk at the strange procession.

Inside the apartment, Rosalyn took off her coat and hung it but held her purse as she sat and pointed to the chair for Sam. He sat. Scarboy sat next to him, looking up keenly at Rosalyn. Sam placed his hands on the table, holding the leash, waiting.

"You've defied me, hidden things from me, and lied to me, Samuel. You stole from my purse. You failed your test. I can only guess at what else."

Try as she did to control herself, she was shaking, and the words were spilling out her mouth. The weeklong wait and her raised expectations now crashing were too much.

"No, I was going—"

"Your '*volunteering*' was a lie."

"It's not that—"

"No. Don't interrupt."

She pointed at but didn't look at Scarboy.

"And you somehow have a dog, against my orders." She paused, glaring. "What kind of lie would you like to tell me now?"

Sam moved his hand to the dog's head.

"I didn't fail the test," he said quietly.

The soft voice struck Rosalyn, and she lowered hers too.

"I talked to the teacher, Sam. She told me." She sighed so that he could hear her. "And I know you were in my purse."

"I didn't want to... I was going to put it back—"

"And you're going to tell me you didn't get a dog? Do you intend to put it back too?" She accented her harsh sarcasm with an abrupt emphasis. "Because you can't keep it."

"I didn't get him. I mean, I didn't mean to get him. I just—"

"You just what?"

The welling frustration was choking his voice and filling his eyes. He stood up.

"Sit down! You're not moving until I get the truth."

But Sam remained standing. Rosalyn stared at the dog now.

"That dog goes to the pound tomorrow. He seems to be the cause of your new enthusiasm for deceit and delinquency, so we'll deal with that first."

Sam had known this was coming. Still, his voice was a dazed hush, and he sank into himself.

"I didn't fail the test."

"I don't want to hear anymore."

"May I go to my room?"

She nodded, her jaws clenched. Sam slid off the chair and into his room; Scarboy followed.

Rosalyn watched, angry and anguished.

◇◇◇◇◇◇◇

Dr. Davis was finishing his final treatments. He glanced at Scarboy's open cage door: Sam had yet to return. Marie walked by, noticing too.

"Maybe they went to the school field," she said hopefully.

Davis nodded. He would wait a little longer. He knew, as Samuel had asserted, that the boy could look out for himself. And he had an incomparable companion in that regard. Anyway, Davis had another thought. He went to the clipboard with the clinic entry sheets, flipping through to Samuel's. Samuel's glum acknowledgment about his mother had been nagging at Dr. Davis. He had a feeling.

◇◇◇◇◇◇◇◇

In the apartment, Rosalyn finished cleaning up the dinner. Samuel had yet to emerge from his room since their battle. She'd gone to the door to summon him to dinner, during which he'd said nothing and not looked up. Afterward, he'd briefly walked outside with the dog before returning to his room. She stared at the dog, shaking her head. How could this be? The brazen defiance enraged her. '*No dogs*,' she'd said over and over, and now he'd brought back the most dangerous type she could imagine. The other scofflaws in the apartment had only tiny dogs. Mr. Sturdevant would surely evict her and Sam.

She went over their confrontation again and again. Could she have handled it better? How did they get to this point? Was it a sign of something worse?

The knock-knock on the door startled her. Good lord, it was the landlord already! She put down the dishtowel, set her back straight, and moved dutifully to it, peering through the peephole. It was a young black man in a suit coat. A lawyer? She opened the door, forcing on a neutral, businesslike face.

The man was slightly taller than her, slender, and stood relaxingly with a slight smile of greeting. She arched her eyebrows inquiringly.

"Hello, Mrs. Broussard?" He didn't wait for affirmation; he sensed this was Sam's mother. Her coiled, tense stare said everything to him. But he wasn't put off.

"I'm Dr. Colin Davis, a veterinarian. I'm just checking in on Sam's dog. We treated him at our clinic."

Rosalyn looked him up and down. Her first thought was, in what way had he conspired in this corruption of her son? He looked like the typical, gullible do-gooder with his suit jacket and mealy smile. He'd befriended and pitied the fatherless black boy. What stories had Sam told him to coax a dog out of him? He knew nothing of her or their lives.

Davis could see the veins of strain vibrating on and under the woman's exterior. Her smile was cold, her eyes colder. But still, underneath the lean sternness, he saw something else: intelligence and concern.

"He doesn't have a dog," she said calmly. "The animal can either be returned to you, if you're responsible for it being here or to the dog pound. One or the other. Tomorrow. If you would like to take it now, that's your choice. They don't permit dogs in this building."

Dr. Davis nodded, and glanced ironically down the hallway just as a few barks erupted. "Did you give him the dog?" she pressed. "Did you enable him to claim the dog?"

His smile and the calmness in his manner both irked and intrigued Rosalyn. It was not what she expected.

"I'm glad we've agreed there's a dog," he replied. "But no, to answer your question, I did not."

"Don't try to be smart with me, please. Samuel didn't just find a dog like that."

She saw his face change, harden a bit, though the smile remained.

"I run a clinic, Mrs. Broussard. I take care of sick animals."

"And my boy just brought in this sick dog to you?"

Davis stared at her for a moment before responding. "Is that difficult to imagine?"

The question, and merely the fact that he would answer her question with a question, felt highly insolent to her. She held back her anger as best she could.

"And this fact didn't concern you?"

"Why would it concern me?" he said. "I was pleased that he made use of our services. People of all ages bring in sick dogs to us every day. We're a veterinary clinic." He held up his hand at the look on her face.

"Please, Mrs. Broussard. My intention is not to be '*smart*.' And I'm not here to aggravate a family conflict. I wanted to check on Samuel and the dog. I'd been expecting them back in our office this afternoon. Sam was walking it and caring for it this week."

"A twelve-year-old boy, alone, with no parent accompanying him?"

"I'm not saying the fact didn't interest me. That may be one reason I'm here. To meet the parent."

She was in no mood for what she saw as his lofty airs and speech. And he wanted to meet her to judge her suitability as a dog owner?! She frowned crossly.

"Anyway," he added. "I believed Sam when he said he found him."

This was too much for her.

"Oh, you believed him? How big of you. How long have you known Sam?"

"He's been working at my clinic all week. I can tell a fair amount about someone from their work."

"Working?"

"He wanted to work off the costs of the care. When I reminded him it was a free clinic, he told me his mother said, '*nothing is free*.'"

This gave her pause.

"Did he ask you to come here?" she asked.

Davis shook his head.

Rosalyn stared at him, her eyes remaining tense and focused.

"I'm trying to raise a son, Mr. Davis."

Davis could feel the weight of emotion and implication compacted within the simple statement. Still, he couldn't resist his urge to correct her.

"It's Dr. Davis."

"Pardon me," she replied with sincerity. He nodded.

"I'm trying to teach him right from wrong," she continued more evenly.

"I would say, based on my brief experience, that you're doing an admirable job."

The compliment flustered Rosalyn. She could only respond with a certain barbed sententiousness.

"You know, it's easy to impress a fatherless boy by being a nice guy and telling him he can have something, or do something, without any mind to the consequences."

Davis understood Sam's mother a lot better now.

"Mrs. Broussard, I don't know if I'm a *'nice guy'* or not. I grew up without a father myself. But I'm not going to give you women all the credit. Sometimes you're given good raw material. Anyway, please tell Sam I stopped by to see how Scarboy was doing. I hope to see them both tomorrow. I'm sure we can come to some arrangement for the dog."

He turned and walked off, and she stared at his retreating back. She closed the door.

She stood in the half-light of the one kitchen lamp. The apartment suddenly felt empty. Sam's closed door radiated rebuke to her. There was nothing to do. But it was promising to have a possible answer for the dog. The vet, this arrogant but seemingly capable Dr. Davis, might be willing to take it. And Sam knew and liked the man.

She walked to Sam's door and opened it slowly.

Sam was asleep. The large dog was on the floor directly beside Sam. It lifted its head, its ears pricked up, watching her. While she felt a quick stab of fear, an atavistic urge to draw back at the sight of a 'police dog'—as it appeared to her—the feeling vanished as quickly. What she saw instead was a guardian, and the image jarred her. She brusquely rejected its reassurance. The dog lowered its head again, between its paws, its ears still erect. She stepped back and closed the door.

Later, Rosalyn lay in bed on her left side, watching the curtains quiver slightly from the crack in her window as she struggled to shut her mind to the day's events. As cold as it was, Rosalyn could not sleep in a room with sealed windows. The quiet and sense of peace was broken by a distant siren, a bottle breaking, and a slurred shout somewhere on the street. After a few seconds, there was silence again. Her eyes closed.

They snapped open sometime later. What was it? It seemed to be a live sound, behind her. For a moment, she wondered if she was in a nightmare, paralyzed, as something crept up on her. She wanted to turn and sit up but, for some reason, could not. Then she heard it again, a low rumbling.

Finally, slowly, she turned. She jerked backward in the bed at what she saw. The dog was staring at her, a foot from her bed. Its mouth was closed, and the growl was smooth and deep. While its eyes were fixed on her, she saw no threat to her in them; instead, she sensed a message. She sat up, and as she did so, the dog immediately turned and moved out of the room. Was it Sam?

She sprang out of bed and into the living room. The dog was at the door to the hallway, sitting in front of it. She let out a breath. For heaven's sake, it had to do its business, that's all. At least it was housebroken, a saving grace for Sam. She would wake him up. The dog was aiming its nose at the knob like an arrow. Suddenly Rosalyn heard a sound outside. Was it whispering? She moved closer and saw the knob turn and the door flex against the lock. The dog growled now more deeply and stood as if readying itself. Rosalyn leaped the six feet to the door and pounded on it, twice. She heard footsteps running away. She checked the locks—the internal lock on the knob and the sliding chain loop. They were intact and locked.

She looked down at the dog.

"Go back to sleep," she whispered.

The dog padded back to the boy's room. She stared after it, shaking her head. Did she talk to a dog?

◆◆◆◆◆◆◆

The dog explored and reckoned the boundaries of the new space to which the boy had brought it. His actions were instinct. It understood the boy's den; it was rich with his scent.

He accepted the woman because the boy did—the dog was attuned to affiliating signals among humans. The woman had authority, and the dog picked up on it, not in a challenging or subordinating sense, just as what it was. Rankings were important to understand.

He identified the kitchen food smells and the woman's den as her scent seeped through the cracked door. He identified the entry door as the point of territorial exposure, detecting the foreign odors under the threshold. He heard the sounds from the hallway and took a moment to interpret them. He decided to lie down by the door. He lay there for a while, having no sense of time but only purpose, when he heard the scraping and the fiddling at the door—a proximate and worrisome noise whose potential threat became real with the movement of the knob. His instinct told him to alert the human. So he made his way into the woman's room—she was closer. The woman had emerged, and he'd been satisfied with the result. The threat was gone. He returned to the boy's room, but he knew he would sleep lightly for the remainder of the evening.

It was Saturday, but Sam rose extra early and walked Scarboy. He could have walked him for hours. It was a release of tension after the fitful night in which he'd stewed about the next, unavoidable confrontation with his mother.

He returned to find the breakfast table set. Rosalyn was fully dressed and stood by the table. She pulled out the chair for him. The moment-of-truth tension hung in the air.

"We'll leave right after breakfast."

He didn't go to the table but stood holding Scarboy's leash.

"Where?"

"You know where Samuel. To the pound to drop off the dog. They'll find him an appropriate home."

He avoided her eyes and shifted Scarboy behind him. He shook his lowered head.

"What is that?" she asked.

"No."

"What did you say?"

"I'm not going. We're not going."

"Samuel. I'm telling you—"

"No."

Sam fully understood the cost of his defiance but somehow sensed the reaction could not be worse than he'd imagined. And he knew he had no other choice; this was his choice, one reached and fortified by conscience.

"Samuel!"

She could see Samuel's grip on the leash. He spoke, and his voice was low and of a timbre she'd not heard before.

"I won't. He's mine. I found him and...." He shook his head, his eyes staring past her. "He found me." He paused and now looked and sounded like a man at his trial, irretrievably lost in his cause and no longer caring about the judge or jury.

"I can't. I won't."

Rosalyn took a few seconds, weighing the character emerging before her.

"You know you can't have him, Sam. It's just not possible."

"I don't know that. I don't believe that."

His breathing became faster. Rosalyn had a sudden image of his chest bursting. *This cannot be happening! It's just a dog!* She wanted to stop and calm him, but at the same time knew she could not relent. But he suddenly brought his breathing down. Now he looked at the dog.

"When I saw him in that hole, I knew he was mine. I felt it; I knew it. I knew I'd bring him home, no matter what, and we'd find a way to keep him. He saw that too and believed it too. I was never so sure of anything. It's why he got better."

Rosalyn sat down at the table. She gestured for him to join her. But he stood where he was.

"You're twelve years old, Sam. You don't know what being sure of anything means. You don't know the responsibility of being sure."

"Yes, I do. Why don't you ever think I know anything like that?"

This caught Rosalyn short. "What are you talking about? And don't think you can change the subject."

"I'm not. I know how to take care of this dog. Why do you think I don't?"

Rosalyn felt the conversation slipping away from her.

"What happens in a few weeks when you lose interest in caring for him, cleaning up after him, feeding him, and walking him?"

"I'm not going to do that. Why do you think I'm going to do that?"

His hand moved to Scarboy's snout, and he ran it up from the scar over and down his head and back.

"I care about him. You said caring about something was all that matters."

"That's not what I said, Sam."

"Yes you did. I heard you say it. You said it mattered more than anything."

Despite her anger at being challenged in this way, she remained calm.

"Yes, it matters to care, Sam. But there are practical considerations to this."

"It's not impossible. It's not. It's a bad rule we can't have dogs. You said bad rules should be broken. You said it was a bad rule you couldn't swim in the pools down in Virginia."

"That was immoral, Sam. There's a difference."

Sam shut his eyes and spoke lowly, adamantly.

"I'm not getting rid of him. If they don't want dogs here, I'll move."

"You'll move?"

He nodded, wiping his eyes, his fury shifting into desperation.

Rosalyn stared, unable to contain her astonishment. She stood up from the chair and moved closer out of an uncontrollable motherly reflex. But he stepped back. She felt a shock of self-recrimination. She saw his right hand clutching something as tightly as his left held the leash. The right hand stretched to the table and released its hold—it was her 'stolen' money.

Sam bent down, putting his arm around the dog, and seemed to be talking to him, not Rosalyn.

"When I was in there, and he saw me, he growled. I knew he was only doing that because he was hurt. I wasn't scared of him." He turned to her. "I was scared of you."

She stared, stunned, at the boy and the dog. Tears stung her eyes. She hadn't felt tears since she was a teenager. She brought her hands up to her eyes, covering them, and leaned forward into her hands.

◇◇◇◇◇◇◇

Sam led the way toward the clinic, Scarboy at his side. Rosalyn followed a few steps behind, watching the boy and the dog and their easy rhythm. The day was almost painfully clear, crisp, and windy. Rosalyn noticed the people making way for them, or sidestepping quickly out of the way.

Rosalyn saw the clinic ahead. It didn't look like much. It needed painting and a new sign. '*Free Clinic.*' Did they make any money? Was it a charity? She suddenly let it go. Who cared? It was performing a service. She was trying to distract herself from feeling ashamed and losing an argument to her son. Oh, was that it? She upbraided herself. '*Losing an argument*'? That was the voice of beaten and bitter pride. And pride was a sin. She was so sure she knew the right way and needed to make all the decisions. She'd blinded herself to any possibility that Sam knew something she didn't, something closer to him than she could feel or imagine, or that he had a will as strong as her own. She should have been nurturing that will. But he didn't seem to need that nurturing. He'd shown it when it mattered to him.

They reached the door of the clinic and entered. Rosalyn was buffeted back by the wild barking and whining from the rear and cringed. But she stood straight and took in the scene. The clinic looked far different on the inside; in fact, clean and bright. Sam led her through the lobby to the back.

Dr. Davis appeared, a light smile on his face.

"Ah, Mrs. Broussard. And Sam. And Scarboy."

Rosalyn offered her hand, and he took it.

"We're hoping we can arrange to house the dog here until Sam and I can work out the next step."

Davis nodded, glancing between her and Sam.

"Of course." He reached down and stroked Scarboy. "Quite a dog, isn't he? I'm glad he won you over."

She smiled noncommittally and stepped back as if that was that.

"Can I show you around our clinic?"

She raised her eyebrows as she looked around.

"That's right," he said. "This is it. But you were wondering about our operations, I'll bet. Is this is a reputable enough facility for young Sam to spend his time? Well, we accept donations from our clients, whatever they can afford. That helps but doesn't make ends meet. We have some larger benefactors..." he interrupted himself with a slight smile, "thanks to some of my after-hours dedication, and now we're part of WGBH's list of worthy public services. We've just purchased a new otoscope, a heart monitor, and an x-ray machine." He shrugged apologetically. "I don't mean to boast."

She nodded. "Yes, you do. But it sounds earned. Good for you. There's no need for false modesty."

She noticed his mouth play out the same smirk that had irritated her. Well, today was different. She could see he was an actual veterinarian. But she was still mildly irritated. He seemed to know that she would capitulate to Sam and the dog.

"So the dog will be fine here, I see."

"His name is Scarboy, mother."

She looked at Sam and at Davis, who nodded in support.

"All right. '*Scarboy*.' That won't be hard to remember."

She shifted and fiddled with her purse. "What do we owe you?"

Davis shook his head. "Sam is working off any costs. We agreed on that."

Rosalyn nodded and looked at Sam, her face softening.

"He's been busy. I had no idea." She looked up at Davis. "Maybe now I'll stay informed?"

He gave a remonstrating look at Sam, which Sam acknowledged. She didn't miss his focus on Davis.

"I'm taking some of the dogs to Blue Hills this afternoon," Davis said. "Why don't you come? Both of you, with Scarboy, of course."

Sam's face lit up. Rosalyn looked skeptical. Davis had anticipated her balk.

"It's not far," he assured. "I take the hike a lot."

"Dogs?" One dog was enough. Rosalyn hesitated. But seeing the two sets of eyes, she suddenly smiled resignedly.

◇◇◇◇◇◇◇

Rosalyn stood at a fork on the hiking path staring down at two dirty beer bottles and a condom wrapper on the over-trodden earth. Dressed in slacks and old sneakers, she already felt out of sorts. On the other hand, Davis looked more in his element here than at the clinic. He stood ten feet away in khakis, boots, and a stylish blue windbreaker looking braced for adventure. A trio of small dogs circled him—two Jack-something terriers and a Corgi (he'd told her). He handled their leashes with confident coordination.

Sam was to her other side, with Scarboy seated next to him, his ears up and watching the perimeter. Did that dog ever not look like he was studying everything around him?

Davis moved in closer.

"Okay, Homer, Butch and Belle." He looked at the others and gestured ahead. "Shall we?"

Rosalyn offered a cordial nod, and they walked on.

The trail alternately widened and narrowed between the lines of the woods, and Sam and Scarboy took the lead. Rosalyn was beginning to enjoy the cool, clean air on her face and in her lungs. She appreciated that Davis wasn't forcing small talk and seemed absorbed in the walk and observing the horizon.

A bend was ahead, and as Sam and Scarboy reached it, Rosalyn heard a sudden scuffle and rush of barking and growling. Davis moved quickly to Sam's side, and she followed.

Three large dogs, two unleashed mastiff mixes and a Doberman dragging a long line, all panting heavily, sped to within a few feet from Scarboy before braking abruptly. The dogs were stiffly posed, slightly to the side, their heads averted, the whites of their eyes showing, their short tails high and flicking back and forth in alarmed readiness. To Rosalyn, the air around the three dogs seemed imminent of violence. As Sam was directly next to Scarboy, feet from the dogs, she stepped forward. But Davis's hand firmly restrained her. She looked at him; he quietly shook his head. He was staring at Scarboy.

She turned and could see the dog's look was markedly different: he stood straight on to the other dogs, his head tilted a little upwards, seemingly unperturbed, and his tail parallel to the ground and motionless. His mouth was open a little in a slow pant.

The two dogs warily sniffed the air as they edged closer to him. One of the small dogs at Davis' feet suddenly barked, and the other two joined. But the mastiffs and Doberman ignored them. Davis made a quick correction, and the little dogs quieted.

The tense mastiffs, keeping heads averted, moved off to the side of Scarboy, a brush of hackles now showing on their upper backs. The Doberman growled, arousing rumbles from the mastiffs. Scarboy was silent, still making slow, relaxed pants. As the mastiffs moved around Scarboy on Sam's side, Scarboy made a slight bodily shift, looked directly at the mastiffs, and made a quick, brief growl with a curled lip. It sounded to Rosalyn like a terse order. The mastiffs sprang back as if stung. The Doberman, taking its cue, cocked its ears half back in submission and stepped back. It was all over.

Suddenly a heavyset man in a flannel jacket, breathless, emerged from an angled pathway. He scrambled to gather the Doberman and hook the mastiffs to their leashes. The trio just watched. The man, making no gesture of apology, walked around them down the path.

"There's a leash law here, sir." It was Rosalyn. The man threw Rosalyn a look but said nothing and disappeared around the corner; Rosalyn let out her breath. She looked down to see Davis' hand still on her arm. He noticed and released his grip.

He smiled. "A little '*draamer*,' as they say in Boston, to get the blood moving."

Sam put his arm around Scarboy with pride, and the two moved up the path.

"This is all a conspiracy between you and Sam," she said.

Davis shook his head. "No, it's just that dog. He's a badass."

She laughed in a quick burst, despite herself.

They jogged to catch up to Sam and rounded the corner to see him fifty yards ahead. He was veering left, descending under a shroud of trees.

Feeling a new ease in Rosalyn, Davis decided to probe a little.

"I see a lot of dogs and owners in my practice, Rosalyn. I'm not sure how this will sound, but I believe that dog chose that boy as much as he chose it."

It was the first time he'd used her first name. She took in his words.

133

"So, Colin, you think I should break the law and risk losing our home?"

"Why don't we just call it *'bending the rules.'* Or a little rebellion for a good cause."

"<u>We</u> can call it whatever we want. But it won't matter to the ones who make the rules."

They reached a turn down into a woodsier stretch. The trees were thick and broke up the sunlight. The track was wider, and they could see Sam and Scarboy ahead.

"Where and when I grew up, Dr. Davis..." she let the implication hang and looked at him. "I'm not risking the life we've built here for a dog. For any dog."

"What about Sam?"

He regretted his words instantly. He'd meant to bring up Sam's interests and needs, but not so soon. The outdoor exercise and their moment of laughter, the door they'd had opened to friendliness, had beguiled him into the blunder.

She stared at him, indignant.

But the sound of voices startled them out of the moment. They looked up.

To their side, set back about twenty-five yards in a raised clearing, was a graffiti-spotted concrete utility shed. Three kids, older teens, Davis guessed quickly, and 'Southies' as he reckoned from their appearance, flouting the weather in their T-shirts, stared truculently at them. One was on the top of the shed, his legs swinging. The other two walked down the sides to approach Rosalyn and Davis. The taller one waggled a beer bottle in front of the little dogs with a heavily tattooed arm and looked up at Davis.

"You're in Quincy, boy."

The other, shorter and skinnier with cropped blond-yellowish hair and a hard look, circled Rosalyn's side. He poked forward toward her purse. Rosalyn pulled back. Davis stepped in with an open-palms gesture of his hands.

"We're just walking. Did you see a boy and a dog a little while ago? We're looking for them."

The one sitting on top, between the others in height, in torn and baggier painter's overalls and a vest over his T-shirt, jumped down and joined the other two.

"Nope," he said.

He moved in toward Davis and stopped a few feet away, smiling.

"No smudges allowed around here."

He pushed out his chest and walked into Davis. The little dogs barked.

"Shut up," the tall one said, making a sideways kicking motion at it.

Davis took a step back, shielding Rosalyn.

Moments earlier, Sam had seen the Southies and stared back. Their eyes had been mainly on Scarboy. Sam registered their potential threat but wasn't worried and felt Scarboy would generate a wake of safety for Rosalyn and Davis, not far behind him. When he reached a bend in the path, he stopped and looked back; his mother and Dr. Davis were nearing the shed. He waited, watching. Scarboy sat, staring with him.

He saw the two, with the dogs, come parallel to the shed, and pause. He saw the three white boys saunter down to them. Their body language as they moved closer was clear to Sam, and when the one boy lunged at his mother, he pulled at Scarboy and ran back down the path.

The three now circled Davis and Rosalyn. Davis handed the dogs' leashes to Rosalyn, peeled off his jacket, and stood, fists clenched.

The boys made '*ooohing*' sounds of mockery as they taunted with lunges, closing in.

They all heard a sharp cry. One of the boys stopped and looked up toward the sound and froze. A hush fell on the others as he made a garbled noise and pointed, then turned to run. His face was panic. The other two now looked up searchingly.

Down the path, they saw the blackish-tan streak of the dog, charging low and fast. The boy was behind him, running to catch up with the leash. The Southies scattered. One scrambled up to the flat roof of the shed, another tried pulling himself up a nearby tree with comical futility, and the third ran with crazy zigzags into the woods as if dodging imaginary gunshots.

Scarboy rushed the shed and circled it. He shot glances toward the woods but seemed satisfied to hold his position.

"Scarboy!"

Sam ran up to the dog, who was sitting, panting. He clipped on the dog's leash and turned to the others, his face beaming.

"I just told him to '*Go.*'"

The dog hadn't needed a command. He understood from the boy's stiff-ened posture, changes in his breathing, his directional focus, and no less from the sight of the two trailing members of his pack encircled by the threatening figures, what to do. The boy's sharp cry merely confirmed it. Once he'd reached the scene and the boys had scattered, his judgment, his sense of task completion, restrained him. He had no reason to pursue or bite the boys.

Rosalyn and Davis looked on with different kinds of amazement. Amazement rarely came to Rosalyn. But to her, the dog's swiftness in reaching them, his efficiency in routing the hooligans, and how he now sat with Sam, calm and unfazed, were something to behold. It seemed to her that the dog had done what he did for Sam. She had no conception of this possibility in this dog or any dog. To her, dogs were scatter-brained creatures of impulse and need, only taking, eating, and making noxious noises and messes, all with total disregard for humans. But this dog looked mindful of something beyond himself, and now, as he sat next to Sam, she saw that maybe he was mindful of her son.

As for Davis, he felt much the same but marveled more at how the dog turned on and off so cleanly. He'd seen dogs that could do this from watching and interning around police dogs in Ohio. They were not close to the decision and self-control he'd just seen in this dog.

They watched as Sam approached them, flicking his hands around Scarboy's muzzle with light, teasing smacks as the dog lightly mouthed him in a gently playful response.

"Maybe we should get going," Sam said.

Rosalyn smiled with a little more amazement.

◆◆◆◆◆◆◆

Rosalyn closed the door to Sam's bedroom. It had been a long and happily exhausting day. After the adventures at Blue Hills, the group had driven into Boston, walked around the Commons, and enjoyed an outdoor lunch. They'd first stopped at the clinic and let off the three dogs, but Scarboy stayed with them. During the walk around the Commons pond, the dog behaved perfectly with Sam, never leaving his side and paying no attention to other dogs. It was all hard for her to believe.

By the time they returned to the clinic in Davis' Buick wagon, no word had been spoken about Scarboy's arrangements; Davis made no motion to collect him nor Sam to lead him in. They said their goodbyes, and Rosalyn, Sam, and Scarboy walked off.

Back at their apartment building, Sam decided to keep walking, and Rosalyn went inside to prepare supper. As she cleaned up Sam's room, she noticed a crumpled piece of paper on the floor just under his bureau. She picked it up, but instead of placing it on top, straightened it out in her hands.

She moved to the kitchen table, reading it in the light of the table lamp.

At the top, Sam's scrawl read '*Budget for Scarboy.*' Below it was a series of line items. They included, among others, '*Food*', '*Equipment*', and the misspelled '*Vetrinary Care.*' The costs seemed realistic to her. He'd done some work to prepare this.

Her palms pressed out the wrinkles on the paper with curating care.

A quiet knock on the door startled her. A little nervous, she went to the peephole. It couldn't be! She should have known; the accounting always comes. She braced as she opened the door on the landlord, Mr. Sturdevant.

◇◇◇◇◇◇◇◇

Sam ate his Wheatena as his mother watched him.

The morning had felt strange. He usually felt out of sorts on Sundays, but on this one he especially did. He'd risen early and walked Scarboy, but Rosalyn wasn't up when he returned. He prepared his own Wheatena, treating himself to an extra section of banana and a scoop of brown sugar in the bowl as he waited for it to cook. After his mother woke, dressed for church, and emerged, she was strangely quiet—with no sense of onus to the silence. When Scarboy greeted her with a nudge of his nose, she touched him back.

Finally, she sat at the table next to him and folded her hands. Her face was solemn but with no lines of tension. Sam waited.

"Mr. Sturdevant came by last night," she said.

Sam looked up, milk running down his chin.

"He told me, Sam...."

She closed her eyes for a moment. Sam stared, apprehending the worst.

"He told me that in the ten years he's managed this building, no one has ever come to him first and offered a probationary period for a dog."

Sam swallowed and wiped the milk off his chin.

"Samuel. I owe you an apology."

Sam looked down, unsure of what to say, how to react. This was a new experience. He turned to Scarboy as if for an answer. And, as he hoped, the dog's look reassured him that it all made sense, and Sam was grateful. The dog's presence was enough at any moment, and he could relax and allow gratitude and instinct to guide him. Whatever he did for the dog, and to ensure that they were together, would work out, and all the people and pieces in his life would somehow come together toward this end because this was his destiny. His mother, for all her resistance, was, in fact, crucial to how it came together, and he knew that.

"I'm proud of you, Sam. I'm proud of you, and I love you very much."

Her eagle eyes softened, and she reached out to touch his arm.

She fought back a laugh as the milk dripped off his chin.

"Now, get ready for church."

◇◇◇◇◇◇◇

On Monday, as Sam prepared to leave for school as usual, Rosalyn started out with him. Sam looked at her, surprised, but fell into stride with Scarboy, pleased; this would mean she would walk Scarboy home. They reached the school, where the students in the yard stared in wonder at the sight of the three of them.

Inside, they reached the hallway in front of the school office, and Sam handed the leash to Rosalyn. She took it tentatively, watching Sam move down the hallway.

Rosalyn turned and walked into the school office.

Five minutes later, she sat across from Sister Jewell. Jewell's interlocked fingers formed a small steeple as she waited for Rosalyn to speak.

"Sister, I'd like to introduce you to the sick friend Sam was caring for while I was at work and couldn't be reached."

Jewell looked at the dog sitting at Rosalyn's side.

"You might have saved us some time by mentioning this at the beginning. But as to any dispensation, I can't bend the rules."

Rosalyn nodded patiently. "I appreciate the value you place on punctuality. Sam won't be late again—if he can help it."

Jewell seemed satisfied that the matter was closed and started to stand. But Rosalyn remained.

"There is the matter of the test. I understand that Sam completed it."

Jewell started shaking her head before she was back in her seat.

"He wasn't authorized to take it at that time. He was in detention. Those are the rules."

"But he took it. Does that deserve a failing grade?"

"Those are the rules. He took it without a proctor to supervise."

Rosalyn nodded. "Rules," she said. "I see. You have yours, and I have mine. We have reasons for them. But it is good to think them over now and then. Thank you, Sister."

She stood. She pointed at the dog.

"This is Scarboy. He is Sam's dog. I had a rule against dogs."

She gathered the leash and walked out.

Walking the dog was easier than Rosalyn had imagined. He kept perfectly to her pace, simultaneously aware of her body while keeping track of the goings-on and people around them. It was almost as if he wasn't on a leash but was still bound to her. She inhaled the morning air deeply. She rarely felt fearful or even insecure walking the streets, but with this dog, she felt almost invincible.

After picking up some items at the local bodega, Rosalyn made her way down the last block before home. Rounding a corner, grocery bag in one hand and leash in the other, she nearly collided with Cuz. He backpedaled, eyeing the animal.

"That dog."

Rosalyn tugged at the leash, but Scarboy didn't move.

As Cuz leaned into him, Rosalyn felt a little nervous: will he take the man's arm off? But when Cuz's arm reached his head, Scarboy consented to the stiff stroking.

Cuz looked up at her and put out his hand with a dull-eyed panhandling plea.

"Any extra change, ma'am..?"

Rosalyn's impulse was to rush off. But for some reason—the dog's indulgence?—she paused and fished inside her purse for a quarter.

A few minutes later, approaching the building, she saw Davis outside the entrance. She walked up behind him; he turned with a start. She smiled at his surprise as he saw Scarboy.

He spoke first. "I don't want to keep you. I just wanted to say something." She nodded. "What I said at Blue Hills," he continued. "It wasn't fair."

"Fair or not, I'm glad you said it." She tilted her head up to the apartment. "I have the day off. Why don't you come up for some coffee."

The two sat at Rosalyn's kitchen table ten minutes later, Scarboy between them. The silence this time, Rosalyn thought, was not uncomfortable.

"So, you don't give all the credit to your mother?" she asked, somewhat impishly.

"I don't know. If she hadn't left Detroit for Columbus, I might not have gone to Ohio State. That's what got me into veterinary medicine."

"So she left your father." It wasn't a question.

"He'd already left. She moved back there to be with family. I grew up around so many aunts, uncles, and cousins that I never even noticed he was gone."

"Really? How nice. Sam didn't have that advantage. A father is important."
"Yours?"

Rosalyn looked straight at him, then down at the dog, reflectively.

"He always had a scheme. His last one was training dogs for rich white folks. Turned out the dogs were no good for hunting, and he was no good for training. Whatever new scheme there was, the alcohol was always the same."

Her eyes went opaque, looking beyond Davis.

"One day, I told him to git."

"'*Git*'"?

She nodded vacantly. "I was fifteen. I was about as tall as he was but skinny as a corn stalk. We were in our kitchen, if you could call it that. Good thing he'd been eating the bacon my mother saved for us on Sundays. It helps to have something like bacon to back up your outrage, don't you think?"

He was captivated by the new tone in her and her remote expression, which he thought was concealing emotion.

"Last I heard, he was in Atlanta. I never missed him for a second. But you could say he taught me some things, like survival." She smiled mirthlessly. "How to stand up."

He sighed, leaning back. "I wouldn't want to tangle with you." He paused, looking into his coffee and then back to her. "Let me rephrase that."

She laughed shortly. "Don't sell yourself short."

◇◇◇◇◇◇◇◇

The months went by. It was May, and Rosalyn, Sam, and Scarboy had settled into a routine pleasing to all. They'd all three walk to his school in the morning, and Rosalyn return with the dog and either drop him off at the clinic or, increasingly, leave him in the apartment for the day. She had become entirely comfortable with his presence there. He was an irreproachably well-mannered living companion.

Sam would work at the clinic after school and bring Scarboy home for play and training. Davis made no demands on Sam to work; it was soon an entirely voluntary effort. Davis offered help in the dog training but was impressed by how much Sam was learning on his own and gave the boy support, only helping if asked. Sam had found some library books, but his instincts seemed uncanny and more than equal to the work. Davis saw that Sam and the dog had rapidly formed a remarkable bond.

Formal training hardly seemed necessary, as the dog reacted as if anticipating Sam's will or command. Thus, Davis felt reaffirmed in his guess that Scarboy had already been through some formative training, probably through a police curriculum; he was sure the dog had a working K9 provenance. If so, he was no ordinary K9.

Rosalyn looked forward to the clinic visits but also respected Sam's preference for the dog to be home. She didn't want to use the dog as a pretext for time with Davis, of whom she was growing fond. '*Fond*' was the only word she permitted herself, for now. But her feelings of safety and trust in his company, feelings long in suspension and almost forgotten were undeniable. Old prideful resistance to intimacy was crumbling. The three along with the dog had made weekend visits, walks around the city, or more ambitious outings, a regular event.

Rosalyn and Sam each felt that they'd never been happier.

◇◇◇◇◇◇◇◇

Sam and Scarboy had been extending the usual ambit of their walks, and one afternoon they caught the eye of a man in a parked car.

Sergeant Brian Doyle stared with lazy malice at some loiterers across the street, wiped his mouth with a wad of restaurant napkins, and made an unsatisfied grunt. He was in his Plymouth Duster, finishing a McDonald's burger. His mouth pursed sourly; he could tell the food wouldn't go down well. Nothing had in weeks. But he kept hoping, returning to his old fast-food hang-outs. He dug into the bunched pocket of his jacket for the antacid tablets.

The months since the fire and the death of Chaser had not been good.

At first, he'd requested sick leave, then filed for disability, citing the re-injury of his back (he'd been treated for a back problem years before).

After a few days of not showing up for work after the fire, he'd told Lockwood that his dog had been stolen. Lockwood, genuinely shocked, had offered the department's resources to help search. While Doyle could hardly refuse, he gave only token support to the effort, citing trauma as the excuse. This wasn't well received, he could tell. But how dare they doubt him! The trauma was real; he was tormented by images from the fire, night after night, in excruciating clarity and detail.

He tried to convince himself he didn't care what Lockwood or others thought, a claim which, no matter how often repeated, invariably fell apart in his sleepless hours of purgatory. The only relief was drinking. In the numbing succor of his stupors, he confessed to an imaginary and forgiving priest that he was weak and a failure and that his career had always been on borrowed time until his true character finally caught up with him.

The dog was at the center of his torment. Doyle knew the dog had been his golden opportunity to escape his fate, to free himself from the weight of unworthiness he'd been dragging around his whole unhappy life. And now it was gone. Had he killed it? Or had it been violently taken from him by inimical fate and its agents? The answer was different each day, sometimes every hour, and even minute.

His father had been right; the old man, the Navy veteran, the electrical contractor who'd worked his entire life to support him and Corrine, knew his son was nothing special. Doyle had always sensed this. His father disdained civil service; it would never be the same as *making it on your own.* Doyle had tried invoking the *higher calling* of police work, but the words didn't impress his father. In truth, Doyle couldn't convince even himself of it.

He had no idea what else to do. He had no skills, practical or interpersonal. He didn't like people; the prospect of meeting strangers and asking for work mortified him. With each day, the pretense of his career and the truth of his failure ate away at him.

He knew Lockwood didn't believe him, which also ate away at him. Lockwood had the intimidating talent of seeing into people, and Doyle knew that he saw into him. Craving Lockwood's respect, Doyle had only ever felt condescension. Lockwood's phony 'mentorship' sickened him.

This was all Lockwood's fault for not trusting him, and supporting him. He wouldn't have felt driven to take Chaser out and set his downfall in motion if Lockwood had treated him with the same respect he did the others.

At least now he didn't have to see Lockwood every day and be reminded of his disdain. Was that some cold comfort? No, not entirely. He knew that too.

His disability claim had been conditionally approved, but there were still more tests. The X-rays confirmed the disc problem. But new symptoms were complicating the picture. The doctors wanted a bone marrow tap. The medical people were sympathetic, and the painkillers they'd prescribed were an unexpected prize. He was surprised and proud to discover he was a very compliant patient. In a way, he thought, he wished to be even sicker. Letting go into the arms of the doctors was an escape from his self-recrimination.

Corrine tried to be helpful but didn't know what to say. Doyle at home so much of the time was awkward, and he discouraged her coddling—once blowing up at her to leave him alone. So she left him alone for the most part. He sensed she knew that he was beyond her now. She had cried about Chaser's theft and blamed the police department for not assigning him a new dog. She'd bought into all his lies, and her credulity only made him feel worse about himself and edgier around her.

No, it was the black activists who'd killed Chaser. They'd set the fire. He'd uncovered their treacherous drug den, and they'd killed his dog, nearly killed him, destroyed all the evidence, and escaped. And there was nothing he could do about it. His rage festered, and soon he began to see all blacks around him as conspiring in his downfall. He'd never thought of himself as a racist. But he couldn't see a black on the street now and not associate him with the night of the fire, his trapped and dying dog, and all the ensuing misery. Maybe he was a racist after all. He didn't care.

Doyle unwrapped the Rolaids and popped several more in his mouth, crunching and swallowing. He reached for the small amber bottle of Percocet and swallowed one, then another, washing them down with the warm Pabst on the front seat.

Lowering his head, he now saw the boy and the dog.

They were fifty yards away. It was an extraordinary sight, for sure; the dog cut a striking figure and was nearly up to the boy's waist. What was a black kid doing with a dog like that? It was too weird. Doyle had difficulty focusing and rubbed his eyes, which only made his vision blurrier. He struggled to pry himself out of the car. Grimacing from the cold, sharp pain around his midriff, he leaned back against the door, breathing hard.

The boy and dog were now in his direct line across the street and heading to his left. From what he could see, the dog looked scarred around its head. That dog, Doyle thought, had the shape, stride, profile, and unmistakable vibe of a professional dog. That the boy walked as if the dog was his prized possession somehow rankled Doyle; something about this was wrong, very wrong. It wasn't only his curiosity that was piqued anymore. He needed to get closer.

The boy turned right and down an alley. Doyle crossed the street, laboring to trot. He reached the other side and could see the boy already turning again. Instead of following directly, Doyle turned right, hoping to track him on a parallel path. At each block, he could see the boy and dog pass by the alley opening. He picked up the pace, breathing harder, and cut left. The two were nearing the sight of the burned building, stirring unease in Doyle's gut. This was getting too strange. Now about twenty yards behind, he watched them cross the street and head toward an apartment building. His eyes were locked on the dog.

His pulse quickened as he soaked in its movements, and the images began to merge with memories. He couldn't believe he was seeing what he was seeing. At first, he felt as if the Percocet had altered his perception, followed by a sense of paranoid unreality. He'd had such surreal panic attacks in the past few months, out of nowhere, when his heart would race, and he felt as if the world around him was a confined space and black walls were closing in on him. It was like a personal *Twilight Zone* experience shot through with guilt, a morality tale of nightmarish reckonings for failing the dog. Was this the ghost of his dead dog? He could feel his beating heart almost outside his chest, in the air itself, a throbbing wrap compressing around him. A car honked, and he came up short on the curb as the taxi lurched past. He could see the boy leading the dog up the steps, and for an instant, the dog's profile was framed perfectly against the horizon light.

It couldn't be possible! But it was. Wasn't it? His dog had come back from the dead. No, that was insane. The dog hadn't appeared in his dream; it was right there, being walked around the city and into a building by a little black kid. He'd seen what he'd seen. Somehow the dog had escaped death. He hadn't killed his dog at all! This boy had found him! A black kid had claimed his dog, the dog he'd found and trained!

His panic receded, and the sudden vacuum was filled with rage. Doyle fought an impulse to follow the boy into the building and seize the dog quickly, violently, and righteously. No, that wouldn't work. He needed a plan. This opportunity was too great and required planning equal to it. After his months of misery, possible justice and redemption were within his reach. Turning around, he'd already started plotting.

◆ ◆ ◆ ◆ ◆ ◆ ◆

Sam sat on the chair by the window, staring out at the drizzle, Scarboy curled at his feet. It was a gray Saturday, and he wanted to be outside. Rosalyn finished balancing her checkbook and looked up.

"Everything all right there, Mr. Sam?"

He nodded.

"Yes, ma'am."

She stood and walked over, peering out.

"It will clear up. I heard it would. You'll have plenty of time. Later we can go over to the clinic. Colin wants to take us out for a Sundae."

She reached down and patted the dog's head. By now, the dog's scar was a smooth, grayish curve. For the hundredth time, Rosalyn felt grateful that whatever had caused the scar had missed his eyes. Also, for the hundredth time, she marveled at his quality of composure.

The dog looked up at the woman. This was now his family, his pack. He was comfortable. While he didn't think back longingly to his work as a K9, a vague yearning for it was still a part of him. The physical challenges, the urge to meet

146

them, to grip and hold on through whatever strength and resistance were put against him, were part of his being and always would be. But equally so was his need to guard and protect the humans he valued. If that meant a quieter life, he would be satisfied and prepared at every instant to fulfill his role should the need arise. The dog didn't worry about such a prospect; worry was not in his nature. Readiness was unconsciously part of him, as breathing was.

An hour later, Sam stepped under the reemerged May sun. He zipped up his jacket against the cool breeze, which fluffed Scarboy's withers. Rosalyn asked him to pick up some groceries at the bodega, and they set out.

Arriving, they saw Cuz in front, standing with a broom. He'd seen Cuz here often, hanging around the store, running deliveries. There was no more friction between them. Indeed, Cuz was fascinated by Scarboy, and since seeing Sam take charge of the dog, he acted with new respect around him. Cuz nodded and watched as Sam tied Scarboy to the bike rack in front, made a head signal of greeting, and walked in.

Ten minutes later, Sam had his bag of goods and, with Scarboy on leash, made his way home. Cuz had decided to walk with them, and Sam didn't mind. The route took them down a quiet and narrow alley in the shadows as the buildings blocked the sun. It was a routine for the two, and Sam's mind wandered as he dropped the leash and popped M&Ms into his mouth. Scarboy didn't need the leash; it was just for other people and the leash laws his mother worried about.

As they neared the end, suddenly Sam saw the uniformed bulk of a police officer. He looked huge to Sam, broad and tall, with his stomach bulging over his belt. He seemed to block their way, and his face wore a too-wide, disquieting smile. He pointed with one hand while holding his other arm behind his back.

"Hey there, son. That's a smart-looking dog."

Cuz shuffled off to the side against the alley wall. Sam looked over, noticing Cuz's fear. He didn't understand; they'd done nothing wrong. Did this have to do with Cuz? Sam heard a low rumble from Scarboy's chest. He looked down. The dog's eyes held a stare Sam hadn't seen before. His body was stiff.

"Where'd you get him?" Doyle said.

Sam didn't know what to say. He knew this was none of the cop's business but didn't know how to force those words out.

"It's a simple question, boy. Some dogs been stolen around here. Someone reported a dog just like that stolen."

Scarboy's rumble deepened, and his head dipped a little. Sam picked up the leash.

"He's not stolen," he said.

"Okay. I believe you. But I need to check."

His outstretched hand now reached behind and took something from the other hand. He tossed it at them. The object landed at Sam's feet with a smack. It was a nylon and brass-hooked device. Sam recognized it as a muzzle. He stared at it.

"I need you to put that on him."

Sam looked up at the hulking authority figure ten feet away. He felt in trouble for the first time. It was more a feeling of alarm than fear. He wasn't scared for himself but for Scarboy. The idea that the cop would demand this made no sense and could only mean something bad. That he, Sam, would attach that thing to Scarboy was unthinkable.

"Go on. It's easy. It doesn't hurt."

Sam's hand moved to the clasp of Scarboy's leash instead. He wanted it off, not dragging. He wanted Scarboy to be free to move without constraint.

"Go on, pick it up."

"Don't." It was Cuz, his voice strangled, his eyes wild with fear, as he pressed his back against the bricks. "Don't!"

"You shut up!" Doyle's voice snapped at Cuz like a whip, his smile gone. He turned back to Sam.

Sam had unclipped the leash and held it as he stepped to the side.

"Run, boy, run!"

Sam wanted Scarboy to flee behind them. But instead, the dog splayed its legs in a plant, lowered its head, and barked deep and threateningly at Doyle.

Doyle stepped back, holding up his visible arm to protect himself. There was a pause. No one moved. Sam saw it all in a freeze frame and feared what might be next.

Suddenly, Doyle's other arm, which he'd firmly held behind his back, flung itself forward. The arm was covered in a padded, training bite sleeve, which Sam had seen in his training books. He guessed the effect it might have on Scarboy, and his guess was correct.

Scarboy lunged at the sleeve around Doyle's arm.

It all happened so fast, too fast for Sam to absorb. Scarboy was clamped on Doyle's sleeve as the boy shouted, "Scarboy, no!" Doyle spun the dog around as his other hand held something pointed—was it a knife? —that he thrust at Scarboy's shoulder. Cuz was yelling and circling Doyle, spastically throwing fists at the air around him. Sam rushed to grab the cop's arm, but Doyle, now finished with its thrust at Scarboy, knocked him sideways, sending him face-first into the asphalt. Sam scrambled back up, dazed and dizzy, and his cheek scraped and bleeding. He could see Cuz clawing at Doyle's back, trying to climb on him. But Doyle had little trouble tossing the skinny figure off and against the building wall.

When Sam was flung to the ground, Scarboy redirected his fury and his bite from the sleeve to Doyle's stomach, tearing through the vinyl jacket, latching on, and pushing into the folds of fatty flesh. The cop cried out. But the heavy dose—four hundred plus milligrams—of ketamine pumped into Scarboy's shoulder was already shutting down his central nervous system. The dog held on beyond the point his eyes closed, growling in a low drone as he clung to Doyle's clothing before finally going limp.

The bleeding Sam, watching his dog lose consciousness—for all he knew, dying—screamed as he rushed into Doyle, arms swinging. Doyle, no longer contending with the dog, swung his baton, striking the boy between the base of his head and back. Sam fell like a sack, landing inches from Scarboy's head. As his vision darkened and closed in on him, his hand reached out to grasp the thick fur of his dog's neck, trying to hold on. His last image before blacking out was the dog's body shifting, being dragged away from his grip, and the black boots of the cop retreating.

Marblehead, Massachusetts
1969

THE SEPTEMBER SUN had reached the girl's back as she sat at the piano, stymied, holding her fingers in mock rigidity over the keys. She couldn't warm up in any sense. She stared at the raised goose-flesh of her spindly arms, shook herself, and stood, kicking back the bench which scraped across the tiled floor. She hated her susceptibility to chill but refused to wear the sweater Sonia kept coaxing on her. She felt tiny and smothered inside it, unable to float and dance over the keys as she needed to; the only thing she could do, the only thing that made her feel right with the world.

She moved between the two potted fig trees in their ivory planters and pushed the wrought iron door of the sunroom. It opened easily. It was warmer outside than inside; it always was this early in the day because of the cooler nights. She walked into the sunlight, threw back her face, stretched out her arms, and spun in a little circle, soaking in the warmth: a few moments of feeling like a nymph gamboling under the smiling eyes of pleased Gods.

Rachel Abedon was fourteen but looked younger (or smaller would be more precise, she thought). Her almost Kabuki-like pale face was a study in extremes: thick eyebrows, sharp and oversized Ashkenazi nose and full lips, and large, wide-apart, and fierce green eyes which put to rout any idea of frailty that her otherwise tiny and vaguely stunted body suggested. A beret tilted over her cropped hair declared the contradistinction.

Sonia had told her many times that she'd be happy to look younger as time passed and her friends aged around her. '*What friends?*' Rachel always replied with irony but without a trace of self-pity. Anyway, Rachel mused, maybe she would be '*happy.*' But she wasn't so sure. That is, she had a feeling that time and whatever future treats Gaucher had in store for her would end up making her look older faster, if still tinier. So what? Only the here and now and whatever composition she could complete as quickly as possible mattered. After all, she couldn't be a prodigy forever. After eighteen, she might be a has-been, a crashed comet whose '*potential*' no longer excited anybody, and she'd be left teaching piano to bored wealthy brats. She didn't have any plan for the '*future*' except her day-to-day discipline of writing music and daring anything or anybody to stop her, including Gaucher (or 'Gaw-cher,' as she would boldly mispronounce to annoy her doctors). She refused to honor it with its surname.

Yes, *prodigy* was a double-edged appellation. The sharpened edge was drawing closer. She was already way behind Mozart! She laughed at herself. It was a complicated laugh—at once humble, haughty, and jeering—at herself for her recurring conceit, at the deaf and dumb world for doubting her, and again at herself for needing to think that they doubted her. So serious! Laugh at the seriousness; it was the best way to secretly sustain it (oh, dear and damned contradiction!).

If she were pure outward seriousness, she'd crack right open or stiffen like one of those stone figures in *The Lion, the Witch and the Wardrobe*. That would come soon enough, thanks to Gaucher. It was such a rude tenant. But still, could she, in all fairness, deny its gifts?

Oh, yes, she was serious! And try and change me, she would declare— addressing nobody and everybody, or rather the deaf and dumb world out there that scared her, no matter how much she sneered at herself for feeling scared. She wasn't going to lie to herself or pretend modesty. She was brilliant and crazy, and she had a right to think so; anyway, true or not, believing it at least in fits and starts helped her with the music. It kept her loose, inspired by the illusion of suppleness, against the fear of the creeping calcification and brittleness (there, she said it). Her greatest fear was paralysis at the piano, the stiffened fingers and arm, and the rest of her extremities finally snapping like dry twigs before her eyes so that she could no longer play or hear or even imagine the music. The only way she knew to checkmate the fear was with her conceits and craziness and the freedom to laugh at it all. It was her prerogative.

She closed her eyes and spun around again until she was dizzy. She drank in the sensation and the power. It was so easy to get dizzy and so wonderful to recover. Maybe she'd faint on the soft grass outside her little sunroom sanctuary.

Max was the only one who knew, in part at least. He knew her talent, but he kept his knowledge to himself, only giving away his secret understanding in sweet winks and glances. That was enough for her. The last thing she wanted was for her father to dote or lavish praise on her. She couldn't bear the self-consciousness or the pressure to please him. It was so much better when she could hide in her work, when she only had her ambition and love for the music to drive her, and she would keep it all to herself, including the fear of failure. Too much talk could only mar the beauty and mystery of the struggle and the music that came out of it. God forbid she would have to explain it to somebody. Max respected the mystery. It was all in her, a mess, and it could only be shared and experienced through the music, not through any other stupid thing she had to do or show the world with her homely, anti-social freakish self.

Max had not pushed her into the piano. Her mother had been a violinist, so he probably just assumed something similar from her. And he played the piano. He was good, better than he thought, and with a risky flair that usually exposed his technical limits. But he didn't practice. He'd be very good, she thought, if he practiced.

He loved what she did and how much she loved it (or was tormented by it but could do nothing else—the same coin, flip side), just as he'd loved Bluma for it. And she knew his torment, that he and Bluma's genes had passed on the gift of Gaucher, and knew it would never go away. But she'd keep trying to make it go away. Oh, what absurd heartbreak this world was.

She fell back on the grass and closed her eyes into the sun, feeling its hot glare through her eyelids. How wonderful!

But suddenly, she felt the familiar, oddly metallic taste, the sudden restlessness, and the simultaneous need to swallow and spit of the coming vomit.

Of course, it would hit her now when she was so happily lost in her happy thoughts. God damn, God damn, God damn! Go away, go-shay. Hah! She pronounced it right!

She sat up. For a moment, the nausea receded. Okay, that's a relief. She loved those moments when she beat it back. She knew deep down she was stronger than the nasty intruder in her body.

She stood and slowed her breathing. Relax. She stared out across the long, sloping lawn, past the hedges, down to the rocky shoreline, and out to the blue-gray surface and feathery chop of the harbor, with the tiny triangles and fluttering sails of the boats.

The squeak of Sonia's nursing shoes on the tiled floor of the sunroom broke Rachel's reverie. Shortly, she heard the unwelcome clatter of a tray of china set on the table. Rachel didn't want to turn. She didn't want to see any food right now; she didn't ever want food or even Sonia in her sunroom conservatory. She'd told her this. But as Max said, Sonia's Slavic obstinacy was part of her charm. Rachel only turned when she heard the rubbery squeak of retreat.

Rachel walked back and stared through the window at the silver tray with its pitcher of orange juice, bowl of cottage cheese, and spread of lox and a bagel. That was it: Rachel gagged.

She walked to the boxwood lining the outside of the sunroom. She felt the first warm-up heaves, leaned over, and mentally freed herself to vomit—a brief chowdery stream ending in stringy bile. She struggled to spit out the last acidic strings. Standing up, she noticed some gleaming, pale-greenish threads of vomit on the lace trim of her blouse. She leaned against the whitewashed brick. Oh, go to hell. I don't care. Give me your worst, you killjoy bitch. I'll puke as often as you make me; I will not give up. I'm going to finish my Sonatina and win the Kohak prize, and even if I don't win because of deaf and dumb judges, I'll still laugh knowing I won.

She coughed, and the effort felt like metal shards being shaken around in her chest. She suddenly burst into a gulping sob with tears, but she choked it all off almost instantly.

She looked back once more across the breathtaking emerald and blue vista and inhaled, then turned and walked back into the solarium, wiped her mouth with the napkin on the tray, scraped the bench into her, and sat at the keys of her beloved Knabe baby grand. She picked up the pencil in the easel gulley and stared at the blank composition sheet. She sat like this for a minute, her pencil poised. She finally put the pencil down.

Not now. Instead, her fingers landed gently on the keys and moved straight into Mozart's Sonata number 10. Screw you, she thought.

◆◆◆◆◆◆◆◆

Max Abedon, forty-one, with a thatch of dark, gray-stippled hair and the same prominent features of his daughter but, in his case, reposing in a gentle, academic mien, stood looking absently at his open suitcase. The rising sound of the piano from the solarium summoned a quick smile.

Perry, his young assistant, came in briskly with a manila envelope. As usual, he looked rattled by worried responsibility. He held out the envelope.

"More. I'll forward these to the local PD."

Max glanced at the envelope and nodded evenly, then at Perry's blondish preppy face, bright with ambition on behalf of his boss (and no doubt for himself) leaking from its pores. Max often thought it was a hyper-Anglo and darker Jew pairing that seemed to work.

"Death threats," Max said. He glanced sharply at the envelope. "Do any of them mention Rachel?"

Perry shook his head.

Max stepped to the window to hear the music better and added, nearly under his breath,

"So I'm part of the really important inner circle now, is that it? Someone who needs to die." He chuckled dryly. "It's where unacceptable ambition will always take you, I suppose. Am I that ambitious? Or stupid?"

Perry chose to ignore the irony. "Professor, I'd hate to see you lose this opportunity..."

Max closed his eyes for a moment, then turned back.

"Because of a sick daughter or because of death threats?"

He brushed away the comment. "I'm sorry. Ignore that. Nothing to worry about, Perry. The opportunity, as you call it, is interesting."

He pointed at the envelope, "I wonder, are they the least of my concerns?"

He gestured at the half-packed open suitcase, shaking his head.

"Right there, you see? I can't finish. Traveling somewhere, even to Washington DC... it's so hard. That's an understatement. It will be my first trip since that misadventure last year. And I vowed no more after that."

Perry seemed ready for this.

"It's only for a few days, and just to Washington. You might meet with the President, and you can finally hand him your report. And his sudden interest in your Mid-East ideas sounds promising. You know Rachel will be fine. She's got Sonia and Karl, and I'll be here."

Max nodded absently. "It's funny. I always believed the vocation of an academic or—" he slipped in a note of sneer— "'*intellectual*,' attracted the self-effacing scholar types who preferred to disappear into the warrens of research and refine their mastery of a subject, away from the public. Maybe they assume I'm more interested in celebrity or public attention. As so many are, I'm learning."

"It's not something you sought, professor. They came looking for you. This kind of attention to your work could do more than any book or even years of lectures."

Max smiled knowingly and sadly. "Perhaps. And maybe increase the number of those who hate Israel even more because of me. Or who hate me."

Max looked at Perry's face and laughed.

"Don't worry. I'm going. But no promises. I want to unload this report, as you say, '*finally*.' As for whatever new plans or reports they have in mind about the Mideast, only after I get a resolution on the Vietnam report. At that point, I'll owe it to this fellow Nixon to listen. Reaching out to me, a so-called liberal's liberal, couldn't have been easy for him."

"He has a lot of affection for Israel."

"Hmm," Max said.

The piano music had stopped. Max patted Perry on the shoulder, left the packing unfinished, and walked down the hall, down the semi-circular staircase, and toward the solarium. He could see the bench askew and the heavy wrought-iron door outside ajar. Beyond, he saw Rachel standing in the sun.

She heard him and turned. She gestured for him to come forward as she shielded her eyes and pointed to the cotton-ball clouds.

"Well," he said as he reached her, "it looks like Mr. Abedon goes to Washington."

"Dr. Professor Abedon, please."

She linked her arm with his. "You're a very important person now."

"Only because I'm your father. And I want you to try to eat something— other than fruit."

"Knishes and kishka and latkes? Max, dear, you're not that kind of doctor, or Jewish mother."

She turned up into the sun. He stared at her pale profile. Even with her eyes closed, he could feel their intensity. He thought it a good moment to discuss his idea.

"Rachel, I've been thinking—"

"That's all you do, sweetheart."

"Let me finish. When I get back, I thought we could look into getting a dog."

She squinted sideways at him like he'd lost his mind, saw his serious expression, and laughed.

"Well, if Sonia and Karl want to take care of it. You know that I'm way too selfish for that."

"If you have to be alone, I'd rather you weren't... so alone."

"And how, dearest father, is being with a dog less alone except as a matter of attending to its needs?"

"This wouldn't be an ordinary dog."

She suddenly laughed. "Well, of course not. Anything you thought of would have to be extraordinary. But I don't understand."

Max paused, suddenly caught in wonderment at his daughter, at the wit and independence that inspired his wonder. And caught short by his worry over her vulnerability, not merely to her condition but the risks he might be exposing her to.

She played with his arm reassuringly as if reading his worried mind.

"I'm not alone. There's Karl and Sonia. Besides, dogs are needy, and I'm neurotic. Not a good mix, Max. And you know I couldn't abide the distraction."

"The dog I'm thinking about wouldn't be needy or much of a distraction, but rather a healthy and..." he searched for a word that wouldn't throw her off. "A supporting presence. I've been researching such dogs, you know. Please think about it. Maybe we could find one that likes Mozart or at least music."

She nodded indulgently but couldn't resist having the last word.

"Oh, dear. A brute of the savage breast to protect me from all the mean Marblehead millionaires. That wouldn't be a distraction?" But she noticed the lines on his forehead and smoothed his jacket. "I'll think about it."

◊◊◊◊◊◊◊

Perry made hurried notes on his pad as he stood by Max's bags at the front entrance. He looked up impatiently and saw Rachel appear. She dawdled, staring at him.

She knew that she peeved him a little; she guessed he saw her as a drag on Max's career, his rising profile. She didn't care whether he liked her and found his resentment—if that's what it was— amusing. She did her best to find amusement in people, to a point. That point was when behavior rubbed up against either Max's happiness or her freedom. She could see that Perry was the sort who could reach that point with her and maybe already had in some ways. But he was helpful to Max. And she was clinging to the view that he wasn't worth her agitation.

She smiled broadly at him. He didn't return the smile, and she walked toward the kitchen.

The house was larger than most houses in the area and exhibited the architectural characteristics of a small mansion. The long, pebbled drive behind the iron gates led to a stately frontage of whitewashed brick. The inside foyer was large and vaulted with a marbled floor and a beveled-mirror surround, opening to the library and living room on the right and beyond to the solarium and the adjoining garden with its sweeping view down to the ocean. To the left were the dining room, pantry, kitchen, and a small servant's wing.

Max's family was wealthy and had been one of the early (and fortunate) Jewish émigrés from pre-war Austria, escaping with most of their wealth. Max had done well by his own lights, entering Harvard at sixteen, the Law School at twenty, passing the Bar at twenty-three, and completing his doctorate two years later. He met Bluma, a first-alternate violinist with the Boston Symphony, at a luncheon where her small classical trio performed. He was smitten with her shy, elfin look and quiet grace and, by his admission, behaved in the most forward manner he'd ever shown with a girl. Bluma had told Rachel that she instantly knew Max was for her but allowed him to carry the weight of the courtship to test if it was genuine and durable. It was.

They lived comfortably and happily at a rambling old Victorian house in Brookline, where Rachel was born and spent her first ten years. This despite diagnoses early of the rare, genetically-inherited Gaucher Disease, of which her 'Type 1' was the mildest, but still produced impairments in the liver and spleen and digestive functions and often affected bone development. It explained Rachel's underdeveloped or 'young' appearance (the spontaneous vomiting was an atypical symptom) and, of course, her fear of losing control and dexterity in her fingers.

For Rachel, the only response was to work harder at music, in her case, the piano. She had delighted in listening to her mother play the violin, admired her virtuosity, and had taken lessons. But the violin couldn't rival the piano for her affections. It was a grand instrument, with its soldierly lineup of ivory and black keys before her, awaiting her orders; it was the definitive musical challenge. She knew that meeting the challenge at higher and higher levels would be her life. The violin was too airy and free-floating for her. She wanted to be planted at the bench and spread her arms in command, to subdue and call forth from that massive eighty-eight tooth beast the orderly and canorous beauty of the classics.

Of course, her diagnosis was a blow, but more, Rachel thought, to Bluma and Max, who had bequeathed the Gaucher genes to her. The disease was more prevalent in Ashkenazis and it took both parents to pass it on. This freak legacy had tormented them. But it only made Rachel more determined to plow her way through it with as much cheer and irreverence as she could muster. It hadn't occurred to her at first that this often made them feel more sorry for her, that they'd burdened such an indomitable girl.

But despite her illness, Rachel remembered those early days idyllically, with Bluma shining in the orchestra and Max gaining more intellectual ground and public attention with his articles and books and his political science classes at BU. Max's passion, as he liked to express it, was applying great Western philosophical ideas to leadership practices and public policy formation. As far as Rachel knew or cared, he was brilliant and wise beyond compare and should be running the world.

But their world had collapsed four years earlier when Bluma was stricken with ovarian cancer and was gone from them in four months. At the time, Rachel, a ten-year-old prodigy, briefly assumed the parenting role as Max left his teaching work, stopped writing, and pulled inward. But he recovered, and they both emerged with a greater understanding of each other and their strengths. For Rachel, it wasn't even a matter of forgiving Max—she was glad for his grief and that he lived through it. As for her, she had spent every minute she could with her mother, and there were no unspoken issues between them. There was nothing she could do. Life is life, and death is death, and Rachel instinctively understood the time for each. The music was her refuge of timelessness and nepenthe.

They'd both agreed on a move and consulted with each other over where; Marblehead offered a dramatic change of scenery while still near enough to Max's work and Rachel's musical needs. Neither cared about ocean activities, but to be close to the water felt different and sort of '*liberating*,' as Rachel put it.

◇◇◇◇◇◇◇◇

Max came down the stairs, took Perry's briefcase and notes, walked across the crushed stone, and climbed in the Mercedes, with his stout Swiss, Karl, at the wheel. Rachel didn't like goodbyes, and neither did he. The car crunched away. As they drove out, Max hardly noticed the large faded-blue linen delivery truck that squeezed past them up the driveway. As the Mercedes reached the road, a ragged clutch of protesters with signs rushed from the hedges. Karl honked, and the Mercedes surged past them. Max saw one sign, the lettering scrawled in red, something about '*Palestine*' and '*Warmongerer*.' They couldn't spell, Max thought. Some soft fruit struck the back window with a muffled thud and slid down the glass, leaving a slimy stream of seeds and pulp. Max felt a stab of worry again about Rachel. He would follow up on his conversation with that Lockwood fellow in New Hampshire about the dog.

◇◇◇◇◇◇◇◇

Back from the airport, Karl Haglund, the Abedon's house man, stared at the video monitor of the front gate and flipped the switch to close it. He'd earlier called the police about the rag-tag assembly of protestors (not the first time).

The new CCTV system—a novel and expensive set-up for a home—was a marvel to him and stirred his Germanic appreciation of technology. He flicked between the multiple cameras and views of the exterior and felt a pulse of pride in managing it all.

Rachel moved past the storage room into the kitchen. She opened the refrigerator door, looking disinterestedly inside, and closed it. She heard the high chatter of women from the pantry, plucked a nectarine from a china bowl, and pushed open the swing door.

It was a regular game of Gin. Sonia, Karl's Czech wife, bosomy and with a cartoonishly over-drawn face—big eyes, nose, and liverish lips—under a pile of tight blonde curls tinged with gray, sat across from two of the neighborhood help, the couple Manny and Verna. Rachel wondered what Sonia and Karl saw in them. Manny, with his comb-over strands of black hair, seemed perpetually dour. Likewise, Verna, whose eyes looked craftily mean.

Verna glanced over quickly at Rachel before turning back. Rachel caught the disdainful glint and was amused that Verna didn't seem to notice.

Sonia shook her head at Rachel.

"Always with the fruit. I made you a chicken salad sandwich."

"I'm fine," Rachel quietly responded, hoping to be ignored and watch. The door swung open, and Karl returned to his chair.

"Karl, wash the rest of the fruit for our Rachel."

Karl looked up at Rachel, winked, and turned back to Sonia.

"You're just trying to break my concentration. That's why you always run the wash when we play."

Sonia heaved a sigh, put down her cards, reconsidered, picked them back up, and bustled down the hallway to the laundry closet, closing the door. She looked down, shook her head at the broken slat at the base, and walked back.

"That door, Karl. How many times do I ask?"

"See?" Karl said to Rachel. "Always with my concentration. I'll get to the door. Many more important tasks."

Sonia gestured to Verna and Manny and said what she always said.

"Rachel, you remember Manny and Verna?"

Rachel nodded.

"And how are the music lessons, sweetheart?" Verna said, not looking up.

Rachel bit into the nectarine and replied noisily through her chewing.

"Pretty well. I'll perform Chopin's Polonaise in A-Flat Major at Symphony Hall on December 15th. Along with a stunning and unforgettable Sonatina of my own." She wiped her mouth with her sleeve and took another bite, the juice dripping. Sonia looked up with pride but winced as she saw the juice on the girl's blouse.

Rachel was enjoying the moment, though she expected no reaction from Verna. Rachel hated her, she suddenly admitted to herself; she wondered, for a moment, at the phenomenon of hate for someone she hardly knew. But she knew enough. It didn't matter. It was what it was. Her instincts were good, and she trusted them. Poor Sonia. Maybe she and Karl didn't get out enough. They deserved better.

Rachel finished the fruit, held the pit delicately between two fingers as she moved to the trash receptacle, stepped on the pedal, and dropped in the pit.

"As painful as it is to admit, my incomparably brilliant Sonatina remains to be written. So I bid you adieu. Adieu."

She pushed through the door, and it swung behind her. Sonia smiled.

"She's certainly full of herself," Verna said lightly and looked up at Sonia. "In a good way, of course."

◆◆◆◆◆◆◆

Completely frustrated at her progress on the piece, Rachel finally tore herself away from the piano. She had tried to grind through the agonizing barrenness, the blank sheets, followed by the busy scribbling of notes that seemed to sound right in her head and give her hope but turned into discordant dead ends on the keys. The more hope she felt, the greater the frustration when it went nowhere.

She realized it was dusk. She felt like working right through the night to outlast the frustration. She looked outside at the pale blue light and shivered.

She sought the stumbling blocks like an intoxicant and likewise the breakthrough moments. The demarcation always gave her a little thrill, like passing through borders of countries of consciousness, between an iron curtain and freedom. The struggle gave freedom meaning. She felt that the endless dichotomy was telling her something and was necessary, if not regenerative. Maybe it was her Jewish heritage, she thought, smiling to herself through gritted teeth. But it was a thrill to float between the worlds of incarceration and liberation, all in this room and on her own. But she was seriously stuck now.

She stood and stretched, and felt guilty—she hadn't earned the stretch.

She moved up the stairs and down the long shadowed hall toward her room. She saw a glow of light midway—Perry's room. The door was ajar. She peered in and saw him working at his desk.

"We're not getting a dog," she said mildly.

He looked up, took off his glasses, and leaned back, assessing her at the threshold.

"You'd rather he worry about you so much?"

"He'll do that anyway. Like I do about him. Some dumb dog won't change that."

She realized that wasn't what she wanted to say. She hated when that happened but didn't feel like backtracking. "And it's not your business."

Perry stared into her combative eyes.

"The dog isn't my idea."

They stared at each other in a moment of mutual measurement.

"My only business is to help him do his," he added. "Whatever I can do to make it easier for him."

"So selfless."

"Your father is a brilliant man," he said, ignoring the jibe. "This is a great opportunity for him."

"And what about you? It's not an *'opportunity'* for you?"

She half expected a rise from this, but he just rubbed his eyes and yawned.

"Sure. It is. But if it were at his expense, I wouldn't want it."

She stood, staring. She wanted to register his words as shallowly artificial but couldn't. She only saw a young man working late and alone. She searched for something to say.

"I would never try to talk down to you, Rachel. I hear you practicing. Of all people, you should appreciate the nuances of ambition. Your father can offer more than just teaching and writing. Look at it this way: your father has a chance to compose different and important music heard by a much larger audience. If I weren't helping him somehow, he'd know that, and you'd know that, and you wouldn't keep me. As to his worrying about you, anything that can help him in that respect, and doesn't upset your routines, is worth considering, no?"

She naturally bristled at any hint of a lecture. But Perry's words seemed to skirt the line; in fact, they fell within plain speaking. She told herself she didn't want to argue. But she wouldn't give him the satisfaction of assent. She moved off down the hall.

She entered the dark solarium and sat at the piano. There it was, awaiting her. It seemed indifferent to her, just a piece of furniture. Or maybe it was sulking because she'd disappointed it. Her fingers pressed down on the C note, and the lingering sound soothed her. No, it was forgiving. She lightly played with a song she remembered from her early childhood affection for stage and film musicals. Her fingers tickled out the tune from '*The Wizard of Oz*'... '*If I only had a heart*,' and she started humming and then quietly singing. Her voice was scratchy and weak—terrible. She couldn't sing or even carry a tune. How funny, another contradiction. But she sang it anyway, in the dark, to herself.

◆◆◆◆◆◆◆◆

Max made his way down the polished marble floor of the Russell Senate Building. It was crypt-quiet, with only faint echoes of a telephone here and there behind the well-varnished oak doors. His eyes followed the austere black lettering until he came to the one he was looking for: *Senator Williston Beadle*.

Ten minutes later, he was seated in the large inner office, which was decorated as he imagined it would be—a stately desk, national flag and state flag of Virginia, plaques, and photos of the smiling Senator with world leaders, military people, other politicians, and an occasional celebrity. Sitting across from Williston Beadle, he realized that the Senator fit his preconceptions too nicely. He was on the short side, with a well-fed paunch under a dapper dark-blue suit. His handshake had been firm, and he brought his other hand over to clasp his. His eyes, Max thought, were not what he expected—with a lighthearted glint that did not seem entirely senatorial. Beadle had sounded very sincere on the phone, and Max wasn't willing to question his hopes yet.

"I can't tell you what a delight it is to meet you, Max. But tell me, I hear you've been gettin' some threats?"

Max waved it off. "They're nothing. I've had them before."

Beadle nodded judiciously. "Join the club. We get them here pretty regularly. Your young man forwarded them to me, and I'll run them past the FBI. Anyway, I want you to know I sympathize. I have a good personal protection service I can recommend."

Max smiled his appreciation. "Thank you, Senator. My daughter's an artist and is rather particular about her... personal space. It's hard for her to develop her talents with too many distractions around her. That's why I'm approaching all this" —he gestured around him – "with circumspection."

"You're a man of high principles, Max. That's why I was asked to make these overtures. The President and I are old friends, and I know he wanted you to feel well-treated in Washington, short of being able to see you himself right now. He is very interested in including you in a pool of advisers and distinguished scholars with fresh ideas on the Middle East conflicts. I'd like you to trust me to help arrange that."

"I appreciate it, Senator. But you can help by arranging for me to deliver my report on Indochina directly to the President, as I promised. I understood that might be happening on this trip."

Beadle nodded with maximum agreeableness, but his eyes held a shiny, vaguely shrewd gleam as if measuring what he wished to say and what would be wise to say.

"Well, you probably know there are rumors about your report, not only what's in it but how it was to be delivered. As I hear, the President already asked you for it?"

"That's not entirely what happened. I received word from an assistant, who asked to have it sent to him. I'd never had any contact with this person before. I reminded him of my promise to the President to deliver it to him personally."

"Yes, right. Of course." Beadle shifted in his seat. "You're a man of your word."

"I thought it was unusual for the President to ask me. But I was impressed that he'd solicit a view from someone outside his world, from another perspective."

"Yes. It was very interesting."

"But I assume you know all this, as you and he are friends."

Beadle shrugged with what seemed to Max affected modesty. He suddenly felt that this talk was not so much an offer to help as a kind of disingenuous pat-down.

"Here's the thing, Max. And I'm speaking as a crusty old insider passing along the tribal rites of DC to a newcomer, to prepare you for what to expect. The President has his prerogatives, of course, as in his decision to reach out to you. But because of the sheer volume of groups and individuals pressing on him for his time and ear, especially with respect to Vietnam, the advisers around him are duty-bound to review, evaluate, judge, prioritize, whatever word you like, what can get through to the man in the oval office. The White House is sort of like a palace, Max, and reports to the President need to go through this process via" —he offered an apologetic smile — "the palace guard. That's just how it works. You're in academia, and there must be a similar process of peer review, vetting and all that?"

Max stared at Beadle, realizing now what this was about. In a way, he'd expected it. He'd also been very clear about his response.

Max nodded pleasantly. "I understand. But it's not how I work. I promised I would delivered this report directly to him."

Beadle tossed his arms up in spirited surrender. But his words didn't match the gesture. He shifted in his seat.

"Some people—not me, of course—are afraid you might make a sort of cause célèbre over this, become a martyr to your old friends on the liberal side. Some, not me, I promise, but some have brought up an opportunistic hidden agenda. You know, due to the nature of your past associations. I don't mean any disrespect, Max; I'm just passing on what I've heard."

Max couldn't suppress a quick laugh. "My assistant almost accused me of not being opportunistic enough." He paused for a moment, gathering himself. "But if I'm just seeking to deliver this personally and be done with it, how can that be opportunistic?"

The question, and the answer, seemed simple to Max. But Beadle looked stumped.

"Let me ask you this," Max continued. "Couldn't we say the same about the *'palace guard'*? That is, could it be that they—I've never met these people, so I can only speculate—see an opportunity to interrupt or mediate the delivery of my report? Since you've opened up the subject of cynical possibilities."

Max was tired, and the veiled verbal jousting, he could sense, was not going to end satisfyingly. He wanted to give the President his report, period. And he'd come to realize Beadle was a point man to persuade him to release it to others. This irritated him. He was also preoccupied with thoughts of Rachel; he wanted to wrap this up. But could he? He'd committed himself to the delivery, and he couldn't quit.

Beadle was focused intensely on Max with glycerin earnestness and sympathy. But as Max finished speaking, the mask of sincerity slipped a little, and he betrayed a knowing smile. He sighed deeply and leaned back.

"Well, Max. Maybe you guessed it, I'm a middle man, just trying to do my President a favor and follow the rules. If you'd like to leave me the report, I promise to read it as a confidante and get back to you about how we might finesse it through the system directly to the President."

Max's face unconsciously hardened. Beadle was forcing Max to make it personal, to risk offending a powerful Senator by admitting his distrust. *'He hasn't been paying attention, or I haven't been clear enough,'* Max thought.

"Thank you, Senator. I appreciate your graciousness in seeing me. I'll hold on to my report for now and trust you will pass on my wish to deliver it to the President."

◆◆◆◆◆◆◆

In the dim light, Rachel sat at her bench in her pajamas, staring at another scribbled composition sheet on the piano easel. A litter of sheets covered the area around her feet. She reached out, closing her hand over the latest sheet, and crumpled it.

She heard the sound of car wheels crunching over the pebbles on the front circle. She moved to the large windows to peer toward the front. It was the Mercedes—Max. She felt the urge to rush out but held back. She didn't want to see him in her frustration.

She suddenly hated everything—herself, the pressure, even the music that was eluding her just when she needed it the most despite all the agonizing devotion she gave to it, all the hours of solitude in this cold, cavernous room. And all the while living with a chronic sickness, the fears of brittle bones and stunted growth and sudden bouts of vomiting. Self-pity welled up inside her. She felt tears, not the expiating kind, but bitter, frustrated tears for betraying her code, i.e., her existential passion, her conceit that the work itself, not the payoff, was the purpose and the glory. No, she wanted the fruits, success and glory. She wanted it to be easier. She was a selfish, egocentric fake. Her small fists clenched into knobby white balls and her jaw clamped. Like her sickly, frail frame, how quickly her vain little world could collapse. She ran out of the solarium and up the stairs to her room.

◆◆◆◆◆◆◆◆

A few weeks later, Max sat at the dining room table, sipping his morning coffee. He stared at the gold rim around the cup. Sonia laid out sliced grapefruit, toast, and some lox. He was waiting for Rachel; she was late for breakfast. Sonia had said she'd been working hard. Max had seen the strewn sheets on the floor and knew she'd been putting herself through the paces. She was a complicated little creature. He'd tried almost everything—or thought he had—to ease the pressure on her, the pressure she put on herself. He'd encouraged more social activities, diversions, and hobbies but had finally given up. It seemed the more he tried, the more she resisted. She'd finally told him that none of those things interested her; in fact, they just sapped the energy from the music. All she wanted to do was play the piano. She'd joked that he shouldn't wonder where she got her focused intensity on work.

So he'd done all he could to facilitate her work for her. And she'd been grateful. But he could feel the pressure for this upcoming contest. Beyond trying to relieve that (probably hopeless), the threats concerned him. Bodyguards were out of the question. He believed Rachel had an affinity for animals. She'd had a cat as a small child—Mr. Cheshire—and adored it. When it died, she was crushed and vowed not to have another. She went all-in, always. Max thought he could work this angle to help her and ease his worries. He knew well her contradictory nature; that is, efforts to make things easier likely would be ignored, rejected, or flipped around on him. So maybe this time, he'd try to mix it up: make his help also a challenge, with enough difficulty to push her into making it work. Of course, there needed to be some appeal to the challenge, an emotional incentive.

Max had called the Lockwood fellow and arranged a visit for that day. Lockwood came highly recommended by a colleague at the University. Their few conversations impressed Max. Lockwood seemed educated: a Masters degree in psychology earned while working as a cop. He was relatively young. His father had been an FBI agent. Lockwood started a pioneer dog program with the Cambridge police but recently left it to operate as a partner in a training facility just over the border in New Hampshire. From what Lockwood described, it was also some sort of dog rehabilitation center. Lockwood seemed to pick up on the nature of Max's challenge and sounded confident they could find a dog to balance protection and companionship.

Rachel walked in, went up to Max, kissed him, and sat next to him. She picked up a piece of toast and studied it.

The swing door to the kitchen opened, and Sonia came out with a plate and put it in front of Rachel. Only a small black velvet box was on the plate. Rachel stared at the box. Sonia smiled at Max and retreated.

She opened the spring-loaded top until it locked and carefully extracted a thin necklace with a tiny gold piano. She delicately moved it between her hands and looked up at Max, covering her gratitude with a smart-aleck sideways stare.

"Okay. So what's the catch?"

"Well, how about a drive today? I want to show you something. Please keep an open mind."

Rachel nodded quickly. "If we take the MG."

◆◆◆◆◆◆◆◆

An hour later, the raffish little gray 1959 MGA roadster with the lobster-red interior, its top battened down under the tonneau cover, zipped along Route 125, nearing Plaistow. Rachel sat jacketed and scarfed, tilting her face into the buffets of wind and marveling at the maple trees shouldering the road in their near-peak pageantry of scarlet and yellow.

"Warm enough?" Max had to shout. She nodded, smiling. It was the fifth time he'd asked.

They sped past a sign that read '*Slow! Horses Crossing,*' and Max compliantly slowed, downshifting with a cough of protest from the exhaust. They saw no horses. But soon, another sign caught his attention; he checked his notepad in the center hip next to the gear shift and turned on his blinker.

"We're almost there."

A few minutes later, they were motoring parallel to a field with a barn and small outbuildings before turning into a long drive. A wooden sign said in carved, burnt lettering, '*Hunde Haven.*' Rachel looked at Max with a resigned smile.

"Okay," she said. "My mind is open."

As they pulled up to what appeared to be an office adjacent to the barn, she could hear dogs barking.

◆◆◆◆◆◆◆◆

Darius Lockwood sorted through the paperwork on some recent dogs to the '*ranch,*' as his business partner Patrick called it, awaiting the appointment with the professor and his daughter. He was tired, in a good way, from the morning workout with some of the dogs. He looked over at the scarred young dog in the narrow kitchenette ten feet away, lying on the old horse blanket in the cubbyhole, and reflected on what had brought him here so figuratively far in such a short period.

After *'Chaser'* was reported stolen (a claim Lockwood had doubted), Lockwood heard rumors of the brass's discomfort with his K9 program. Doyle, the cause for the concerns in Lockwood's mind, then seemed to disappear on medical leave; but this didn't quell the unease. He shortly got word from Captain Bixby that the pilot program was axed. Budget concerns were cited, but Bixby averred that it was political—even a rumor of a dog biting black college students was a public relations horror-show, he said. They weren't going to risk it. Lockwood knew the brass mindset and didn't try to lobby to save the program. He'd been thinking of leaving the force for some time. He didn't enjoy police work enough to sustain a career without the dogs.

He'd been corresponding for a few months with one of the oddball characters common to the fringes of the dog world and realized he was developing a friendship.

Patrick Cornichierre was a young, effervescent French émigré who'd spent many years in Canada before coming to America. He'd loved America from afar and seemed to love it more now that he was here. Son of a wealthy corporate CEO, he'd always been interested in his family's farm animals and herding dogs. Resisting his father's pressure to enter the shipping business, Patrick turned to dog sports and police dog training. One of the youngest titlists in Schutzhund's history at fourteen, he was already developing training theories and practices that were turning the ironbound tradition of compulsion-based training on its head—just the sort of theories Lockwood had been working on himself. Patrick had read about Lockwood's program, a system of inducements of play and intense, sensory-engaging activities to shape and modify behavior. The two struck up a friendship over the phone. Patrick had recently purchased, with family money (about which he was refreshingly frank), a large tract of land in New Hampshire to open a facility and was very interested in Lockwood's involvement. He especially liked his idea of rehabilitating damaged and aggressive dogs of certain working breeds.

Both liked and trusted dogs more than people and laughed about it. They finally met, and the friendship and partnership were sealed.

The day before Lockwood was formally to leave the department, he received a strange call from a woman, her voice hoarse and broken. It shortly became clear she was Brian Doyle's mother. Lockwood hadn't heard from Doyle in months. The woman said Doyle was *'dying to see'* him. No, that wasn't it. He was dying and needed to see Lockwood. The woman, he realized, was stuttering through her tears. She pleaded with him to visit her son at the hospital.

Lockwood made it that afternoon. He was directed to a large room with about twenty beds behind portable cubicles marked by aluminum poles on casters. Lockwood understood it to be a terminal ward. He was led to Doyle's bed, more of an Army cot behind pale-green translucent curtains. An IV tube from a hanging clear plastic bag, and another tube from a lighted machine, ran down into Doyle's arm.

Lockwood barely recognized him. Doyle's cheeks were caved in, his skin yellow and seemingly stretched to a tearing point, his lips cracked, and his hair thinned out. His eyes floated vacantly, in a drugged daze. Suddenly he felt a presence to his right and turned into Doyle's mother. She was short, with a flushed, sharply-featured Irish face. She stared at her son with hopeless tears, then up at Lockwood. Lockwood was unsure why Doyle's mother had called him; why would Doyle have even mentioned him, or how could he have done so in his condition?

With surprising, bony strength, the woman steered Lockwood outside the rectangle of pseudo-privacy as if to confide a secret. What did it matter? Lockwood thought; it was not as if Doyle could hear them. But she reached up, tugging at his sleeve to lower his ear to her mouth. He did and caught the heavy scent of tobacco on her breath.

"Pancreatic cancer. Pancreatic, it's the worst, the doctor said. He's brave."

Lockwood nodded. He was about to ask her what Doyle had said to her when he suddenly saw Doyle's eyes shift and settle on him. The dying man's dried lips moved slightly, briefly—or more like trembled. Doyle's mother nudged Lockwood to move in closer. Lockwood did so that he was over

Doyle. Now Doyle's lips worked, trying for words. Suddenly Lockwood felt Doyle's hand on his forearm, the weak prong-grip of his fingers.

"I'm sorry."

Lockwood saw the man's arm shake in a loose palsy before the hand let go and dropped to the sheets. Doyle's mother beamed at her son, then at Lockwood. Her hand circled and gripped Lockwood's arm.

She insisted that Lockwood follow her to her house. It was very important, she said. After that, she wouldn't bother him anymore. Lockwood sensed there was an answer for him ahead and agreed. He felt obliged at this point anyway.

When they entered the house, Lockwood recoiled at the oppressive stuffiness. It was cool and pleasant outside: how could anybody endure this closed space? As of sensing his reaction, she quickly led him to the back, through the kitchen, to whatever she had to show him. He could see through the kitchen window a large, screened-in porch. She opened the door.

The odor of fecal matter and urine was a blow; Lockwood felt sick before he stepped in. He tried breathing through his mouth, but the odor blasted right through the blockade. She made way for him to peer inside.

Inside was the dog, Chaser. Stretched on his side, he was asleep or dead, and Lockwood wasn't sure at first. He'd lost probably twenty-five pounds, his ribs seeming to break through his chest, his hip area concaved. His coat, matted with dried feces, was dull and shedding. He had what looked like new contusions around his head. He lifted his head slightly to stare at the new person. Did he recognize Lockwood?

Lockwood, fighting against his revulsion, moved in decisively and leaned over the dog, holding his hand over its midriff. The dog's lips curled back. Lockwood heard a weak rumble from the dog's chest.

He turned back to Corinne Doyle. She was leaning against the door, her hand at her mouth, biting it. Tears were in her eyes.

"He left him here," she said, with pleading helplessness. "I didn't know what to do. I should have called someone, I know I should have. I was afraid Brian would get in trouble. I'm sorry. I fed him. I gave him water. I'm sorry."

Lockwood understood her torment and shame but was beyond interest in apologies. He just needed to get the dog out of there.

He did and took Chaser to his vet. Afterward, he brought him home as he prepared his move. And so it was that Chaser came with him to New Hampshire. From what Lockwood could gather, Doyle had beaten Chaser regularly. In what manner Doyle lost the dog, Lockwood didn't know (he assumed it was Doyle's negligence or fault), but when Doyle had recovered it, he probably came to see the dog as a reminder of his failures—of what he'd lost and couldn't regain. Doyle couldn't come clean to Lockwood or the department, which probably exacerbated his frustration and displaced rage. Abusing the dog became a kind of crutch or addiction, he supposed. Doyle, he learned, was an alcoholic. Lockwood didn't like even imagining such a state of being. But that's how it must have been. The mother had not beaten or abused the dog.

Chaser's physical health had returned rather quickly, along with his weight. But he didn't recover in the way Lockwood hoped. He seemed broken in some way, at least in a social sense; he wanted nothing to do with anyone. No exceptions. He tolerated Lockwood but met any extended attention or contact with avoidance or a mild growl. He looked healthy enough but still lacked the alertness and authority which were his distinguishing features.

Lockwood made no overt effort to befriend him, preferring to allow him the time and space to develop trust on his own. He did try to work with him a little on the tugs. Chaser would soon lose interest, less physically than emotionally. As Lockwood saw it, this dog placed enormous importance on trust and leadership and had been profoundly betrayed. Maybe the dog had found a person meaningful to him during his absence from Doyle, and Doyle had ripped him away and then tried to beat the memory out of him. Lockwood could only speculate. In the meantime, he thought it appropriate to rename the dog but hadn't decided yet on what.

◆◆◆◆◆◆◆

Lockwood heard the grumble of the MG and moved out of his office. He left the horizontally split farm door unlatched, the top open and the bottom loosely ajar.

Max's first impression of Lockwood was encouraging and what he'd assumed from the phone calls: bright, professional and cordial.

Rachel nodded her greeting, her hands firmly in jacket pockets. She scanned around. At the car's arrival, clamorous barking had erupted, now subsiding. Her eyes sought the source of it.

Max asked if it was safe for Rachel to walk and look around. Lockwood nodded. "All the dogs are up." Rachel ambled off.

Lockwood turned to Max. "I'm honored you looked me up, professor. I know we've talked a little, but why don't we go over your lifestyle patterns, how you see a dog fitting in, what you would expect of it, and want or not want in terms of personality and behaviors for you and your daughter."

Max nodded. "I'll do my best."

Max reiterated that he needed a dog capable of responding to any physical threat without hesitation. But his daughter, a concert pianist, worked alone much of the day with great concentration and couldn't feel cramped or distracted by a needy dog. That was it. He expected few social interactions for the dog, just the household help and occasional guests. Max didn't care if the dog got along with people as long as he knew the difference between a threat and a non-threat. Max wanted to be comfortable that his daughter was watched and guarded, period.

"Do you have a dog that fits the bill?" he concluded.

When Max had finished, he looked up to see Rachel. She was strolling along the line of kennels.

Lockwood knew most of this but wanted to hear it directly. He listened patiently throughout, occasionally glancing up at Rachel in the distance. He was surprised more of the dogs weren't barking.

"Dr. Abedon, thank you for that. I believe we can help. You've concisely suggested what makes the personal protection dog so unique. You see," he invited Max to walk with him down the lane. "Training a dog to bite or attack a human being starts essentially as a game which exploits the dog's natural drive to chase, bite and fight, what we call *'prey drive.'* It's all fun and games, working with pads and such. Challenges are added; dogs are pushed harder, and ultimately, the dog can recognize danger and is willing to bite and subdue a person on command. Most of the dogs for this work are tough, high-drive dogs but generally also well-balanced, even socially outgoing dogs. They can fit into the everyday world and the lives of their people. Most can, anyway.

"The difference with a personal protection dog is simple. It needs to make judgments much faster and often on its own, sometimes without a command. It needs to make clear decisions in distracting social circumstances. Compare this to a police dog hunting a criminal. That dog can be wound up for that one task, to find and seize that criminal.

"But a personal protection dog might be strolling happily along with a mother and her child in a park. Suddenly a man tries to snatch the kid. The mother isn't looking. The dog has to act instantly, on its own, from zero to sixty in half a second. It has to be calm and socially disinterested one second and a terror the next."

Max took all this in. "I think I understand. It means an extraordinary animal. And probably an expensive one," he added, smiling.

Lockwood nodded. "That's not what I was getting at, but yes, they are expensive. Good ones are, anyway."

"I understand the concept of value, Mr. Lockwood. Above all, it's my daughter's call. She must feel a bond. The dog must feel it too, to understand it's her that he's protecting."

Lockwood nods. "Yes. But that's easier than you might think. With the right dog."

"So, do you have such a dog?"

"Not ready to go at the moment, but we have some in the works. I want to show you, both of you."

◆◆◆◆◆◆◆

Rachel had been strolling along the line of twenty or so wired kennels and dogs. Clouds now covered the sun, and she hunched forward in her bulky jacket against the chill. There'd been scattered barking as she approached, with some dogs leaping up in apparent anticipation of release. Each dog seemed a little different as she neared its kennel, some nosing through the wire, some circling excitedly, some simply sitting and staring with inscrutable intensity. All displayed highly alert looks and postures; Rachel realized she liked this, the alertness. She thought, yes, this was also admirable in people. So few people were alert like this. Maybe because it would make them look crazy? She smiled at the thought. Well, they needn't be this alert. But still, alertness was an attractive characteristic. Too many people were the opposite.

On each kennel was a clipboard on a hook. She looked closely and saw a name and brief information about the dog... age, background history, and notes on behavior. It seemed a lot of these were *'problem dogs.'*

She wondered what would eventually happen to all of them. She would ask. She didn't want to admit that none of the dogs seemed to be one she could imagine in her home, living with her. But none did. She came to the end of the row. She glanced back and saw Max still talking with the owner. The owner had a friendly face. She looked up at the barn and attached office. Curious and feeling a sudden need to escape the chill of the sunless breeze, she moved toward it.

The large A-frame barn was a quiet and mostly empty space and oddly felt colder than the outside. The ground level held a few more kennels against one wooden wall; on the opposite side were stacks of equipment, including plastic teepee-like things, segments of disassembled dog jumps, and, most interesting and amusing to her, bulkily padded jackets and pants, along with removable heavy sleeves and leg attachments. She assumed these were for dogs to bite.

She moved past a few more dogs. These looked older or perhaps more infirm than the ones outside and silently watched her, a few wagging their tails.

She wasn't sure she wanted to see anymore. It struck her suddenly that this wasn't an idea that would work. A dog like any of these in their home... how? She'd kept an open mind; yes, she had. She now felt sorry for Max. He was trying. She needed him to realize he didn't have to worry about her. She was who she was, and it wasn't going to change, but it wasn't a cause for worry. She would talk to him on the way home. Seriously, as to the threats (yes, she'd known about them. Perry was not good at keeping anything from her. She was alert!), who was going to bother with either of them? They were safe in Marblehead.

She reached the other end of the barn, to a small set of steps and a latched door. Opening it, she saw a rough hallway leading straight through to where Lockwood had emerged to greet them. Through the far door, she could see a gray slice of the MG. To the left, halfway down the hallway, was a horizontally bisected door.

She walked down the corridor and paused as she came even with the door, its top section fully open, the bottom just ajar. She peered over the flat panel on the lower section. The room looked to be an office, with a desk dead ahead and a narrow oblong opening to the left hidden from view.

Rachel held her stare on the opening and didn't know why. She felt both stuck in place and driven by a strong urge, with an accompanying tingle of nerves, to move closer, to step inside and look down the narrow space.

The room was the man's office. Perhaps the urge was natural curiosity at peering in on a private space. No, she thought, it was more. But what? She just stood there, hoping Max would suddenly call her outside.

Her hand lightly pushed at the lower section, and the door creaked as it moved inward on its hinges about one foot. It didn't slip back. The stillness felt dense and portentous. What was this? She'd never felt anything like it. She wanted to believe it was her imagination, but nothing about the setting or the barn lent a foreshadowing atmosphere. The feeling had come out of nowhere. Rachel was aware of how much her presentiments affected her. She often felt afflicted by them and wished not to have them or only to have them when they were helpful, as to her music. This was the first time she'd felt one so strongly and compelled to take action, to follow it to an end. The compulsion relieved her, as in removing her choice.

She placed her foot over the threshold. Two more steps were required to be able to see down the opening between the wooden cupboards. She took one; the old barn-board floor made no sound. She didn't try to crane her neck around but committed herself to the next step and slowly turned to face the opening.

She sensed something there before she saw it. The narrow space was about ten feet long, with cupboards and a waist-high countertop lining each side. To the left, near the end, was an opening below the countertop. Out of it, she saw a dog's dark, russet paws. It appeared from their position that the animal was lying down with its head up.

There was no question about moving closer; Rachel took three careful steps until she was a few feet away. The inside of the space was darkened, and she would have to kneel to see inside. She did.

The dog was unlike any of the others she'd seen or had ever seen. Her first impression was the grayish mark of a scar between its eyes and running down the bridge of its snout, her second was the dog's unique mix of colors. But it was the eyes she quickly locked on to—richly auburn with steadiness and sense of depth that was, at least in her experience, singularly undog-like; a suffused light seemed to leak around their edges, as if from an underlying, smoldering source. The dog's stare was unreadable to her.

She instantly identified with it; she couldn't turn away from it. She also felt, as palpably as any physical sensation, that the dog was dangerous—i.e., was capable of abrupt and committed violence as extreme as its stare and manner were composed. She didn't know how she knew this but just did. One extreme could not indwell the dog without the other; it was too preternaturally motionless not to be dangerous. Maybe that was why the dog was here, in this space, she thought. It wasn't meant to be approached. It was the man's private dog. It was an attack dog trained to protect his office. That must be it. But why hadn't it barked or lunged at her? Surely it had sensed her approach and now could see her. But she also knew that '*attack dog*,' if it was one, couldn't be all that it was.

Her eyes now explored the dog's flanks and could see the marks, the patches of scars.

"Damaged boy," she said quietly, in an observational, matter-of-fact voice. She somehow knew it was a boy, and her intuition told her that sympathy would be neither appropriate nor welcome. There was something *'more'* about this dog, some secret it carried of the history of dogs, which strangely thrilled her. It didn't know it, couldn't express it, and only carried it. And she saw it.

This was THE dog, she said to herself. It was why she was here. The certainty shocked and excited her. It was life surprising her.

But how was this possible? Wasn't she going off on one of her ecstatic jags?

She was torn between reaching out to the dog to test the reality of the moment, and marveling at him, maybe until he moved closer to her. But he wouldn't, would he? No, he wasn't a reaching-out kind of dog.

She slowly held out her hand.

The dog's eyes remained fixed on her eyes, not the hand. Rachel's hand hovered over the dog's paws. She watched the mouth. The dog's lips quivered and drew slightly up, showing a glint of teeth. But his head was unmoving, his eyes holding on Rachel. She stopped and held her hand in place.

She began to hum at first, then to sing the words, barely audibly...

"*I'd be tender, I'd be gentle...*"

Her hand settled on the leg. She held it there and stroked the paw, now sliding her hand up its leg. The dog's lips lowered.

"*...I'd be awful sentimental, regarding love and art; I'd be friends with the sparrows, and the boy who shoots the arrows...*"

Outside, Lockwood and Max had both looked up to where they last saw Rachel, by the kennels. Lockwood scanned toward the barn.

"Is she all right on her own?" Max asked.

Lockwood nodded. But something was nagging at him.

"Let's go inside."

Lockwood jogged up the concrete block steps, opening the door. Ahead he saw his office door, the two panels open wider than he had left. Damn! He quickened his pace, Max following.

The dog was now in his third month with Lockwood after his removal from the woman's porch. He had physically recovered from the dehydration and intermittent beatings from Doyle. To Lockwood's credit, the dog soon understood the ordeal was over. During the first two weeks, he did little but sleep and walk outside the barn area on a long leash. He accepted Lockwood's walking regimen, just the two of them. But his mind, with his natural genetic drives, and his defining sense of purpose to work and bond with a human, lapsed into a sort of sullen torpor.

The memories of his last wild minutes before the stab in his shoulder, and the crowding blackness over his eyes and loss of muscle control—seeing the boy that had saved him and who he would have died for on one side and on the other, the handler he had been trained to serve but now felt driven to kill— were increasingly fitful, and fading. He couldn't know that nothing would be the same again for him or express this as a bitter certainty through his behavior. But nothing was the same for him anyway. He was alive, that was all.

The man proved to be patient and methodical in his work, but the dog did not sense the leader he sought in him. This was a man for many dogs, not one, and not him. This was something he just knew.

The days passed, and the dog fell into a routine. He spent most of his time with the man, if not walking with him, just the two in the office. There had been no interaction with other dogs after he'd badly wounded a dog who'd approached him in a dominant manner. The dog tolerated the few humans who came around, and the man was careful about these interactions. The dog routinely paid initial attention to a guest, probing for the familiar scent of the boy, the mother or the veterinarian, but when there was none, he retreated into his cubbyhole in the office. While he was a resilient dog with great genetic powers of recovery and had 'recovered' as it were, the losses of those people, of being stripped of those relationships in so violent a manner, left an emotional scar.

When he heard the sound at the door, he sniffed. The female presence and odor were identifiable, and he lowered his guard slightly. Females were not as much of a concern. The fact she didn't walk right in aroused his curiosity a little. He waited. As she approached, he saw she was small, a child, like the boy. He watched her, interested. She was here, in his space, as if she knew it was his but was also making some claim on it. And where there was one child, there might also be the boy. She stared. Ordinarily, since the shattering event, he would not tolerate too-long eye contact from humans. But hers was not concerning and gave him time to read her. The fact she sat so still and stared began to take on some importance. Her shape was not 'of a piece,' not especially well-conformed or suggestive of physical competence; he could see she was not a dog-training person. When her arm reached out, his first impulse was repulsion. He would not allow touch. But somehow, the awkward way she was crouched, and the gentleness radiating from her, gave him pause. The hand touched his paw, and he didn't pull back.

She began humming. The sound to him did not seem associated with any particular intention. It felt to be FROM her more than AT him, but also to include him. And it reminded him of the boy. It was not a sound to worry about. While this small person did not present herself as a leader, with the typical characteristics that stirred his urge to bond, there was something beyond actions or gestures, the simple 'being' of her, a presence he hadn't felt since the boy. For the first time in a long time, he felt a revival of his guardian instinct.

Rachel heard the door open sharply behind her and quick footsteps, then the heavy breathing of men.

"Rachel—" It was Max.

Rachel turned casually. She pointed at the dog.

"This one," she said, smiling.

◆◆◆◆◆◆◆

Astonished, Lockwood led her back to the area of his desk. Max wasn't sure what to think; he could feel Lockwood's tenseness. Lockwood was even more astonished when the dog stood, walked behind Rachel, and sat down.

Max looked between the dog, Rachel and Lockwood, waiting. There was a long silence while Lockwood watched Rachel as she put her hand on the dog's head. What was wrong here?

After a few minutes, Lockwood said, "Let's take a walk."

The four moved outside. Lockwood didn't make any sign to Chaser, just studied him. Lockwood moved behind Rachel as they walked away from the kennels to a path bordered by pine trees. He had them start and stop, again and again, each time Chaser close to the girl, and after fifteen minutes, they returned. They went again with Max between Rachel and the dog and holding Rachel's hand. He asked Max to touch the dog's head. The dog accepted the hand without flinching.

Back by the car and the barn office, Lockwood stared at the three of them with a bewildered look, let out a sudden laugh but wiped the smile away as suddenly.

"Dr. Abedon, I'm not sure this is the right dog for your daughter."

"He is the right dog," Rachel said. She turned to Max. "He's the dog."

Max knew that look and tone of voice. He turned to Lockwood.

"Why don't you explain to both of us."

"I..."

But Lockwood was genuinely speechless. He didn't know what to say that wouldn't unfairly indict the dog. His mind was scrambling to take in the idea of releasing Chaser into the hands of a young girl.

Max turned to Rachel. She was quietly shaking her head over and over.

"He's the one," she repeated.

Max looked back to Lockwood. "Is he trained to do what he might have to do?"

"Yes. I'm just not sure of his...." Lockwood didn't want to say '*stability*.'

"Don't most of the dogs here have pasts?" Max asked.

Rachel took this as support and defiantly furrowed her brow at Lockwood.

Lockwood's precautionary mindset (including his worries of indemnity risk) was waging an internal debate with his feeling that the dog might be suitable for this girl. He'd always felt Chaser was extraordinary, a dog with uncanny judgment and character. In truth, he hadn't seen anything from him in the two months that pointed at a breakdown of his psyche; it was more a case of the dog keeping to himself and biding his time until he decided to live life again in the way he was capable. What Lockwood saw in the dog's body language with the girl was incredible. It was the dog he'd known; it was more than he'd seen from the dog in all their time walking and working. His ego smarted for a second, but his admiration for the dog overcame the ding, and a sense of reassurance in their pairing overcame his doubt.

Lockwood nodded, at last surrendering. Rachel smiled with triumph and looped her arm around the dog's neck.

Lockwood suggested they return in a week while he worked with Chaser to refine the commands. Rachel would have none of it.

"He comes back with us today. It needs to be today. He's ready to be with us."

Lockwood looked at Max, but Max just shrugged.

"Then I'll come down to you in a few days," Lockwood averred. "After he settles in, we can review the protocols and commands."

Rachel looked at the dog, then at Lockwood.

"He won't need commands. He'll know what to do."

Max smiled but told Lockwood to call them, and they'd set it up. "It's a good idea," he said to Rachel. "It will be important for me and Sonia and Karl."

Lockwood looked at the dog. He suddenly realized Chaser was mired in place and complete recovery wasn't possible there. Perhaps because of Lockwood's association with Doyle, and that Chaser couldn't ever dislodge the tangled memories. Dogs were creatures of association, for better or worse.

Lockwood was partly correct: the dog would never be entirely comfortable around Lockwood; he couldn't help feeling the shadow and immanence of Doyle, the expectation of his re-appearance. The dog had resolved to kill Doyle if he saw him again. This was not an easy vow for him or any dog with ancestry as steeped in dedication and service to men. It left him on constant edge. By contrast, the dog was already feeling comfortable with the girl in a way he hadn't since the boy. He associated her with the boy somehow. He was prepared to go with her.

For Rachel, the drive back was a somewhat ridiculous yet wonderful event, with the dog towering over them up against the wind in the rear 'seat' (more a cramped platform behind the front seats). She studied him as she thought of possible names. He looked aged and wise beyond his years. Her hand stroked his shoulders. It suddenly hit her.

"Elijah," she said, turning to Max.

"Elijah," Max repeated approvingly.

She leaned back, closing her eyes. "He was hidden away in the wilderness a long time, but when summoned by God, came out fearlessly. And he called forth fire."

Max glanced at her, surprised.

She laughed at his face and her flourish. "You didn't think I remembered anything from my religious education?"

They approached the sign for horse crossing; there was a car in the other direction, having come to a stop. Max slowed.

Just then, two huge chestnut horses crashed out of the thicket on the left, and Max slammed the brakes. The lead riders wore cardinal red jackets with yellow trim, skin-tight tan jodhpurs tucked inside long gleaming black boots, and rounded black riding helmets. The horses, jerky and high-stepping, with lather at their muzzles and flecked across their withers and the whites of their eyes showing, circled anxiously, chuffing hard. Suddenly, like a blast of canine buckshot, two dozen black-and-white hounds exploded from the path, barking and baying. They packed the strip of asphalt in a manic mass, their heads bent to the ground to catch the lost scent of the hunted.

The dogs rushed around the MG as they yowled. Both Max and Rachel stared, fascinated at the bizarre spectacle.

"Hold Elijah!" Max said, shouting over the noise.

Rachel was delighted that Max had used his new name. But she didn't need to hold him. The dog was watching the scene without moving a muscle. He must realize, she thought, that this wasn't his concern. Still, his composure amazed her. The hounds seemed too absorbed in their pursuit to notice him.

Another rider, heavy and low in the saddle, blasted from the thicket. He wielded a long whip and started cracking it expertly, inches over the dogs' heads, attempting to herd them across the road.

Suddenly the hounds caught the scent they were seeking and, as quickly as they had appeared, poured out through the funnel-like opening on the other side and were gone. Max and Rachel could hear a new eruption of baying, this time of frantic pursuit. The riders on the two chestnuts followed, along with a dozen or so riders in mostly black coats who'd been trickling in from the thicket. The fat rider with the whip spun this way and that before his horse backed up, raised its tail, and deposited a mixture of road apples and steaming liquid dung on the hood and grill of the MG. It then shot off after the others.

Max sat up and examined the mess. "Here's to the fox," he said.

◆◆◆◆◆◆◆

Once home, the orientation process for Elijah, which Max had been worrying about on the drive, turned out to be a non-issue. After they'd circled the pebbled frontage and stopped, he'd lightly hopped out on his own, waiting for Rachel. The two walked the perimeter, with the dog marking spots here and there, and then she'd led him inside. He made a thorough walk-through with her, sometimes going off on his own to smell something but shortly returning to her.

Perry wasn't home. When Rachel led Elijah into the kitchen, Sonia drew back with a start. Karl, however, moved right to him and held his hand forward. Elijah sniffed it neutrally and sat beside Rachel.

"What on earth?" Sonia said.

Karl nodded admiringly. "*Deutscher schaferhunde.* A fine addition to the castle, I can see. Congratulations, dear." He made a formal bow.

Rachel smiled. "He's Elijah, that's all. We'll need some food for him, Sonia. No dog food, but our food. Beef, bones, and other good things."

"Of course," Karl said. "Only the best."

Rachel waited to introduce him to the solarium. She was a bit anxious—selfishly so, she acknowledged. The sunroom was where they'd be spending most of their time. He couldn't be anything but perfect, or perfectly quiet, there.

She walked him again outside, around to the side and the solarium. She doubled back into the house, down the long hallway, unlocked the door, and walked straight to the piano. She turned. He waited at the threshold and sat.

"It's all right; you can come in."

He remained where he was. Rachel walked back, her feet tapping on the tiles, echoing slightly. Perhaps it was the odd space—the tiled floor and unusual acoustics, the lone piano in the center, nothing else. It had always been her room, and she jealously asserted her prerogative. Everyone in the house understood this. Was it in the very air of the room, and he sensed it? She stood next to him. Now she kneeled and placed her arm on his back.

"This is our room, Elijah. Ours."

She stepped over the threshold, her eyes and body abandoning her claim. She meant it. Her heart was lightened. The idea of the sanctum suddenly felt silly, childlike. He stepped in with her, and together they walked to the piano.

She held her fingers over the keys, thinking newly about the Sonatina. She'd been too concerned about its form, the strict injunctions of the Clementi model. But it was her work. She'd always wanted to do more, and the tension was cramping her. She would try what she'd always wanted to do: to challenge, stretch, experiment. This might take some deception in the preliminary submission process (about which she'd already received notice of an advance interview). She didn't care. The work would fit their needs close enough. She would stick to the proper exposition but add a richer and extended development section. Instead of a pure recapitulation, she would add a contrapuntal passage, a shock that would evoke the exposition, as expected, but also challenge it. Then a back-and-forth skirmishing between the motifs, with a furious close to decide the winner. Why not? It would be only a bit longer than the standard Sonatina. Just longer and different enough.

But enough thinking about it. It was time to bear down on the project.

Not tonight, though. She stretched her fingers and started in on Chopin. The day away had done no damage. She was so paranoid about not practicing. Maybe she could surprise them all and play the most difficult Polonaise. No, that would be an unseemly stunt. She wanted to do something original, to break the rules while still following them. That sort of finesse excited her. It would be more demanding, so of course, more rewarding. She wanted it so.

She suddenly paused from her mind-walk and looked for Elijah. She scanned the perimeter. Had he left? She leaned back and peered under the piano. He was stretched out on his side. She smiled and sighed.

She practiced for another forty minutes and stopped abruptly. Elijah sat up and looked at her. She pushed back the bench, and the two walked down the hall and into the kitchen.

Sonia was preparing supper. Rachel watched her glance apprehensively at the dog.

"You don't have to be afraid of him, Sonia. He knows you're part of our family. I can tell."

"Well, I'm glad," Sonia said. "But I have some not-so-happy memories of... dogs like him."

"Tell me," Rachel said.

"I'd rather not. But I will try not to be afraid. Mr. Max tells me he is here for you." Her face brightened. "I have something for him."

She reached for a handful of sliced stew meat and held it out. Elijah, seeing the motion, stood and walked forward to sniff. She opened her hand, and he took it gently, swallowing without chewing.

"Ah!" Sonia said. "Where there's good food, there is goodwill."

◇◇◇◇◇◇◇◇

Only Perry was left to meet. When Rachel heard Perry's car returning home, she went to set up a surprise. She stood in the front hallway with Elijah in the darkness. She heard Perry fumble with the door and slide his hands up to the switch. With the light, she saw he was carrying a heavy load of books and papers. He turned. His face went white, and he dropped the stack and fell back.

Elijah barked once, deep and echoing in the hallway. It startled Rachel, and her hand went to the dog's head. Elijah's body was stiff and aimed forward.

"It's okay, Elijah."

The bark brought Max from his study and Karl. Perry leaned against the wall, shaken.

They all stood as if waiting for the explanation. Rachel wasn't sure what to say.

"What is that?" Perry said, pointing.

Max introduced the dog. Rachel went to lead it to Perry. But Perry drew back.

"No, no thanks. It doesn't matter. I'm not... I'm not a dog person. I don't need to...."

Still, Rachel walked forward with Elijah, and Perry stood frozen. Elijah leaned in, sniffed once, and stepped back, looking up at Rachel—as if the matter was settled. Max led Rachel aside. Rachel spoke first.

"It was my fault, Max. Perry startled him. Dogs read fear, I think."

Max nodded. "Well, let's ease Elijah into all of this. When Lockwood comes, we'll go over it all."

◆◆◆◆◆◆◆

Rachel and Elijah quickly found their routine. Breakfast, practice in the solarium, a walk around the two-acre grounds, casual rounds through the house, more practice, more walking, and sometimes, between practice and walks, wool-gathering on the window seat along the solarium side wall. Dinner in the kitchen, or a snack with Max in his office, and to bed. The dog would stand at the end of the bed while she prepared for it, then lay on the small rug. She had invited him onto the bed once, but he had no inclination. She somehow understood. When Max looked in on her, he would see the dog's eyes gleaming from the hallway reflection as he sat up and stared back before easing back down.

The visit by Lockwood was ten days later. Lockwood had come with his partner, Patrick. The latter was a lean Frenchman with a merry expression and a shock of prematurely grayish hair. He charmed Rachel instantly, and Elijah seemed uncharacteristically receptive to him. They chatted as the two trainers walked the grounds with Rachel, Max, and the dog. Lockwood was pleased with how Elijah had adapted, casually referencing his '*past*.' Max asked him to elaborate, but Rachel interrupted.

189

"The past is the past. He's Elijah now."

Lockwood nodded, accepting the reminder. "It doesn't matter," he said to Max. "It wasn't anything he did, but what was done to him."

They returned to the driveway, and Patrick opened the rear of their Jeep. "Time to get down to business," he said in his French accent.

"*Vous allez maintenant voir Elijah*," Rachel said, smiling.

Patrick nodded, pleased. "*D'accord.*"

Rachel watched as they removed some of the gear she'd seen in the New Hampshire barn, the bulky padded sleeves and suits. She noticed Elijah's pricked-up ears and intense stare. They carried the gear to a small square of lawn between rows of pear trees. Patrick suited up.

"I want to show you what Elijah can do," Lockwood said. "It's been a while since he had any rigorous training, so he may be a little rusty. I suggest some refresher work every few months, at least."

Rachel wanted to say, '*he'll do fine*,' but didn't.

Lockwood moved to slip a leather harness around Elijah. The dog stepped back. Lockwood held out the harness for the dog to sniff. But Elijah looked up.

"It's all right, Elijah."

Rachel offered to take the harness; Lockwood looked at Max. Max nodded. Rachel took it and easily slipped it over Elijah's head. She looked to Lockwood to help her snap it, but he directed Max. The dog was soon strapped, and Rachel attached the fat, leather lead line Lockwood had given her.

Lockwood nodded to Patrick. Patrick, one arm secured inside a thick quilted sleeve attachment, the other holding a splintered bamboo swizzle stick, moved twenty feet away and stood staring at Elijah.

He suddenly slapped the sleeve, yelped, violently shook the stick as he leaned forward and moved menacingly toward the group.

Elijah stared, motionless. Patrick repeated his actions even more vigorously. Elijah still didn't move. Max looked between the trainers. Lockwood signaled to Patrick to pause.

Lockwood turned to Max. "He knows it's simulated. I told Patrick, but he didn't believe me."

Lockwood went to Rachel, leaned in, and whispered in her ear. He stepped back and motioned to Patrick to resume.

As Patrick slapped the sleeve and shook the stick, Rachel shouted, "*Blitzen!*"

The change in the dog was instantaneous and electric as if his muscles and mind were somehow circuited into Rachel's voice. He launched forward. Rachel let go of the line, and Elijah slammed into Patrick's sleeve, knocking him over. Rather than thrash at the sleeve, he bit into it, gripping nearly the entire width to the back of his jaws and pressing down. Patrick tried to clamber up but slipped. The dog wasn't letting him up. Patrick shook the swizzle stick around the dog's head. Elijah was oblivious; all focus only on bearing down.

Lockwood whispered again in Rachel's ear, and she shouted, "*Aus... Fuss.*"

Elijah instantly let go, stepped off, and trotted back to Rachel in the heel position.

Max stared, stunned. Rachel grinned, her hand on Elijah's head, stroking it. Elijah's mouth was open, his tongue out and panting as if nothing had happened. Patrick had slipped off the sleeve and was rubbing his arm. But he was grinning.

Lockwood explained to Max and Rachel the unique, natural sense of threat assessment and discrimination of their dog. "He's one in a million. But what matters," he pointed at Rachel, "is how he recognizes you, your command."

They spent another thirty minutes reviewing the different commands. Lockwood told them it was good to keep it simple. '*Fuss*' was the heel, '*Aus*' was the out command, and '*Blitzen*' was for an attack. To merely be alerted was '*Watch it*.' He admitted that he'd somewhat bastardized his commands from the purist vernacular and that Elijah had also been trained in English. But he used '*Blitzen*' instead of the German for attack, '*Fass!*'

"I think it means '*lightning*'," Rachel said.

"That's close," Lockwood gave her a thoughtful look. "It's less likely to be confused with '*Fuss.*' You can't mistake '*Blitzen.*' You did well. You spoke with authority."

She sighed. "He was performing for us. He knew it wasn't serious. He wanted you to see he was fine. He won't need my commands."

"You're sure of that, are you?"

"I know the look. That's all."

Lockwood examined Elijah for a long moment, then started packing away the gear with Patrick. It would be all right.

◇◇◇◇◇◇◇

Rachel sat vacuously at the piano. Nothing. She'd worked on dozens of openings to the Sonatina, each lapsing into a confusing mishmash, going nowhere. To counter the frustration, she'd play something classic and simple or even a pop song. This was part of the process—the trial and failure. Or was it failure and then suffer the trial? But did it have to be so predictable and punishing?

It was Thursday, and something was nagging at her. The meeting with the Philharmonic lady—was it today? She'd lost track of time. She needed some air, to take a walk. She stood and moved to the door. Elijah was up from his position under the piano and beside her. Then she heard Sonia's voice down the hall.

◇◇◇◇◇◇◇

Rachel sat in the drawing room adjacent to the solarium, next to Helena Ordspring from the Philharmonic. '*Assistant to the Director of Special Performance Events,*' she looked the part. She was Scandinavian, Rachel thought, with her short whitish-blonde hair and brows, pert nose, and perfect skin. She was thin and in a long, prim pencil dress accentuating the thinness. Just now, she was trying to hold to her status of officialdom against the distracting sight of Elijah in a rather minatory posture at Rachel's feet.

Ordspring held the cup of coffee from Sonia elegantly in two hands, a smart leather case across her knees.

"But of course, Miss Abedon... your solo composition you'll be performing, as we indicated in our correspondence, Mr. Van Guersling would very much like to see it..."

Rachel said nothing, just smiled.

"We're a week past the deadline," Ordspring continued.

Rachel's eyes lit with sudden animation.

"I very much appreciate your patience, Miss Ordspring. It's really coming along beautifully, but I'm superstitious about showing it before it's finished. If I could have a little more time..." It was her most calculatedly solicitous voice.

Helena Ordspring, anxious about returning completely empty-handed to her notoriously short-tempered boss, grabbed hold.

"Can I tell him you'll have it next week?"

Rachel smiled sweetly. "I'll do my best."

Helena, as satisfied as she thought was possible, stood. Elijah stood. She sat back down. Now Rachel stood, putting her hand on Elijah's head, gesturing it was safe.

"May I ask what you're calling your piece?" she asked, making conversation to cover her nerves.

An hour later, Rachel was again at the piano. Her fingers came down on the keys like ten tiny hammers, and the pounded dissonance reverberated.

"I'm calling it '*Upchuck in E-flat*,' Miss Ordspring."

◇ ◇ ◇ ◇ ◇ ◇ ◇ ◇

The next day, aware of Rachel's stymied state, Max invited her to accompany him to lunch with a colleague in Topsfield. Rachel at first begged off, but Max said she could bring Elijah.

"Morris has a good spread of land, and you and Elijah could take a long walk. He'd love to see you and your dog. He made a point of it."

The worst of all social outings were the daytime ones (in which it seemed harder to hide or steal away), and especially ones in which there were expectations. Would she have to play the piano? Maybe she could fake a broken finger, and tape her hand? She laughed, knowing she'd done it before. Normally Rachel would have held firm. But the thought a new bit of landscape for Elijah appealed to her. He could really run.

The greetings and small talk weren't terrible, she found. Morris was a friendly, donnish widower, much older than Max, tall and thin in well-pressed gray flannels and a sizeable old cardigan. His handshake was careful as if he understood her vocation. He joked about asking her to play but spent several minutes mapping out the property and where she could walk: a path through a thicket of pines would lead to wide field next to a stream and a horse lane. Very safe, '*no lions, tigers or bears*,' he said. He told her she might see some horses; an actual live fox hunt crossed his easement.

He looked at Elijah with a keen appraisal. "Mighty impressive companion you've got there."

"If you want to wait, we'll come with you," Max said. "You could have a bite to eat first."

She wasn't hungry and politely declined. She thanked Morris and started off.

She found the path, and once they'd walked under cover of trees, the atmosphere changed—the breeze vanished, the light dimmed, and a sense of quiet closed around them. Their feet padded noiselessly on the pine-needle carpet. It was like an enchanted forest, she thought. She was soon lost in thoughts of music.

"I know what greatness is," she said aloud. "It's a glorious piece of music that lasts forever."

She stopped and looked at Elijah. "Long after I'm gone."

"There's not enough time. I need to relax. But I can't write when I'm relaxed. I need pressure. I need fear. It's perverse." She gestured around at the forest. "Life is perverse; maybe you know this too. Not all the time, but enough of the time. And this..." she swept her arms around. "This doesn't help me. Nature. I don't find music here; I lose it. I need the cold emptiness of my space, feeling just sick enough so that vomit is at the edge of my thoughts, music the only way out, the only way into meaning. I'm crazy, aren't I?"

She leaned against a tree. She could smell the pine sap. Elijah sat next to her. Her foot stroked his side.

They resumed walking and emerged from the pines into the meadow Morris had mentioned. They walked on fifty or so yards. The wind was tickling the long, tufted grasses.

Rachel noticed Elijah had stiffened. His eyes searched the perimeter before locking onto something. Now Rachel saw a rushing movement, along with a chafing sound, through the grass. Suddenly, thirty yards off, a red fox, its tail as long as its sleek body, streaked past, vanishing again into the grasses behind them.

Elijah didn't chase; he just stood motionless. His nose remained aimed at where the fox first appeared. Now Rachel felt a faint pounding beneath her feet; a second later, a high trebling horn, loud and too close, then a familiar baying of hounds.

She saw the hounds and horses burst from the far edge of the meadow. The bellowing pack was mad after the scent, followed by two dozen riders on huge horses. Rachel watched the hounds charging in their direction. Where could she and Elijah run to or hide? The forest line was too far back. They were as likely to rush into the path of hounds and horses as not. They could only stand where they were.

The hounds caught a scent and veered away upwards of them, the horses following.

But suddenly, a few of the closest hounds snared the new scent. This rogue group tripped over the others to break toward them.

As Rachel cried out, Elijah bolted straight at the oncoming rush. The hounds, seeing Elijah, parted like billiard balls before his headlong charge. The riders were suddenly spinning, shouting at the hounds, and struggling to rein in the flustered horses. Elijah circled back to Rachel and again speared out at loose hounds, which had now lost all sense of unity or purpose.

Several horses reared as the fleeing hounds dodged Elijah and pin-balled off their legs. Scattered hounds were making opportunistic stabs at Elijah, like hyenas at a male lion, but would yelp and turn tail when he spun at them.

Rachel couldn't do anything but watch, with her hands at her face, both terrified and thrilled; she was marveling at Elijah's agility and precision, routing the hounds as he darted among the general anarchy.

Suddenly, through some weird synesthesia she'd never experienced, she felt the ambient noise quiet, and she began to hear quick pulses of mental music, of piano notes, set to the scene. Elijah's movement and focus seem to set the timing and tone, with dramatic *allegros* as he sped toward one dog, quick *staccatos* as he jerked to the sides to catch the thrust of a hound and drive it off, a transitional *tenuto* as he paused and freshly appraised the scene; a *grazioso* as he pranced back to check in with her; then a revived *animato* as he rushed back in.

She was filling the spaces of the scene with her transitions and instantaneously teasing it into something cohesive.

It was a phenomenal product of adrenaline over her fear for Elijah and her awe at his supple, quicksilver display. His poetry in motion demanded from her and inspired a musical similitude.

Elijah stood arched up in the grass and scanned the milling group, now about thirty yards off and re-assembling itself after the chaos. A rider dressed in gray and black emerged behind the others and leaped toward him. His left hand at the reins, he was dragging a whip in his right hand. He brought it up from his side and, with alarming quickness, whipped it towards Elijah. It cracked a few feet over his head like a gunshot. Elijah reared up, his teeth bared, holding his position as if challenging the rider. The rider curled the whip back, readying it anew; Rachel could see his determined grimace.

She screamed. Her voice caught the ears of the other riders, one of whom, dressed in red, shouted at the 'whip-master' (as Rachel had named him in her mind). Another blew the horn, and the hounds and horses retreated up the meadow. The whip-master snapped the whip's handle toward her before moving off, but not before casting a haughty glance back.

Rachel yelled for Elijah. He came up to her, panting. A new look was on his face—of primal satiation.

◆◆◆◆◆◆◆◆

They walked back to the house in what Rachel felt was a silent, shared thrall. Each time she looked at Elijah next to her, the sounds became clearer and more resounding. The tune was playing in her head, the notes filling the mental musical bars. She didn't want to interrupt the phenomenal freshet. Maybe it was all her conceit and would amount to nothing, but she couldn't stop.

She said little at Morris's house, thanking him while trying to hold her concentration on the music. Max noticed the flush on her face on the drive home and how she leaned forward in the car seat, no longer huddling. In Max's Mercedes, Elijah had ample room in the back.

Back home, after feeding Elijah a bowl of stew meat with some chopped and boiled carrots prepared by Sonia, Rachel almost ran to the solarium. Elijah followed and lay down under the piano. He listened to the tapping and torrents of notes and chords until he fell asleep.

Back in his study, Max looked out the window at the gathering clouds. They'd returned in time. He turned around when the phone rang and saw the light on the extension flicker. He waited. Perry entered shortly, his eyes eagerly gesturing to the phone.

"The Senator."

Max nodded and picked up the receiver, but without Perry's enthusiasm. "Hello, Senator."

"Good to hear your voice, Max. I trust all is well with you and yours?"

"Fine, Senator. Thank you. How can I help you?"

"Well, you may have heard, Senator Cray has made noises about calling you before his committee in a closed session. He's hinted this may be before the recess in December."

Max hadn't heard. He looked at Perry and motioned for him to pick up his extension. Perry turned and ran back out to his office.

"Max. I'm your ally in all this. So is the President. To really help you, we need to see your report."

"I believe I mentioned, Senator, I'm happy to submit my report to the President. Personally."

There was a brief pause. Max could faintly hear wheezy breathing.

"Please, Max, call me Will. Or Willy. And certainly, Max, I'm sure we can arrange that. Why don't we have you come back to DC very soon."

"All right, Senator."

Max hung up. Perry trotted back in, excited, out of breath.

"Sounds like they've agreed to your conditions."

Max stared back, not wanting to spoil Perry's almost childlike look of hope.

"Why don't you make arrangements. Just be mindful of Rachel's performance—no conflicts with that."

Perry nodded. "Of course not, professor."

◆◆◆◆◆◆◆

A week later, Max and Rachel sat in the office of Dr. Bernard Minkum at Beth Israel Hospital in Boston. It was a testing day, and Rachel hated them. And she had nearly finished her composition after her breakthrough; this was a pointless interruption, based only on stupid '*protocol*' for Gaucher Disease, so she was always told. Five years of this, and she'd had enough.

Elijah sat next to Rachel. Some contretemps over the dog had taken place at the entrance when Max's explanation that Elijah was Rachel's '*service animal*' had not sufficed. Minkum had walked down and smoothed it out. A former classmate of Max's at BU, and the youngest department head at the hospital, Minkum was highly popular among the staff and was known for his excellent '*bedside manner*.' Best of all, as the hospital directors saw it, he was their premier fundraiser.

Minkum was very fond of both father and daughter; he considered Rachel a '*pistol*.' He could feel the girl's balled-up tension.

"Well, team, how are we? You look like you're doing well, Rachel. Am I on the mark?"

Rachel nodded.

"Okay. Well, we'll do some blood work and a liver tap and you'll be on your way."

"This is my last time for this," she said, her eyes levelly on Minkum.

Max leaned back. He'd decided to let her handle it.

"You know, Rachel, the tests are important."

"No, they're not. Not if I'm feeling well. I wasn't always feeling well. I am now. I've never felt better. I have work to do."

Minkum smiled, looking between them.

"Well, with the tests—"

"There's nothing to do about it. I've got Gaucher and always will. If I'm not feeling well, the tests will just tell you I'm not feeling well. I could tell you that. Whether it's my spleen or liver or anemia, it's just Gaucher. I don't care. I don't want to know anything else. There's nothing else to know."

Max looked at Minkum and spoke in measured tones.

"She's doing as well as I've seen, Bernie."

"Since Elijah," Rachel said, expressionless.

"Elijah?" Minkum asked.

Max pointed to the dog. "Elijah."

"Elijah," Rachel repeated.

Minkum stared at the two stony faces, then arched his neck to peer over the desk at the dog. He settled back judiciously.

"I see. Well, I won't dismiss anything that is helping you feel better. Maybe we should look more into this 'Elijah Factor.' In the meantime, since we're all here, let's do our tests, and you can be on your way."

An hour later, Rachel, feeling chilled and fragile in the hospital gown, lay on the examining table in the fiercely white-lighted treatment room. There was no place she wanted less to be. She leaned her head over the edge and saw Elijah curled on the linoleum floor beneath the table. She grinned with satisfaction at this victory, at least. Yes, the last time.

Minkum and three young interns came in, and they went through the same routine: the injection of the anesthetic, then the liver probe, and its strange, deep pressure (her mind unable to resist the mental image). She suddenly wondered, what if she cried out, would Elijah snarl at the doctors? Would he drive them out of the room? But maybe with the needle still dangling out of her body? The thoughts amused her. But of course, he wouldn't do that. She tried locking on the image of Elijah under the piano as she sat and played.

◆ ◆ ◆ ◆ ◆ ◆ ◆ ◆

Another week had passed. Rachel was at the window seat in the solarium, huddled under a blanket and staring at the drizzle and dirty wads of clouds. She felt the cold through the glass. She was at the penultimate moment in her composition but wasn't ready to finish. Something was missing—perhaps some last spasm of anguish to bring it all home. It had gone so well, almost too well. She'd hardly even paused to question or doubt any of it. It had just poured out of her. The moment and images of Elijah charging the hounds, spinning with agile efficiency, controlled ferocity, returning to her, back again, rearing up at the horse... the music followed the proper Sonatina sequence and form: of statement, exposition, recapitulation, and final evocative flourish. It was brilliant. Hah! She dreaded to go back over it, now having freed her caged critic. Let loose, he would cry havoc and force her to eat her rash fanfaronade. He always did. '*Brilliant*'?! Would she never learn?

She shivered, drawing the blanket tighter. She looked at Elijah. Why had he permitted her into his life as he had? He had faith. As she had in him. It had been that simple, hadn't it? Faith. Based on nothing but the sight of each other.

The dog's eyes rested on her. It was comforting to do so; the comfort had become a valued resource to the dog. He knew she wasn't the same as the boy, but the difference was still pleasing. She wasn't a leader in the same way the dog was coded to follow. The boy had also saved him. Other than Lockwood, the girl was the first to approach him after the trauma and had done so fearlessly and with intention and need. Lockwood had no need. The girl was like the boy, and that might have been enough. But he saw in the girl physical differences—defects and frailties—which struck another guardian chord. Her voice had calmed him. So had the music. He felt a latent strength in the girl, comparable to the boy's but different. He'd made an association: the girl with the boy. He would protect both with his life, and one would ultimately lead to the other.

Rachel suddenly stood, staring at Elijah, and tossed off the blanket. She turned to the piano, rubbed her hands together, and sat on the bench.

She brought her hands up an hour later, made some final scrawls on the composition sheet, and dropped the pencil. She stared at the rows of marching black notes, looked down at Elijah under the piano, and took a deep, satisfied breath.

◇◇◇◇◇◇◇

Karl stood at the video monitor in the cramped closet. The screen was slightly fuzzy and flickering, but the image of the long sedan at the gate was clear enough. The bell had rung, signaling a guest, and Sonia had summoned him. He heard the house phone ring in the kitchen, which Sonia answered, and her muffled response. Seconds later, she was at the door.

"It's for Dr. Max. You're to let him in."

Max had received the call from Senator Cray the night before. Perry had taken it and, looking somewhat confused, informed Max.

"Senator Cray. He said he's in town, in Boston."

Cray wanted to meet, to have a friendly chat. He could be there in an hour.

"Fine," Max said and gave him the address (though he suspected Cray already had it).

He'd assured Perry that it would be all right. He understood that Cray was no friend of the President, but he only intended to listen. There could be no harm in that.

Senator Leland Cray was in his mid-70s, lean and as stately-seeming as a Senator could hope to appear. He wore no overcoat and though slightly bowed, moved with the looseness of a former athlete (he'd played basketball at UVA). Max led him into the library and offered him tea, which Sonia had already prepared. He sat across from Max on the sofa, his eyes crinkling up as he studied him.

"I won't waste your time, professor. May I call you Max?"

Max tipped his head. "Of course."

"Very well, Max. There is an awful lot of interest in your report, and a lot of rumors. My committee is investigating certain operations of the war effort which, sources tell me, are examined in your report."

"I'm beginning to regret I wrote it," Max said quietly.

"Because it might embarrass the President? Or not embarrass him enough?"

Max flared. "My personal feelings about the President have nothing to do with it or why I agreed to the task," he said sharply. He took a breath; this wasn't like him. "I apologize. Let me re-phrase. I'm just weary of the attention and talk. I wish to submit the report to the President and let him decide what to do with it. Until then, it is entirely off limits for discussion."

Cray had been watching Max closely and put down the tea.

"Max, I'm the one to offer apologies. I'm a veteran of the shining city of hidden agendas. And thus, I often assume the same of everyone else. I was aware of your liberal leanings from some of your writings, and it crossed my mind you'd learned some things in producing your report that would support our efforts to hasten an end to the war."

"Is your hidden agenda to embarrass the President, Senator?"

"No. It's my overt agenda. I'll be clear, Max. This war sickens me. And I'll do what I can to try to end it."

"That's fine. But are you sure that politically damaging the President helps end the war? After all, he inherited it."

"It might, Max. I don't know yet."

"Well, that's an agenda that doesn't interest me. Perhaps I'm not politically experienced, realistic or cynical enough, but I want the truth to end the war. I'm satisfied I am offering the truth in my report. It will be up to him to make use of it or not. He took risks in asking me to do this. I was not a supporter, but I will not exploit his trust in exchange for approbation from his political enemies. So I'll be clear, Senator. Until I hand it to the President and he reads it, I won't talk about it. I may not even do so afterward."

"I appreciate your honesty, Max."

"I appreciate yours. So there we are."

Cray nodded, smiling. "So it appears." He sighed and appraised Max. "You know, you came to my attention with your article about the Arab-Israeli mess. I thought it was pretty brave and bold."

Max's eyes went inward. "The Arab side calls me a Zionist; the Israelis call me an appeaser. There's no winning. Apparently, it's also what brought me to the attention of the President. My misfortune."

"Let's hope not, Max."

◊◊◊◊◊◊◊◊

In the kitchen, Rachel sat, spent and loosened by relief after her completed work, sipping a cup of tea. Elijah was at her feet. Sonia was working on slicing potatoes next to the deep-dish sink. Manny, Verna, and Karl were in the nook, playing Gin Rummy. At Karl's side on the table was a fly swatter; his eyes tracked a house fly flitting about the table and a bowl of fruit. He picked it up and took a swipe, brushing the edge of the table, missing.

Elijah's ears pricked up at the sound.

Irritated by Karl's failed attempts, Manny stood, rolled up a shopper's newsletter on the counter, and moved out of the nook to stalk the fly. Rachel could see Elijah eyeing Manny wielding the paper tube, raising it, and bringing it down hard on the counter with a resounding smack.

"Aha! That's how you do it."

Rachel saw Elijah sit up now with a hard, furrowed stare. Hearing him growl, she neatly stood and walked with him to the door, carrying her cup. They passed through the swing door.

Sonia made a clucking sound of disapproval at Manny and gestured for him to put down the paper. Manny shrugged and pointed at the door as if to say, *'they're gone.'*

"Why would a nice little Jewish girl want a dog like that?" It was Verna, in a low voice but with a full intention to be heard.

Sonia looked at her sharply. Verna's eyes slid away as she shrugged.

As Rachel and Elijah passed through the dim hallway, Max emerged from the library with Cray. Cray stopped short.

"Whoa there, Miss." He looked between Rachel and Elijah.

Rachel approached. She was a little surprised when Elijah moved to Cray and stood still when the stranger leaned over and rubbed his head.

Max stepped forward. "Senator, my daughter, Rachel. Rachel, this is Senator Cray."

"Nice to meet you," Rachel said, offering a plastic smile. She sized him up and pointed to Elijah. "His name is Elijah. Are you familiar with the Old Testament?"

"Probably not up to your standards. But am I safe in assuming by that—" Clay pointed at Elijah—"you mean the prophet?"

Rachel said matter-of-factly, "He suffered loneliness and despair in the wilderness. Now he's with me."

"I see."

Rachel enjoyed moments like this to provoke and experience the reactions. She'd also overheard Verna's comment, was smarting from it and felt like venting. It was the first thing that came to her mind to say to some stuffy old man meeting with her father. But Cray seemed to take it in stride.

"It is an admirable thing to offer a dog a new life," Cray said.

Rachel nodded, impressed despite herself. They stood in a circle for a moment.

"I have a ranch back home with a few of my own. Collecting misfit dogs—not to suggest your fine friend is a misfit—is a hobby of mine. Perhaps we can arrange a visit with you, your father, and of course Elijah sometime soon."

Rachel nodded again. He put out a large hand, and Rachel shook it briefly. Cray followed Max out the door.

◇◇◇◇◇◇◇

Rachel reviewed and practiced her composition over the next few days. She'd yet to hear back from the Philharmonic blonde and hoped the issue had been dropped. Rachel had no intention of offering her work for review in advance. She didn't know if there would be a problem with its extended length and altered form. But she didn't care. She wanted it to be a surprise. The event was on the Saturday of the following week. Rachel felt no apprehension; one blessing, or irony, of her neurotic temperament, as she told herself, was zero performance anxiety. Any pressure and angst she felt were exclusively in preparing, writing, and practicing. She could play almost anytime or anywhere, if she willed it, without nerves. Rachel did feel slight tension over the one condition she intended to demand once she was at the scene and over which she had vowed not to compromise.

Perry and Beadle's office had scheduled Max's visit to DC for the Thursday before the event. Max wasn't happy, but Perry said Beadle assured them the meetings would only take one afternoon. Max would be home Thursday night or Friday morning.

Wednesday evening, Max took Rachel out to dinner. She'd wanted to bring Elijah.

"We'll be home soon," Max said.

They sat at a slightly wobbly wooden table in the fish and burger shack near the water. The atmosphere was working-class and easygoing, with lanterns and fishing props along the walls.

Max wanted to explain what these trips to DC were about; he felt Rachel would understand. She, of course, knew about his three-week research trip to Southeast Asia the previous summer, though he'd not gone into detail about it. As he told her about his trip to DC, warming up to a longer explanation of the project, she nodded knowingly.

"You're a VIP. I know. Your very important report is probably embarrassing to the bigwigs, and that's why they're trying to put pressure on you. But you won't give in."

He stared at her, only briefly surprised. "I should have known," he said, smiling.

"I listen and watch. It's all in the air." She paused, munching on a celery stick. "I know you don't want me to worry. I'm not worried." She looked off to the side, then back. "Will it be all right? You'll be back in time?"

"Of course."

"Can you tell me what the report is about, why they care so much?"

Max stared back. She looked different in the light from the small lantern on the table—older and serious. Was it disrespectful not to tell her more?

"It might be embarrassing, as you say. It might upset people in government and the military. It's important that I release it to the man who asked me to write it and that I don't talk too much about it. Whatever he decides, even if he wants to flush it down the toilet, that's the end of it all for me."

She listened, nodding. "Someone came to you with information. Someone who trusted you."

It was a statement, not a question.

"Yes, that's about it. He came to me, not to anyone else in the group."

"You believed him."

"Yes. It wasn't only about believing him, but his facts. He had proof."

"He trusted you. I know why. And you trusted him." Her eyes closed a little. "It's about that thing in people's eyes and faces. Not just people, you know. Like with Elijah. We can see each other."

Her eyes opened wide, and she looked brightly at Max. "I hope you can give it to him and come back tomorrow."

He smiled and put his hands on hers.

"I will."

◆◆◆◆◆◆◆

Max arrived in DC at eleven the following morning on the Eastern Airlines shuttle and was escorted from the airport to Beadle's office with encouraging efficiency. *'Let's get this over with,'* he said to himself. However, Beadle wasn't in, and Max was soon led by Beadle's aide and two others—an Army officer and a plainly suited man—outside, where they walked around the side of the massive ash-gray building into a lower floor entrance.

The hallway here was quiet—no one else seemed to be around—and their heels on the marble floor echoed. They made a turn, up a short set of stairs, then through some double doors, and finally into a room marked '*HR-A*.' Max assumed this meant 'Hearing Room A.'

Inside, it looked just like a hearing room. Six men—four military officers and two in dark suits—sat at a panel of raised central desks. They faced a desk at the near edge, with an empty chair. The Army officer gestured for Max to have a seat. Max moved to the desk, sat, and stared back at the six unsmiling faces. So this was it, he thought—the inevitable inquisition he'd imagined. He wondered if he should ask for a lawyer or if he was too far into the outer limits for such relief to be possible.

The men stared unwaveringly. Max waited. The man in the center, about fifty, with a flattop crew cut that looked like steel bristles, and dressed in a gray IBM suit, shuffled some papers as he kept his eyes on Max.

"Dr. Abedon. Did you know there are thousands of US intelligence agents in Vietnam? But not one of them has reported anything remotely like what's in your report. Can you explain that?"

Max had suspected that they'd always known some elements of his report and assumed this was now an effort to bluff him into revealing more or releasing it to them.

"No. Can you? Everything I saw was openly visible." Max looked at each of the men before him in turn. "Would you care to introduce yourselves?"

The door opened with a quiet click, and Beadle entered. He avoided Max's look and sat toward the back, behind the others facing Max.

A man at the edge, younger (almost too young looking, Max thought), in glasses and with the look of a hungry Junior Achievement badger, snorted. He said through the side of his mouth to the uniformed man to his right: "The closest he's ever been to a war zone is a college faculty conference."

Crewcut spoke again. "Dr. Abedon. Please. We know the gist of your reported 'findings.'"

"All right. Then you don't need me, do you?"

"Why don't you just tell us the source of this perfidious fiction."

One of the younger officers to his side put his hand toward him in a pacifying gesture, smiled at Max, and spoke silkily.

"Now, we're sure a man of the Doctor's credentials wouldn't offer a report he couldn't substantiate or be willing to reference. Not if he cared about his... professional viability."

Max ignored the men in front and looked back toward Beadle.

"As I've said, but maybe you haven't heard, the President trusted me with a certain confidence regarding my findings. They are for him to read."

Crewcut didn't allow a second of pause.

"The President reads what we give him to read."

The young officer again took the milder tone but tinged with condescension this time as if talking to a child.

"You know, Dr. Abedon, we've also been entrusted with something. A war—"

Crewcut interrupted sharply, "A war, not an academic debate, not an occasion for phony 'fact-finding' excursions under the misleading direction of self-serving, self-appointed investigators with axes to grind and happy to take advantage of gullible intellectuals puffed up with importance by '*presidential request*.'"

The young officer to his right, seemingly giving up efforts to contain the wound-up Crewcut, pressed.

"Not to mention, professor, how you've been associated at one time or another with every anti-war activist on the east coast."

"Associated? How?" Max calmly replied. "Because my essays may have appeared in the same journals as theirs?"

"Perhaps the irony will amuse you, professor, as you intellectuals seem always to appreciate irony, but what if this 'report' you thought would advance your career instead turns out...."

He left the threat dangling. The officer saw an opening to bring the point home.

"I'm sure it's occurred to you that if we can wage war 6,000 thousand miles from here, we can...." Another dangling implication.

Max stared into his eyes, speaking evenly.

"But that's the point, isn't it? You can't wage such a war. And the shame of it is, it takes someone like me to tell you." He paused, taking in the others. "Yes, I went to a war zone. I took a Kodak Instamatic and a steno pad and walked the streets beyond the air-conditioned confines of your secured compounds, and now I'm back. And I do sympathize with you; I can see your bind. How will it look if word gets out that an egghead professor exposed the most obscene military mismanagement and corruption in maybe, well, history?"

"I take it that's a threat to go to the media, to go public?" Crewcut asked.

"With what?" Max asked. "My phony report?" He looked at each of them in turn. "Have any of you been to Qui Nhon? Well, that's where you offload K-rations: clothing, guns, cannons, grenades, and of course, the real essentials of war: TV sets, washing machines, and stereos, funneled into the black market under the noses of your 6,000 CIA agents. The entire time I was in Vietnam, I never heard anything about '*the war*.' Everybody was too busy trying to turn a profit. Convoys of goods hijacked straight into the jungle. American material stolen from the docks and sold in shopping stalls a hundred yards away. But who cares? There's always more where that came from—more money, munitions, material, and more men. You want me to trust you? What trust are you keeping with the young men giving their lives for this profligacy and corruption?"

He stood. "Have the President call me to arrange receipt of my report personally." He collected his small briefcase and moved out the door. As he reached it, he heard the man stand up and bark at him.

"We know you've been talking with Cray. We'd advise you to be very careful about any involvement with his committee. Do you understand?"

◇ ◇ ◇ ◇ ◇ ◇ ◇

Rachel stared out at the bleak December day. The bare poplars seemed to shiver in the wind. The weather had such an effect on her. Was it the same with others? A glimpse of the sun would cheer her; its concealment behind clouds a second later would sink her. She was so weak and impressionable, she thought. She rubbed her hands into Elijah's thick coat. '*It doesn't bother you,*' she thought; '*you're impervious to such vagaries.*'

Max would be back tomorrow, Friday, he'd said on the phone. The event was Saturday. It was all fine. She didn't want to practice now, maybe not even again until the day of the event. Sometimes little breaks like that would help sharpen her. What to do? She would tease Sonia.

"Let's go," she said to Elijah.

◇◇◇◇◇◇◇◇

The dark, wiry young man, Z, sat in the driver's seat of the linen van. He checked his watch: fifteen minutes to go. The two others, V, and X, with whom he'd never worked, were squatting in the back, smoking tensely. Typically, Z would have refused the addition of others he didn't know. Still, he accepted the conditions, incautiously he admitted, because of the money and the relative simplicity of the job. Yes, he knew no job was ever simple; he knew from experience. But still, the money. He'd been out of circulation for too long. He needed this and looked forward to its refresher test.

He saw his work as a form of high athleticism. He had tried out for his country's Olympic track team in 1968 and though eliminated, had done quite well. It was a small, personal challenge, and he'd satisfied himself that he was good enough to make it if he'd really tried, if it was all he did like the others competing. He was very fit, far more so than the flabby and pampered American radicals he'd met and worked with briefly at the 1968 convention (what a sad education that was). At five-eleven and a hundred and forty pounds, he was naturally lean, quick, and, he told himself with a certain self-aware immodesty, lethal should the need arise. A veteran of the Army, he'd just missed the '67 war due to appendicitis. Good luck or bad luck, he wasn't sure. Friends had died, and he could have too. He didn't kid himself that he wanted to be a martyr. But he wanted to make a mark. Secretly, he saw himself as a future legendary terrorist. At twenty-eight, he felt he was coming into his own. With the help of his group, he'd dissimulated himself as a foreign-exchange student at Boston University and had been biding his time for the right opportunity, keeping careful contact with an intermediary in Paris. He'd made his interest known in joining the Popular Front for the Liberation of Palestine and was looking for a dramatic calling card; this could prove to be his entrée.

The contact for this job, he'd been told, was a rogue figure, unaffiliated with any known group but still legitimate, according to his handler. The legitimacy seemed rooted in deep pockets; Z sensed from the tone of the exchanges that the figure was domestic and maybe governmental, which lent a certain weighty and baleful feel to it for Z. The prep and intelligence had seemed solid, and the money was real. They put him in charge of the operation. He was thrilled. They offered him two assistants; one was Egyptian and the other Jordanian, both embedded at BU. The two accepted their subordinate roles. Of course, Z made them feel more important than that. Z prided himself on being a leader. This was what had been so maddening about the Americans of Weather Underground he'd met—their disdain for good leadership and all their slobbering over 'equality.' And the women, the ridiculous and vulgar women clearly unfit for the work. He didn't hide his contempt, and they surely hated him for not sniffing after them like a horny dog as the other men did. Too bad. Never again with those arrogant, over-privileged children. After this assignment, he'd go back to Paris.

He knew about Abedon, had seen him on campus and interviewed on PBS and despised him without needing to know more. He despised Jews, especially the effete, intellectually superior and moneyed Jews who craved celebrity and felt it was owed them for being Jews. And Abedon was a Zionist to boot. But he wasn't the target (not directly); it was the daughter. She was small and sickly, the intelligence had reported. Some sort of musician. The job would not be difficult. They had next to zero security at the house, just some fancy new cameras (which their inside man would take care of). Abedon himself was away from home; the girl was essentially alone. There was a middle-aged, German housekeeping couple—they would be no threat. There was a dog, apparently, but, again, no big deal—a pet. The inside man was taking care of that too. Get the girl, get out. After that, there'd be a drop-off, and he was out. Five thousand dollars for him, a thousand already paid. Hopefully, the Jews would be killed or their lives ruined, or if not, bled of their ill-gotten wealth.

They hadn't told him to bring a weapon, but he brought his anyway—a Browning Parabellum. He checked his watch. It was almost time. He made a clicking sound with his tongue. V stubbed the cigarette and moved to the back of the van with X. The tape, bag, and tie-strips were in a box. They all slipped on their balaclavas.

◆◆◆◆◆◆◆◆

Sonia ladled some soup in a hot bowl in front of Rachel, then reached down to hand Elijah a stew bone. Elijah sniffed it and started gnawing one end.

In the nook, Karl suddenly stood up from the card game with Manny and Verna. Manny looked at the clock, then at Verna.

"Where are you going? We're almost finished. I'm winning."

Karl brushed it off.

"I'm restless."

The bell for the front gate rang, a brief, shrill clang over the freezer.

"Who's that?" Karl asked.

"Find out," Sonia chided him.

He moved to the equipment closet. Manny stood, stretched, and followed him. Verna watched, her hands tightly clutching the cards.

Karl pushed open the door and examined the monitor. The blue linen truck was at the gate, its fender almost touching.

"It's not their day, is it?" He was about to turn to Sonia, but Manny pointed to the machinery.

"I'd love to see how this works."

Karl grunted and turned back to the small screen. He put his hand on a large lever dial and moved it a quarter turn. From the video, he could see the gate swing open. The truck slowly entered.

Rachel hadn't vomited in almost two months but suddenly felt sick. It seized her all over, with a simultaneous sense of agitation and weakness. She turned pale and stood, then quick-stepped to the bathroom off the kitchen. Sonia saw Rachel's face and motion and put down her slicing knife.

"Are you all right, sweetie?"

Rachel leaned over the toilet, waiting. This was strange; after doing so well for such a long stretch. But now, it seemed to be passing. She stood straight, staring at herself in the mirror. The other strange part was her premonitory, out-of-body sensation, as much of a panic attack as nausea.

Outside the door, Elijah sniffed at its base and then sat, waiting. He whined once and looked around the kitchen. The movements of the people were out of the ordinary. Verna had walked out toward the hallway as Sonia came toward the bathroom. Manny was now following her. Karl was watching the video, his back visible from outside the closet.

Karl frowned as the truck sat in the front circle, no one emerging. "Sonia, come here."

Manny now returned from the hallway. He reached into his pocket to pull something out and walked quickly to Elijah at the bathroom door. Elijah felt the presence behind him, and looked over, alert.

Wump. A heavy wad of beef hit the floor in front of him. He stared at it for a moment. An image from his memory flashed before him: of Doyle dropping bits of meat in front of him, his arm poised to smack him if he made a motion toward them. A growl rolled up from Elijah's depth as he stared at Manny, who was mistakenly making a frontal challenge of eye contact.

Elijah now swiveled and barked. It was a shock of sound in the room, and everybody turned. Rachel opened the bathroom door as Manny back-pedaled, stumbled, and fell. The motion, along with Rachel just behind him, triggered Elijah's protection instinct, and he barked again, lurching forward toward Manny.

Verna, about to re-enter the room from the hallway, stopped. Manny stood and retreated toward the hallway; Elijah was barking now like a repeating rifle at each step, each bark guttural and reverberating in the space. Manny screamed and, reaching the hallway, stumbled into Verna. Rachel now had Elijah by the thick collar. The dog's body was rigid, and she could feel the taut muscles and the barely restrained force in his shoulders through her grip.

Manny now straightened, holding on to Verna.

"That dog's crazy! He tried to attack me. He's crazy!"

Verna looked behind her toward the front door, whipped her head back, and shouted wildly, her wildness calculated but convincing.

"I saw it. He attacked Manny! For no reason! He's mad! Lock him up!"

"Lock him up!" Manny echoed.

Sonia had come up behind Rachel and put her arms around her shoulders, looking confused. Karl appeared from around the corner.

"Lock that dog up!" Manny repeated.

Sonia steered Rachel and Elijah to the large laundry room, past the cowering Manny and Verna; as Elijah went in first, she pulled Rachel back and shut the door quickly.

"No!" Rachel cried.

"Just for the moment," Sonia urged her, "just let's wait. We don't want anything to happen here to Elijah."

Sonia turned to the couple and glared at them.

"What happened?"

A shadow fell over Rachel and Sonia. Rachel began to turn, moving her head a few inches before glimpsing what seemed like several men. One clasped a hand over her mouth, cutting off her cry, while another threw a heavy canvas bag over her head. Another did the same to Sonia, and her cry was strangled. Karl charged the men but was knocked over by Manny. Karl struggled, but one of the men in masks held his hand up to strike him, and Karl fell back.

Manny and Verna stepped back as the third man wrapped up Karl quickly and expertly, gagging him.

Rachel was hauled backward by the men down the hallway, past the laundry room.

The entire break-in had taken less than forty-five seconds.

Inside the laundry room, Elijah tensely listened, unsure. But when he smelled the three men and heard Rachel's high, cut-off cry, he erupted in a frenzy of barks, with each bark hurling his chest forward until his snout struck the door. His teeth were entirely bared, and saliva sprayed from all sides of his mouth.

Turning to the gap at the base of the door, he now shoved his nose under it, snuffling for scents and trying to jam his head through. In between barks of raging frustration, he forced his snout under a little further, scraping and tearing his muzzle and gums, trying to grab at whatever of the panel he could, carving off slivers of wood with savage growls. His mind and body had fused into a primal force of determination and fury.

As Rachel was being clutched and dragged, she was able to slip her mouth from under the canvas and scream once, "Elijah!"

The cry was too much for the dog, and he spun in circles, throwing himself against the door futilely and trying to bite off the handle. He quickly returned to the base of the door, realizing this was his best chance for escape. But he couldn't get a position from underneath to fully grip the panel.

Upstairs at the far end of the house, Perry, wearing Dictaphone earphones and typing up Max's notes, had not heard Elijah's first bark or Manny's shouts. Initially, there had been nothing else to hear. But several seconds later, at a pause in his replay, he heard the more resounding, rapid-fire barking. He tossed off the earphones and ran out.

Coming down the stairs, he saw nothing at first; the men had moved outside his view of the foyer at the door. But he heard Elijah's clawing, growling struggles from the laundry room. He moved fast toward it, past the foyer, and nearly stumbled into Z, the man holding Rachel. In a quick, fluid motion, one of the men struck Perry on the side of the head with a collapsible baton. Perry went sprawling across the floor toward the laundry room.

Dazed and already nauseous from the blow, his head flat on the ground sideways and angled toward the laundry, Perry could see the base of the door, the dog's shoveling snout, its bared teeth gnawing at the wood in between its feral yelps and growls.

Perry heard the front door behind him thrown open and felt the blast of cold air. His arm reached out, trying to pull himself against the tile as his legs worked to push toward the broken door and the dog. His fingers finally curled under the panel. Elijah, at first lunging at the fingers, caught the familiar scent and whined at a higher pitch. He could see the fingers turning white with strain. The panel was cracking and, at last, snapped. Elijah now had his head through and, his shoulders lowered, pushed off more of the panel, and finally, with a splintering crack of wood, he broke through with a wild yelp.

Outside, Z and V were carrying Rachel lengthwise, her upper body covered in canvas now circled with duct tape at her waist. X came running around from the kitchen door side. Z grinned harshly—almost done. Not perfect, but they had the girl.

Inside, Elijah's legs flew on the ice-rink surface of the tile, unable to gain traction. He slipped twice, his rear end spinning out as he twisted toward the front door just closing. He leaped into it, his forelegs slamming and clawing at it. He turned back, uncertain for an instant, then instinctively spun and accelerated toward the kitchen, the scene of the violence. He sprang over Perry. Perry pulled himself up against the foyer wall and limped toward the library and the phone.

Elijah scrambled around the kitchen, quickly sniffing the prone shapes and muffled moans of Sonia and Karl. Manny and Verna were gone. No Rachel here. He raced toward the solarium, past the open door of the library, where Perry clicked the dead receiver.

Elijah charged to the solarium window, jumped up, and scanned the front area visible to him. He could see the corner of the truck and two men lifting Rachel inside. Elijah circled the room in a fit, the glass vibrating to his booming barks.

As Z and V pushed Rachel inside the truck, she thrashed and shouted.

V raised his fist to strike the shape of the head under the canvas. But Z checked him.

"Wait. We get out of here. Then tape her again."

Suddenly they heard a loud crashing sound of broken glass.

V looked at Z. "What was that?"

Z shook his head, pushed V away, and moved to yank down the truck's sliding rear panel.

"Let's go."

V turned toward the passenger side as the back panel clattered down on its pulley. From the edge of his vision, he saw a blot, a swiftly moving dark shape; his primordial senses understood the threat before his vision could interpret it. He backed up, raising his right arm in defense, the adrenaline twisting his panicked face into an anticipatory rictus of pain.

The dog had ten spearing feet of air, its jaws at forty-five degrees and lips entirely drawn back, before it hit the man in the upper left of his chest where breast met armpit. The teeth cut two inches into the flesh beneath the shirt, and the jaws closed and simultaneously dug in, bearing down at two hundred and fifty pounds per square inch. But it was not so much the pressure that did the damage, it was the commitment of the bite, and Elijah's was the bite commitment of his young life.

V tried to scream, but his breath escaped him as he was knocked back against the pillared middle of the truck.

Elijah wasn't growling anymore as his entire energy poured into the bite. It was an innate matter of focus and force. Still, this wasn't his ultimate purpose, and once he'd sawed into the meat of the man and torn sideways, he released his grip and shook out the bloodied fabric from his jaws. The man had turned on his side, curling up as he screamed and tried to crawl under the truck.

Z had heard the attack and guessed what had happened. He should have shot the dog when he had the chance. Pulling out the Parabellum from his waist as he backed up toward the front of the truck, he dropped the keys. Cursing, he looked down among the crushed stone for them.

Elijah reared up to the back, sniffing at the edges of the canvas bundle snagged under the panel's rubber skirt. He pulled with his teeth at the wrapping. Rachel could hear him and feel the tugging.

"Elijah!"

At her voice, Elijah made a high whine and snuffled harder. But remembering the other man, he stepped off quickly into a spring-loaded landing and spun to the front.

Z had just scooped up the keys and stood, but couldn't steady the gun in time. He saw the dog wheeling around from the back, the shape low to the ground and moving faster than he'd expected. Naturally conditioned to a human target, his aim was high; by the time he'd lowered the barrel, the dog was too close and the bullet overshot him by a foot. Z backpedaled and twisted himself around belly-up against the closed door as the dog's jaws landed on his upper thigh. But the bite was not solid, as Elijah had to adjust to the spin at the last second. Z partially turned and brought his gun down to fire into Elijah's head, but Elijah released his grip and lunged upward, seizing the man's forearm. Screaming, Z dropped the handgun. Wrestling to free his arm, he groped for the door handle with his other arm. Elijah yanked on the man, trying to drag him away from the van. But Z managed to open the door and force one leg into the cab, gritting his teeth against the tearing grip on his arm. Half inside, one arm stretched out in the dog's jaws, he could just turn the key with his other hand, start the engine and stretch his leg for his foot to reach the pedals. He slammed the van's automatic shift into 'Drive,' and the van jolted forward a few feet, Elijah moving along with it as he held his grip. But realizing the vehicle was too much for him now, and remembering Rachel still in the rear, Elijah let go. Z hauled himself into the driver's seat and now floored the pedal, the truck's wheels spinning and spewing gravel.

Perry had followed Elijah to the solarium and saw the broken glass. He moved out the door and toward the truck as quickly as he could. He saw the man wounded by Elijah's bite crawling to reach and open the passenger side door, and then Elijah's legs at the rear of the truck. A second later he saw the third man running toward the wounded man, pulling him up and inside the passenger side. Perry reached the back of the truck as Elijah disappeared around it after the driver. A second later, Perry heard the loud crack of the gunshot.

X had been watching this drama unfold from the hedges to the side of the front door. After Elijah's attack on V, he drew back in fear. When the dog moved to the back, he saw his chance. He ran to the truck and dragged V into the passenger side.

Perry, at the rear, hearing Rachel's shouts, yanked up the panel and grabbed her bound figure just as he heard the scream of the driver. Elijah had bought him enough time to wrestle Rachel out, and as her legs hit the ground, the engine roared, gravel sprayed up at them, and the truck heaved off down the driveway.

◊◊◊◊◊◊◊

The phone was out, but Perry had made it to a neighbor's house. In ten minutes, two local police cruisers arrived, and within thirty minutes there were five, along with an ambulance, and within one hour, four state police vehicles, two unmarked. Perry informed the huddled group—Karl, Sonia, and Rachel—that the FBI would be coming.

Sonia and Karl were fine, though shaken up. Karl had a bruise on his neck. Perry's injury seemed the worst, an ugly contusion. A medic attended to him, and there was some official urging that he go to the hospital. He refused. Rachel told him he should, that Max would want him to and that she did too. But still, he just silently shook his head.

There was no word on Manny and Verna. They were not at their residences, the nearby estate where they worked. Alerts had been issued for them.

There was much concern over Rachel, but she also begged off the attention. Nothing had happened to her, she said; she was unharmed. A plainclothes female officer made mention of '*shock*' and '*delayed shock*.' Rachel just shook her head. She'd surely know if she was in shock. She lived at the edge of shock all the time, she thought to herself. She'd been coping with notions of her own mortality most of her life. She processed them through her music and probably would in this case too. But who would understand that? She also sensed that once such a kidnapping attempt was made and failed, the likelihood of another would be next to zero.

Most of all, and strangely, she'd never felt in danger; the entire event felt like some sort of stunt. (This worked for her, at least for a while. In time, she was to realize it was indeed a form of denial.)

Elijah, sat, stood, or lay down at Rachel's side through the various questioning as if nothing had happened. She had the medic examine him for cuts or bruises. They found only some blood around his scraped gums. Most of the police minced their steps around him while casting awed glances. She'd told them what she could, and they'd seen the broken window. One officer said it was a miracle the dog hadn't been sliced up by the glass. But another said no, it was a funny thing; he'd seen people crash through glass and suffer no injury. Something to do with an attitude of commitment, or sometimes even drunkenness, as well as the point and force of the impact.

Rachel realized it was Elijah's determination that had protected him. She told the female officer who was so concerned for her that she'd never doubted Elijah would take care of her. She also knew, however, that it was Perry who'd pulled her out of the truck seconds before it wheeled away; she advised the police that he should be awarded a medal if they did that sort of thing. Rachel told them to be sure to pass this message on to any reporters.

The officials and Karl were all trying to reach Max.

◇◇◇◇◇◇◇◇

Max learned the news from a call from the FBI at his hotel. The caller, Agent Eckhardt, had a quietly dire voice and Max, not prone to flights of fearful imagination, momentarily felt his blood freeze and time stop. Once he understood that Rachel was unhurt and safe, he wanted to hang up and call home. Then the urge seized him to know whether the kidnappers had been caught. No, they hadn't. Eckhardt was not forthcoming with details. Max, who considered himself a supremely rational person, felt assailed by more emotions, mental images, fears, and (entirely new to him) stark paranoia, than ever in his life.

Who had done it? How had they disappeared so fast and completely? Who was behind it? Was the FBI concealing something? Could it have something to do with his report? Those men in the meeting—they looked and sounded the sort capable of anything. That is, cold, faceless apparatchiks with vast and shadowy resources at their bidding. What did he need to do? Should the family move? Where? Where would it be safe? His mind and heart were racing out of control. Rachel—she had to be kept safe. Nothing was more important; nothing else mattered. He'd inflicted her with a life-long incurable disease; he'd never forgive himself for that. Now this?

His work and public profile had exposed her to another kind of disease, of refracted hatred. Whether purely political or anti-Semitic, it was more threatening and almost impossible to treat.

What about Elijah? Where was he during all this? Did Max need to hire a team of dogs? Max couldn't stop his mind from throwing up fears and questions. He needed to get home.

On the plane, he realized the centrifuge of emotions and panic into which he'd fallen.

He must not allow it. He must show control—for Rachel. He could only guess at her emotional state. He had difficulty imagining her losing control, but she was fourteen and physically fragile. His entire life Max never had a problem controlling his emotions. It was a point of pride for him; there was always a logical and rational way through anything. His calmness always calmed others. So it must now.

When he arrived home, he found the scene implausibly normal, aside from a police car in the driveway. The house looked the same. He saw the broken window at the solarium, but Karl had cleaned up the glass and neatly tacked up pieces of cardboard to cover the openings.

Rachel, Perry, and Elijah were in the library. Rachel smiled saucily at him as he went over to hug her. Despite her look, she hugged him back with a quick, hungry clutch which he felt. She laughed at his expression when she stepped back.

"Everything is fine, Max. It was just an adventure."

Sonia and Karl came in and fussed over him. She had tea for him and said she would bring some stew after he settled in.

"I'm calling it 'kidnap stew,'" said Rachel. "She was making it when it all happened."

Karl soberly shook Max's hand, put his arm around Sonia, and gestured to the other three.

"There are your heroes."

Rachel shook her head and pointed to Elijah, then Perry. Perry shrugged and pointed to the dog.

Max said nothing and sat down, rubbing his face.

"It's all right, papa. It's over."

Max looked up. She hadn't called him that since her mother had died. Max felt tears coming but forced them back. He cleared his throat and asked each of them to recite the events.

Twenty minutes later, he'd heard four accounts, all roughly jibing. Sonia included some unique embellishments and quietly hissing curses for Manny and Verna. Max insisted on detailed descriptions of the kidnappers, but they could only tell him what they told the police and FBI: they appeared thin and fit young men; none had spoken, so no accents were detected, and their faces were hidden under ski masks.

A quiet settled. Sonia brought in Max's stew and left. He put it aside, took a breath, and leaned forward, addressing Perry and Rachel.

"We're going to need to do something here."

Rachel stroked Elijah.

"We don't need to do anything, Max. He—" she tapped the dog's head— "took care of it. If he hadn't been put into the laundry room, he would have stopped it right away. So all we need to do is tell everybody, '*Elijah never gets put up, ever.*'"

Max suddenly felt it wiser not to make a case at the moment. He smiled and looked at the dog at Rachel's feet. He'd leaped headlong through a window. Max turned to Perry. He'd faced the kidnappers and pulled Rachel from the truck.

What if it had all been pure luck and a fluke of circumstances? In any case, he couldn't put them in that position again. He would remove himself entirely from public or political activity, even indirectly. He'd already decided.

Perry excused himself to go to bed. Max took his hand, then brought him into an embrace.

Perry seemed abashed but smoothed his hands on Max's shoulder.

"As Rachel said, professor, it's all over. I don't think anybody will try it again."

When Perry left, Rachel placed her hand on Elijah.

"I saw him in my mind the whole time. I knew he'd find a way to reach me. I never doubted it. And you know, they weren't going to hurt me anyway. I could tell by the way they moved me. I wasn't scared, Max. Really, I wasn't."

She stood, and Elijah stood with her.

"I'm going against my religion of superstitions to tell you this," she said, "but I finished the piece, and I'm happy with it. That sounds impossible, I know. I'm ready for Saturday."

Max looked stunned.

"You're not going to perform." It was more a statement of toneless astonishment than a command.

"Yes, I am," she replied. "Yes."

Max tried to gather himself. He couldn't conceive of this after what had happened. He stared at her but saw not the slightest trace of either over-compensating bluff of courage or defiance, just plain resolve.

Max played out his hand with a poker face. "We'll talk about it in the morning."

"Okay," she said with a merry lilt.

❖❖❖❖❖❖❖

The dog had felt troubled when Rachel retreated to the bathroom. His vision and hearing had suddenly sharpened; the world bifurcated into threat and non-threat. He'd always seen something wrong in the body language of Manny and Verna. And the context for the inducement of meat was a final wrongness. He didn't wait for more. Once he was separated from Rachel, he was beyond any form of control. The bite on the man by the truck had been both disturbing and satisfying. Elijah did not wish to bite a human, but this met the call of necessity. Once she was safe, he was satisfied, his purpose, for the moment, was fulfilled.

❖❖❖❖❖❖❖

Max was up early and on the phone with the various agencies. They'd found the linen truck on an isolated stretch near the shore in Swampscott. They had no fingerprints. Nor were fingerprints found on the gun. No trace of Manny or Verna either. It appeared they'd prepared a departure in advance, as they'd withdrawn all funds from their bank. Their employers reported that both had talked about relocating to Canada someday. Max felt acutely frustrated. He needed to know the plot's origins and that the danger was over.

The FBI routed him to another person, a woman agent; she seemed less forthcoming or engaged in the investigation than Eckhardt. And the State Police were equally unhelpful, referring any further questions to the FBI; it was *'their case.'* Max sensed he was caught in a bureaucratic loop of incompetence or maybe worse, stonewalling.

He wanted to hire some guards for the event the following night but knew Rachel would have none of that. If he hired them anyway, it would backfire.

As if reading his mind, she came to him that afternoon. She looked confident and healthy, her voice clear and decisive. He could hear her joke in the making—something about *'a kidnapping a day keeps the doctor away.'*

"Max, this will be a public event. There will be guards and officials there. And I'll have my escort." She looked down at Elijah.

Would they even permit a dog? But Max wasn't worried about that. He now wanted the dog with her—everywhere. And she, they, would make it happen. Seeing her confidence and spirit, he felt more at ease but even more protective.

The evening came. Rachel was dressed in a midnight blue velvet dress Sonia had fabricated and sewn, with a white corsage. Karl, who'd repaired the windows, had the Mercedes 190 idling in the driveway. Rachel invited Perry to come; he'd balked at first, but she and Max insisted. Now the three, along with Elijah, climbed into the Hunter-green saloon.

Rachel sat with her cracked leather music folder on her knees, tapping her fingers, her mouth moving silently to the notes in her head. Elijah was to her right, poking his nose out the slightly open window.

Floodlight beams crisscrossed the grand brick front and arched sections of Symphony Hall, and a line of attendees stretched from the ticket booths down two blocks. Karl dropped them off on Mass Avenue in front. Rachel held Elijah on a short traffic leash in one hand. Max offered to carry the leather folder, but Rachel tucked it under her other arm. People stared at the peculiar sight of the trio and the large German shepherd led by the diminutive girl in the velvet gown.

After a few words at the door with a tuxedoed usher, they were led inside, across the marble foyer, through a curtained arch down a hall to a large staging room adjacent to the theater. Performers mingled with their families and friends. Rachel moved to a sofa with Elijah and sat alone, Max and Perry following.

"You may have to wait here with Elijah while I perform," Rachel said.

"Of course," Max replied. He noticed that she looked pale.

"Is everything all right?"

She nodded. But it wasn't. She was suddenly nervous. While not cold in the car, bundled in her bulging down jacket, she noticed she was shivering in the warm, even overly warm, room. When she closed her jaw, her teeth clicked. She took a deep breath, talking to herself: *this was nothing, just a performance, playing notes she'd practiced beyond any point of uncertainty.* But she couldn't control it. She would have to. In a sense, it seemed entirely physical. But she knew it was more. She looked at Elijah, who was calmly surveying the room as he lay at her feet, his mouth slightly open, tongue out. She noticed that the crowd in the room (mostly self-centered and eccentric musicians, she surmised) weren't paying any attention to Elijah.

As she put her hand on his flank, the change was sudden, as if she were folding herself into a source of deeply soothing warmth. The shivering stopped. He was part of some secret struggle and shared solace between them; she knew it, and knowing it was enough at the moment. He was there when she broke through her musical block, silent and abiding; now he was here, and it was the same. She could be in any new or strange place, and she was still with him, and he with her.

It was true also in some way between her and Max, but different; she couldn't share silent secrets with Max. She had to be another Rachel. But flailing and frustrated and crazy lost-then-found Rachel, child of the music, she had never shared with anybody until Elijah. Before, she hadn't even known she had been withholding herself, or what she was withholding, or that it mattered. And the discovery was accidental.

She stared at the big animal with his erect ears lying so confidently at her feet, so reserved yet so deceptively ready. She tried to soak up his image before the moment she had to go out alone. She closed her eyes.

Max watched her intense and abstract look and at her hand holding the dog as if he were a talisman. He stifled an urge to laugh—at the absurdity and beauty of the moment. She was his daughter, and she came from him and Bluma (*'two oddballs ourselves,'* he mused). But she was her own and inimitable, and she could do anything she wanted to do. He knew she would never doubt what that was, but would still wonder, search and find. The thought that the dog might outlive her or that she would outlive the dog and be forced to live without him pierced his heart.

He reached out to touch her arm. She looked up.

"I'll take care of Elijah while you're out there," he said, smiling. "Don't worry."

◆◆◆◆◆◆◆

Rachel willed her mind to go blank as she waited. Finally, her turn came, and she heard the host (some TV morning show celebrity) begin her introduction. Rachel was the last performer. Max said this was because she was considered the star. She didn't process the notion at all; such things were beyond her control. She knew enough about her physical frailty and the solitude of her studies to realize all of that was music's ephemeral, public trappings.

There was quiet from the Hall. She could feel it. Helena Ordspring now approached, holding her arm out, a nervous fixed smile on her face. Rachel stood, and the dog also stood as if to follow her. But she put her hand out in silent command, and passed the leash to Max. The dog stared intensely at her as Ordspring led her away.

As she neared the stage side entrance, Rachel could hear the clear, amplified voice.

"Ladies and Gentlemen, to conclude our STAR program, it is our pleasure now to hear the premiere of an original work by one of the area's most talented young artists, performing her... '*Sonatina to Elijah*'... Miss Rachel Abedon."

Applause. This was it. She walked out holding her folder. One second she was in the closed comfort of the staging room, and the next, as she moved beyond the massive crimson drapes, the scene, the world, changed with dazzling totality. With one step, she was open to the vast theater—rows of seats filled with blurry heads over formal dress stretching back into a darkened, depthless distance, and stacks of private booths on each side packed with people, all clapping (clapping before she'd played a note).

She walked to the piano as the clapping, one solid buffeting sound on her left, continued. The massive piano squatted alone under the lights. It was a glistening black Steinway grand. Grander than grand. She moved around it, opened her folder, and arranged the composition on the easel as the clapping now ebbed, as if by a slow dialing-down of a master volume control. Amid the isolated coughs and leftover claps, she sat on the bench and looked down at the keys.

Suddenly, from the direction of the green room, she saw a figure emerge and walk to the center of the stage. It was Helena Ordspring. Ordspring took hold of the microphone at the stand and studied Rachel with what Rachel saw as a weirdly proud and unnervingly awkward smile. Ordspring turned to the audience.

"Ladies and Gentlemen, the Symphony needs to offer a special thanks to Miss Abedon for her appearance tonight. As many of you may be aware, she and her family recently experienced a frightening criminal event at their home. Fortunately, all are safe. We at the Symphony believe that Rachel and her family showed great courage in not bowing out of our event. Her father informed me that Rachel never hesitated in her plan to perform tonight. So we all extend our admiration and deep appreciation."

There was a new wave of even higher-pitched applause. Rachel had no idea of this announcement. The effort to empty her mind and focus on the piece fell apart instantly. Her heart started racing as she tried to regain focus as the applause went on. But as she reached for the music, it seemed to recede as if in a nightmare. She stared at the composition sheet; it was a blur of distant, jumbled specks. Where was the beginning? She moved her finger up, trying to locate it, but her eyes flitted here and there to the quickened beat of her heart. She tried to breathe to bring it down but couldn't; she only hyper-ventilated. She looked out to the audience. It was a mass of shapes; worse, expectant, demanding shapes. The applause now ended. Silence. She couldn't take her eyes off the crowd to look at the keys or the music, as if that would commit her to blunder. How long could she do this?

She suddenly began to imagine the kidnappers in the audience, having slipped capture only to follow her here, to make their move as she sat alone on stage. If they could nab her at home, they could nab her here. That had to be their plan. They would storm the stage and steal out the other side, away from the staging room, before any silly people in their silly formal wear could do a thing about it. The speed with which her mind slipped into a paranoid frenzy adrenalized her panic. Thirty seconds now of silence as she stared at the audience. She began to hear murmurs.

The police lady had been right—this was '*delayed shock*.' Rachel wasn't courageous; she was a coward and a fool for not admitting her fear. Of course she'd been terrified. She felt the heavy hands around her mouth now, the rough canvas coming down over her head. Oh, God, she felt sick. Would she vomit on the piano keys? She had to get off the stage —now!

She stood. The bench scraped back on the stage floor, echoing throughout the hall. She straightened herself and turned toward stage left. Every eye was on her, she knew. She just wanted to get off and go home, back to her solarium with Elijah. She started walking toward the side drapes. How many more steps; it was endless. The murmuring grew louder. As she came within ten feet of the eaves, she saw Helena Ordspring, her face a pale mask of bewilderment.

But now she saw another figure, no, two figures, just beyond the stage. One was Max. He was smiling. She saw clear understanding in the smile. But something else—confidence and challenge in the eyes. Elijah was at his side. Now, flying in the face of her comprehension, he held out the leash to her.

Rachel took in the image, and at once, reality returned. This was real. Max knew, and Elijah knew, and she knew. This was how it was meant to be. It was what she had wanted. How many times had she vomited and come back to write more music and play better? Nothing ever happened the way it was planned, except when she worked hard enough for it; there would be a proper end even though there might be all sorts of twists and turns and reversals, but it would be right and proper if she worked hard enough. And she had worked hard enough. And this was right.

Half visible to the audience, she reached behind the line of drapes and took the leash. She turned back and walked across the stage with Elijah.

The murmurs picked up, now mixed with gasps of surprise and bursts of chatter and laughter. Leading Elijah past the now twice-bewildered Ordspring, Rachel moved deliberately back to the piano and sat on the bench. Elijah looked out to the audience, turned around, and put his head on her lap. The audience made a loud, collective sigh, which turned into a new wave of laughter and applause. Elijah walked to the piano's center, stepped under its massive, ebony wedge, circled once, and lay down. Now there were cheers. Rachel did not acknowledge them, but took a deep breath, moved her fingers to the keys, and began.

MAY 1970

ROSALYN BROUSSARD WALKED out of her Cambridge apartment's bathroom wearing cleaning gloves. The living room was bare but for the stacks of boxes. She stood stock still for a moment, staring around her with satisfaction. She closed her eyes and took several long breaths.

It was happening, this move. It had been a year since the attack on Sam and the loss, or theft, of Scarboy. How could she have ever imagined what the loss of a dog would mean to her son or her? And not just how the trauma would change their lives but to what the dog itself had led: meeting Colin Davis, their decision to marry, and of all things, a move back to the South. Would this have come about if not for Scarboy? Rosalyn knew her Bible and understood that travail and providence, pain and deliverance, were intertwined and often beyond reckoning. It was her, or man's, lot to bear either way and to appreciate any gifts of grace.

But she could not force an understanding on Sam. It was about him that she worried, his stoic grief—and grief she was sure it was—and his determined fantasy that Scarboy was grappling with a demon in some dark underworld region and would return to him when the time was right, triumphant.

After the Cuz character had found her, they'd gone to Sam, who was conscious and propped against the alley wall. They'd taken him to the hospital; x-rays showed no serious injuries. He soon recovered from the abrasions without issue. But he'd refused to talk about what happened in any detail. They had to rely on Cuz's account, a rather colorful and lurid tale—that a monstrous figure had jumped them and stolen the dog. Rosalyn wondered if it was the dog's original owner who'd come across them and seized him back (though she'd kept this suspicion to herself).

Sam had quit working for Colin. Sam didn't reject Colin or resent him in their lives; he just refused to take an interest in any other dog or activity with dogs. Whatever he thought, he kept it to himself or inside the black composition book, which he also kept to himself. She'd only found out about his fantasy when she'd sneaked a look at it.

So Rosalyn, Colin, and Sam had become a family. They ate together nearly every night, either at her apartment or his. Rosalyn quit her house-cleaning jobs and started working—or being trained to work—as Colin's assistant. This was another bizarre turnabout: her working around dogs and animals! But she wasn't that surprised to find it as rewarding as it was challenging. Mainly because of her admiration for the way Colin worked. She took care of the accounting and purchases of supplies, some client relationships, and general business and lab organization. With her innate sense of order, frugality, and discipline, the work proved somehow natural to her.

Quitting housecleaning, she'd felt a huge weight lifted and a binding tension in her body fall away. Strangely, as Sam withdrew into himself, she emerged more out of the tough, rigid persona she'd constructed for herself. House cleaning was all she'd known, she was good at it, and she had gritted her teeth, tightened her shoulders, and braced for a lifetime of it.

Colin's trust in her threw all that off.

But was this all because of Scarboy? Or because of the loss of Scarboy? If the latter, as she sometimes thought, she could not help feeling at least a little guilty.

She admitted to herself she'd been attracted to Colin from the start. But she'd been guarded, untrusting. Her first husband had wronged her, and she also had to think of Sam (with what became, she admitted, excessive protectiveness). When she assumed Colin had invited Sam into his life and work '*behind her back*,' she'd been angry. Attraction vied with resentment and raised the stakes. It was a personal challenge for her, and she'd been relieved when she'd suddenly let go to acknowledge her gratitude. Her affection soon deepened. Colin never pushed or shrank before the barriers she put up. He was honest, responsible, and clear-headed (if sometimes flippant about his values and ambitions). That was fine, just a male characteristic—and perhaps that was his way of being guarded. She came to realize he was a rare man. After the Scarboy incident, she knew she was in love when she saw his deep concern for Sam. No girl love, but a complete and confident womanly love of respect and longing to open herself without reserve to whatever end. It had been so long that she'd wondered—or more accurately, had almost stopped wondering—whether she could experience such a thing.

She was determined to be the best assistant he could have, and she studied the textbooks in her spare time and asked endless questions while managing the books with scrupulous thrift. Thankfully, Marie had shown complete support, and no jealousy, as Davis assured the girl that nothing would change for her. Indeed, Marie was to become more involved in treatment and consulting with the clients to support her goal of veterinary school.

During all this, Sam had been her only genuine concern, a worrisome riddle: outwardly keeping up his responsibilities and healthy habits but otherwise reticent. She knew he'd been shattered. How could it not show itself in symptoms? Rosalyn didn't press him. Indeed, she loosened her tight reins on him. She'd discussed with Colin about a psychiatrist. Colin was neutral. He said it would take time, that's all. Sam was a strong kid working through his loss in his way.

Then came the offer and the life-changing decisions.

Colin's mentor at veterinary school, Dr. Boyd Carleton, had formed a business partnership to open several vet clinics in the South. Carleton wanted Colin to manage a new one in Virginia. He'd been aware of Colin's success with his free clinic and considered him one of the most capable and promising vets he'd ever taught. He wanted Colin to meet his partners. He was the future, he said, and just the sort to be one of their managers.

If Colin was excited, and Rosalyn could see he was at least interested, he kept a subdued exterior; he had doubts about leaving the free clinic he'd started. He was a community fixture now. Moreover, he was not in his vocation for the money or to surrender his autonomy to a corporate model. Rosalyn had been prepared for this reaction and knew how to handle it. She said that while it was always hard to let go, opportunities like this needed to be appreciated. Colin knew Carleton and respected him, and vice versa:

this was a show of trust. He was still a vet and would manage the work the way he wanted. She believed that he wasn't in it for the money. But wasn't he really in it to help animals and people? And, if Colin was doing this on a larger scale, why shouldn't he make more money if it was offered? It would also mean more responsibility, but he was more than capable. She told him to be sure the agreement was to his satisfaction and didn't involve any compromise of principles. There was no conflict between helping people and operating according to a sound business model.

Colin was also concerned about the two of them. Hadn't they escaped the South to make a life in Boston? That was true, she replied. But that was before she met him. She wasn't the same person; nothing was the same. She wouldn't be returning to what she'd feared and fled but making a new life, in a new place, with the people she loved.

Sam showed no strong reaction to the move either way; he nodded his head in unemotional agreement with the plans. She wasn't sure if leaving the area where he'd found and lost Scarboy would be painful or a relief. He gave no indication. But after a few days, Colin told her that he'd been asking him about where they were going, showing curious interest.

Informing her housewife employers on Beacon Hill elicited mixed and telling reactions. Two had responded similarly, with tight smiles, clenched teeth, and frosty eyes of repressed resentment. They'd wished her well and offered her small bonuses.

Abigail Fitch's response was dramatically different. She was pained as if losing a bosom friend and ally but also sincere in her warm wishes. At this response, Rosalyn felt obliged to disclose details about her marriage to Colin, his career, and their opportunity. Abigail seemed genuinely delighted. After a slightly awkward hug, Abigail told her to wait for a moment as she retreated into one of the back rooms, then returned with a sealed envelope and a glimmer of tears in her eyes.

When Rosalyn arrived home, she found five hundred dollar bills inside, with a scrawled note—'*Love, the Fitches.*' Rosalyn briefly felt the urge to return the money but thought it might be insulting. Instead, she drafted a letter of thanks and used the money for the moving costs.

As for Sam, his heart sank at first when he learned of the decision to move. He'd visited the crawl space almost every day since Scarboy's disappearance in that violent, surreal blur. He would look in with his flashlight, crawl in, imagine Scarboy's shape, and sometimes for an instant, believe he saw the darkened outline of the dog or heard his growl. Everything else was the same, the dangling insulation, broken pipes, rotting sections of plank, or bits of trash just where he remembered them. He would close his eyes and pray that when he opened them, there would be Scarboy. He knew it wasn't to be, but he couldn't help himself. He wondered where his dog was and prayed he was happy. He couldn't imagine being happy with the man who'd stolen him.

He came to believe, with growing conviction, that Scarboy was no ordinary dog but a mythic animal, one meant to face tremendous and dangerous tests to achieve some glorious destiny. The memory of the final moment didn't fade away to leave a haunted residue like a nightmare but instead transformed into a series of dramatic images gaining continuity and animating detail in his head, like a series of storybook illustrations come to life.

This enabled another conviction—that being torn from Scarboy was part of their shared mythic journey and fate. It was the story of Scarboy, of which he was an essential and ongoing part. That might mean his part was not over, as anything was possible in myths. He unconsciously reiterated and solidified this notion so it felt more real each day.

Soon after he learned of their plan to move, he saw a sign posted at the site of the burned building. The bodega owner at the corner confirmed it: the building and its adjacent building above the crawl space had been purchased and would be demolished. For Sam, it was a sign. He didn't want to live there anymore with the building gone.

His mother was happy, Sam knew. He would not give her cause to worry anymore. That was not heroic. Colin Davis was his friend, and life with him as a stepfather would be as good as it could be wherever they went. Wherever Scarboy was, he was fulfilling his destiny, and Sam sensed that he couldn't try to stand still and hold on in this place anymore; it wasn't befitting the legend he'd been constructing in his mind. He must allow himself to be led where destiny would lead him. He must show Scarboy's courage; it was his best and only chance to ever meet him again, in whatever form. That's how myths worked.

Colin came into the apartment and saw Rosalyn staring out the window. He walked silently up to her and wrapped his arms around her from behind. Her hands came up and held his forearms. He felt her suddenly shake with two quick, quiet sobs. He said nothing; he just waited it out. When she turned, her eyes were wet with tears but at peace.

❖❖❖❖❖❖❖

Rachel's performance and piece won the first prize at the Philharmonic event. She was pleased but hadn't appreciated Ordspring's impromptu announcement and suspected this led to sympathy votes. The suspicion bothered her, but she knew it would motivate her to work harder. Rachel accepted perverse motivations, anything to beat back perilous self-satisfaction.

Rachel admitted she craved winning but found the feeling to fall short in the end. She was more deeply pleased with how she, her father, and Elijah had come together in the moment.

The months passed. After the New Year, Rachel returned to academic studies as part of her novel school-at-home program. It was not difficult for her; it had never been. Elijah was with her always, and they would break up the day with walks. She no longer thought much about the kidnap attempt; she realized that her spasm of fear the night of the performance was unique to the moment, more of a cascading panic attack of multiple causes.

She was worried about Max, though. He couldn't seem to get over it. He was always on the phone about the matter, and although he tried to keep his conversations from her, she picked up on them. It looked like he'd lost some weight. She told him that the '*stupid, clumsy kidnapping event*' wouldn't, couldn't happen again; no one would assume that they weren't taking precautions.

Max was exasperated at the lack of results or answers in the investigation. It seemed no one cared. His calls weren't returned promptly or at all. The

FBI was worthless, he decided (and kidnapping was supposed to be their specialty). He'd talked to four different '*special agents*' and had to reacquaint each with the case. He couldn't help wondering if politics were behind it, behind more than merely the indifference and poor results. This suspicion grew. He had begun to consider hiring a private investigator or agency and had even talked to a few.

He'd been dodging Senator Beadle's communications. Beadle had sent sympathetic word about the home invasion, but Max ignored it.

Max offered Perry a teaching assistant position at BU in his department. And in April, he sent him on a long, overdue, and paid vacation. Perry chose to go home and visit his parents in Vermont. Before Perry set off, Rachel— of all people—organized with Sonia a small party for him. Max thought Perry would cry.

Around this time, he got a call from Senator Cray. Max received the call coolly. As if prepared for this reaction, Cray assured Max that the call was only a courtesy to see how he and Rachel were doing, nothing else. He'd been impressed with Max's integrity and equally so by Rachel '*the prodigy*' (he'd heard about her prize). Max acknowledged his graciousness.

As Cray talked, Max found his tone genuinely warm. Maybe it was his disarming Southern drawl or the sudden realization that Cray's manner was entirely different from Beadle's. He forced himself to remember that Cray was a politician and therefore must have a hidden motive (and Cray had already made known his interest in Max's report). But still, he couldn't help welcoming the chance to confide. Frustrated by his dealings with the authorities, he opened up to Cray, a little at first. Cray listened, with only a few noncommittal but sympathetic responses. Max went on to tell Cray he suspected the FBI was purposely refusing to investigate the matter. Either that, or they were starkly incompetent.

"Is that possible, Senator? Could there be some political pressure behind all this? You have oversight on these people, don't you?"

"Anything is possible, Max," Cray replied cryptically. But instead of elaborating, he switched his tone.

"Max, I've got an idea. Why don't you, your splendid daughter, and her stellar dog come down to my ranch for a little R&R. I've got plenty of space; it's just me and my animals. Not to strum the self-pity fiddle, but I'm a recent widower and could use the company, especially of the edifying sort. I have a feeling you and Rachel would enjoy the getaway. No strings attached, Max. I hope you'll give it some thought."

Max thanked him and said he would discuss it with Rachel.

At first, Max brushed aside the idea of a vacation at a politician's home in Virginia. But as the week went by, he considered that maybe it was what they needed: a real break. So what if Cray was still interested in the report? It was a non-issue. But still, he'd be sure to let him know it before accepting.

At breakfast, he mentioned it to Rachel. She listened thoughtfully—which pleased and surprised him a little. Then she started nodding as if to some musical beat in her head. Her anti-social quirkiness could be hard to predict.

"It would be good for you," she said, looking up at him.

He smiled at her serious face.

"Maybe good for all of us."

"Elijah too. You said he has a ranch?"

"Uh-huh. One hundred acres."

She looked at Elijah at her feet and ruffled his neck. She smiled with sudden decisiveness. "Why shouldn't we? How will we get there?"

"He'll send a plane. He wrote me."

"We're VIPs."

And so, Max wrote Cray and clarified that the report was not open for discussion. Cray sounded as if he already knew (Max thought—my snubbing of Beadle must have made it through the senatorial grapevine) and made light of it.

"Ah, yes, the notorious report. Honestly, Max, one of the reasons I'm fond of you is how you told them all to go to hell."

"Senator, I didn't quite say that. But thank you. I just hope they didn't see it some *casus belli,* their suspicions of which might be ratified by a trip to your ranch."

Cray laughed. "You don't strike me as a man to whom that would matter."

"It doesn't, to me. But I have a daughter."

"Point taken. If you have second thoughts, I understand."

"No, Senator. We're coming."

VENICE BEACH, CA
1970

JEREMY LOOKED OUT from the porch at the Venice Beach pad he and Dev were sharing toward the flat blue-steel line of the ocean in the Southern California haze.

He'd decided—enough of Los Angeles and California altogether.

It had been a year out west, more than a year. It was almost scary how fast the time had gone. Was it a peculiarity of California—i.e., the monotony of the weather which failed to account for time passing? Just a kind of seductive spell in which the impossibly perfect weather colluded? It seemed almost that way. He didn't care for it. It was part of his growing sense of concerted decadence.

Despite the high expectations not long after arriving with Dev in San Francisco, or probably because of them, nothing had seemed 'right' to him. He knew he was a harsh judge of...everything. He hadn't said anything to Dev, who remained excited by the whole scene. Dev found the two a place to crash in Oakland with friends of friends (good old Dev, once again). Dev didn't waste time striking up a friendship with a girl and helping her take inventory of a garage full of used books.

Introduced widely by Dev as a '*poet and writer*,' Jeremy was quickly befriended by an aspiring '*activist*' with alleged contacts in the SDS. But as far as Jeremy could see, '*activism*' amounted mostly to rap sessions in mari-juana-suffused dens with alienated college kids; the boys mumbling radical slogans, the girls looking like zoned-out Rapunzels, their eyes peering glassily between long draping hair flattened to each side. '*Flower power*' didn't seem to jibe with anything he'd read or had come to mythologize along with much of the American youth.

As a writer, Jeremy viewed himself as an eager and curious student of the human condition. So he fought past his first, possibly unfair, impressions to steep himself in the hippie counter-culture. But he soon couldn't escape the sense it was mostly a lot of self-righteous loitering, interrupted by ecstatic calls to nature and a communitarian Utopia, on the one hand, and fulminations against the '*the Man*' on the other. He also found the hippie's condemnation of '*capitalism*' and affluence, in conjunction with their covert obsession with '*bucks*' and '*bread,*' wildly hypocritical, though weirdly beyond their alleged self-awareness. He'd never been around a concentration of people so preoccupied with money.

It all felt shallow, boring, and even somewhat degrading.

However, the thought crossed his mind that even he was an unconscious slave to '*the establishment.*' He wasn't going to dismiss the possibility.

But something else was bothering him, driving his astringency; he just wasn't sure what it was.

He'd hated Boston for its hidebound caste traditions and the physical correlative of its miserable climate and had wanted to get away. So now he was '*away*' and unhappy with the change. This internal conflict and debate soon became his main question to figure out.

He met a few sweet, guileless hippies who seemed to have stepped out of a popular rock or folk ballad. But they also seemed hopelessly out of sync with reality. The leading anti-war activists were mostly graduate students, and he attended some of their protests. He hadn't thought much about the war and mostly agreed with what he heard: war was terrible, and this one was unnecessary. But he paid more attention to the psychological and personality clues of the protestors. These were more important to Jeremy than the flags people waved or slogans they shouted. He felt something else was going on behind it all—a destructive, Dionysian frenzy in the culture. Rallying to the cause meant condoning this mindset, and he couldn't. After a while, he quit paying attention.

Jeremy finally understood that he wasn't a rebel and missed his old life, mostly the work—the routine, the simple, orderly, gratifying craft of house painting. That is, the cleaning, the preparation, the careful application of the colors, and the clean-up. The results were always a fresh and rewarding revelation. People were happy. He was happy. Best of all, the work exercised and satisfied one part of his psyche, clearing the way for the other, which required contemplation. It didn't seem like this new culture appreciated mundane order or valued discipline, in anything. It was all so mellow, groovy, and undefined. What about the *'uptight'* suburban housewives and husbands who wanted clean, nicely painted rooms for their children or their homes and cared about appearances and what the neighbors thought? Were they all materialistic, soulless conscripts of capitalism?

'*My God, relax,*' he told himself.

An insight struck him. In some inverted and ironic way, maybe coming out west was his path to self-discovery after all; that is, rubbing up against the elaborately embroidered but spurious façade of *'spirituality'* and realizing the selfishness behind it was proving to be clarifying therapy. He was indeed *'getting in touch'* with himself, i.e., clearing out the deadwood of naïve illusions and discovering his inner clarity and ruthlessness!

With each day, he cared less about California as anything other than self-education, a preparation for the next thing, whatever that might be.

Dev, who seemed to miss the routine of work himself, came to him one day with the idea of trying out Los Angeles. His girlfriend had introduced him to her brother, who was about to start work as a 'PA' (production assistant) on a TV show at Warner Studios. He said they were always looking for good help, and the work paid well. It could open up doors to bigger production jobs.

So they were off to LA. The brother had friends with a loft over a shop in Venice, where they crashed. Jeremy found it a similarly communal environment, with little privacy or standards of domestic order and hygiene. The weather was better. They both landed positions right away, and Dev took to his well. Jeremy admired Dev's uncomplaining nature and ability to take orders. To Jeremy, it was unsatisfying work, and he didn't like those giving or barking the orders. Many were their age or just a little older, assistants to producers, and too full of themselves.

He attended a few poetry readings in coffee houses and bookstores. The poetry was stridently political or insipidly Utopian. It was all about revolution, one way or another. A quote came suddenly to his mind: '*it is not religion but revolution which is the opium of the people.*' He thought about reciting his work but held back. It wasn't due to nerves, just that he felt like a spy, enjoyed the feeling, and didn't want to 'blow his cover.'

He thought about writing song lyrics to get his mind off it all. He knew almost nothing about music, but did it matter? How much did Jim Morrison know about music? He was a poet.

Jeremy spent a few nights trolling through the nightspots along the beach, imagining he'd run into a musician and experience some sudden artistic synergy and produce a hit song. After a week of hangovers and feeling like an idiot, he quit and morosely sat on the beach most of the day, marinating in mingled self-pity and a general alienation over Los Angeles with its film-world atmosphere of manic fatuousness.

He was willing to play out his disappointing experiences according to Dev's timetable.

But that '*something else*' continued to nag at Jeremy, just beyond his grasp. One day he blew off a PA job and took a long hike up the canyons. Watching a young couple walking their dog, it suddenly hit him.

It was Tory that hit him. It was not only his lingering feelings for her, which he'd been denying but his regret for how he'd behaved and how they'd parted. But it was something else, too, and he hadn't realized it until now: it was the dog. The thought startled him. Yes, it was not only his spontaneous act of violence against it but that he'd allowed the dog to be stolen. The self-recrimination was still there, and he felt even worse for burying the recognition for so long. It didn't matter that it wasn't '*his*' dog; he'd been responsible for it. It was an innocent dog. The whole episode was a personal disgrace. Yes, he'd tried to find the dog, but what of it? He'd lost it through his selfish negligence. And then he left town '*to find himself.*'

After this, he couldn't stop thinking about Tory and what had happened. He knew his thoughts were useless and hopeless, but he still thought. Of course—the vain *'what ifs?'*

Then one afternoon, he received the two life-changing letters, forwarded in a third envelope by his mother.

One was a Selective Service notice instructing him to report for formal induction; his number had come up in the recent draft lottery. He felt an odd absence of shock; he even felt relief. After his rudderless drift over the past year, the letter felt bracing in its bluntness and finality. He had not sought a deferment. If induction was going to happen, it was beyond his control. He'd tossed around with Dev the idea of Canada. But he didn't seriously consider it. Now he would have to. But to his surprise the idea of serving interested him. It didn't mean Vietnam, necessarily. Anyway, now he was forced to decide.

The second letter was more shocking. It was from Tory. As soon as he saw the fine, female cursive on the envelope, he knew. He wondered how she'd learned his address. But he remembered telling her about his mother's home in Malden. She'd figured out the rest. The envelope was small, the flap sealed with a tiny heart-shaped stamp. He opened it carefully, peeling back the flap, sliding out the small, cream note paper, and unfolding it from its quarter fold. It was brief.

'Dear Jeremy: I hope you are well. Where are you? I've wondered. Did you make it to California? I hope you did, but I hope you haven't yet. I'm still at Radcliffe. I think about you and our unusual trip last year. How is our dog? He's your dog now, I guess. I wanted to say I am sorry for my behavior. You didn't deserve it. I feel real sadness and regret about putting that burden on you. I felt so much pressure. I didn't handle it well. Truthfully, I keep thinking about how to break free of this place, this world I'm in, and how you helped me believe it was possible. I hope you don't feel this is inappropriate for me to share. You're a strong and decent person. I need that gentle strength in my life. That's all for now. I hope you get this, and I would love to hear from you. I have your poem and read it often. It is dear to me. You're very talented.

My best, Tory.'

Jeremy held the letter in front of him for fifteen minutes, re-reading it. The two letters at the same time were almost too much. Was this a dream?

Her words forced him to reflect again on his regrets. He'd wanted something from her and fixed himself on it, disregarding her personal crisis. There had been openings for him to show his strength and understanding, especially that night in the hammock and with Drake. He'd tried, perhaps shown a little. But he'd been confused, even scared. Her beauty, and his desire for her, had paralyzed him at times. As a confused girl experiencing some nameless pain, why would she have been attracted to that? Then he'd thought she might be unstable, and he'd become more scared and uncertain. It was such an odd experience. Finally, there was the mortifying scene on her doorstep and his abuse of the dog. He had only been able to see the dog as the representation of her betrayal. What '*betrayal*'? He had no right to feel that. She was a stronger person than she thought. He could help her understand. He could help her. The ineffable sense of attraction to her was still there, and it was deeper than mere lust. Was it love? He didn't know, but he wanted to know.

He'd learned that love wasn't a poem, an image within one, or some momentary feat of strength; though they can be part of it, they can be where it begins. He was not the same person he was then. He didn't have to try to prove this to her; he just had to be with her. She would see it.

He shared the notes with Dev that night on a bench on the Venice Beach boardwalk. Dev seemed even more floored by it all. He hugged Jeremy, then sat back, shaking his head.

"Man, that's all heavy. I don't know what to say. Tell me anything I can do, whatever you want me to do."

Jeremy had made up his mind. He would start the next day for Boston. He had yet to decide about the induction notice but intended to contact Tory anyway. He would have a plan by the time he arrived. He would play it as it came. Whatever the plan, it would involve commitment. It's what he wanted and needed now, one way or another.

If he had to go to war, he would go. Plenty of writers and poets went to war and became better men for the experience. It would be an existential more than a patriotic decision. If he decided to dodge the draft and paint houses in Canada, he would do so only if he knew it was conscientiousness and not cowardice that moved him.

He told Dev that he planned to dogleg off the straight path and into the South again and track part of the route they had taken before, at least from Virginia. He said he'd thought about living in that area once events shook out. The east was done for him, and the west was no longer appealing. The die was cast.

The two best friends since junior high school shared a long silence. Jeremy could see that Dev was torn over whether to join him, so he made it as clear as he could that it wasn't meant to be: Dev was doing well working as a PA, had made many friends and contacts, and maybe had even found his place, for now at least. Jeremy insisted it wasn't the end of anything, just a turn in the road for each. Dev finally nodded, then led him out for their last night.

June 1970

THE COLOR GREEN had made its robust return to the Virginia land-scape. It was Rachel's first impression—the richly green and rolling land, so much softer and open than Massachusetts. The private jet experience and flight from Logan Airport had been fun; it was just the three of them, with a stewardess in the cabin treating them like royalty. Elijah was unfazed by it all. When they'd stepped out and down the stairs to the tarmac, the embrace of humid heat and thick aromas felt new and delightful.

On the drive to the ranch in the sleek Cadillac, chauffeured by '*Johnnie*,' as he introduced himself—a sixtyish black man dressed in what Rachel found to be a whimsical clash of work denim and a formal chauffeur's cap—Rachel powered down the back window for Elijah. The mingled scents of mown fields, cow manure, and varied flora seemed equally entrancing to him.

After about forty-five minutes, they turned between two high and wide white gates into the 'ranch.' It looked vast to her. She could see geometric patterns of picket fences bordering lanes and split rail fences marking off large fields. One hundred yards ahead was a two-story, flat-roofed, col-umned house with an extended porch on both floors. The Southern Beaux Arts style was familiar to Rachel from television shows and movies. It felt simultaneously stately and congenial.

As they stopped on the packed, reddish clay of the front circle, Cray emerged from the front door and briskly hopped down the steps to greet them.

"Greetings, Yankees. You've met Johnnie. Johnnie, to make it official, this is Dr. Max and his daughter Rachel. And that, of course," he pointed at Elijah, now springing out next to Rachel, "is Elijah."

"Yessir, yes, miss. We all met."

Now with the time to take in Elijah fully, he gazed at him admiringly.

They heard a sudden commotion and looked up to see a posse of dogs running toward them from a small barn. The dogs bounded up but pulled short when they saw Elijah. The three medium-sized hound and retriever mixes, along with a dachshund and a medium-sized German shepherd female, minced around him, craning necks to sniff.

Elijah ignored them, walked to the fence, and lifted his leg, leaving yellow streaks on the white post. As he was doing this, the dogs circled to his backside for more sniffing. When he turned, most scattered, but one dropped down before poking his head back. Elijah quickly, efficiently pinned him by the neck. The dog yelped once, and Elijah let him up, then went and stood by Rachel.

Cray laughed. "Well, we can see who's in charge."

He moved among the dogs, and they gathered around him, milling and whining.

"That wasn't the introduction I wanted, and I apologize. I told Billy to keep them in until I could introduce y'all properly."

Johnnie nodded glumly and glanced toward the barn.

"You should let me send that no-count boy packing, Mr. Leland."

Cray cheerfully ignored this and pointed out the dogs for Rachel.

"We've got Beau, Jeffy, Lu Lu, Clematis, and here's my little darling..." he scuffed the German shepherd's neck and picked up her front legs. The dog licked his chin.

"This is Daphne."

Rachel saw a tall, sandy-haired boy, about eighteen or nineteen, saunter down to them from the barn. He was shirtless, his torso thin and muscled in a wiry fashion and his large baggy work pants belted by a dirty cord. His eyes were half-closed, and his physical manner seemed vaguely insolent. She wondered if the others felt that too.

He stood there, his stance slightly bent, waiting.

Cray saw him without turning and said softly, "Take 'em back to the kennels, Billy boy."

Billy gathered up the dogs and, stealing looks at Elijah, walked back toward the barn.

Rachel blinked up into the blazing sun and breathed in deeply.

"That's right," Cray said, "It's the smell of the South. Good for the soul."

At the barn, Billy placed the dogs in the kennels and the leashes on nearby hooks. He picked up his wadded, torn T-shirt and mopped the sweat off his chest and stomach. He walked out and leaned against the barn clapboards, stared toward the gathering, pulled out his Marlboros, and lit one, sucking in deeply. He squinted as the smoke seeped out his nose and mouth. *'No smoking around the barn'* —sure thing. So who were the guests? He didn't care. Just more self-important city people, outsiders, Yankees, probably from up in Washington. The dog looked trained. But that little girl didn't train it. She had no business handling a dog like that.

He tossed the cigarette, ground it into the dirt, stared at it for a moment, then picked up the mashed butt and flicked it away from the barn over the fence. He moved tiredly to his battered '59 blue Ford pickup, climbed in, and turned the key. It screeched for a moment (the starter motor, he told himself), then wheezed and turned over. He slipped it into gear and moved down the driveway, turning right, and peeling out of the drive kicking up gravel dust, a sour grin on his face as he looked in his rear-view mirror.

He made a left down a narrow dirt road, then a right onto the old state highway, with farmer Mason's field on the left bordering the river. After about a half-mile, the great tree stood, a massive and gnarled copper beech tree dating to the Civil War. Scarred and partially split by an epic lightning strike, the gash opening its trunk to its marrow, it stood at the base of a rising outcrop—a thirty-foot section of hard earth that angled up like the roof of an open jaw and married up to a flat shelf of rock. It was an odd site in the field and the scene of a Civil War battle, one if not historically decisive, still bloody and costly. The tree and location had been dubbed *'Bloodied Beech'* and was a local landmark (its name often misidentified by visitors and Yankees as *'Bloody Beach'*). At times driving past it, Billy would imagine the flashing sabers, booms of recoiling canons, and the desperate clinches of men closed in battle, with bodies strewn as heroic rebel soldiers staged a last stand on the rock platform, the tree at their backs. The long field spreading out to the distant horizon always looked picturesque to him, especially framed against the great tree; the contrasting images fired his imagination.

The truck reached a bisection of the field, and Billy made a hard right up a slight rise and disappeared into a darkened, piney thicket.

◇◇◇◇◇◇◇◇

Two miles away, across the field and on the other side of the river, a cleared section of land marked off as the subdivision '*Golden River View*' was taking form. About a dozen foundations had been laid on the fifteen one-third acre plots. Two houses were completed, standing on bald rectangles of packed dirt.

Just short of the subdivision, at the line where the vegetation, ash trees and natural, uneven contours of land ended, was a free-standing old farmhouse, built in 1925 and recently renovated. In addition to the ash trees, two old oaks stood as corner sentinels on the one-half-acre property.

Inside the newly clapboarded house, Rosalyn was finishing a casserole. Her kitchen window offered a view between an opening of the trees to the river and the field beyond, and if she closed her right eye, she wouldn't see the ugly naked plots and squares of concrete with their jutting rebar poles. '*Oh, stop it*,' she told herself, opening her eye. It wasn't so bad. People have to live, and how did this neighborhood compare to the one around their apartment in Cambridge? There was no comparison. '*Count your blessings*,' she told herself.

The move had gone smoothly. The house had been empty and clean, with new appliances, and the moving van had arrived as scheduled. It had been fun arranging the furniture and making plans for painting. Colin had been delayed in Cambridge, handling the transfer of ownership and management of his free clinic to the city. But now he was here, spending most of his days at the new office and clinic. The building was impressive and felt more like a hospital than a vet clinic, with its gleaming new equipment, furnishings, and spacious client lobby. Dr. Carleton had come down to greet them. She could see his fondness for Colin and his trust in him. Two weeks later, they were open. Business was still slow but growing. She thought there might be a reluctance to accept a black veterinarian (though Colin had a white colleague), and perhaps there was some of that, but so far, so good. She believed Colin was too capable and personable not to build trust within the community.

Sam seemed to be adjusting. She knew he clung to his memory of Scarboy, and she had no intention of prying him from it. It was his prerogative. All she could do was maintain a loving, stable household for him. And she would do that. Colin felt the same. She sensed that if Sam wished to confide, it would be first with Colin. She accepted that. Colin was his father now, or stepfather, or at least his father figure. They'd found a school for Sam, a Christian school, and the administrators had been welcoming.

Sam had taken to tramping about the local area on his own. She'd asked Colin about it, and he wasn't worried. There was much open country around the farms, and the river had several tributaries; he said it was an ideal area for a boy to explore.

At that moment, Sam sat on his bed, holding his composition book with his notes and pictures of Scarboy. He stared out the window at the short gravel driveway and the road beyond. It was a world half real and half of his imagination. He would accept what he had to accept, but he would privately hold onto his belief that Scarboy was waiting for him somewhere, in some shape or form. It was not something he could confide to anybody or wanted to; that would risk it dissolving away, his greatest fear. He didn't want to put his thoughts or longings to the test of a sympathetic adult audience with its tender but barren admonishments of reason and reality.

He would keep up his end of practical responsibility in every sense, but his secret world of faith and hope was his own.

◆◆◆◆◆◆◆◆

The following morning, Rachel, outfitted in jeans and a man's white shirt folded up at the elbows, was high-stepping across a rolling green meadow bordered by the S-shaped river.

She stopped, out of breath but invigorated. The morning dew had reached through her sneakers, and she could feel the first squish of wet socks. She didn't mind; the day promised nothing but sun and heat. Ahead of her, she could see the grasses bend as Elijah made quick bounds, paused, looked back, and bounded on. The two reached the split-rail fence at the road. They slipped through the fence, crossed the road, and stepped down into the next, lower section of meadow.

Just as the two fell out of sight from the road, they heard a car approaching. Rachel didn't look back as the battered Buick station wagon swept past the spot. Colin drove with Sam in the passenger seat. Neither glanced in her direction; they had no reason to. They were off to the clinic, something Sam had requested. It was his first visit. Davis glanced over at him and smiled.

An hour later, Rachel and Elijah had made the long and slightly uphill walk back to Cray's ranch. Rachel recalled their modest walks in Marblehead and felt pleased with their accomplishment. Elijah looked happy and tired, his eyes relaxed, his tongue lolling out the side of his mouth.

They moved toward the small barn, saw Billy's pickup, and heard the sound of dogs. Rachel moved inside. She had thought yesterday that Billy had a complicated, unhappy face, and she'd been intrigued.

She heard the dogs in the kennels but didn't see Billy. She spotted a fiddle on a shelf over some stacked hay. She went to it and lifted it, weighing it. It was old but looked well-made. She plucked lightly at a few strings. She was familiar with stringed instruments through her mother and had even started music lessons on a violin. She heard a muffled voice from behind a slatted divider from the kennels. She walked closer and peered through a crack in the slats.

She could see Billy in front of one of the dog kennels. He held out a bone to one of Cray's dogs. As soon as the dog neared it, he yanked it back.

Rachel struck a few notes on the fiddle. He turned quickly and walked around the partition. Seeing Rachel with the fiddle under her chin, and

Elijah sitting next to her, he stared for a moment. Rachel scratched out Beethoven's famous opening four notes, which sounded amusing to her on the fiddle, and looked up brightly.

"Is this yours?" She picked out some threads of a spider web from its center.

"Leave it."

He stepped toward her. A low growl from Elijah stopped him. Rachel gave Elijah a quick touch on his crown, calming him. Billy noticed the easy signals between them. Something was not right about such a little girl being able to do that, he thought. At the same time, he couldn't help feeling envious.

She examined the side of the fiddle, where she saw an etched name.

"Is that your name? Cuthbert?"

"It was my daddy's fiddle." His face was stone.

"It's nice. Could use some tuning."

She improvised a quick, country barn-dance tune, ending with a flourish.

"I don't like country music," he said.

She lowered the fiddle.

He pointed down to Elijah. "You gonna breed that animal?"

Rachel took her time with the question. "I haven't thought about it." She gestured to the back of the barn. "You must like dogs to work with them."

He shrugged. "Take 'em or leave 'em. It's part of the job."

She lifted the fiddle back, thought for a moment, and flung the bow across the fiddle, playing the opening of the Beatles song, '*Help!*'

He snorted, but he half smiled.

"Billy! Where'd you go, boy?"

It was Johnnie's voice from the back of the barn.

Billy backed up, turned, and was gone. Rachel put the fiddle back on the shelf.

◇◇◇◇◇◇◇

June 1970

Sam was widening the range of his explorations around the countryside. He recorded scenic details in his head as he roamed and sketched a rough map in his composition book, accompanied by colorful, blunt commentary in the vein of a footloose wanderer marking memorable scenes of once or future adventure. The fields, dirt lanes, river veins, and ponds became places of possibility and mystery, calling forth from him bold claims of discovery and conquest. The landscape lent itself to such boyhood flights of imagination.

One day he followed a break in the river to a small bowl of a pond, with an active stream flowing in and a small trickling waterfall leading out. The water was clear, with the sandy bottom visible at its four-foot depth. Thick grassy banks led to the water's edge, crowded with orange tiger lilies. To his mixed thrill and disappointment, he saw an old rope tied to a branch of a fat oak tree overhanging the pond. This must mean it was a known, if not a popular, swimming hole and not his unique discovery. At the same time, he was excited to try the rope swing. The pond would indeed go on his map.

◊ ◊ ◊ ◊ ◊ ◊ ◊ ◊

Rachel, Max, and Elijah returned from a long walk. They'd gone farther this time at Rachel's urging. She was becoming a more ambitious trekker, not just for herself (her stamina was growing daily), but for Elijah. He delighted in the exploration and always returned with a look of euphoric exhaustion.

Max had been concerned she was pushing herself, but he'd never seen her looking so healthy. He'd spoken with Dr. Minkum about her test results before they'd left; Minkum was pleased and a little astonished by them, guardedly, of course—weren't doctors always guarded?

She and Elijah came to the pond from the opposite side. Elijah trotted down the bank and circled the pond, stirring some sunning frogs to leap and plunk into the shallows. Enchanted at first sight, Rachel walked down and tested the water. It was chill but not icy. Was it swimmable? She vowed to return and try it.

Later that day, she and Elijah took another walk around the fence lines with Cray, accompanied by Daphne. Daphne circled and playfully poked at Elijah. Elijah, who had previously ignored her, poked back, occasionally pinning her down with mild growls before letting her up, which only excited her more. Cray puffed at his cigar, crinkling his eyes as he looked down at the sparring dogs.

"Looks like your loner boy has a girlfriend."

She stared at Elijah and placed her hand on him. "Yes. He's a loner. He has a past to explain why."

Cray nodded, smiling.

Rachel looked into his eyes. "Your wife was named Daphne?"

Cray eyed her acutely. "And that little girl..." he gestured with his cigar at the dog... "was born a week after the funeral. The tiniest one, tough as nails and sweet as sugar. Just like my wife."

Elijah pushed his way into their twosome. Releasing a puff of smoke, Cray spoke softly. "And we have Elijah."

She looked up at him, shrugging, her eyes remote.

"I may not have the right to name him. He had a life and a name before me. I feel sometimes he will outlast me. That does not sadden me."

Her arms were looped around each dog. Cray studied her face.

"My dear, that is entirely too melancholy from a lovely girl on a lovely day. Let's beat a retreat for home and a nice rest with your father on the porch."

Cray decided to overlook Rachel's spell of despond. He said to himself that she was an artist and subject to moods and, given her age, to bouts of adolescent melodrama. She was also clearly a brilliant talent. She had on occasion sat down at the old Wurlitzer upright in their drawing room, on which his wife had played and taught children; he'd never seen or heard anything like Rachel's virtuosity. One night she'd played, from memory, Cray's favorites—six of Chopin's preludes.

That night he and Max sat on the porch after dinner, observing Rachel and Elijah walking down the driveway fence line.

Neither had raised the issue of the report. Max felt by now that Cray fully understood and respected his censure of the subject and that the invitation was not a ploy to wangle access to the report. But for Max, it wasn't settled. He still wasn't sure what to do with it—it was undoubtedly something powerful people wanted or wanted to suppress. And he couldn't help but think it was somehow associated with the kidnap attempt. The notion of leveraging Cray's influence had occurred to him. As if sensing his friend's mental agitation, Cray broke the soft silence of the evening.

"Max, would you like to know what I'd do?"

It was that blunt and simple. Max waited a moment before looking up at the eyes behind the cigar smoke.

"I would."

"Exactly what you told me you were going to do. Put an end to any involvement in Washington. Make this publicly clear to all if you haven't already. Go back to your life. This isn't for you." He paused. "But as to the report, this is what I suggest."

Max waited in suspense as Cray looked over the field, tilted his head, and puffed on the cigar. The last evening light was fading, and Cray had yet to turn on the outside lamps. Max watched the glow of the cigar.

"You know, Max, I'm done myself. Thirty-five years in the senate for this old whore is enough. I decided that this week." He made a subtle nod to Max.

"I grew up here, in this county. I'm from a good, not particularly wealthy, family. I did well in tobacco, invested well, and, against my better judgment, made use of my influence to compound those investments. Yup, I did, I admit. I stood up for the people of my state as best I knew how. My wife was my conscience, a far more refined one than mine, and I never told her the worst of what I did, which wasn't as bad as it would have been without her. My love and respect for her kept me in line, for the most part. The one thing I despised, we both despised, was Jim Crow, and I'm honest enough to admit my party's role in it. After we passed those laws, I should have gotten out. But then this damn war came along. Anyway, I'm saying this to back you up. I'm gettin' out of this filthy business too."

He took a long, deep breath.

"Max, give me the report. I'll seal it in a safe deposit box. I'll tell all the powers that be that I have it, and if your name ever comes up again or anything happens to a hair on you or your daughter's head, I'll take the damn report and... well, I'll leave it to their imaginations."

Max listened and, at that moment, decided to agree. This was all bigger than he was. For better or worse, he cared about Rachel more than he cared about anything in this world, and he was willing to accept the verdict of bailing out. But he had one more thought.

"Senator, thank you. I will break my pledge to the president as he's broken his to me. I tried twice to fulfill my promise, and twice my plans were blocked or undermined. The report is yours to do with what you will."

Cray nodded, and the two returned to gaze out at the fading magenta blur of the sunset.

◆◆◆◆◆◆◆◆

Later that night, in the stillness of the old house, Rachel lay in bed, over the covers, feeling the faint brush of air on her skin from the whispering overhead fan. It wasn't the heat keeping her awake. She looked down at Elijah, sleeping on the pine floor. Some fuzzy, unsettling feeling had been flitting at the edge of her consciousness the last few days. She pressed in on it now, trying to identify its first appearance, its associations of time and circumstance. Mood shifts, sudden swells and troughs of emotion, fleeting forebodings, and fantastic projections of anxiety were not new to her, to her everyday existence. It was part of living with herself; she had come to understand and accept the cost of her unilateral life, living solely for music. There had always been Max, of course, but there was nothing or nobody else—until Elijah. She had no close friends. She didn't mind this fact. She knew she couldn't keep up with the emotional demands and didn't wish to be cruel in her parsimony. She'd struck up a dear and damning love with music, with the musicians and composers in her practice, and it was a troubled, enriching and consuming relationship. It had been enough, all she could handle.

This was about Elijah, she thought. She cared too much about him—perhaps that was the problem. But she also cared about Max, also probably too much, and this fact hadn't ever stirred currents of unease. Max was entirely hers; she was his, and they were bound in an original, total and fateful way beyond her control. Instead, with Elijah, she felt there was an incompleteness; he also belonged to another place, time, and person or people. She'd felt this from the beginning, but only lately had the feelings become intrusive, inciting odd anxiety, and feelings of covetousness and jealousy—foreign states of mind for her. And for no objective reason she could define. But she knew she did not entirely occupy an objective world or defer to objectivity. At the same time, she felt a pressure to accept that Elijah was not original to her, but was a blessing possibly as transitory as it was dear. Her sickness and the uncertainty it brought her had inculcated a sense that an end, the end, was a real thing, not something reserved for other people or some point in the infinite distance.

She suddenly climbed off the bed with the blanket and pillow, spread it next to Elijah, and lay next to him.

The dog didn't concern himself with why or where he was going with the girl and her father; they were his people, she was his human, and he went where she went. He remembered the older man and adapted to the house. The other dogs were no issue once he'd established the hierarchy. He had no hesitation about doing so, just as he had no interest in or felt no need for conflict. He knew there would never be a dog who would dominate him, but it was important to make clear what conduct was acceptable or not. The hiking and running made him feel stretched out, and looser, and rested his mind.

◆◆◆◆◆◆◆

Sam broke through the tall grass on the embankment overlooking his pond. The sun was high and hot, and he had on his shorts, prepared for a swim. He moved down the bank, but then paused. He'd heard soughing sounds from the other side—someone walking through the grass. He waited.

"I know you're there," Sam said loudly.

Rachel emerged alone; she paused at the weedy crest and stared at him. "Hello," she said.

Sam walked around the curved bank until he was a few feet away. He looked her up and down.

"Can you swim?"

Rachel snapped the bathing suit strap under her shirt. Sam, satisfied, turned back to the pond.

They said no more, and Rachel peeled off the overalls to her one-piece suit. Her legs were pale as candlesticks. She put her foot in the water and shivered.

"It's not that bad," Sam said as he stepped in and waded up to his waist. He held his arms up. It felt cold, all right, but he wasn't going to show it. Rachel walked in up to her knees. Sam suddenly dropped down underwater, then leaped up.

"There are no snakes."

Rachel nodded evenly.

"Only snapping turtles," he said.

She stepped back for a moment, and he grinned. She joined in the joke with a smile.

"I think that's enough for me anyway," she said, moving back to the bank, toweling her legs and slipping her overalls back on. She looked at the rope swing.

"Did you put that there?"

Sam shook his head. He moved to it and pulled himself up, swinging for a second before dropping back to the water. Rachel noticed he hadn't brought a towel and offered hers to him. He waded to her side and took it.

"Thanks."

He stepped fully out, dried off, and put his shirt on.

Rachel sat down. "I was here yesterday with my dog." She gestured with an arm swipe behind her. "We're staying with a friend."

Sam looked where she gestured.

"We live back there," he said, gesturing in the opposite direction. "Why didn't you bring your dog this time?"

"He was sleeping. It's boiling hot anyway. He's been getting a lot of exercise. My name's Rachel."

"I'm Sam." He looked gravely at her. "It was never too hot for my dog. He'd been to Hell."

Rachel took this in with equal graveness. "That's very interesting. Is there more to tell?"

Sam, not expecting the reaction, thought for a moment.

"He fought the Devil. Their fight shook the ground and opened a crack, and he crawled out. I found him, just like I was meant to." He studied her expression. "I don't care if you believe me or not," he said, with a subdued tone, short of defiance.

"I didn't say I didn't. I'd like to meet your dog."

"I have drawings," Sam said, his eyes staring ahead.

"Oh. Well, I'd like to see them sometime."

Sam nodded. He'd not felt this free to talk about Scarboy before. But he wasn't sure what to say or how to say it, which brought a new, livelier pressure.

"Scarboy." It was all he could think to say at the moment.

"That was his name?"

"Who he was," Sam said. "And always will be."

They sat for a few minutes in silence.

Thirty minutes later, as Sam and Rachel walked out of the bowl of the pond and struck to the dirt lane beside the oak tree, Billy's battered blue pickup streamed down the old state road. Billy drove, the front seat crammed with his cohort, Jason, Seth and Toby. The fair-haired brothers Seth and Toby worked at the lumber yard in town. Jason, darker and a little older at twenty-three, and recently dishonorably discharged from the Army, lived in an apartment at the edge of '*darky town.*'

Jason's father owned a junkyard, and the property was Jason's inheritance; however, he'd failed to maintain its business license, and, now forgotten as a local resource, it had become a '*drinking and plinking*' hangout for the group. It also served as a rough kennel for Jason's collection of mastiff mixes—three of which were now secured by cross-tied chains in the truck bed. (Jason entertained dreams of competing the heavily-muscled, square-headed beasts as fighting dogs, something he'd attempted to interest Billy in, but nothing yet had come of it.) Jason bounced between part-time jobs, most recently working on a landscaping crew for the new veterinary clinic.

Jason nudged Billy and pointed as they passed the intersection with the lane leading to the swimming hole. They all stared at the small figures of Sam and Rachel walking away.

Billy squinted and leaned back with a sour look.

"It's the rich kid from Boston staying at Cray's house. The one with the dog."

"Who's the colored boy?" Jason asked.

Billy shook his head.

"Want to head down, give 'em a scare?"

"Nah," Billy said. "Not now."

◆◆◆◆◆◆◆◆

Max thought it might be time for their *'vacation'* to wrap up. He realized that Rachel had never seemed healthier or more relaxed, so he'd been forestalling the decision. It had been an open-ended invitation, but Max was sensitive to becoming an imposition. Still, Cray appeared to delight in the companionship and conversations on the porch or while ambling about the property. Max had been given an indefinite leave from his work at BU, so there was no pressure to return. He inquired about Cray's schedule, offering the Senator an out, but Cray waved it off.

"Schedule? To be right here right now with you all."

Late that afternoon, Cray and Max walked the fence line around one of the alfalfa fields (Cray leased some of his lands to farmers); Rachel and Elijah were ahead, slipping through the fence posts. Rachel had asked about Daphne, and Cray told her she was penned up at the moment, as he suspected she might be *'coming into season;'* Rachel understood. Cray was waiting for Johnnie's thoughts on the matter, but this was his day off. Billy was up at the barn, or should be, Cray added dryly.

Elijah and Daphne had become quite attached, Rachel noticed. It wasn't simply that Elijah was rebuffing her less; though that was something in itself,

Rachel and Max joked to each other, as Elijah did not easily make friends—human or canine.

Suddenly, they heard a rush of light, galloping steps, and Daphne was racing among them excitedly, greeting all in turn.

"Dammit," Cray said, turning and scanning toward the barn. "Damn, Billy."

Daphne pushed at Elijah, who half-heartedly fended her off, one paw boxing at her withers or resting on it. The sight amused Rachel. Soon the dogs were taken up with new scents in the high grass. Daphne hopped through the posts and started foraging. Elijah watched, not wishing to negotiate his larger bulk through the rails.

Suddenly Daphne yelped and sprang back, striking a post, and scraping through the gap. She stood on the lane; her front leg curled and lifted as she whined. Almost simultaneously, Elijah leaped between the rails and speared his head into the high grass. There was a ferocious thrashing; the grass stalks swished and fell in a circle around the violent motion. His head suddenly shot up, the four-foot length of the brown snake in his jaws as he whipped it about, terrier-like. He stopped as quickly as he'd started, and the snake drooped limply from his closed mouth. He repeated the shake, just for a few seconds, to be sure, then stepped back through the fence, daintily this time, and dropped the rope of lifeless snake on the lane. Rachel drew back, but Cray and Max stepped in, Cray closely examining the hourglass markings along its side.

Cray went to Daphne to check her leg as Max stared at the fat snake with its thick wedge-shaped head.

Cray stood and looked toward the house.

"Billy?!" He waited a moment and shouted the name again. There was nothing. He turned to Max.

"Billy is supposed to be here. We'll need a vehicle to get to the vet. That's a copperhead."

Max ran up to the front circle, glanced at the barn, and saw Billy's truck. He called once without a response. He found the keys where Cray told him to look and drove the Cadillac back down.

Within ten minutes, they were packed into the large car, Max driving to Cray's directions. Cray sat in the front seat, holding Daphne. Rachel and Elijah were in the rear, leaning over and looking down. Daphne's paw was crooked and hanging in the space between Cray's lap; she was quietly panting, her breathing slightly raspy. Her half-closed eyes had a watery, dazed look.

They reached the intersection of the state highway and the outskirts of the commercial area, where on the left, they saw a freshly white adobe-style building on a newly developed lot. A large red sign announced '*Virginia PetCare.*' The building was surrounded by elaborately landscaped grounds, thick plantings in perimeter rows, and islands of brick-red bark chips.

"Haven't been here yet. Heard about it," Cray said. "Doc Cash would be another thirty minutes."

Max wheeled the car into the vacant parking area, and they piled out, Cray carrying Daphne. Rachel watched as Elijah followed Cray, his head arched up and sniffing at Daphne.

They approached the front desk. Aside from the lone female receptionist, the lobby was empty and smelled of fresh paint. Seeing Senator Cray cradling the dog, the receptionist quickly stepped out.

"Copperhead bite," Cray said.

"Yes, sir," said the short, bobbed-hair girl ('*Brenda*' on her nametag), and without another word, ushered them back into a more brightly lit examination room with a gleaming chrome exam platform. She patted it for Cray to place Daphne.

"Dr. Millard is on duty. He's in the back; I'll get him."

It all seemed very efficient, Rachel thought.

Cray looked around. "If they're as good as they smell, look and sound, we came to the right place."

The middle-aged Dr. Millard came in with a professional smile and, without introduction, bent straightaway to Daphne. Brenda stood behind him and made nervous glances at Cray. She knew he was the Senator, Rachel guessed; she wanted the doctor to acknowledge him. The doctor looked up at the men.

"How long ago was the bite? And you're sure it was a copperhead?" Millard did not have a Southern accent.

"A half an hour," Cray said. "And yes, sir, I know my Virginia herpetology. I have personal experience with Mr. Copperhead."

The doctor smiled. "I'm to understand that you're our distinguished Senator. Pleased to meet you. I'm Richard Millard."

Rachel placed his accent as mid-western. He held Daphne's paw. Just then, they heard a low growl from between her and Cray. Millard stepped back and peered around the platform at Elijah. He looked at the assistant.

"Is this a concerned relative?"

Rachel tapped Elijah and made a shushing motion.

Millard stepped back and took a deep breath.

"Well, judging from the elapsed time and mild swelling, it doesn't look too serious. She's a larger dog, and the bite was in the leg, so that's good. We'll wrap her leg and put her on an IV with some antihistamine and antibiotic. We'll keep her overnight to monitor. How does that sound?"

Cray agreed and thanked Millard. He turned to Max and told him he was getting old and worried like a woman because they did nothing at all in the early days for copperhead bites. Max put his hand on Cray's shoulder. Rachel knew that it was all about what Daphne meant to him.

As they started to move out of the waiting room, and Brenda prepared to lift Daphne, Elijah resisted Rachel with a quick but firm pull. He looked at her, then up to Daphne, holding his ground. Rachel peered through the open door to the back area, which appeared stark and clinical.

"Where will Daphne be, back there?"

"Oh, in a nice clean kennel with a bed," Brenda said. She waited as Rachel looked at Max.

"Can Elijah stay with her?" Rachel asked.

She wasn't happy to leave Elijah. But she knew Elijah's attachment; she could feel his need, and thought it would help Daphne in what Rachel sensed would be a cold, isolated setting away from home. Elijah could handle it. It would be a comfort to Daphne and, thereby, to Cray. She felt it was her obligation. (That it was against her will, i.e., her selfish and exclusive claim to Elijah, seemed to affirm the decision). Elijah was her gift, and such a gift demanded to be shared.

Brenda had gone back to check with the doctor. Max, however, wasn't comfortable leaving Elijah, and Cray said that it wasn't necessary. Rachel looked at Elijah. She loosened her hold on him, and he stepped toward Daphne. Rachel said nothing, just retreated from the room.

Brenda returned.

"The doctor says that's fine. We'll need you to sign some paperwork. We can put him in the adjoining kennel. There aren't any other dogs back there, so it will be quiet tonight. We have a night assistant who checks on the dogs." She smiled. "That will be me tonight."

◆◆◆◆◆◆◆◆

In his home office, Cray sat back wearily in his father's old cane-back oak chair. They'd returned from the vets with no one saying much. He felt bad about little Rachel, but she hadn't relented; he didn't want to make more of a scene. He knew she was doing it for him and Daphne. She'd gone to the car. He and Max had stayed until the dogs settled in their clean, new kennels, Elijah dropping against the mesh as if satisfied and Daphne up against his back.

Now Cray had to deal with Billy. He'd put it off long enough. He pulled out his checkbook and pen and waited.

Billy knocked once and entered. He walked boldly to the desk and stood, silent. Cray folded his hands on the desk.

"You understand why I must let you go, Billy?"

The young man said nothing. His untidy, brown hair fell over his right eye, leaving only the half-closed left to stare back with silent animus.

"I've been clear about the standards here," Cray continued. "You've shown consistent indifference to them. The responsibilities are not overwhelming; I know you can live up to them. I know you're better than this. But you choose not to be. That's your choice. I can accept mistakes when they're honest, when there's a willingness to listen and improve."

He put opened his palms in a gesture of surrender.

"For now, there's nothing more for me to do. You allowed Daphne to escape today. She's at the hospital now. And I understand from Johnnie that you persist in smoking in the barn."

"You '*understand*'?" Billy's tone was sarcastic.

Cray ignored the response. He opened the checkbook, wrote a check, carefully peeled it from the book, and offered it to Billy. Billy kept his hands at his side. Cray laid the check at the edge of the desk, a foot from him.

Billy picked up the check, held it loosely as he examined it, and then let his arm drop again.

Cray kept his eyes locked on Billy. "I know you blame me for what happened to your father. I've tried to explain and offer amends beyond any measure of debt or decency. This is something you will have to learn to live with, Billy. When you grow up and feel ready, I hope you'll come back, and we can discuss your—"

"'*Grow up*'?!" Billy's eyes opened wide before returning to a hard squint. He pushed his hair back, tucking it behind his ear and glaring at Cray. The hair fell back again.

"You don't own this county. Lot of us don't like these changes goin' on so that you can be a big man in Washington takin' the colored side against your people. You loved it when you had a chance to sic your sheriff against my daddy."

Cray laid his hands back on the desk and stared back.

"I can't explain it any more than I have, son—"

"I'm not your son."

Cray took a breath. "I'm sorry about your grievance. I've told you what happened. Your father made choices in what he did, and I made mine. There must be law and accountability."

"Yeah, accountability," Billy said, smiling darkly.

"I suggest you read again the letter I gave you when all that happened. It was the truth."

Billy shifted, and his eyes swept the room—the Oriental rugs, the oak paneling up to the high ceiling and its carved molding, the smoothly-ticking brass fan, the full library shelves behind Cray. He looked down at his muddied khakis and stained T-shirt, and back at Cray.

"I shouldn't be here." His voice was low, of mixed anger, shame and sadness.

Cray let the words sit for a moment.

"You can belong anywhere you'd like to belong, Billy. I'd like you to work for me again. I just need—"

Billy shook his head back and forth. He lifted the check again, studied it. It was more than he made in a month. He didn't understand. All he could come up with was patronization. He must maintain solidarity to memory. He put the check back on the desk and walked out.

It was a quiet dinner, and Rachel went to bed early. She'd wanted to play some piano and knew it would make the adults feel better, but she couldn't sit at the keys without Elijah in sight. She soon admonished herself for being silly and selfish, but it wasn't enough to change her mind. She just wanted the night to be over.

She lay awake listening to the chirring insects. One moment they lulled her, the next they seemed intent on keeping her awake. Always the infernal contradictions! But tomorrow, all would be back to normal.

◆◆◆◆◆◆◆◆

Colin Davis arrived at the clinic early, Rosalyn with him. Millard had informed him the night before of the copperhead bite on the Senator's dog. Davis agreed with the treatment protocol. Venomous snake bites were not something Davis had dealt with, but he'd been studying. So had Millard, as Colin instructed. As Rosalyn had said the night before, a Senator as a regular client would be a welcome boost to the business.

He saw Brenda's car and parked the old Buick wagon next to it. It was their first overnight case. They entered an empty lobby. Colin saw the door to the back open and heard noises. Brenda walked out. Seeing her pale, stricken face, he didn't wait for an explanation and walked past her through the door, Rosalyn following. The long line of kennels was empty, two with wide open doors, and the back door to the outside was a few inches ajar, the knob and lock mechanism gouged off. A small mess of equipment and tin bowls from the built-in counters littered the floor.

A struggle had taken place; the dogs were gone. Davis went to the far outside door, pushed it open, and looked out. There was only the sloping open section of landscaping leading to the side access road.

He turned back to Brenda. The cute, apple-faced, and reliably cheery Southern girl looked devastated. Colin and Rosalyn led her into his office, sat her down, offered her some of his McDonald's coffee—which she refused with a trembling hand—and asked her to tell him what happened.

"I don't know," she said weakly. She'd made nightly checks at eleven p.m. and three a.m., and everything was fine. The male dog had merely looked up when she came in. Daphne was resting comfortably. Then she'd arrived one-half an hour ago to discover the crime scene and missing dogs. "I don't know," she repeated numbly.

Rosalyn stayed with Brenda while Davis returned to examine the back door. The simple doorknob lock had been pried off. It appeared nothing else had been taken—no surgical instruments, drugs, or other equipment—just the dogs. Davis thought for a moment. He had to call the police. Then the Senator. He felt a spasm of sick fear twist his gut. He fought it off. There was nothing else to do. It should never have happened, and he was responsible. Nothing else mattered now but the fact of the loss, responsibility for it, and recovery of the dogs.

He had never even thought of security or dog theft before. He hadn't worried about it even in Cambridge. Now he was paying for his inattention, or others were. He should have considered security when he'd learned it was the Senator's dog. It would never happen again, but that was useless now. He needed to make phone calls.

Cray took the call. Davis's voice was matter-of-fact, and he asked the Senator if he would prefer to call the police or sheriff himself, as he might have more influence. He also volunteered to help on a search or in any way he could. Cray listened without saying a word. Cray could hear from the vet's voice that he was black (which he knew about) and guessed Davis thought this would reflect poorly on him as newly arrived and operating a business based on trust. Cray told him he would handle the call but would refer Sheriff Turnbull to Davis. He also agreed to meet immediately at the vet's office. Cray hung up. His concern now was informing Rachel.

Cray was sure that Billy was involved but decided to keep this suspicion to himself for the moment. He walked into the foyer and saw Max sipping coffee on the porch. Down the hall, through the door to the parlor with the piano, he could see Rachel sitting at the piano but not playing. There was a still-life feeling to the scene—tranquility about to be shattered.

Cray gestured to Max, and they retired to his office; he told Max the same way Davis had informed him. Max listened as his face etched itself into grimness. He walked out without saying a word. Cray sighed. And now to call Bobby Turnbull.

Max moved down the hall. About twenty feet away, Rachel turned and stared at him. How was it, he thought later, that hers was not a look of greeting but foreknowledge? His mouth went suddenly dry, and he rested his hand on the smooth top of the piano. Max didn't want to say the words. But she spoke first.

"I knew it," she said quietly. And one finger struck a lower note softly. She tapped the note again and again, repeating, "I knew it," lower each time until it was a hush. Finally, her head sunk forward for a moment, then pulled back upright. Her eyes returned to hold on to Max, now with a pure daughterly appeal.

"What do we do?"

Johnnie drove them in his old Land Rover to the clinic. Max and Cray had resolved to take the most positive outlook. It was a small town, and this must have been an act against either the Senator or the black vet to damage his reputation before he got started. They doubted the dogs had been taken far. That they would have been killed or would be killed seemed unlikely: that could have been accomplished at the clinic.

Sheriff Turnbull's car was in the parking lot. Davis greeted them and led them to the back area, where they met Turnbull. In his mid-fifties, a former linebacker in Division II college football now gone a bit soft in the stomach, though still solid in the upper regions, with cheeks veined and reddish from the standard Southern diet plus three beers an evening, Bobby Turnbull's eyes were still keen and his constabulary sensibility sharp and fair. He prided himself on his competence and honesty, as Cray and the community did.

Through the open door of Davis's office, Rachel saw a thin black woman standing, her arms folded, one hand under her chin, worryingly. It must be his wife, Rachel thought.

Cray, Max, Davis, and Turnbull stood looking at the scene. Turnbull seemed respectful of the vet and asked the basic questions: Who had access? Did Davis have any enemies? Receive any threats? Or had anybody suspicious been hanging about? Did he have any ideas at all about motive or opportunity? Max didn't sense that Turnbull was playing up to Cray, but only that he sounded capable and serious.

As an afterthought, Davis mentioned a landscaping crew working outside, but they'd completed work about a week before. He had no reason to suspect any of them. He gave Turnbull the name of the company. There was silence.

Rachel noticed the black woman had stepped into the room. She moved beside Davis. Davis introduced her, "Rosalyn, my wife."

"Is Sam your son?" Rachel asked suddenly.

Rosalyn turned quickly to her. "You know him?"

Rachel nodded. "We just met."

It broke the mood for the better.

"Well," Turnbull said, "we'll start asking questions. And we'll put the word out." He pulled the Senator aside. "What about that Cuthbert boy working for you? You've had trouble with him in the past, I know."

Cray gave a considered nod. "Yes, I'd go talk to him, Bobby." Cray now handed the Sheriff a small piece of paper. "There's a reward. For a safe return. No questions asked."

Turnbull unfolded it, and his hard eyes widened before he could control them.

"Yes, sir. We'll let that be known."

Davis looked at Max, Cray, and Rachel, in turn. "I will join in the search and do everything I can. This is my responsibility."

Rosalyn moved closer to him. "I will too. I think Sam will be happy to as well. We'll find your dogs."

Cray nodded. "We appreciate that."

Rachel moved around them out the back door and stood on the stoop. She stared out at the sun-washed yard. The world looked and felt vast and bleak. Where was Elijah? She tried to imagine the event in the darkness, the figures slipping in. How many? How had they managed to snare Elijah? What was the point? She closed her eyes tightly to clear her mind. It didn't matter. It was beyond her understanding, and she didn't care to know. Only that he was gone and somewhere out there. And Dr. Davis wasn't responsible. She was. It was her idea for Elijah to stay there. She'd felt some force of fate and surrendered her leadership role. Elijah depended on her to look out for him, to see past his impulses of the moment. Was it that she had so much respect for him and did it for him? Or a stupid, misguided need to refute her weakness, to prove she didn't need him for one night? It had been so easy in one sense, almost a reflex, i.e., from being sick for so long and taken care of by others. She couldn't face the fact she was now taking care of him and accept what this required to be the leader. She had felt paralyzed to act on her instincts, or maybe sick of all the fears and phantoms and eager to stomp on them. Now, one had come true. And Elijah had paid. And Daphne.

But what if she'd taken Elijah home? Would Daphne have been stolen anyway? Did they want him, her, or both of them? At least now, maybe Daphne had Elijah to look after her.

She was suddenly angry at those who did this. This wasn't some fate she had to accept. She wasn't going back to the house to seek refuge at the piano or in bed to be pitied or pity herself. She would find him.

◆◆◆◆◆◆◆

Hours before, Billy had been nursing beers at *Holler*, the roadside bar a few miles out of town, when Jason and the others had shown up. Seth somehow knew about Billy losing his job, and the others offered sympathy. But Jason's eyes were alight. He'd heard from a friend of Brenda's that the

Senator's dogs were being kept overnight at the new clinic run by the colored vet. Why not steal the dogs, hold them for a while, and shake up the high-and-mighty Senator? It wouldn't be hard at all. The clinic had no security. Jason had worked the grounds and seen the flimsy lock on the door. The idea seemed justified and exciting—even irresistible. They had a few more beers and, with Jason's egging, headed out.

It was true that it had been easy to break in. A small pry bar did the trick. The space inside was too brightly lit for their comfort, but they moved fast, if a little sloppily. Slipping the female dog out was easy, but the big one was another matter. Jason found a catchpole in a closet. They cracked open the kennel, looped it around the dog's neck, and straight-armed him out and into the truck. Seth had sat in the back, holding the dog with the pole.

Jason had suggested taking the dogs to Billy's house, but Billy was adamant; once they found the dogs missing, he would be the first suspect. The defunct junkyard was the only possible place. No one would think of it, and it was tucked far back off the road. Jason had no problem with this. Billy had left the others at the clinic at four a.m. and driven home.

◆ ◆ ◆ ◆ ◆ ◆ ◆ ◆

When Sam rose, his mother and Colin had already gone to the clinic. He enjoyed these mornings on his own. He was eager to visit the pond, hoping to run into the girl again. They'd agreed to meet this day. He walked outside. The sun was blazing; it was already hot.

The thick, dewy sward left itchy slashes on his bare legs, and he was sweating, with a squadron of deerflies circling him and defying his swats, by the time he reached the bank. But then he was there, the little stream trickling into the tea-water pond, as perfect as he remembered. She wasn't there. Well, it was early. He watched the pings and tiny ripples on the surface as dragonflies hovered, dipped and strafed.

He slid down the embankment, surprising a few frogs camouflaged on the weedy sliver of the shore. He scooped his hand into the water—it was delightfully cool. He took off his new sneakers, put down his book in the grass, and waded in.

◆◆◆◆◆◆◆◆

Billy woke with a sick, hangover headache. He'd been unable to sleep. What the hell had he done? But it was done, anyway, and he'd committed himself to it. Oh, to hell with it. How much was he supposed to take? They were just dogs.

He drove to the junkyard. With no work, he had nowhere else to go. And he had to go somewhere to escape the cramped shanty he shared with his mother. He knew a visit from the Sheriff was looming. His alibi—their joint alibi—was that they'd been at *Holler* and then gone home and passed out at Billy's. Jason said he had nothing to worry about. There was no evidence, no fingerprints, if it even came to that.

He found Jason fiddling around his rough kennel and his dogs. Two slipped out as he cleaned and ran to the interior fence where the two shepherds were. They paced along a section where they could see them, barking, lunging into the wire, flinging foamy saliva off their heavy, flapping flews. Jason collected them and put them back.

So here they were. Billy stared at the large German shepherd, who sat next to the female watching him.

◆◆◆◆◆◆◆◆

The female dog had interested Elijah from the moment they'd arrived at Cray's farm; he'd recently sensed her readiness to breed. He'd begun a crude courtship by bullying her a bit to demonstrate his strength and intentions. He was unschooled in this sort of thing. Still, instincts compensated for inexperience, and he knew from her whining and coy, agile dances of avoidance and re-engagement that she understood what the future held.

He had dispatched the snake with quick fury by pure instinct. He only knew it as a danger to be dealt with. He also knew the female had been injured; he was compelled to act.

When he heard the cracking noises at the clinic door, he knew it was trouble. He was up. He smelled the boy from the barn and the alcohol he remembered from Doyle, and he could also see the threat in their jerky body language and urgent voices. He'd never seen a catchpole and tried to fight it, but it was impossible. He accepted the capture and waited for his moment to fight and free the two of them. There would be no wasted energy.

◇◇◇◇◇◇◇◇

"So now what?" Billy asked dully, rubbing his eyes.

Jason put his arm on Billy's shoulder.

"We'll throw some food in, slip some water bowls through the gate, and give it a few days." He winked at Billy. "Maybe we'll have some fun later. I thought I'd put Huey in there and see what happens."

At about fifty pounds, Baby Huey was the smallest dog in the group; he looked more like a low-slung pit bull than the heavier mastiffs.

Billy nodded unenthusiastically.

"Listen, man," Jason said, bearing in on him. "After what that sumfa bitch did to your pa, this is nothing. He thinks he's better than us, always has... that he can live here next to us and rub it all in our faces. Are we supposed to do nothing, ever?"

Billy shrugged. "Yeah."

"Hell, yeah." He nudged Billy toward the truck. "Let's get some breakfast in town. You'll feel better."

Soon they were back on the old state highway in Jason's truck, approaching Bloodied Beech and the long field. As they neared the turn-off to the lane that led to the pond, Jason tapped Billy's arm.

"Let's check it out. I've got a feeling."

Billy nodded, thankful for a distraction, and Jason took the turn.

273

◆◆◆◆◆◆◆◆

Sam was up to his waist, near the center of the pond. Looking down, he could see his feet stirring up little clouds of silt. He stooped down to his neck, then submerged himself. It was a whole new sensation. He held his breath for as long as he could, then launched.

He opened his eyes and saw the figure atop the embankment through his watery blur. For a millisecond, he thought it might be Rachel. But the shape was too tall, a man. A second figure joined it, just as tall. They stood still, at a slight cant, and as he cleared his eyes, he could see the smirks on their faces. Rednecks, he thought.

"Don't you know the rules, boy?" It was the one on the right, the dark-haired one. He picked his way down the bank, stopping a few feet from the water.

Sam could see them more clearly now. They were not men, more like older boys. The crooked smile was still on this one's face. Sam waited.

"No coloreds in this swimmin' hole."

Sam looked around. "There's no sign." The words sprang from his natural, invariable honesty without a trace of challenge or combativeness.

"There don't need to be a sign. It's the rules." It was the straw-haired boy behind him. He made no motion to walk down.

Jason noticed the pile of Sam's clothes and book and moved to them, putting his boot squarely over them.

"You goin' skinny-dippin with white girls?"

"I'm alone," Sam said.

He wasn't scared. He felt somewhat safe in the water. He didn't believe they would come in after him.

"You know," the dark-haired one said as he reached down to pick up the clothes and book. "We got dogs bred to track boys like you. You come back here, we'll use `em."

He held out the clothes, then sniffed them—a hint of what he would offer the dogs. Sam instinctively knew it was useless to say more. He just hoped the boy would leave some clothes and the book.

But the dark-haired boy turned, holding the bundle, and started walking back up the slope.

"Please leave the book," Sam almost shouted. He couldn't help himself.

The dark-haired boy stopped, and lazily turned back, holding the book out curiously. He opened it, flipped the pages, studied it with mock focus, and shut it. He suddenly Frisbee-tossed it over Sam's head. It fluttered in the air and smacked the surface. Sam spun and splashed toward it.

Jason laughed and trotted up the bank with the clothes.

"It ain't funny," Sam heard the fair-haired boy say. "That was our swimmin' hole once."

◆◆◆◆◆◆◆◆

Cray, Max, and Rachel returned home. It wasn't the same place, Rachel felt. The yard, the fences, the house and the furnishings seemed cast with a cold light, stripped of their homey warmth. Rachel suddenly wanted to be away, back home, but the urge only made her feel worse. How could she leave without Elijah? As awful as feeling what it was like here and now, how awful would it be to travel back without him, to return home alone? She felt a sick chill in her bones. Simultaneously, she felt a manic need to move, to take action.

As soon as they were out of the car, Rachel walked to the fence and looked over the fields. Max followed. They stood together, silently sharing the moment. Max could feel her restiveness and sensed what was coming.

"I'm going to walk and look. Search."

"I don't want you to go alone. I'll come."

Rachel looked up at him. "You should stay with Senator Cray. You can do another kind of searching, with cars and phones. I have to... search. I have to move."

"You shouldn't go alone."

She nodded. "I won't be alone. There's a boy who will help me. He had a dog that he lost too."

"What boy?"

"You know, the vet's son. His name is Sam."

Rachel had already started walking down the lane.

◆◆◆◆◆◆◆

Sam was naked, and his home was a mile away. He had to get there before Rosalyn returned. He had nothing but his composition book, which he'd pulled off the water and laid in the grass under the sun for ten minutes. It was swollen, with most of the print and images washed out or bleeding. He walked up the bank and crouched in the higher weeds. He tore off clumps of weeds and set them in a pile on the ground, packing them down with his feet, tossing water on them, and trying to fabricate a solid mass to hold around his middle. He thought for a moment: what did it matter? He'd never seen anybody on the walk, and he'd be trekking across open fields.

Suddenly he heard a sound and could see a shape moving on the east side where the boys had emerged. He slipped back into the water up to his waist, with the clump of weeds held over his middle.

The figure emerged. It was the girl, Rachel. She stared down at him. She waited a moment, and walked down to the water's edge. She looked different, he thought. Her face was flushed, rashy from the sweat, or was it tears?

"What's wrong?" he asked.

She tilted her head, perplexed.

"I... what's wrong with you?"

He looked down.

"They took my clothes. Can you go to my house and get me some more? No one should be home. I can tell you where to go. It's not far."

She nodded, "All right. Then can you help me?"

"Yes."

And so Rachel, carrying the book he'd asked her to put on the bedside table in his room, made the hike to his house. She looked about her the whole time, having conditioned her eyes to the image of Elijah. As he said, in twenty minutes she was at the house and could see the back door. No car was in the small dirt driveway. She was nervous and excited as she cautiously stepped inside and found Sam's room. She opened the drawers and pulled out some underwear, shorts, a shirt, and old shoes from a closet as he'd directed. She looked at the bedside table and placed the book on it. She paused and carefully opened it. The pages were still damp, but she could leaf through some. She saw sketches of a dog, his dog—or more like a fantastic image of one, something from a crude comic book without the color. On top of the page, in bold, graphic lettering, it read 'Scarboy'. It was a German shepherd, she guessed, oddly not unlike Elijah. Of course, maybe not so odd, as all German shepherds looked somewhat alike. The dog had bodily streaks and scars, including a vivid one on its face—vaguely similar to Elijah's.

That Sam had owned and lost a dog like hers suddenly confirmed her sense that he was someone who could help her, even that she'd run into him for a reason. She closed the book and hurried out of the house.

One-half hour later, Sam, freshly dressed, tied his shoelaces and ran up the embankment where Rachel stood staring out over the long field. In the eastern distance, through the wrinkled haze of heat, they could see the craggy beech tree, the rock tabletop in front of it jutting up over the field like the prow of a ship.

"What happened?" he asked.

"My dog was stolen from the vet's clinic. I'm going to find him." She turned and looked at him. "Will you help me?"

Now close to her, he could see she'd been crying. Her eyes were puffy and bloodshot, with a swirl of smeared grime on her upper cheek where she'd been rubbing. But her expression made it seem they'd been angry tears.

"The vet clinic?"

She nodded.

"My step-father is the vet," he said flatly.

"Dr. Davis," she said, not a question.

He nodded.

"He's nice," she said, also flatly.

"Where should we look?"

She shook her head. "I don't know. Everywhere. It's good to start with one chord."

"Okay," he said, unsure what she meant but still satisfied.

❖❖❖❖❖❖❖

The Sheriff's cruiser pulled up to the shotgun shack with the unmowed yard. Billy saw it through the frayed muslin curtain and moved to the door. To hell with it, he thought. He picked up the empty beer can and shuffled to the door, opening it.

"Sheriff," Billy said laconically.

Turnbull put his foot on the bottom step of the landing and looked around slowly.

"Hello, Billy. Some dogs of the Senator gone missing. You know anything 'bout that?"

Billy arched his eyebrows and swung the door wide as he stepped sideways. "Take a look if you like."

❖❖❖❖❖❖❖

An hour later, Billy drove up the incline, through the narrow, winding lane shadowed by pines, and parked next to the junkyard shack. He suddenly realized he didn't want to be here anymore; he wanted nothing more to do with this stunt. The others were there. Billy got out and walked up to the threesome. Jason was staring into the enclosure.

"I've been tossing in hunks of meat," he said. "The female dog is eating. Not the big one." He turned to Billy. "So what happened?"

"Nothing. Sheriff came as I reckoned. Asked a few questions. That was it."

"Like I said," Jason said. "No big deal. They can't tie it to you."

Seth looked at Billy and Jason in turn. "There's a five grand reward for the dogs. Janice heard from the dispatcher."

Toby's eyes widened, but Billy just shook his head.

"I could return them," Seth said. "Say I found them wandering on the Beech field. We can split the reward."

Billy shook his head. "No."

"Five K," Toby reiterated.

"It doesn't matter," Billy said, straightening. "I'm going to take them back. I'll say it was my idea. I won't mention any of you."

"Think about that, man," Jason said. "He'll do to you what he did to your daddy."

Billy stared ahead beyond Jason, bringing his eyelids down to a slit.

"My old man deserved what he got. I messed up on my own."

Jason shook his head disgustedly. "Oh, man. That's wrong. Don't let them beat you down. They've got everything, own everything, all the power."

Billy turned abruptly back to the truck.

"I don't know. I'll come back later."

He climbed in, reversed, and drove off. Jason looked at Seth and Toby.

"Don't worry. He won't do anything. Anyway, let's have a little fun. I'll get Baby Huey."

◆◆◆◆◆◆◆

Rachel and Sam came up to the small porch of Sam's house and sat tiredly. They'd walked across the southeastern portion of the town, their side of the old state highway. They'd stopped at farms and talked to everybody who passed their way and would give them the time of day. The sight of a white girl and a black boy stirred curiosity and talk, but word had reached most that she was the Senator's guest and the boy the new veterinarian's son.

Sam went into the house for a moment and returned with his black book. He laid it on the concrete step; it looked yeasty from its dip in the pond.

She watched him. The few minutes of rest seemed to have restored him, she thought. He sat compacted into himself, breathing quietly like a little machine, staring at the countryside with a determined boxer's eyes.

"Thank you," she said, "for going with me."

"We'll go over there..." he pointed toward the northwest... "tomorrow."

She nodded. He didn't seem to hear her. It was almost as if this was his mission now and he didn't need thanks. This didn't displease her. It gave her strength. This was all Elijah's doing, his aura at work. Sam understood him somehow, felt a kinship through his dog. She considered that his dog must have been remarkable.

Yes, they will do the same tomorrow. What else was there to do?

Rosalyn walked out the screen door and handed each an icy glass of lemonade. She looked down at Sam's feet, at the old brown shoes.

"Where are your new sneakers, Samuel?"

Rachel watched him, wondering what he'd say, sensing and hoping he'd fib. He'd already told Rachel that he would get his sneakers back no matter what and didn't want his mother to know, didn't want to go to the police.

But he was saved from a response as Colin stepped out to join them.

"I'll drive you home, Rachel."

She stood. To the surprise of Rosalyn and Davis, Sam stood and reached around Rachel with a quick hug, picked up his book, and went inside.

◆◆◆◆◆◆◆

Rachel had been trying to tamp her anxiety about returning to Cray's. She hoped for good news but knew there wouldn't be any. The search for Elijah would not end so quickly or neatly; she was somehow sure.

Cray had been making calls, and Max and Johnnie had driven around to the feed stores and local merchants putting up a flyer with the reward notice. Turnbull reported that Billy seemed to be in the clear. Otherwise, he had no new information. He thought but didn't share that the dogs might be on their way to some other part of the state or country by now.

Their dinner was quiet. Rachel couldn't bear it but had no idea what to do. She ran through the typical behavioral options as if from a menu. None made sense or felt natural. She fantasized about screaming or bursting into tears as if she were another kind of person. But it wasn't possible for her, and she knew it wouldn't accomplish anything anyway. All she could do was allow the dread and emptiness to have their way, for now, and to keep looking.

Max came to her bedroom and stood looking out the window as she sat up against her pillow. She glanced down at the spot where Elijah would be sleeping.

"I think Sam is going to find him," she said.

"Oh"? Max turned, surprised.

She nodded and shrugged. "I don't know. He seems like someone who finds what he's looking for."

"You do too. The two of you make a team."

She looked up, and words came out she didn't expect and with an energy of their own.

"I don't find things; they come to me. I'm very fortunate that way. I try to be ready. Music comes to me; I don't search for it. I didn't find Elijah; he came to me. I was there, that's all. I didn't expect it. He was your idea...."

And the last thing she expected was to cry; it came all at once from deep in her chest, the back of her throat, and her eyes, wrapped around her vocal cords and the anguished words she wanted to stop but couldn't.

"I didn't... he came to me... he came to me... I didn't...."

Max sat on the bed, reached out, placed both hands on her shoulders, and pulled her into him. He felt her warm cheek against his chest. The tears stopped, and she breathed deeply. She leaned back, rubbing her eyes. She looked at him, blinking away tears.

"Don't worry," he said. "We'll find him." It was all he could think to say.

Max watched her as she closed her eyes, her hand slid down his arm, and she turned over on her side.

Hours later, Rachel woke. In a dream, she'd seen people praying around a bed, the people and the figure in the bed unidentifiable. She'd walked away in scorn, then felt awful, but when she returned, the bed was empty and the people gone. All her dreams were a mess of images, and they made no sense to her except for their seeming associations to her anxieties of health— of dying young or becoming debilitated—and her insecurities and needy self-torments around music. Her subconscious was an imponderable, and she was fine to keep it that way. She honestly didn't care to know more, or so she told herself. She had to deal with life and work, and those challenges were crystal clear to her. She was grateful for this and didn't wish to tamper with the equilibrium. She wanted nothing to do with psychoanalysis. She considered the riot of sensations of her dreams, the guilt, shame, and fear, to be the price of being who she was. She'd accepted her particular wretchedness as long as she had music.

She wondered about prayer and her avoidance of it. She'd never prayed, not even when her mother was dying. She refused to lower her head, close her eyes or repeat mantras at the few Temple services she'd attended. In her mother's case, she realized later that prayer would have admitted the seriousness of her illness. She also felt it was beyond her, in a way, beyond prayer. The world had to spin, people had to die, and we could only do what we could. She loved her mother; the love was there no matter what, prayer or no prayer, and her mother knew that. If prayer were some way to sanctify her love, no, she would have no part of that. She didn't need intermediaries, rituals, or other affirmations of what she knew was true. It was hers, too deep and private for others to understand (just as she was not to understand others), and the mystery was sacred. She knew the prayer would fail, that is if the purpose of it was to save her mother. She knew her mother was dying and would die. Why should her mother be saved just because she prayed for it? Didn't we all have to die, after all? She wasn't going to go through the pathetic and futile motions. No, thank you. She was going to prepare for the worst and show strength.

Her honesty made her realize that her mother's death had compelled her to work harder with her music. It had motivated her, perversely. The enormity of the implications disgusted her, but she didn't shrink from them. She felt wretched and more driven. It was necessary for her to regularly contemplate her wretchedness as it was to contemplate the illimitability of her artistic potential.

No, she wouldn't pray and would accept the consequences.

In a way, her music was prayer. Her work was a prayer. She was wondrously open to music and opened herself to it with tireless and humble practice. It was all the prayer she had inside her. Music made her humbler and stronger, she knew. She wasn't caught up in some delusion that genius would take care of everything. It was out of her control. Only work was within her control.

Or maybe her music was an inversion of prayer, turning it inside out, she thought. She wasn't asking or pleading but declaring and sacrificing. Not from arrogance because she was unique or better, but from simple duty and dedication to art, sublime and beautiful, the highest thing she knew. She wasn't asking for anything from God. She would work for everything. Do what you will to me, she thought. She wasn't going to pray for her disease to go away. *I'll work through the damn disease.*

I'm a miserable wretch, and you can break me if you want; it will be easy, I guess. Physically speaking, I'm weak and brittle, but I won't pray for salvation, here or later. I will do my work such as I understand it.

She felt braced for a few minutes. But it was still wrong.

She suddenly threw off the covers and fell on the rug on her knees.

I'm grateful. That's what it is. I'm overwhelmed with gratitude for Elijah, Max, and my music. Elijah brought it all home to me. He asked for nothing from me, gave everything, and I'm sick and weak with unworthy gratitude. Save him for his infinite, innocent goodness, not for me. I never saw such strength and goodness. Just save him and bring him back, if not back to me, to someone who can love him even better. This isn't a prayer, she whispered fiercely; *it is a demand. I demand it. Please.*

◆◆◆◆◆◆◆

Seth and Jason pried the dog Huey from the bunched, yowling pack, all crazed to free themselves; they squeezed him through the opening and slammed the gate shut, shaking the entire structure. Jason led the low-slung, muscular dog up the incline to the junkyard enclosure, Seth following. Toby watched dubiously from the porch of the old office shack.

As they approached the pen, Huey first caught the smell and then the sight of the two shepherds and lunged, nearly yanking Jason over. Jason recovered his balance, chortling.

Toby stepped back. "You sure about this?"

Jason ignored him yet stood by the door as if deciding. Huey leaped up at the gate. Jason nodded to himself with increasing emphasis, and suddenly unlocked and unwrapped the chain, lifted the horseshoe latch, opened the door, and unsnapped the dog's rope leash.

Elijah, hearing the latch, stood. The dog, half the height of Elijah, came in like a blue-gray bottle rocket. Elijah had time to gauge speed and aim and was ready. He could see the compact dog coming in low for his throat. At the perfect moment, Elijah sidestepped, arched up, and came down. The other dog's open mouth and bared teeth grazed the fur on Elijah's throat as Elijah's jaws clamped over the base of its skull and upper neck. He bit down, shifting his legs and balance to bring the full force of his shoulders down on the dog's head. The dog howled shrilly in pain and thrashed. He was a quick, slippery dog and spun and twisted, but Elijah held on, agilely adjusting his position for balance and pressure.

Daphne had backed up behind a large tractor wheel and watched, growling and whining.

Baffled by the quick end to the fight and his dog, Jason shook and kicked the fence in frustration.

"He's going to kill Huey!" Seth shouted.

Jason shot glances around the ground, saw and grabbed a jagged chunk of concrete half the size of a brick. He opened the gate, stepped in a few feet, screamed, and flung it. Elijah was a large target, broadside and only twenty feet away. The chunk struck his upper flank with a dull thump; Elijah grunted, fell back, and for an instant loosened his grip. In that instant, Huey broke free. But rather than stepping away and recalculating for a new, better angle of attack, he twisted his head up and grabbed for a tenuous hold between Elijah's eye and the side of his neck. His teeth punctured the soft margins around Elijah's eye; Elijah's cry quickly lowered into a savage snarl. He spun, whipping his head around to break Huey's grip, and lunged at the soft region of the dog's neck. He bore in deep and deeper still until the back of his mouth felt the dog's fur and flesh to the point of choking. He made two violent shakes. The second tore Huey's trachea, cutting off the dog's last yelp.

Knowing it was over, Elijah released his grip and backed up.

The dog made crawling circles in the dirt, struggling to breathe, a wet, reedy sound coming from its mouth and blood from its nostrils. It seemed to realize where the gate was and groped toward it.

Jason rushed inside and dragged the dog the remaining distance before slamming the gate. He stared at Elijah with a mixture of scared shock and hatred, then down at Huey, who was gasping and dying at his feet. Toby and Seth glanced down at the dog and up at Elijah, who sat in front of Daphne and the tractor wheel, staring impassively back at them.

"Shit," Seth said.

"I'm gonna get my 30-30 and finish this," Jason said.

"Why don't you wait for Billy," Toby said. "It could mean a lot of trouble. And there's still the five thousand bucks. I think we can convince Billy."

"Why do we have to convince him? It was my idea to take him. Who said he was the one deciding things?"

"And it was your idea to let Huey in there," Toby said. He was now sick of all this and his involvement in it. It was getting out of control. And Jason wasn't part of their original group; trouble seemed to go with him. "Let's wait," he said.

Jason stared hotly at him. He suddenly backed up a step, his eyes sliding away.

"I've got to bury my dog."

◇◇◇◇◇◇◇

Max and Cray walked to the end of the drive, and both leaned against the fence in the shade.

"We have to leave soon," Max said. "I have to tell Rachel. I don't know what more we can do." Max's voice ended on a questioning rise, and he watched the older man. Cray's face was hard to read.

"You know what, Max? Maybe I'm getting so old that a lifelong cynicism is fermenting into the moonshine of stupid optimism, but I'm strangely hopeful. Something tells me we're going to find those dogs, and soon. I'm not saying it will be easy, but staying the course here may be important."

"For Rachel."

Cray winked. "For you both."

Max understood and smiled thinly. If not wisdom, he thought, Cray was offering something like it, and he was right to listen. He couldn't say he felt something similar; he was too preoccupied with worry for Rachel. She was focused on the search for Elijah to the degree that could only mean disaster if they all failed. What would it mean to her health, the new joy and resilience he'd seen in her? He couldn't remember last when she'd gone months without daily symptoms. Could it all be because of the dog? But the dog couldn't live forever. No, it was more, something more enduring that the dog had given her. Listen to me, he suddenly thought; I sound idiotically fanciful. But still, the evidence was there in front of his face.

"We'll stay," Max said. Now seeing Cray's pleased expression, lightened by the sun breaking through the shifting of branches in a cooling breeze, he nodded firmly. "As long as we have to."

◆◆◆◆◆◆◆

The next day was hotter, though the sky in the distance looked ominous, with a solid and foreboding band of greenish-gray stretching across the horizon. There was a rumor of heavy storms later. At noon though, the hazy sun and light breeze belied any threat.

Sam and Rachel agreed to meet at an intersection of the old state highway near the landmark Beech tree that afternoon. Sam hung up the phone with her and stolidly went to his room to prepare.

Rosalyn wondered if she should worry about Sam's new obsession with finding the young girl's dog. But Colin had calmed her.

"It's a good thing he's doing. It's a purpose. Boys need one."

He was right, she thought.

"He's growing up, that's all," he added. "He's had to grow up hard and fast. He's handling it well, better than I would have."

June 1970

◆◆◆◆◆◆◆

By two o'clock, Sam had reached the edge of the field, the tree a few hundred yards off. He was hot, but the heat wasn't slowing or bothering him; conversely, he felt loosened, unimpeded, as if he was beyond the reach of the heat, even feeding off it. He looked behind him through the heat haze over the asphalt. Where was Rachel? Sam wasn't sure of the time. He would wait here for her. He looked at the sky, careless of the glowering band of liverish green in the west. He felt or thought he heard a quick, faintly whistling gust, an omen of change. But still, the hazy sun beat down, invincibly it seemed.

◆◆◆◆◆◆◆

Billy stared out through the screen door. He'd woken up late. The sun glared off the pickup, and he blinked away the sunspots in his eyes. The day ahead looked empty. What, another trip to the junkyard? What to do about the dog? He'd re-read the Senator's letter the night before in a semi-drunken state. He spotted it now on the ground next to the tattered recliner, covered with bottle caps and Ritz cracker crumbs.

He shuffled to it, picked it up, brushing the crumbs away. He realized it was not what he remembered. Last year, in the bitter aftermath of his father's arrest and suicide, he'd found it to be only a bunch of patronizing, useless, self-serving words, just a way for the Senator to excuse his betrayal of his father to the Sheriff. All the flowery language about *'responsibility'* and his holier-than-thou hopes for Billy's future had disgusted him. He was sure of what he knew.

Now it seemed shorter and more direct, neutral, and even honest. The uplift at the end seemed more earnest than contrived. Why did it feel different now? Was it just time? He'd worked for the Senator for a year; Billy knew he'd been a resentful, shiftless employee. He had to admit it; the beers couldn't dull the reality—he would have fired himself sooner.

He looked at the empty bottles on the table. His mother had said nothing about them that morning. He felt depressed and ashamed by the fact. Maybe she'd given up on him? The silence was worse than the nagging—it was desolating.

"Shit," he said.

◆◆◆◆◆◆◆

Rachel rose early, felt her stomach ache, and almost vomited. She didn't care; it wouldn't stop her. She went with Max and Cray to meet the sheriff in the next county. Everyone was respectful to Cray, and the sheriff had been no different, promising to look out for the dogs. They returned by one o'clock. Cray went for a nap, and Max made calls to BU.

She had some iced tea and took an apple with her as she walked out. Max wanted to drive her to meet Sam, but she declined. There was something pure about the two of them meeting up as they did, like a naturally forming coalition of forces. She sometimes felt as if she were inhabiting a fable. She felt entirely hopeful when she was with him, as if he was a living refutation of disappointment and defeat. It wasn't anything he said (what he did say was either to the point and honest or, on the other hand, declaratively, provocatively absurd). She liked both of these Sams; both were very serious. She liked unaffected seriousness. He didn't seem to care what people thought about him. This didn't mean he was disrespectful in any way to his mother or his stepfather (she'd seen him around them enough). He valued who he was and what he knew; that was enough for him. She felt inspired; that was it, she realized, somewhat to her surprise—he inspired her. That was not easy; perhaps the secret was he didn't seem to be trying.

Jason and Seth had spent the evening at *Holler*. After helping Jason bury Huey in the woods behind the kennel, Toby begged off. While Toby's words left a mark on him, Jason stuck to his decision to teach the German shepherd a lesson. He couldn't let it pass. It was about justice. But he wouldn't shoot it; that was his concession to fairness. There would be another fight with one of the larger dogs. He was thrilled at the prospect of a battle with one of the big mastiffs. He imagined the beasts' deep primal cries; the pure, brutal clash with life-or-death stakes. That's what it was about. He was excited as he finished his half-day of landscaping a new home in a subdivision. The afternoon was his.

Rachel could see the small figure of Sam at the fence. In the distant sky behind him was the horizontal band of green thickness. She thought she saw a filament stab of yellowish-white in its midst, an electric wire flash that spread in veins through the green. A few seconds later, she heard the muffled crack of thunder and felt its sonic throb in the air around her.

She came upon him just as he turned. He silently gestured toward the west, toward the darkening horizon. They started walking alongside the gravel shoulder over the culvert in a wordless alliance.

They went on for about ten minutes, slowly closing in on the great beech tree with its bone-smooth, bisected trunk. Sam kicked a rock; it skipped and rolled until it struck a gray-pinkish lump poised at the ditch's edge. The two walked up to what appeared to be the bloated corpse of a badger or raccoon, flies buzzing over its eye sockets.

They heard the sound of a vehicle and looked up. A half-mile ahead, they saw the square shape of a pickup. It slowed, turned left, and melted into the shrouded tunnel, leaving a dust cloud. Rachel noticed the replacement fender on its right side.

"I know that truck. It was driving away from the swimming hole when I met you."

Sam looked at her, holding her eyes. He moved toward the turn-off with purpose.

◆◆◆◆◆◆◆◆

Toby and Seth were on the porch. Jason pulled up short of the large junk-yard enclosure with the stolen dogs. The penned mastiffs started whining and barking. Jason climbed out and walked up, looking at them, then back at the enclosure.

"Where's Billy?" Seth asked.

Jason shrugged. He gestured toward the enclosure. "It's up to me to settle all this."

"Settle what?" Toby said. "It's Billy's call."

Jason walked to the fence and looked inside. Elijah was where he was before. Daphne was up and sniffing around, dragging the unwrapped bandage from her leg.

◆◆◆◆◆◆◆◆

Sam reached the intersection. He looked over at the behemoth beech tree, its tangle of upheaved roots at the base of the rising shelf of rock. He looked back: Rachel was lagging behind about thirty yards. He realized he'd been walking too quickly for her.

The wind had picked up. The sun was now covered by the outer edge of the roiling clouds, and the ambient light had taken on a strange, greenish cast—a sense of unnatural, premature dusk as in an eclipse. Sam turned up the darkened lane.

A minute later, Rachel came to the turn, saw Sam moving around the first bend, and followed. Once under cover of the pines, the light dimmed further. Rachel glimpsed through the branches at the dark, dense clouds. The wind seemed to funnel up and swirl about her. There was another millisecond flash of lightning, and the crack of thunder was closer. She felt the first spit of rain breaking through the pine sieve.

Sam rounded the final corner before the opening. He took in the unkempt, rustic scene:

two pickup trucks;

the rough chicken-coop pen with the ominous profiles of large dogs inside;

a partial view of the enclosure's chain-link fence up ahead;

and adjoining it, the run-down shack with the figures on the porch.

Sam moved forward slowly, and the dogs started barking.

The wind was now wild, in whistling bursts whipping the pine branches and the kudzu vines against the borders of the lane.

Sam walked toward the shack, the needle-like rain in his face. Seth and Toby stared. Jason had turned and now also saw him.

"You took my clothes and new sneakers," Sam said clearly, flatly. "I want them."

A new uproar of barking from the coop made them look up to see Rachel approaching the clearing.

Jason walked to his pickup and looked around in its rear. He reached down.

"You're in luck, boy."

He pulled out the bunched clothing, then the small sneakers, and held out his arms. He walked to the junkyard enclosure and tossed them high over the fence. The clothes fell and draped across a rusted farm till, and the sneakers bounced alongside in the dirt.

Sam walked to the fence.

The rain and wind suddenly and eerily stopped, as the sky grew even darker. Sam looked back once, turned, and started climbing the fence. The fence jangled and swayed with each toe-hold as Sam scaled the ten feet. He swung one leg over the top bar with its single line of barbed wire, carefully straddling it before bringing his other leg over and beginning the descent. At around four feet, he dropped, stumbled the landing, and fell into a pile of hubcaps with a clatter. He stood quickly, looked back at Rachel, and moved to collect his clothing.

Rachel watched the boys, who didn't move. She had a quick, unclear premonition, a collision of light and dark flashes.

"Sam!" she shouted.

Behind the tractor wheel, the dog heard the shoes drop and the thud and clatter of the hubcaps. Daphne alerted to it but waited for the big dog's reaction. He stood and bent around the wheel to look. His right upper body was sore from the blow of the concrete chunk, and his eye swollen shut from Huey's bite wound. He limped slowly around to see the small figure at the fence line. The rain had resumed, violently now as if in some cosmic resolve to deliver on its forebodings, obscuring his already impaired vision.

The dog stepped forward. Something, some evocative scent, was in the air. He held his nose out, trying to gather more clues, slowly moving closer as he did.

Having gathered the sneakers and clothes and ready to climb the fence again, Sam sensed a moving density in the space behind him, and turned. He squinted through thick striations of rain and could see a large dog, low like a stalking wolf. It occurred to him that the clothes thrown in the enclosure had been a trap by the rednecks.

He dropped the clothes and tossed first one sneaker and then the other over the fence. He gripped the wire, preparing to climb. But again, he paused, and irresistibly turned back.

The dog moved closer. He was fifteen feet away, hunched and sniffing. The scent was potent, a sensory barrage arousing rich and wrenching associations. He instinctively growled, not from fear or aggression but from undetermined emotion.

Sam wiped his face and cleared his eyes through the rain and wind. He could see the dog's head more clearly, the wounded and swollen eye. And something else—the markings, the slashing grayish scar. His heart skipped, and he quickly felt that it had even stopped, and he unconsciously put his hand to it.

This scene wasn't real—it was a cruel trick, a price for all his fantasizing, and stoked by the adrenalin of his confrontation with the rednecks. He wanted and willed the dog to look like Scarboy. Of course, it was a lie.

He couldn't move. He kept wiping around his eyes as the rain came at him in horizontal blasts driven by even fiercer gusts. The dog was now ten feet away, its lips drawn back, teeth bared, a deep growl rolling up from its chest. The growling suddenly stopped. It moved its head down to sniff a piece of the dropped clothing.

He singled out the scent, and it was overwhelming. But it still wasn't enough. He moved closer. He heard the word spoken low, and the sound rode in with the scent and crushed the dog's doubt to dust. It could do nothing but go down on all fours.

"Scarboy!" Sam said.

The dog closed the distance, and Sam reached down and placed his hand on the head. He moved his hand gently along it and down along its snout.

"Scarboy!"

The dog slid forward on his stomach until his head was under Sam's bent legs, then lifted himself and moved between his arms. His nose pushed in under Sam's chin, and he inhaled his scent. He made a slight whine, and Sam cupped the dog's head between his hands and pressed his face again his snout.

Nothing else mattered to the boy as the rain lashed at them. Daphne approached hesitantly and was soon wagging her tail and nosing Sam. Sam finally stood and moved to the fence; he stared at the dumbfounded boys, waiting. With Scarboy at his side and Daphne just behind them, he pointed to the latch chain and lock.

Toby looked at Jason and moved to the gate. He stared at the boy and the dog for a long moment before removing the chain. He opened the gate and stepped aside.

Rachel had watched this from her distance. She'd seen Sam's standoff with the large dog through the rain and wind-swept pine debris and the dog's slow approach and submission. In that instant, it was shatteringly clear what this was: the dog was Elijah, and he was Sam's lost dog, the dog, '*Scarboy*.' Of course. The simultaneous impossibility and musicality of the moment made awful, beautiful sense to her. It was emptying and fulfilling at once. Everything she'd been feeling for days, both the spells of dull despair and the bouts of energized pursuit with Sam, had been the cross-currents of her portents.

She felt a stab of heartache and yet a flood of relief. Elijah was here and safe, and Sam had led her to him, just as she knew he would (without knowing exactly why or how). It wasn't '*bittersweet*,' she thought; it was painfully glorious. This was life, the unexpected, surprising her again. But it was the truth, and therefore had to be beautiful whatever she felt. It would always be so. He is Sam's dog. That is the truth, one that cannot be denied. She longed to deny it, but the longing was testimony to the beauty; it was the opening to acceptance. She knew it even then. The worst was this moment, but even now, she felt both the urge and the need to embrace it.

She moved in and stood beside the three just outside the gate. She put her hand on Scarboy's head, stroking it around the swollen eye. Scarboy pushed into her. She stroked Daphne, pulling off the trailing bandage wrap on her leg and throwing it aside. She looked at Sam and had to speak up over the howl of the wind.

"Take us home."

They started walking back down the lane.

Jason had observed all this with increasing, helpless frustration. It was ridiculous and humiliating. It wouldn't stand. He moved to follow. Toby put out his arm.

"Let them go."

Sam, Rachel, Scarboy, and Daphne reached the first bend. The sight of Scarboy and Daphne had sent the five mastiffs into new paroxysms of fury, and they slammed up against the fence. The largest, a male, was jamming its heavy, square head under the fence while the others turned to dig at different spots.

Their sounds merged into a savage frenzy of overlapping barks, cries, and howls. Sam picked up the pace to move out of sight. Even as they rounded the last corner, they could still hear over the roar of the wind the mastiffs' cries and claws against the structure, the desperate canine clamoring to be free, chase and fight, and the rattling of the tin roof as the commotion shook the coop's steel support poles.

.The group emerged from the narrow tunnel of pines. The punishing waves of diagonal rain almost obscured their view of the field and the tree. The culverts on each side of the road were already full, foamy brownish rivers. The sky looked like a surreally overhanging ocean of livid green and mottled umber; the clouds blended into an angry, churning mass. Jagged, multi-pronged spears of lightning split the horizon, followed lockstep by frightening, Olympian booms of thunder. What should they do? Rachel wondered. Sam urged them forward into the wind and rain.

At the shack, Toby looked at the wild stirrings of the dogs.

"Go shut them up," he said to Jason.

But Jason was transfixed on the kennel, his eyes eager as he nodded his head in little jerks of excitement. Toby looked back at the ramshackle kennel. Was it shaking off its footing? Toby started toward it, and at that instant, the largest of the dogs hit the wire door; it swung open just as the front of the kennel collapsed. Toby shouted, running toward it as the dog, seemingly buried, emerged from under the scraps of corrugated tin and, electrified by its release, bounded down the lane. The others, seeing his escape, howled in frustration as they fought through the tangle of wood, wire, and tin. Two more finally crawled through it and tore off after the first. The remaining two scrabbled against the debris with desperate cries.

"Leave them!" shouted Jason to Toby, his cry too late to matter.

Sam and the group were a hundred yards down the road, twenty-five yards from the tree. Rachel and Sam had heard the distant shout. Sam looked back at the lane opening. Rachel saw the sudden urgency in his eyes. She turned just as he yelled.

"Hurry, run!"

He led them toward the tree. Rachel, throwing glances back as she ran, still saw nothing. But clearing her eyes from the stinging rain blasts, she now saw something—a fleeting dark shape. She caught up with Sam and the dogs. Sam grabbed and pushed her to the ground against the rock table and into a tight, angled crevice, jamming Daphne in next to her. Rachel forced herself back to make more room, feeling the loose dirt and rocks give way. From her cramped, supine position clutching Daphne, she had a partial, ground-level view of the road and field before her. She couldn't yet discern the dogs through the lashing rain. Maybe they'd been called back or given up and returned?

They hadn't, and Sam saw one now, moving hell-bent, shoulder muscles rippling with each pounding stride. Scarboy was also watching and lowered himself, his focus intense, his lips curling back. Sam leaned back against the broad tree trunk into its curved hollow. He picked up a rock and sought purchase with his bare feet to push himself up but kept slipping. So he moved behind Scarboy, arm cocked. He knew there was nothing else he could do for him.

Sam watched his dog readying himself, unflinching before the oncoming charge and certain violence. The lead dog came on, forty yards, thirty, twenty.

The mastiff was fixed on Scarboy and didn't slow as it reached the edge of the rock shelf. Sam flung his arm forward, and the dog must have seen the motion as it veered a little off its trajectory. The rock grazed its back and careered into the grass. The fractional dodge by the dog gave Scarboy a chance, and Sam heard the impact as Scarboy struck the dog on the upper flank.

The two dogs rolled onto the field just off the ledge, almost in front of Rachel.

The wild, desperate snarling, flashing white teeth, and the violent jumble of fur and limbs horrified Rachel. Suddenly the dogs broke off, and she could only see the coal-black mastiff's legs and Scarboy's head, his lips curled savagely, and his slits of brown eyes as he leaped up. There was a strangled howl as the fight shifted onto the rock out of her sight.

Sam saw Scarboy with his jaws at the dog's throat. Scarboy's smaller size and flexibility were a momentary advantage, as the more ungainly mastiff couldn't maneuver at the precarious edge of the rock. Their struggle pushed them to the brink. Scarboy lowered himself under the dog's throat, re-gripped, twisted upward as he rammed forward, and let go. The dog soundlessly fell. Sam waited tensely for the dog to emerge from one of the sides with renewed rage, but there was nothing. Scarboy knew something he didn't. The clash had taken less than fifteen seconds.

Sam now saw the two other dogs streaking across the field and zeroing in on Scarboy.

He was poised to hurl another rock, but the second dog abruptly veered toward him. Sam fell back into the scoop of the tree. He didn't see Scarboy charging until the collision and the clamp of his jaws low on the dog's neck. The second dog stretched its neck up just as the third dog, a leaner creature with a shiny gray coat, hit Scarboy broadside but bounced off. Incredibly, Sam saw Scarboy roll away but quickly re-grip the second dog closer to the throat. The dog leaped up to free itself, and his motion carried him over the side of the ledge. Scarboy turned to face the third dog. The dog charged in; Scarboy caught him full on the face, his teeth raking across until he found a hold around the ear and side of the neck. This smaller and more agile dog spun, Scarboy lost his grip, and the dog now latched onto Scarboy's hind-quarters, shaking and tearing. The second dog had raced back up, and both dogs now had their jaws on Scarboy, one on his shoulder and the other on his rear, thrashing and sawing with their heads. To Sam, Scarboy suddenly looked tiny against the blockheaded mastiffs over him. There was a mad welter of cries and growls.

Sam shouted, ran out from the trunk, and threw himself at the dog holding Scarboy's hindquarters; the dog's grip loosened, and Scarboy twisted away. Sam fell and scrambled back to the tree. Struggling with the one dog, Scarboy bent and carried the fight to the opposite side. Sam saw Scarboy's mind at work, dragging the dog to the edge until its rear dropped off and it let go. Scarboy turned in time to face the charge of the dog Sam had struck. The two grappled at the ledge, now both dropping out of sight seven feet to the ground. Sam could hear the raging tangle through the sounds of the elements.

Seeing flashes of the struggle from her crevice, Daphne was barking and struggling to break free; Rachel could barely hold the dog's writhing sixty pounds. The sound drew the other dog to their hide; it snarled and pushed in at them, its bared teeth and lathered snout inches away. Rachel frantically scooped and threw handfuls of dirt at it, shouting, and it backed out. But she lost her hold of Daphne; the female tore free, rushing out toward the dog. The two rolled away in a flurry of growls and cries. Rachel screamed.

Sam ran to the ledge and looked down for Scarboy. He was under the dog's straddled legs, the dog's jaws on the back of his neck. Scarboy wasn't moving. Sam could see the blood and saliva matted on his back as the dog tore away at him.

"Scarboy!"

Scarboy suddenly threw his snout up, knocking the dog off balance, and latched on to its underside. The dog howled and let go.

Sam now saw the dog Scarboy had first thrown off the ledge, lying motionless in the grass ten feet away.

There was a new, crackling sound as chunks of hail smashed onto the rock table.

As Sam, feeling the first blows of the hail, saw Scarboy bolt around toward Daphne and her struggle, something on the road caught his eye: two more dogs were now racing toward them.

'We're finished,' he thought.

A blinding white flash lit up the world around them and shook the ground. The beech tree seemed to explode, and smoking branches crashed around them. Sam leaped off the ledge. Rachel winced at the blast of blinding light, feeling it through the ground and rock, and shuddered a half-second later when the thunder boom reverberated like a close-range cannon shot. The lightning spared the dogs but scared off the mastiff straddling Scarboy; the dog bolted into the field. Also shaken by the lightning explosion, the two remaining dogs racing in from the road split off into the field.

Another huge branch fell around Daphne and the dog. Daphne slipped away as Scarboy, a sable and tan blur, hit the dog hard in the soft indent between hindquarters and ribs. The dog yelped and ran off.

From her crevice, Rachel could see Scarboy in complete profile as he stood next to the smoldering branch. Blood was matted everywhere over him. He was bleeding from his slashed snout, and his rear leg looked shredded as he held it up. He was panting wildly, and his eyes lost in primal abandon.

"Elijah," she said and scrambled out of the space.

Suddenly, one of the dogs from the field hit Scarboy, and the two tumbled away in a new round of savage snarling as Rachel shrank back against the rock. The dog shortly had the exhausted Scarboy by the throat. Scarboy struggled to stand.

Suddenly Rachel saw Sam, wielding a heavy smoking branch, charge and strike the dog again and again. Scarboy broke free. Sam stepped back, waving the branch at the crouching dog.

Seeing the exposed Sam, Scarboy rushed forward, and the dogs re-engaged in a tumble; Scarboy locked on the dog between the shoulders and the neck. The fresher dog stood and tried to shake Scarboy off and nearly succeeded, but one of his thrashing motions enabled Scarboy to re-grip closer to his throat. Too tired and battered to thrash, Scarboy could only hold on as the dog wildly jerked its upper body around to free itself. Scarboy's eyes rolled back as he sank every last ounce of effort into his bite. The dog's motions slowed, and it dropped to its side, feebly struggling and finally going limp.

The fifth and last dog, shaken by the lightning blast and the smoldering litter of branches, circled from a distance in the field. It tentatively approached the body of the first dead dog, sniffed, and retreated toward the junkyard.

◊◊◊◊◊◊◊◊

Sam stared at the battlefield.

He moved to Scarboy, lying still, his chest heaving. His fur was soaked and streaked with red. Open areas of bare skin showed where clumps of his coat had been torn away; one leg was mangled, and gashes on his nose and head were oozing blood. Rachel joined Sam. Daphne whined as she nosed the motionless Scarboy.

Rachel fell to her knees and touched her hands to Scarboy's chest.

Sam looked up into the hail and rain. In the distance, he saw a break in the roiling dirty clouds and a sliver of pale blue. The liverish green taint over the world was lifting.

Seeing a vehicle's headlights moving toward them from the west through the veil of rain, Sam ran toward the road.

◊◊◊◊◊◊◊◊

Jeremy saw the young black boy waving from the field and slowed the VW van. The boy was drenched. In the distance, he could see other figures by the large, riven and smoking tree. He reached over and started cranking down the window, but instead unlatched the door. The boy rushed to open it, walking along with the van until it stopped.

"We need help."

He breathlessly pointed to the scene. His face was more determined than desperate, but Jeremy could see the need.

Jeremy nodded, pushed the parking brake, jumped out, and ran after Sam.

It was as strange a sight as he'd ever seen: the scattered bodies of dogs around the trampled and smoking ground, the two children huddled around one sprawled, injured—or was it already dead?—German shepherd. And the other dog moving around them, whining. Jeremy understood.

"Wait."

He ran back to the van, dragged out a canvas paint tarp, and ran back.

He laid it out flat, and all three found purchase points under legs and body and moved or slid Scarboy the few feet onto the canvas. He was breathing, Jeremy could see. Without a word, each knowing where to hold and lift the canvas, they hauled the eighty-five-pound Scarboy, step by careful step, over the uneven field to the back of the van.

Jeremy looked at Sam.

Sam said, "I know. My father is the doctor. Let's go."

The rain had reduced to a drizzle, and the sky to the west was rapidly lightening. They'd been so intent on the loading that they hadn't noticed the pickup pulling up behind them, its tires sloshing to a stop. They all turned, but Sam tugged at Jeremy.

"Let's go."

Jeremy nodded but paused. Rachel saw Billy step out and run up to join them. He looked at each in turn and Scarboy flat in the back. He glanced behind him toward the lane to the junkyard, then back to Rachel.

"We're going," she said. Sam tugged again, and Jeremy climbed in. Sam ran to the passenger side while Rachel and Daphne jumped into the rear next to Scarboy. As they drove off, Rachel saw Billy standing in the rain, staring after them.

◆◆◆◆◆◆◆

Dr. Colin Davis was at the clinic, and when he saw the soaking wet figures of Sam and Rachel and the stranger burst through the door, all carrying the limp shape of the large dog, he led them straight to the back. In five minutes, the dog was on the aluminum table in the surgery area.

It took Davis a minute to apprehend that the dog was Sam's Scarboy. While the familiar markings first caught his eye, the recognition passed from impossible to unlikely to undeniable, confirmed by the look on Sam— it was Scarboy. But he didn't have time to marvel at the miracle; he was instantly probing the dog, assessing vital signs and the extent of injuries. All the while, he was shooting glances at Rachel and Sam. Sam's eyes were fixed on the dog; Rachel's went back and forth between the two. They both looked almost comically bedraggled, soaked as dish rags yet as alive as crackling high-voltage wires. They needed to get dry. Davis told Brenda, who was next to him waiting for orders, to call his wife and have her come down with dry clothing for Sam and to call Senator Cray and bring the same for Rachel. Davis glanced at the young man who'd driven them, who stood silently in the back, watching.

An hour and a half later, a small group quietly gathered in Davis's office— except for Rachel and Sam, who stood vigil with Scarboy. Daphne was at Cray's feet. Jeremy, who'd introduced himself, decided to remain as long as no one objected. Cray and Max had arrived, with Billy, who'd followed them in. Davis soon understood that Billy had gone directly to Cray's and told him what he'd seen on the road and also confessed to his responsibility in the kidnapping of Elijah, or Scarboy. Cray mentioned this to Davis confidentially and suggested they sort out what to do about it afterward. Max knew of this and withheld judgment or word, awaiting Cray's consideration. As with Max, Rosalyn had brought the dry clothes, and Sam and Rachel now wore them.

The room was quiet. Rosalyn sat close to Colin and looked at him. He took a breath.

"Well, his injuries are not life-threatening. I'll want to do x-rays. As best I can tell, no bones are broken, though he may have some cartilage and tissue damage from the bite wounds. From what I've heard, he was in a violent fight with several large dogs, and it appears to be a remarkable thing that he isn't more damaged. I gave him an anesthetic and a sedative. But given my previous experience with his powers of recovery, I'm not concerned and won't be amazed if he's shrugging this off soon enough.

"The question is, what name do we call him?" He looked around and glanced back toward the open door to the surgery room.

The silence was broken by a deep, hearty voice of a woman coming from the lobby.

"Who's minding the shop here?! Anybody? I've got a sick goose."

Brenda suddenly leaped up. "I left the lobby empty!"

The voice and footsteps grew closer. A short, stout woman in a man's shirt and blue jeans stepped around the threshold. Her wrinkled but lively face and bright flashing eyes took in the scene, then peered into the surgery room.

Brenda moved to usher the woman out; the woman side-stepped her as she looked over the group.

"I heard about the new clinic here. I could have driven on to Doc Cash but thought I'd give you all a try. I've got me an ailing goose in the truck...." She slowed and stopped as her eyes settled keenly on Jeremy in the back.

"I know that yonder fella. I know you."

Jeremy squinted out a look of bewilderment and stepped a little closer.

Brenda glanced to Davis for guidance over the interruption, but he made a calming gesture, a sign to wait.

"Yes sir, you and your lady friend bought my last pup," she said with new certainty. She looked around. "Where's your little lady friend?"

Jeremy, the awareness coming slowly, shook his head with total astonishment. He hadn't been sure why he'd chosen to stick around after delivering the dog, perhaps to satisfy his curiosity about the scene at the tree and to know that the dog would survive. Maybe this was why. It was all too bizarre.

But before he could answer her, the woman shifted her attention to the surgery room behind her; a new, cloudy look passed over her face. She stared at the dog on the table with the IV tube and the black boy and white girl standing next to it.

"That all couldn't be my little pup, could it?"

She turned back to Jeremy, then stepped into the surgery room, now out of Davis's sight. She stopped a few feet away from the table and the children. Davis stood and walked in, with the others following in turn. At this point, every person was, if not expecting, at least prepared for some new, startling turn of events or discovery.

The woman, Opal, nodded her head. She turned back to the group with a satisfied smile.

"Yes, indeed. I always know my own. That's the pup, 'aint it?" She fixed on Jeremy, then Davis.

Jeremy didn't know what to say. Cray suddenly made a sweeping arm gesture for the group to go back to Davis's office.

◇◇◇◇◇◇◇◇

Beginning with Jeremy's account, the saga of Scarboy unfolded. Jeremy told of how he'd come to own the dog by default. He was honest about his failure and the loss of the dog in the towed van in November of '67; it was the last time he'd seen the dog. Davis couldn't confirm the origin of Scarboy but recalled his assumption that the dog had police training and probably had been claimed by a policeman before Sam rescued him.

Rosalyn stepped out and brought in Sam and Rachel, saying they should hear this; she asked Sam to recount where and how he'd found Scarboy. Sam did so in a spare, factual telling but with straight-faced references to heroic myth and destiny as if they were facts themselves. When he reached the moment that Scarboy was lost to him, Rosalyn could see him stutter, and his eyes closed a little, and she interrupted.

"He was taken from you by a policeman, isn't that right, Sam?"

Sam just nodded.

Rosalyn moved over and sat next to him. Rachel moved to his other side.

Now Max spoke, his eyes reflecting how the pieces might fit together.

"I'm guessing that was about a year ago, or just a little longer? This may be where our part comes in. We found him in New Hampshire at a police dog rehabilitation center. The man in charge had recovered him in Cambridge." He gestured to Rosalyn and Davis. "This was where you were living?" Not waiting for their response, he continued. "Yes. He became Elijah. He... saved my daughter's life."

Rachel looked at Max, then Davis.

"I named him Elijah. I didn't know any other name that would fit. I didn't know where he'd been or who had him before me."

The room grew quiet.

"And now we're here," she finished, turning to Sam. "And he's home at last."

Max put a hand on her shoulder.

Opal, against the wall, dabbed her eyes and looked up at Jeremy.

"I told you his line was nothing ordinary. But I'll be damned. This beats all."

◆◆◆◆◆◆◆

Neither Sam nor Rachel wanted to leave Scarboy alone, but Davis assured them that he'd hired a night guard for the clinic and he would be safe. Still, Rosalyn had to talk to Sam to convince him. Cray invited everybody back to his ranch, including Jeremy and Opal, and offered both rooms for the night.

As for Jeremy, he felt a load had been lifted. He couldn't get over that he'd cut across the old state highway on his way to a friend of Dev's and had been the first vehicle at the scene. What did this mean about the rest of his trip or his future? Was it supposed to mean something? Maybe the event itself and its effect of expiation were enough. He didn't know. He knew he couldn't wait to tell the story to Tory; even if nothing else came of their reunion, this might be enough.

He'd also resolved to accept his fate of induction into the service. What he felt about Vietnam didn't matter, he'd come to realize. It was a personal challenge he had to meet, a life experience which, even if a shock to his system, felt timely and necessary. He felt that time would bear it out as it was meant to be.

Rosalyn and Davis thanked him for what he did. He thought but didn't say, '*what else was there for me to do?*' He remembered the image of the small figure of Sam running toward the road, toward his van, set against the smoking tree, and how something had flashed in his mind—a sense of imperative, an aching need to stop. The need was selfless and entirely selfish. It was a painting composed at that moment and wouldn't have been complete without him.

Rosalyn couldn't help thinking about her long-ago doubts over Scarboy and his meaning to Sam. As far as she was concerned now, Scarboy was a blessing. She understood what had to be Rachel's anguish in relinquishing him and knew that something must be done about this. Davis felt the same, not knowing he would soon have an answer.

Max watched Rachel closely that evening as the love and worry crowding his mind and heart became almost too much. But he only saw acceptance in her eyes. He understood how, around Elijah, she had recovered from nearly all symptoms of her condition, and he couldn't help fearing a relapse. What about her music? He knew another dog was not the answer, not the immediate one anyway. But should he still call Lockwood? Maybe there was some extraordinary dog ready to go? Or would it be too painful to return? He would call him, if only to talk.

Cray asked Max to stay on for another week. Max wasn't sure. Would it be better to depart now rather than to force Rachel to be in torturous proximity to Elijah/Scarboy, and in the hands of another? He would leave it up to Rachel. As it was, Rachel decided without hesitation to stay on until Scarboy was on his feet. Sam told her that he was memorializing the *'fight at the tree,'* in which Scarboy survived a lightning strike and an army of demon dogs, in his sketchbook. Both seemed remarkably reconciled to what had happened in their lives and to have become friends.

Opal, happily provided with medication for her goose, told Sam about Scarboy's history and said she would mail him a copy of the pedigree papers. She invited him to her little cabin and farm anytime to see her wall of photographic history. Sam was pleased, and Rosalyn thanked her. She and Jeremy left the following day after breakfast, his VW van rattling out the driveway just behind her International farm pickup.

As Davis predicted, Scarboy recovered enough to be walking in a few days, though he retained (and would the rest of his life) a slight limp from the blow of the concrete chunk on his shoulder. Davis said he would sport several new scars on his face and flank, though the fur would grow over the latter. Otherwise, he seemed to carry no ill effects.

Rachel recounted to Cray and Max the scene at the tree, the savage fray, the whipping rain and hail, and the near-miss lightning strike—most of all, Scarboy's surpassing valor. Sam remained silent, letting her tell the tale. Cray suggested, half-kiddingly, that they memorialize it as *The Fight at Broken Beech,* and officially rename the field after the dog. Sam said nothing, and Rachel knew that both thought it was really their shared, private story, a compact of profound and unique understanding about *their* dog. Rachel knew Sam also felt the triadic bond; they were bound forever. It gave her some peace against the shadowing sorrow of her departure.

Cray had talked with Billy. The agreement was that he would reimburse Davis for the damage to the clinic and provide some volunteer work for six months on the honor system. Davis was not going to press charges, nor was anybody else. If this informal, indentured parole worked out to Davis's satisfaction, Billy could return to work at the ranch. Billy agreed. Billy had already visited Davis, Rosalyn, and Sam and offered his apologies, which were accepted. He had thought it would be the hardest thing he'd ever have to do: humble himself before a black family. It was, at first. But as he sat in Davis' office, watching them watch him, the sense of mingled shame and contempt seemed to vanish or transmute into relief. He realized it was more about his amends, his need to set things right within himself. There was no other way. The idea that difficulty signified meaning, in proportion, became clearer to him than it ever had before.

Billy refused to implicate any of the others. He eased himself out of his friendship with Jason and made no more visits to the old junkyard. Seth and Toby sensed the change and made their own orbital shifts away from Jason.

◆◆◆◆◆◆◆

It came time for Max and Rachel to leave. Rachel didn't want Sam and Scarboy to come by, so she had withheld the hour of departure. But Cray betrayed her, and Sam and Rosalyn came with Scarboy. Daphne pranced about the scene, smitten with Scarboy.

Rachel did not know how to say goodbye—she felt overwhelmed and wished to pretend it was nothing. She looked at Scarboy and wondered what he knew, what he felt. He just stood next to Sam, quietly watching. She walked over and put her fingers on the crown of his head, tracing them lightly back and forth, as she had done when she first met him at the barn in New Hampshire. It was all she could do. There was a sudden silence among the group, and she turned and embraced Max, burying her face in his coat.

Max held her. He saw Scarboy move up to her and sniff her side, then make a slight sideways nudge with his nose. He then sat beside her. She felt the light pressure, knew it was him, felt his presence. But she didn't turn and pushed Max toward the Cadillac and climbed inside as Max followed. Scarboy watched and looked up at Sam. Johnnie backed up the car and drove off down the lane.

The dog did not have discrete or detailed memories, as humans do. When struck by certain associations and stimuli, he recalled vivid moments and impressions in his life, good and bad, and the feelings these evoked. As called forth by his breeding, the dog was drawn to humans for particular reasons of character, leadership and strength. Children were not naturally those to whom he was drawn. But lived experience can break through genetic biases. The girl's touch at this parting stirred memories of that first meeting, that is, the startling new tranquility he felt; those first touches had not led to affection so much as an opening to trust. In time, he saw a different kind of strength in her, a human character to match his own.

Ultimately, given her constancy, strength and gentleness, he developed devotion equal to what he had felt for the boy—a rare phenomenon for a dog such as him, coded from birth to trust and to give himself only to one leader for a lifetime. It was a conflict that he felt as she drove off. It was not what he was born to understand or experience. But now he was with the boy. To be with one or the other would be enough. It had to be. There could be no others anymore.

◇◇◇◇◇◇◇

Max and Rachel fell back into their routine at home. It was welcome for Max, and he had much work at BU to catch up on. Perry had returned, was at the house, and was eager to take on his new responsibilities. He had class schedules and lecture dates worked out, along with a host of speaking invitations for Max to consider.

Cray was shortly in communication with news of Max's now-infamous report. Cray had informed his colleagues, namely Senator Beadle, that he had the report and that Max had entirely entrusted him to dispose of it as he wished. He made no further promises or aversions. It was clear, Cray told him; Beadle and others understood it was now his secret cudgel. He was confident, he told Max, that this would end any further importunacy from Washington.

Max remained concerned about security at home and did contact Lockwood. Lockwood was fascinated by the story of Scarboy and, for the first time, filled Max in on the details of Scarboy's time with Doyle, such as he knew. Lockwood said that he always had good dogs available, though those that would work in family settings with young people were rarer. Max reminded him that Rachel was no ordinary young person. Lockwood understood. It was up to Max when he wanted to bring Rachel back.

Just as Max was preparing to raise the subject with Rachel, Cray let them know some good and surprising—or not so surprising—news: Daphne was pregnant. She'd gone into heat and was at her peak breeding moments during their captivity at the junkyard. Scarboy was the father. They would be having puppies in the next few weeks. Max was elated.

Rachel had made the transition back to her musical practice. The event at Symphony Hall had rippled through the musical world, and she had many invitations to perform awaiting her. Rachel was pleased but chary about what she accepted.

Rachel herself felt physically and mentally well. It was a matter, she felt, of not feeling so precarious, on edge, exposed to outside forces she couldn't control. She knew why: because of her experiences and, mostly, because of Elijah. He had been her guide, her light, out of some sustained, trembling darkness of insecurity and anxiety. One partly driven by her ailment but mostly from phantom fears that self-perpetuated in the absence of any means to check them, to find or locate in herself a stable, durable equilibrium. It wasn't that she felt supremely in control or entirely confident in all things or even in any one thing, but she now had a new sense of personal fortitude; nothing was the end of the world that it used to be. She'd seen and lived through things most never do, and seen a faith and strength emerge in her, and in others on her behalf.

But still, she would look down under the piano at the empty little rug and feel a sudden ache of emptiness. She found herself playing and practicing through it; it was the only decent way to respond, to honor the strength that had been offered to her and which had indeed saved her. She couldn't just get up and go outside and quiver and vomit. No, that wouldn't work. So she grew a little stronger each day from the effort.

One night at dinner, Max mentioned his call from Cray and the possibility of a visit back to Virginia soon. Rachel felt an almost forbidden thrill at the idea but then, immediately, a harrowing caution. How could she go back and then have to leave again? She couldn't. And would it even be fair to the others? Sam and Scarboy were now at peace together in their world.

Max nodded; he understood. He had another idea.

A few weeks passed, and Max received the package he'd been expecting. He opened it, revealing the eight-millimeter film. He had Karl set up the projector in the study and, after dinner, brought in Rachel. Karl turned it on, and they saw the images of Scarboy standing with Sam in Cray's barn. The camera view widened and shakily approached a wooden whelping box, Daphne and her eight puppies now coming into focus. The black, chubby little shapes suckled as Daphne stared up docilely into the camera.

They watched silently for a few minutes. The camera shifted to Sam and Scarboy, with Rosalyn and Davis behind him. Sam looked squarely into the lens, then raised his hand with a faint smile. The screen went black as the film slapped around on the reel. Karl switched on the lights.

Rachel turned to Max with a look of both serenity and seriousness that riveted his attention.

"My dear Papa." She smiled and placed her hand on his chest. "I cannot. You know, there will only ever be one Elijah. But it's all right. It's more than most people have in their whole lives."

She turned to go to her solarium and, for an instant, felt again the nearly unbearable loss. It was followed even more quickly than the last time by the healing promise of making music.

THE END.

CPSIA information can be obtained
at www.ICGtesting.com
Printed in the USA
BVHW05202324022 3
659186BV00010B/219